Welcome to

PARADISE COUNTY

where danger and desire entwine . . .
in Karen Robards' critically acclaimed,
bestselling novel of romantic suspense!

🕊 🕊 🕊

"An engaging read. . . . Suspenseful and atmospheric,
another winner. . . . Readers will cheer and care for her
protagonists."

—*Publishers Weekly*

"Karen Robards has a unique writing style that provides
readers with a fresh voice with every new novel. . . . *PAR-
ADISE COUNTY* is a high-caliber romantic suspense novel
featuring realistic characters struggling with a rainbow of
feelings. Robards knows how to raise the temperature on
several levels with a strong tale that will excite readers."

—Harriet Klausner, ReaderToReader.com

**A Literary Guild Selection
A Doubleday Book Club Selection
A Rhapsody Book Club Selection**

Also Available from Simon & Schuster Audio

✦ ✦ ✦ ✦

"A fast-paced, suspenseful novel."

—*Library Journal*

"Robards expertly balances an intensely sensual love story with a truly chilling suspense plot set against a colorful Southern backdrop. *PARADISE COUNTY* will have readers on the edge of their seats until the final page."

—Amazon.com

"Sizzling suspense. . . . A page-turner of the highest order. The sex is hot and the flames of passion leap high, as do the flames set by the crazed killer. Robards provides plenty of chilling moments to occasionally cool things down."

—Barnesandnoble.com

"Along with exceptional heroes and heroines, Ms. Robards has delivered wonderfully drawn secondary characters. This makes her tales of romantic suspense feel all the more satisfying."

—*Romantic Times*

"Ms. Robards leads us down the path of intrigue, suspense, and romance, with a touch of paranormal thrown in. You'll find this thriller hard to put down. Don't miss it!"

—*Old Book Barn Gazette*

Books by Karen Robards

Ghost Moon

The Midnight Hour

The Senator's Wife

Walking After Midnight

Heartbreaker

Hunter's Moon

Dark of the Moon

This Side of Heaven

Maggy's Child

One Summer

Paradise County

KAREN ROBARDS

PARADISE COUNTY

POCKET BOOKS

New York   London   Toronto   Sydney   Singapore

POCKET BOOKS, a division of Simon & Schuster, Inc.
1230 Avenue of the Americas, New York, NY 10020

Copyright © 2000 by Karen Robards

Originally published in hardcover in 2000 by Pocket Books

ISBN: 0-7434-6723-X

First Pocket Books paperback printing December 2001

10 9 8 7 6 5 4 3 2 1

POCKET and colophon are registered trademarks of Simon & Schuster, Inc.

For information regarding special discounts for bulk purchases, please contact Simon & Schuster Special Sales at 1-800-456-6798 or business@simonandschuster.com

Cover illustration by Lisa Litwack
Cover photos: Thomas Winz / Index Stock Imagery,
    Michael Mahovlich / Masterfile

Printed in the U.S.A.

This book is dedicated with love to my husband, Doug,
and our three boys, Peter, Christopher, and Jack.

It is also dedicated to Caroline Tolley and her new son,
John Andrew Malabre, Jr.;
Lauren McKenna, who was patient;
and Steve Axelrod and Damaris Rowland, who believed.

One

The instant he stepped inside the dark barn, Joe Welch knew he'd found the source of his urgent sense that something was wrong.

Someone was in the barn. Someone who had no business being there. The thoroughbreds were restless, moving agitatedly about in their stalls, not quiet like they should be so late at night. One—he thought it was Suleimann—whinnied to him softly. There was an indefinable heaviness in the air: the weight of an unseen presence. He could feel it, tangible as the scent of smoke that still lingered outside from the burning of a pile of brush that afternoon.

Standing in the rectangle of moonlight that streamed through the wide door he had just rolled partly open, squinting down the long row of stalls, Joe searched the shadows for an intruder. At the same time, his fingers slid along the sanded-smooth planks, groping for the light switch. He found it, flipped it—and nothing happened. Figured. The lights were out, which wasn't all that unusual. The wind had been up earlier, and sometimes, out here in the county, that was all it took to knock down a power line. Or maybe a fuse was blown. That happened sometimes too, when too many lights were turned on at once. Lots of lights were on up at the Big House tonight; he'd seen them as he'd walked across the field. So it was probably a fuse.

Damn.

His gaze continued to search the darkness as his hand dropped to his side. After a moment he found what he was seeking: a darker, denser, human-shaped shadow that seemed to be sitting on the soft raked sawdust of the floor. The figure's back rested against the left-side wall. Its legs were stretched straight out in front of it, solid black logs against the pale umber of the sawdust. In the darkness, Joe might have missed it entirely, except that it was the one shadow that remained motionless amid all the other shadows that shifted and danced just beyond the reach of the moonlight.

Suleimann—he was sure it was the big roan now—called to him again, anxiously.

"You there! Identify yourself, please!" His challenge was peremptory, but not altogether rude, on the off-chance that it might be his employer or one of his employer's guests sitting there on the ground.

No answer. No movement. Nothing.

Joe took a deep breath, steadying himself as his muscles tensed. Billionaires and their pals didn't sit in barn shavings as a general rule, so he thought he could pretty much rule out that possibility. Which left—what? A couple of these horses had been purchased just a few months before at Keeneland's July sale for around a million dollars each, the rest were more or less valuable to some degree, and an intruder presented a host of possibilities, none of them good.

As he prepared himself to scare or beat the bejesus out of whoever had invaded his barn, Joe suddenly recognized, along with the expected smells of hay and manure and sweet feed and horse, the unmistakable odor of sour mash. It slid up his nostrils and down his throat, and left a distinct taste on his tongue. A taste that, over the years, he had come to know and hate.

His tension dissipated as anger and frustration took its place.

"Pop?" The smell was a dead giveaway. Who else was it likely to be at this time of night but his dad, drunk as a skunk as he was always swearing he would never be again? When liquored up, Cary Welch sometimes visited Whistledown's barn, imagining that he was the big-time thoroughbred trainer he had been once, instead of a drunken has-been with a damaged reputation that no owner would let within spitting distance of his horses.

Including Charles Haywood, Joe's primary employer and owner of Whistledown Farm, whose barn and horses these were.

No answer except another agitated whinny from Suleimann and the restless stomping of hooves. Still the sitting figure didn't move. But there was no mistaking that smell.

"Damn it, Pop, you got no business in this barn when you've been drinking, and you damned well know it! I oughta kick your scrawny ass from here to Sunday and back!"

The shadow didn't so much as twitch, didn't respond in any way. Had his father passed out?

Swearing loudly, Joe headed toward the motionless figure. Horses snorted and nickered at him from both sides as they came to the fronts of their stalls en masse.

"You think I don't see you? I see you plain as day, you old fart." His booted feet were surprisingly loud as they stomped through the sawdust. The shadow—his father—remained as still as a rabbit in the open with a dog nosing about. "I'm telling you right now, I don't need this crap."

It was shortly after one A.M. on a frostbitten Thursday in early October. Joe had gone to bed at eleven, just like always. He'd even fallen asleep, dead to the world as soon as his head touched his pillow, just like always. But he'd woken with a start at 12:38 A.M., according to the glowing green numbers on his bedside clock. He never woke in the middle of the night anymore—a long day of hard, physical work was, he'd found, the ultimate cure for insomnia— but tonight he had. Groggy, cross, filled with an indefinable sense of unease, he'd made the most obvious mental connection: something was up with his kids. Rising, pulling on the jeans and flannel shirt he'd left draped over the chair in the corner of his small bedroom, he'd padded barefoot out into the old farmhouse's drafty upstairs hall to check on them.

Jen's room, right across the hall from his own, was his first stop. Poking his head inside without turning on the light, he discovered his eleven-year-old daughter sleeping soundly on her side facing the door. Her knees were drawn up almost to her slight chest beneath the tattered red and blue, horse-appliquéd quilt that she loved. Her short, feathery brown hair was fanned out over her pillow. One small hand cushioned her tanned cheek. Ruffles, the fat beagle mix that was Jen's constant companion, lay on her back at Jen's feet, all four legs up in the air, her long black ears spread out on either side of her. Unlike Jen, she was snoring lustily. She roused herself enough to open one brown eye and blink at him.

Joe made a face at himself as he closed the door again. No trouble here. Not that he had expected any. Not really. Jen had never caused him any trouble in her life that he could remember. If occasionally the thought occurred that she was her mother's daughter, Joe put it out of his mind. It was he who had the raising of her, not Laura. Laura was long gone.

Josh and Eli were a different story. The room they shared was half a dozen steps down the hall, just past the bathroom. One of them was the more likely cause for this gut-sense he had that something was amiss. Not that they were bad boys—they weren't—but they were boys, and as such no strangers to mischief. He opened their door, looked inside, and discovered sixteen-year-old Eli, still clad in jeans and a T-shirt, fast asleep, sprawled on his back on the rumpled twin bed. His feet in their once white but now laundered-to-gray athletic socks extended past the end of the mattress by a good three inches, one arm trailed off the side of the bed, and headphones were clamped to his ears. Eli was almost as tall as Joe's own six-foot-three, with a lanky frame that had not yet started to fill out. His mouth was open slightly as he snored, and a textbook of some kind—algebra, probably, he'd said he had a major test tomorrow—lay open on his chest. Against the far wall, fourteen-year-old Josh's bed was rumpled but empty.

Ah-hah, Joe thought, congratulating himself on his finely tuned parental radar. Years of being both father and mother to this trio had rendered him acutely sensitive to his children. If Josh was up and about at this time of night, secure in the knowledge that his old man usually slept like a rock, he was about to get one heck of a surprise.

The lamp on the battered oak nightstand between the twin beds was on. The volume on the stereo beside the lamp had to be cranked up high, because, despite the headphones, Joe could hear the whine of tinny guitar riffs and the rhythmic thump of a driving bass.

As he'd said to Eli on countless occasions, maybe he'd do better in his classes if he just once tried studying without the stereo blasting his eardrums into the next state. Of course, Eli claimed that the music helped him concentrate. Not that he could prove it by his grades.

Mouth twisting wryly, Joe stepped into the room and

removed the book from Eli's chest. Closing it, he put it on the nightstand and turned off the stereo. Lifting the headphones from his son's head—Eli never so much as twitched—he put those on the nightstand, too, switched off the lamp, and left the room, closing the door behind him.

Now, where was Josh?

As soon as Joe started down the steep, narrow staircase that led to the bottom floor, he heard the TV. A gentle bluish glow illuminated the arch that led into the living room and turned the well-worn floorboards at the base of the steps a weird shade of brownish purple. Frowning, Joe stepped into the patch of purple and looked left, into the living room. The TV was on, volume low, tuned to what looked like one of the Terminator movies. Still dressed in the ratty gray sweater and faded jeans he had worn to school, Josh lay on his back on the couch, his black head pillowed on the comfortably worn, brown-tweed arm as he followed the action on the screen.

"Hey, buddy, why aren't you in bed?" Joe asked gruffly, moving into the room, relieved to find his most trouble-prone child no farther afield than this.

Josh twisted around to look at him.

"Eli's got to have the light on so he can study." Josh's voice was bitter in the way of put-upon younger brothers everywhere.

"Bummer." Joe crossed to the TV and turned it off, then looked back at Josh. "Eli's asleep. Go up to bed. You've got school tomorrow."

"Dad! That was Arnold!" Josh protested, sitting up. At about five-eight and thin as a blade of grass, he still had a lot of growing to do. He ran his fingers over the short stubble of his severely crew-cut hair in frustration. The hairstyle, Joe thought, was Josh's attempt to make himself look as unlike Eli as possible, which was hard when the brothers bore so close a resemblance. Josh frequently teased Eli about what Josh mockingly called his older brother's long, beautiful hair. Eli was vain about his nape-length, slightly wavy black locks, and such brotherly attempts at humor were generally not well received.

"Too bad. It's almost one o'clock. Go to bed."

"Can't I please watch the rest of it?" Josh's blue eyes were pleading as he looked up at Joe, and there was a wheedling note in his voice.

"Nope. Go to bed. Right now," Joe said, unmoved.

"Please?"

"You heard me." Josh was the one who could be counted on to test the boundaries of his patience every step of the way, Joe reflected. Sometimes when he had to tell Josh something fifty times before he was obeyed Joe found himself one deep breath away from making his point with a swift kick to the boy's butt, but underneath he understood his second son's need to assert his individuality. Just as he understood his need to differentiate himself from his older and, to Josh's eyes, more accomplished brother.

"If you'd make Eli turn out the light at a decent time, I'd be asleep right now. But no, you never make Eli do anything." Josh's voice was sullen.

"Joshua. Go to bed." Crossing his arms over his chest, Joe mentally counted to ten.

Josh looked at him, and Joe looked levelly back. Josh snorted with disgust, stood up, and shuffled from the room, the too-long legs of his baggy jeans dusting the floor as he went.

After watching his son disappear up the stairs, Joe shook his head, then turned slowly around in the dark living room.

The kids were fine, it seemed. Had he heard something,

then, the TV maybe or some other noise Josh had made, that had been out of the ordinary enough to wake him up?

Maybe. Probably. But while he was up, it wouldn't hurt to check on the horses. He was almost as attuned to them as he was to his kids.

Horses were his livelihood, and his passion. He bred them, trained them, cared for them. His own, in the shabby, black-painted barn out back, for love and what he could wrest out of the business, and, for a steady paycheck, those of Charles Haywood, in the immaculate, twin-gabled white barn up the hill.

Listening with half an ear to the noises Josh made getting ready for bed upstairs—toilet flushing, sink running, floor creaking, the opening and closing of doors—Joe moved from the living room to the hall and then to the kitchen at the rear of the house. Sitting down in one of the sturdy, white-painted kitchen chairs, he thrust his bare feet into the lace-up brown work boots he had left just inside the back door, tied them, and stood up. Grabbing his University of Kentucky Wildcats blue nylon parka from the coatrack, he let himself out the back door, locked it behind him, and headed across the cold-crisped grass for his barn.

It was a beautiful night, bright and clear, colder than usual for October, which was generally mild in Kentucky. Overhead dozens of stars twinkled in a midnight blue sky. The moon lacked only a sliver of being full, and shone round and white as a car's headlight, illuminating the gently rolling countryside with its scattering of houses, barns, four-board fences, and two-lane roads.

His thirty-three acres marched alongside Haywood's six hundred and seventeen, but because his acreage had once been part of the Whistledown Farm property—the manager's house, to be precise—the two barns were within easy walking distance of each other. His, on the little rise behind his own house, and Whistledown's, atop a bigger hill and separated from his property by a single black-painted fence, were no more than half a dozen acres apart.

As he approached his barn, the triangular-shaped pond to the right shone black in the moonlight, reflecting the night sky as faithfully as a mirror. The covered training ring, a three-quarters-of-a-mile indoor oval that allowed him to work his horses in inclement weather, sat silent and deserted at a little distance to the rear, looking for all the world like a long, curved, black-painted train tunnel. Beyond the ring, an owl hooted in the woods bordering the back of the property, and from some greater distance still a coyote howled. Near the edge of the woods, just visible as a solid dark block against the variegated charcoal of the timber, stood his father's small log cabin. The lights were out. No surprise there. Like himself, his widowed father was a horseman, which meant he was an early-to-bed, early-to-rise kind of guy.

When he wasn't drinking, that is.

Joe stepped inside his barn, flipped on the light—an evenly spaced lineup of cheap fluorescent fixtures overhead, not fancy but adequate for the job—and looked around. Silver Wonder came to the front of her stall, blinking and snorting a soft question. Drago and Timber Country were next, thrusting their heads out of the open top of the Dutch-style stall doors, looking at him curiously. Down the row, more horses, some his, some boarded, popped their heads out. They knew the schedule as well as he did, and plainly wondered what had brought him to their domicile in the middle of the night.

"Everything okay, girl?" Joe walked over to Silver Wonder and rubbed her well-shaped head. The ten-year-old brood mare nudged him, wanting a treat, and he felt around in his coat pocket for a peppermint. Silver Wonder loved peppermint.

Unwrapping it, he held it out to the petite gray. She took the candy between velvet lips, drew it into her mouth, then chomped contentedly. The scent of peppermint filled the air as he made a quick circuit around the stalls. Built in a rectangle, the barn housed approximately forty horses in two rows with stalls facing each other on each side, an office area at the front, and an open area at the rear. The utilitarian layout provided what amounted to a small track around an indoor core of stalls and tack rooms so that the horses could be cooled out indoors when necessary.

It was obvious from the demeanor of the horses that there was no problem here.

"All right, go back to sleep." Ending up back where he had started, Joe patted Silver Wonder's neck affectionately, resisted her nudging hints for another peppermint, and left the barn.

Probably Josh being up was the only thing out of the ordinary on this starlit night. This was Simpsonville, Kentucky, after all. Population 907. The heart of the horse country that was Shelby County. Paradise County, the locals called it for the beauty of the landscape and the tranquility of the lifestyle. Crime was so rare here as to be almost nonexistent.

Yet Joe had felt strongly that something was wrong. And, he realized, he still did.

He would check on the Whistledown horses, then walk once around his dad's house before turning in again.

It was a simple matter to scale the fence. Actually, he did it an average of a dozen times a day. A boot on the lowest board, a leg flung over, and it was done. He climbed the hill to the accompaniment of his own crunching footsteps and the more distant sounds of nocturnal creatures going about their business. On the horizon, silhouetted against a stand of tall oaks, Whistledown, Haywood's white antebellum mansion, glowed softly in the yellow shimmer of its outside security lights. With Mr. Haywood and a party of friends in residence for the Keeneland races, the usually empty house was lit up like a Christmas tree. Diffused light glowed through the curtains at a dozen windows. Four cars were parked in the long driveway that most of the year held none.

Must be something to be so rich that a place like Whistledown was used for only about six weeks a year, mainly during the spring and fall Keeneland races, Joe mused. Horses were nothing more than an expensive hobby to Charles Haywood, and Whistledown Farm was only one of about a dozen properties he owned. Of course, Joe was sure the guy had problems, *everybody* had problems, but with money like that how bad could they be?

He'd like to try a few of the problems that came with being richer than hell, instead of constantly worrying about covering expenses. The most important things in his life—his kids and his horses—both required a lot of outlay without any guarantee of a return.

Unlike his own admittedly shabby barn, Whistledown's was shiny with new white paint, two stories tall, and embellished with the twin scarlet cupolas that were the farm's trademark. Reaching the door, Joe unlatched it, rolled it open, and stepped inside.

Moments later he went stomping furiously down the length of the barn, the smell of whiskey drawing him like a beacon, cursing and ready, willing, and able to put the fear of God into his dad.

His patience was at an end. Six weeks ago, after Joe had hauled him out of Shelby County High School's kickoff basketball game, where Cary had seriously embarrassed Eli, who was a starting forward, and his other grandkids by bellowing the school fight song from the middle of the basketball court at halftime, Cary had sworn never to touch another drop of booze as long as he lived.

Yeah, right, Joe thought. He had heard that song before, more times than he cared to count. They all had. But this was the last straw. His dad knew—*knew*—that he wasn't allowed near the horses if he'd been drinking. Especially the Whistledown horses. Especially with Charles Haywood in residence.

It was so dark that it was difficult to be certain, but the motionless figure seemed unaware of him as Joe stopped no more than a yard away and stared hard at it. A flicker of doubt assailed him: maybe it wasn't his dad after all. The man looked too big, too burly, but then maybe the dark was deceptive. Suddenly, the only thing he was sure of— fairly sure of—was that whoever it was, was a man. Shoes, pants, the individual's sheer size—all looked masculine. Legs thrust stiffly out in front of him, the guy was sitting on the ground, head turned a little away, arms hanging at his sides, hands resting palms up on the ground. Joe thought his eyes were closed. Again, it was too dark to be sure, but he thought he would have seen a gleam of reflected light or something if the guy was looking at him.

"Pop?" he said, although he was almost positive now that the sitting figure was not his father. He caught a whiff of another smell foreign to the barn. It was sharper and more acrid, if not as familiar, as the booze. His voice hardened, sharpened. "All right, get up!"

The man didn't move.

The reddish-brown sawdust looked almost black in the darkness. But all around the man's right side, in a circular shape that seemed to be spreading even as Joe stared at it, was a deeper, denser blackness, an oily-looking blackness. . . .

Joe's eyes narrowed as he strained to see through the darkness. Moving nearer, crouching, he laid a wary hand on the man's shoulder. It was solid and resilient—but, like the man, totally unresponsive.

"Hey," Joe said, gripping the shoulder and shaking it. Then, louder: "Hey, you!"

The man's head flopped forward, and then his torso slumped bonelessly away from Joe, his leather coat making a slithering sound as it moved over the wood. He ended up bent sideways at the waist, limp as a rag doll, his head resting at the outermost edge of the oily-looking circle.

That posture was definitely not natural, Joe thought. The man had to be dead drunk—or dead.

Oh Jesus. *Dead.*

All around him now horses stomped and snorted and called in a constant, agitated chorus. He could feel their nervousness, their recognition that something was wrong in their world. The hair on the back of his neck prickled as he felt it too: the sensation he had first experienced upon entering the barn. The best way he knew to describe it was the weight of another presence. Glancing swiftly over his shoulder only to see nothing but shadows and moonlight and the bobbing heads of horses behind him, it occurred to him just how very isolated the barn was.

There was a movie Eli liked. Joe couldn't remember the name of it right off the top of his head, but the tag line went something like this: In space they can't hear you scream.

That about summed up how he felt as he crouched there in the dark beside the slumped, motionless figure. He felt the touch of invisible eyes like icy fingers on his skin, and glanced around again. He could see nothing but the horses, and the shadows, and the moonlight pouring through the door. But a sudden fierce certainty that he was not alone seized him.

"Who's there?" he called sharply.

There was no reply. Had he really expected that there would be? Mouth compressing, he turned his attention back to the man before him. Touching the oily sawdust, he discovered, as he had suspected, that whatever had discolored it was sticky and wet—and warm.

Blood. The sharp, rotting-meat stench of it was unmistakable as he held his fingers beneath his nose.

"Jesus Christ," Joe said aloud, wiping his fingers on the sawdust to clean them. Then he reached for the man's neck, feeling for the carotid artery, for a pulse. Nothing, though the flesh was warm. At the same time he leaned over the still figure, squinting at the shadowed features.

By that time, his eyes were as adjusted to the dark as they were going to get. He could not see everything— small details escaped him, and colors—but he could see some things. Like the fact that the guy's eyes were definitely closed, and his mouth was open, with a black froth that could only be blood bubbling up from inside.

Charles Haywood. Joe took a deep, shaken breath as he recognized his employer. There was a blackened hole about the size of a dime in his left temple, a growing circle of blood-soaked sawdust around the right side of his upper body—and a handgun lying not six inches from his left hand.

What he had smelled along with the booze was the acrid scent of a recently fired gun, Joe realized. Haywood had been shot dead.

Two

✤

The predator watched hungrily from the shadows. He could still smell the blood, feel the warmth of it on his fingers, taste the saltiness of it on his tongue, imagine the rich, deep claret of the life force draining from his victim's body. But it left him empty rather than satisfied, like inhaling the scent of a meal cooking without being able to consume the meal itself. This taking had been unplanned, an act of necessity rather than pleasure.

But it had awakened his craving for pleasure.

Speculatively he eyed the man crouched beside his prey. It was dark, and they were alone—but no. Caution raised its head. He had been doing this for years, preying on the unsuspecting, taking them swiftly and silently in the night to a place where their screams could not be heard, where he could play and indulge himself and enjoy their pain and terror at his leisure. This man was handsome, with good features and smooth, unblemished skin, but he was not the right type: he would be only marginally more satisfying than the first, if indeed he could be taken at all.

Youth and beauty were what he craved.

The predator slipped swiftly and silently out of the barn. Bent low, hugging the black shadow of the fence, he skirted the fields to where he had left his vehicle hidden from view. He was panting and sweating by the time he slid into the driver's seat, because he was a big man and a little out of shape, and because he had not quenched the thirst for excitement aroused by the ultimately unsatisfying kill.

He wanted more. He needed more. He had to have more. His need was as clamorous as an addict's for a drug. He could not wait.

He had not come out tonight prepared to take prey, but no matter, he thought as he started his specially modified Chevy Blazer and pulled out onto U.S. 60 with a swish of tires. Prey was easy to come by if you knew what you were doing, and he did. The interstate was just about five miles up the road, and on the interstate, so closely situated to his home that it almost had to be fate, was a rest stop. Sometimes he thought of himself as a spider, a big hairy spider on the prowl in search of a meal. The rest stop was part of his network of webs. In time of need, he could almost always find something appetizing at the rest stop.

As he drove he cracked open the window, breathing in the cold air, the scents of passing farms and animals. Now that the hunt was on, he felt more alive than he did at any other time. His senses were sharpened; the familiar euphoria made him smile, and turn on the radio to his favorite, golden-oldies station. The Stones' "Satisfaction" was playing. The appropriateness of it was not lost on him, and his smile broadened.

He would have satisfaction soon.

The two-lane country road was lightly traveled at this time of night; his headlights swept across rolling fields and black board fences, illuminating an occasional horse or cow grazing near a fence bordering the road. It was after midnight. The county was, to all intents and purposes, asleep. He knew it well: he had been born and raised here.

Sometimes it amused him, to think how safe and secure his neighbors felt slumbering in their beds. He had lived among them for almost his entire life, and yet they had no idea that he even existed. There was a dark underbelly to their beloved Paradise County, and none of them—well, none of them except those he took—would ever know.

He turned right, pulled out onto the interstate, and traveled east for about three miles until he reached the rest stop. Easing off the road, he checked out the cars parked in front of the rest area as he drove slowly past the brick building that housed the rest rooms and vending machines. There were two, a black Camry and a blue minivan. A family of a mother, father, and two groggy-looking children were heading away from the van toward the rest rooms on either side of the dimly lit building. They didn't interest him.

At the far side of the rest stop he drove off the pavement and into the surrounding wooded area that was a favorite haunt of local deer hunters. There he parked. Getting out of the SUV, he went around to the back and extracted his folding motorized scooter from the cargo area in the rear. Later he would use it to return to his car, but for now he pushed it silently in front of him as he walked back toward the building. The funny thing was, the scooter never seemed to raise any red flags in the minds of the few who saw it. It looked as innocuous as a child's toy, and he, big man that he was, looked comically harmless riding it.

He had his favorite spot in the deep shadows at the very edge of the woods: a fallen log on which he could sit and watch the comings and goings at the rest area without anyone seeing him. Sometimes he had to wait a long time to get what he wanted, but then, he never minded waiting. Waiting was part of the hunt.

Sometimes he didn't get what he wanted, and had to go home unsatisfied. Then he would hunt the next night, and the next, all over his far-flung web, for as long as it took, anticipation building inside of him all the while.

Sooner or later, he always got what he wanted.

He sat there in the waning of that cold October night, patient as a trapdoor spider at the mouth of its lair, watching as the moon rose high in the sky and sailed toward the west, watching the shadows of the tall pines shift clockwise across the edge of the parking area, watching as cars and trucks and vans and SUVs pulled in and out, disgorging and then reclaiming their passengers.

When they came, he almost didn't recognize them. There were two of them, a young man and a girl, college-age he guessed, in a new, pale blue Volkswagen Bug that the girl was driving. He would have let them pass—two were twice as hard to take as one, after all, and twice as likely to be missed, and he wasn't a fool, getting caught was not on his agenda—but when the girl walked through the diaphanous glow of the streetlamp he saw that she was beautiful, so beautiful in just the way he liked. She had long straight blond hair that shone in the light, and she looked unbelievably slender and lithe in a tan car coat and jeans. She was laughing, laughing back over her shoulder at the young man, her straight white teeth gleaming, the sound of her laughter merry in the cold night—*ha ha ha.*

"Can I help it if I always have to pee?" she asked, and laughed again.

He was a sucker for beautiful laughing blondes. Even beautiful laughing blondes that had to pee.

The young man answered something, but the predator barely noticed him, except in terms of sizing up possible resistance: maybe five-ten, thin, a kid. Not expecting trouble. Not prepared for any.

Piece of cake, the predator told himself, and, leaving his scooter behind, stood up and walked briskly over to the brick building. He looked around, assured himself that the blue Bug was alone in the parking area, then followed the kid into the men's room. He would deal with him first; on her own, the girl would be easy.

The kid was at the urinal, taking care of business. In response to the sound of the opening door the kid glanced back over his shoulder. For a moment their eyes met.

Predator and prey, he thought, amused, although the prey didn't know it yet.

"Nice night," the predator said aloud, stepping inside and heading for the sink as though to wash his hands. In the silver-framed mirror he saw himself: an ordinary-looking fellow with a friendly smile. Nothing about him to suggest a threat.

"Kinda cold," the kid answered, finishing and zipping up his jeans. Turning on the rusty water full blast to mask any possible sounds, the predator was disappointed when the kid headed toward the door without bothering to wash his hands.

Nasty habit, that. Germs were everywhere.

"Take care," the kid said, and reached for the door handle. But the predator was ready, had been ready since entering the bathroom. He could leap on the kid and simply overpower him, but this way was more fun.

"Ah-ah-ah," he gasped just as the kid's hand curled around the silver handle, and slumped forward over the sink, clutching at his heart with one hand. The other was already sliding into his pocket.

Watching his prey through the mirror, the predator was pleased to see the kid behave as expected. He turned to look at the stricken middle-aged man, a concerned frown on his thin young face.

"Mister. . . ."

"My pills," the predator groaned, clawing at his chest. "In my shirt pocket."

The kid left the door and came over to help him. As soon as he touched him, the predator struck. He grabbed the kid's wrist with his right hand, yanked him across the sink, pulled his taser from his pocket with his left and jammed it against the kid's side, all in a lightning blur of movement. A sizzling sound, the slightest smell of burning—sweet, tantalizing burning—a faint cry covered by the rush of the running water, and the kid was his. Eyes rolling back in his head, the prey collapsed in the predator's arms. From experience, the predator knew that he would be out cold for a good quarter of an hour. By the time he came around, it would be too late.

The whole exercise had taken perhaps a minute and a half.

Supporting the kid as he slumped to the floor—he would have let him drop but didn't want to risk any injuries to the head—he crossed quickly to the bathroom door and stepped into the yellowish pool of light just outside. If the girl was out already—she wouldn't be, girls never were, they took altogether too much time in the bathroom—he would summon her to the men's room to aid her mysteriously stricken boyfriend. If another car had arrived in the meantime, which was always a possibility and added a certain fillip of danger to the excitement of the occasion, he would simply walk away. The kid wouldn't remember much of what had happened, and no one else had seen him. But in the absence of these two possible variations to the scenario, he would surprise the girl in the ladies' room, hit her with the taser, and carry them both off in the blue Bug. When he had them secure, he would return on his scooter for his car, and they would all three vanish into the night without a trace.

The young couple in the blue Bug would never be seen again.

Humming under his breath, the predator walked around the building, pleased to see that the Bug was the only car in the parking area. Everything was going according to plan, just as if it was meant to be. In fact, sometimes he wondered if his victims' fate *was* meant to be. If he was their destiny, so to speak.

If so, they must have been very, very naughty in a previous life.

Just as he reached the sidewalk leading to the ladies' room, the girl emerged, shaking back her long blond hair. His heart rate increased at the sight of her. What a truly beautiful creature she was; well worth the extra effort of taking her boyfriend too.

Their eyes met. Hers widened, in instinctive fear, he thought, at encountering a strange man in a deserted area so late at night.

Girls were so wary nowadays.

He smiled at her.

"Did you pee?" he asked genially without ever breaking stride. He was almost upon her. The brick wall that provided privacy for those entering the rest room blocked her escape.

"Eric!" She stopped in her tracks, calling, he presumed, to her incapacitated boyfriend. Then she whirled, her hair swirling around her like a cape, tugging frantically at the handle of the ladies' room as if she thought to escape him by running back inside.

"Silly," he said almost fondly, and grabbed her arm, jabbing the taser into her side.

Three

✤

I t was cold, far colder than she would have expected Kentucky to be in November. She always thought of sunshine and horses and acre upon acre of lush green grass when she thought of Kentucky—but then, she'd only ever been to Whistledown Farm in the summer, and hadn't been there at all for seven years.

Now tragedy had brought her back.

Alexandra Haywood shivered as she stepped out of the big white Mercedes that was one of several vehicles kept garaged on a year-round basis at the farm. Her hip-length, charcoal gray wool jacket had a black Persian lamb collar and cuffs and was belted at the waist. Zipped to the throat and worn with a black cashmere turtleneck, formfitting black leather pants and high-heeled black ankle boots, it should have been enough to keep her warm—but it wasn't. She was freezing, forced to clench her teeth to keep them from chattering. Since the funeral she had lost weight, maybe as much as ten pounds from her five-foot-seven-inch frame, so that now she verged on skinny rather than slender. Her beauty had dwindled too, dimmed like a lamp with the wattage turned down. Her skin had lost color until it was almost milk white, paler even than the expensive platinum blond of her straight, shoulder-blade-length hair, pulled back now into a sleek chignon at her nape. Her fine features had become pointier, pinched-looking almost, and the dark blue of her eyes was repeated in the shadows beneath them. She tried to hide the worst of the ravages grief had wrought, painting her lips Chanel red and patting concealer beneath her eyes, but the fact remained that she looked like a ghost of her former self. And felt like one, too.

It was a gray morning, with overcast skies threatening icy drizzle later in the day. The ramshackle barn on the muddy rise in front of her and the circular, covered-train-track-looking building behind it had weathered to a color that was almost as much graphite as black. The iced-over grass in the surrounding fields, the small pond to the right, the leafless clump of trees stretching skyward like gnarled hands to the left, even the narrow asphalt drive-way on which she stood, were all varying shades of gray.

Her whole life had turned gray, she thought, and the thought brought with it a great burst of sorrow like blood gushing from an open wound. Alex winced, bracing herself as she had learned to do until the rush of pain subsided. A movement in the partially open door of the barn drew her eyes and attention, and, thankfully, she felt the acute stab of grief start to fade away.

A scalped-looking teenage boy in a navy Polartec pullover stood staring at her, hands thrust deep into the pockets of his baggy jeans, apparently drawn by the sound of her arriving car. Methodically, on autopilot as she had been since the funeral, Alex closed and locked the car door. It was too hard to remember that she was in Simpsonville, Kentucky, rather than Philadelphia and didn't have to lock anything at all. Facts like that kept slipping away from her; she just couldn't seem to concentrate. Meanwhile, the boy turned and disappeared back into the barn's interior, yelling "Dad!" at a volume that made her wince.

Maybe that was a good thing, though. Maybe her hearing at least was beginning to return to normal.

Since the funeral, she had tended to experience her sounds, like her colors, as muted. This dulling of her senses was, she thought, nature's anesthetic. It was meant to help her cope with crippling pain.

Her father was dead, a suicide. That's what they said, all of them, the coroner and the lawyers and the police and all the other officials who'd been called in to give their verdict on the death of such a wealthy and prominent man. She'd read the autopsy report, seen the pictures, pored over everything, tried to learn any little detail she could about her father's final minutes, hoping to understand, to salve her grief with knowledge. Nothing she had found had contradicted the ruling of suicide. But she still found it impossible to believe.

But then, everything that had happened over the past five weeks was impossible to believe. Like Alice, she seemed to have stepped through the looking glass. What existed on the other side was an alternate universe to the life she had known.

The boy was back in the doorway again, his gaze fixed on her, his expression openly curious. A man stood behind him, a head and more taller than the boy, a hand on the boy's shoulder, his eyes narrowed as he watched Alex approach. The wintry sun was at her back, and she assumed his frowning, squinty-eyed expression was the result of staring into it, and not because of anything to do with her. He conformed to the general description she'd been given—a big man, tall, black-haired, late thirties—and she guessed that he must be Joe Welch, the farm manager. *Her* farm manager, now that her father was gone.

Alex's informant was Whistledown's longtime house-keeper, Inez Johnson, who had also described Joe Welch enthusiastically as "dead sexy."

If he was, Alex was in no state to recognize it. Like her ability to enjoy food and sleep, her ability to enjoy sex, or even the infinitesimal pleasure of recognizing and responding to a sexy man, had been stolen away by grief. Oh, she could see that this man was handsome enough, with a strong-featured, square-jawed face rendered even more formidably masculine by what looked like a couple of days' worth of black stubble, but she did not feel the lit-tle tingle of male-female awareness that once would have told her that he was attractive. He was simply a tall man in a blindingly blue goose-down parka that made him look massive through the shoulders and torso, with narrow hips and long, muscular legs encased in faded jeans.

At least the parka was bright enough not to fade to gray like everything else in her line of vision. Fixing on it like a homing beacon, Alex headed toward it, placing her feet carefully on the pavement which she feared, from the tem-perature of the air and the icy frosting on the grass and pond, might be slick.

He remained unsmiling as he watched her approach, and Alex wondered if he knew who she was—and why she was there.

Probably not. Her father's death had made all the major newspapers' financial pages, along with reports that he had killed himself because of a cataclysmic business rever-sal. But there had been no pictures of her or any other family member, and barely any mention of them, either.

Strange to think that it took no more than a small rise in interest rates, a few bad investments, and a suicide, and it was gone, all gone, a billion-dollar empire fallen in upon itself like a house of cards. Bankruptcy was such a hideous word. She had never, ever thought it would apply to her family, or their business. Haywood Harley Nichols, her father's wholly owned health-care firm, had been building hospitals and nursing homes and HMOs all over the world for almost half a century. But her father's lawyers—no, her lawyers now—informed her that *if* they were lucky and were able to sell everything for a decent price, there might be just enough to pay all her father's debts, with a little left over.

If not, bankruptcy seemed the only other option. Which would leave nothing at all for herself, her sister, and her current stepmother, as her father's heirs, to divide. Mercedes, her father's sixth wife and his widow, had been having serial hysterics at the prospect of impending poverty since learning the truth shortly after the funeral.

Alex had a feeling that if her emotions weren't so numb, she might be having serial hysterics herself.

There was a black four-board fence surrounding the field in which the barn stood, and a red metal farm gate separated the driveway from the barnyard. Reaching it, Alex dropped her gaze from the blue beacon to fumble with the latch. The metal was painfully cold to her fingers; she couldn't seem to get them to work properly no matter how hard she tried.

Hearing footsteps approaching on the other side of the gate, Alex glanced up to see the man she presumed was Joe Welch striding toward her down the graveled walkway that led up to the barn. His brown work boots seemed to have no trouble finding traction on the gravel.

"Mr. Welch?" she inquired when he was close enough. Her voice was low and husky, with the curiously flat intonation she seemed to have developed since the funeral. It sounded exactly the way she felt: lifeless.

"That's right." His voice was deep and just touched with

a slurring Southern drawl that under other circumstances she might have found intriguing. As he reached the gate their eyes met, and she saw that his were blue, a light, bright shade of near aqua set off by a fringe of black lashes. They were unsmiling, and, she thought with a gathering frown, unwelcoming as well.

"I'm Alexandra Haywood."

"I know who you are." His voice was as unwelcoming as his eyes.

He had unlocked the gate without effort and now pushed it open, inviting her wordlessly inside. Walking around the gate into the barnyard, her ankles wobbling a little as her high-heeled boots crunched through the thick gravel, she held out her hand to him with the automatic good manners bred into her by years at the most exclusive boarding schools. His mouth tightened as he glanced down at her extended hand, and she got the impression that the gesture did not please him. But he took her hand and shook it. His hand was big, enveloping her own much smaller one, and his skin was faintly rough and very warm. Alex shivered involuntarily as he released her cold fingers. Warmth was something she could not seem to get enough of these days. Sometimes she didn't think she would ever be truly warm again.

"Have we met?" she asked, wondering again if he could possibly have an inkling of why she was there. He seemed almost hostile toward her—or perhaps, she thought, he was that way toward everyone.

"At your father's funeral." He closed the gate and latched it again.

"Oh." There seemed to be nothing to say to that. If he had been there, she didn't remember him, which surprised her, because he was the kind of man she would have thought one automatically remembered. But then, she didn't remember much about that day. She folded her arms over her chest and tucked her hands beneath her elbows to ward off the biting chill as she looked up at him. "I'm sorry. I don't remember. Everything from that day is such a blur. . . . But thank you for coming. Philadelphia's a long way from Simpsonville."

He nodded in acknowledgment. "I'm sorry about your father, Miss Haywood."

Alex had heard those words so often over the last five weeks that she felt as though they were permanently engraved on her heart.

"Thank you."

He stood just inside the gate looking at her. As the land sloped upward, she was at a slightly higher elevation than he was, but still he dwarfed her. The sheer size of him, and the fact that he remained unsmiling, could have been intimidating if she'd been the type to be easily cowed.

"I presume you're here to see me?" She *wasn't* imagining his unfriendliness. It was there in his voice.

"Yes."

"Come on up to the barn then. I'm in the middle of something."

He started walking up the slope, his boots crunching over the gravel. She fell into step beside him, her gait just a bit unsteady as her heels sank into the inches-deep rock. Seeing her difficulty, he slid a hand around her elbow to provide support. She could feel the size and strength of that hand clear through her jacket. His grip was both impersonal and hard.

Four

✦

I have to admit, you've kind of caught me by surprise, turning up here like this. What can I do for you?"

Her ankles wobbled as her feet sank into the gravel. His grip tightened in response. Alex took a deep breath, drawing in the cold, damp air along with the smell of mud. Gritting her teeth, she pushed away the ever-threatening fog of grief and reminded herself of her purpose. Her voice was determinedly brisk when she spoke.

"I realize it's Saturday, and I apologize for encroaching on what is very probably your personal time, but—there are some matters concerning the farm that need to be dealt with as soon as possible. The girl who answered the phone at the number I have for you said I could find you up at the barn behind your house, and I should just come on over. So I did."

"Horsemen work seven days a week, Miss Haywood, so you don't need to worry about encroaching on my personal time. And you most likely were talking to my daughter, Jenny." His voice was dry. They had nearly reached the barn now, and Alex was surprised to hear the urgent beat of Black Sabbath emanating from somewhere inside. Hard rock music didn't seem compatible with this man, somehow—but of course there was that teenage boy who still watched them from the barn door to consider. Probably the music was his.

He continued, "If you'd left a message, I would have come up to Whistledown to see you. Saved you chasing me down."

"That's all right. I felt like getting out. And since I'm only planning to be here over the weekend, time is a factor."

They reached the barn. The boy moved out of the doorway, and Alex stepped inside. Welch released her elbow and followed her, rolling the door shut behind him with a loud rattle. The air was warmer in the barn, but only marginally. A line of battered light fixtures overhead gave off a meager amount of illumination. A smell, earthy but not unpleasant, greeted her. Perhaps a dozen horses looked out from the twenty or so stalls that she could see. To her left was a raw plank wall in which was centered a closed door, and to her right was a large open area. In the open area a big red horse, so skinny she could see every single one of his ribs, was tethered by a long leather strap to an iron ring affixed to the wall. Although his coat was dull and he looked half-starved, he was eating from a hay-filled manger, and a curry brush and comb lay on an overturned bucket near his feet. Still munching a mouthful of hay, the horse had his head up and was watching her with liquid brown eyes. Alex moved toward him automatically, drawn by his gaze and the obvious signs of his neediness. Two men, a slender one in a tan hunter's coverall and a stockier one in jeans and a black leather jacket, stood near the horse's hindquarters. Both turned to look at her as she approached, watching her with as much open interest as the animal had displayed.

Alex ignored them as she reached the horse and stroked his big head, then sought Welch out with her gaze. He stood at the mouth of the open area looking at her, the boy at his side.

"Is this animal ill? Why is he so thin?" she demanded, her voice raised to be heard over Black Sabbath's dirge-like chorus. It was very possible that the animal belonged to Whistledown Farm, and was, thus, technically hers. But whether he was hers or not didn't really matter. She loved horses, and could not bear to see them mistreated.

"Turn the music off, Josh," Welch directed. With a sullen twitch of his mouth the boy headed toward a yellow boom box on a bale of hay near the door. Welch moved to join Alex and the horse, one hand reaching into his pocket. When he withdrew it, he was holding a peppermint, which he began to unwrap. The music stopped abruptly and for a moment the sound of crinkling cellophane filled the void.

"My own personal theory is that horses run better when they're hungry," Welch said, voice and expression bland, meeting her gaze as the boy reappeared beside him. Alex's eyes widened in outrage. The boy spoke up hastily before she could reply.

"We just got him in here this morning," he said, shooting Welch a reproachful glance before looking at Alex out of eyes of the same luminous shade of greenish-blue as the older man's. "The man Dad bought him off of swore there's nothing wrong with him. He said he's just naturally sorry-looking."

The horse was stretching his head out toward Welch now, eager for the candy. With a mocking glance at Alex, Welch gave it to him, patting the too-thin neck as the animal crunched and the scent of peppermint filled the air. Indignant at being made fun of, Alex glared at him. If he noticed her ire at all, it didn't seem to bother him.

"I can't believe ol' Cary talked you into payin' thirty

thousand dollars for this fellow, Joe," the man in the leather jacket said. Alex glanced at him. He was about six feet tall, more homely than handsome with auburn hair brushed straight back from his brow, twinkling brown eyes and squashed-looking features that somehow matched his stocky frame. He and the other man had been watching and listening to the proceedings with interest. Now they were looking at the horse. "What's his name, Victory Dance? I reckon you *will* dance if you get a victory out of him." His gaze shifted to Alex and as their eyes met he grinned suddenly. "By the way, hel-*lo*, sweet thing! You doin' anything for the rest of my life?"

Taken aback, Alex's eyes widened on his face. Beside him, his coveralled friend grimaced and walked around to the horse's other side as though to distance himself from the conversation. The horse snorted, bobbing his head up and down and nudging Welch's arm, clearly asking for another peppermint.

"The fool with the big mouth here is Tom Kinkaid, our local sheriff," Welch said brusquely to Alex, reaching into his pocket as he spoke and extracting another peppermint, which he proceeded to unwrap. "He's about as smart as he acts, but it's an inborn condition and he just plain can't help it, so I hope you'll be kind enough to overlook him. Tommy, this is Alexandra Haywood. You know, Charles Haywood's daughter."

"Oh, jeez," the sheriff said, making a face. The scent of peppermint was once more strong as Victory Dance crunched into the candy. "Sorry about your father, Miss Haywood."

Alex nodded acknowledgment, and held out her hand to him. Kinkaid shook it. But instead of releasing it immediately, he hung on to it and grinned at her again. "If the rest of my life is out, I'd still like to take you to dinner tonight."

"Thank you, but no," Alex said firmly, pulling her hand free. She glanced up at Welch, meaning to request a few minutes of his time alone so she could say what she had come to say and be done with it. Before she could get the words out he spoke again.

"While we're making introductions, that's Ben Ryder, our local dentist, over there behind the horse, and this"—he rested a light hand on the shoulder of the boy beside him—"is my son Josh."

There were handshakes all around and a murmured exchange of words.

"Dad, can I *go*?" Josh asked impatiently as soon as the introductions were finished.

Welch focused on his son. "You get all those stalls mucked out?"

"Yeah."

"Horses fed and watered?"

"Yeah."

"Tack all clean and put up?"

"Yeah."

"Am I ever going to catch you smoking another cigarette?" There was a sternness to Welch's face and tone that would have made Alex quake if she'd been a kid and they'd been directed at her.

"No sir."

"Then I guess so. Put Victory Dance up, then you can go on back to the house and help Jenny and Grandpa with that school project Jenny's working on."

Josh's eyes widened on his father's face. "Dad!" he protested. "I've been grounded for a week! I did everything you told me to! I won't smoke any more cigarettes, I promise! *Please* let me go!"

Welch frowned as he seemed to consider. Then he nodded once.

"Okay. Put Victory Dance up and you've done your time. Tell Eli I said it was okay for him to drop you off over at Burke's on his way to basketball practice."

"*Yes.*" Josh pumped his fist. Turning, he moved to untie Victory Dance. Alex patted the big red horse one more time before he was led away.

"Is there a place where we could talk—privately?" Alex asked Welch in a low but determined voice before he could fall into conversation with the other two men, who were discussing the merits, or rather the lack of them, of the retreating animal.

"Sure. Come on into my office." He nodded toward the closed door opposite. "Such as it is."

"Cary must've been drunk as a damned skunk! That's the worst-looking animal I've 'bout ever seen." This, addressed to the dentist and accompanied by a woefully shaken head, came from the sheriff in a disbelieving undertone.

"Just let it go, Tommy, would you?" Welch overheard, and his eyes glinted ominously as he looked at the sheriff. Again Alex registered the man's intimidation potential.

"Sorry, Joe." The sheriff sounded repentant rather than intimidated. Welch's expression didn't soften as he glanced down at Alex.

"This way," he said, nodding toward the door.

Alex moved toward it, her boots sinking soundlessly into the well-raked sawdust. Welch reached around to open the door for her, then stood back, allowing her to precede him inside.

The room was small, perhaps eight by ten feet, and certainly not fancy, with white-painted drywall, a gray-speckled linoleum floor, and a suspended ceiling crisscrossed with strips of aluminum to hold it in place. A single frosted light panel in the ceiling provided unflatteringly bright illumination. In the center of the room stood a metal desk with a wood-veneer top that was cluttered with papers. A black vinyl desk chair on metal casters sat askew behind the desk, and another table with a switched-off computer and a telephone was pushed up against the rear wall. On the left were do-it-yourself shelves holding a motley collection of trophies, photos, books, and papers above perhaps half a dozen black metal file cabinets. Two more office chairs—metal arms and legs, molded vinyl seats and backs—had been placed in front of the desk.

"Have a seat." Gesturing in the general direction of the two visitors' chairs, Welch unzipped his coat without removing it and walked behind the desk, pulled the black vinyl chair into position, then glanced at her and hesitated, obviously waiting for her to sit down before he did. Southern men were known for their manners, but Alex wouldn't have expected this man to be so punctilious. She sat and he followed suit, rolled his chair close to the desk, placed his hands flat on top, and looked at her levelly.

"Shoot," he ordered.

Slightly uncomfortable and annoyed at herself because of it, Alex stalled for time, crossing her legs and placing her folded hands on her raised knee before meeting his gaze.

"There's no pleasant way to say what I have to say."

His eyebrows rose.

She'd done this what seemed like a hundred times since the funeral, but it was still not easy. The staffs of four houses had been dismissed, and the houses themselves had been put on the market. The crew of her father's yacht had been told to seek other positions, as had the crews of his private planes, and the boat and planes were in the process of being sold. Accompanied by a phalanx of lawyers, she'd addressed the employees of each hospital, each nursing home, each HMO, personally delivering the bad news that they would be sold or closed, although her lawyers could and would have done it for her, without any need for her presence. But as the only family member named as an executor of her father's will, as well as his oldest, closest child, she had felt that it was her responsibility to speak for him now that he could no longer speak for himself.

As she must speak for him now. Alex took a deep breath. "Mr. Welch, I'm very sorry, but I'm going to have to let you go."

Five

✦

His eyes narrowed as that sank in. "Are you saying I'm *fired?*"

"That's what I'm saying." Alex's voice was steady and her gaze never faltered. "I'm giving you thirty days' notice, which I believe is more than fair."

Welch's lips thinned and he leaned back in his chair, rocking in it a little, his gaze shifting to fix unseeingly on the ceiling. He looked very big sitting there, and very— Alex supposed the word was "daunting," although she didn't like to admit that she felt vaguely unnerved in the face of his sudden tense silence. His unshaven jaw had grown hard, his lips had compressed into a thin line, and all the muscles in his powerful body seemed poised for action. It was obvious that her news had caught him totally by surprise. After a long, nerve-racking moment his gaze snapped back to meet hers. Placing both hands flat on the desktop, he leaned forward. His eyes were grim.

"You can't be serious."

She had not expected him to argue with her. No one so far had *argued.* Of course, this was the first time she had delivered the bad news in such a one-on-one setting. Usually she gave a little speech to a gathering of the dismissed, with lawyers at her back, and was whisked away the moment she was done. This time, for very personal reasons, she had decided to tackle the job completely on her own.

Possibly she'd made a miscalculation.

She gathered her courage and her wits, and met his gaze head on. "I am completely serious, Mr. Welch, believe me."

"You got somebody to replace me?"

"No. The position is being eliminated."

"The position is being . . ." He broke off as if words failed him, shook his head, and then continued, looking at her very hard. "What do you mean, the position is being eliminated? You can't eliminate the position! There's six hundred and seventeen acres of farmland I manage for you, Miss Haywood. Each year we do about a hundred fifty acres each of corn and soybeans, and a hundred acres of tobacco. You know anything about tobacco quotas or crop rotation or seasonal workers or anything like that?" Alex gave a tiny negative shake of her head. "I didn't think so. Plus I got four of your horses stabled at Churchill Downs, two out there in my barn—in foal, I might add— and more up the hill in Whistledown's barn. Are *you* planning to take care of them?"

"The horses will be sold."

"*What?*" Suddenly he looked like he was ready to jump out of his chair, come around the desk, and throttle her. "You can't do that! You don't know damn anything about what we've been trying to do here with those horses! God damn it to hell, we're almost where we want to be!"

Alex's chin went up as anger sparked to life inside her. She was not used to being spoken to like that—and she was definitely not used to being sworn at. "Oh, yes, I can do that, believe me. And I don't *care* what you've been trying to do here with those horses. The point is, you won't be doing it for me any longer."

Mission accomplished. Alex stood up.

"You got a buyer?" The question was flung at her like a rock.

"That's your job, Mr. Welch. Selling the horses, that is. I expect you to complete it within the thirty days of your notice. The farm will be sold as well, but you don't need to concern yourself about that. My people will handle it."

"You're selling Whistledown?" He looked, and sounded, as stunned as if she'd slapped him. Manners either abandoned or forgotten in the heat of the moment, he remained seated although she was now on her feet staring icily at him. He leaned back in his chair, the fingers of one hand drumming the desktop. His gaze never left her face. "Do you have any idea what a jewel you have here? Whistledown Farm is one of the few properties of any size in this area that is still almost entirely intact. Six hundred and seventeen acres of prime Kentucky bluegrass! What, are you going to sell out to a developer? And let him turn it into a subdivision, with a house on every quarter acre? Your father would turn over in his grave! He loved this place. Hell, I love it! During the eight years I've been managing it, I've spent every single day working my ass off to make Whistledown pay its own way. Damn it to *hell*, we've been making a profit on the land for the last five years! Do you have any idea how hard that is? And we're just now getting the racing stable built up to the point where it's worth a crap! I've got two mares in foal to Storm Cat in that barn. Another one . . . Ah, you don't understand a word I'm saying, do you? I'm wasting my breath talking to you."

"There's nothing you can say that will make a difference, Mr. Welch. The farm is going to be sold. The horses are going to be sold. And at the end of thirty days, you're going to be out of a job. End of discussion." Alex's voice was cold. In the face of his anger, hanging on to her composure was difficult, but she was determined to do it.

"The horses are going to be sold." He stood up then, his mouth tight, his voice bitter, and thrust his hands into the front pockets of his jeans. The edges of his coat parted even more with the sudden movement, and she noticed in passing that he wore a red-and-gray plaid flannel shirt beneath, over a white T-shirt that contrasted vividly with the bronze of his skin. "You realize you'd get a hell of a lot better price for the horses if you waited until the summer sale at Keeneland? Or at least until after the mares have foaled?"

"I have no intention of arguing with you, Mr. Welch. You have thirty days to liquidate inventory." Alex turned away and started walking toward the door. There was no point in prolonging this. She'd said everything she had to say, and the bottom line was that he could like it or lump it.

"Liquidate inventory! Jesus!" He came around the side of the desk and caught up with her in two strides, grabbing her arm, swinging her around to face him. She was five-foot-seven, a good height, and with her high-heeled boots on she probably stood around five-foot-ten. Yet he was still far taller than her—she had to tilt her head back to meet his furious gaze—and far bigger, too. The breadth of his shoulders and chest dwarfed her slender frame, and as his hands gripped both her arms she realized that they were big enough to wrap around them twice. She could feel the hard strength of his fingers through her jacket, and had the unpleasant sensation that he was looming over her, doing his best to intimidate her with his sheer physical size.

Alex began to lose her temper. She liked being man-handled even less than she liked being sworn at. He was glaring at her, biting off each word. "See, basically we got two problems when it comes to *liquidating inventory*: First, there are the horses that your dad just bought. He laid out one point two million for one and nine hundred and eighty thousand for the other. Then there are the mares in foal to Storm Cat. They're worth a pretty piece of change, too. So are a few others. Finding buyers for that many high-end horses at this time of the year isn't going to be easy: there are only so many players at that level of the game. Which brings us to the second problem: The rest of 'em you won't get jack for. We're talking glue or dog-food factories here. Your father kept them, kept paying for their feed and care, long after their careers as racehorses were over, because he appreciated what they'd done in the past, and he flat-out loved them. You'll be selling animals he loved by the pound, Miss Haywood. Are you sure that's what you want to do?"

"Get your hands off me." She spoke through her teeth, her eyes blazing into his, daring him to disobey. Too angry to feel the least bit cautious, she tried to jerk her arms free of his hold. She didn't succeed; he was too strong. But then he let her go, letting his hands drop away from her arms and taking a step backward although he still looked as blindingly angry as she felt. "Don't try to manipulate me with sob stories, Mr. Welch. It won't work."

"I'm not trying to manipulate you with anything at all." His voice was low and hard. His eyes were bright with fury as they met hers. He jammed his hands into the front pockets of his jeans as if to keep himself from grabbing hold of her again. "I'm trying to get you to see what an impossible, idiotic, damned *inhumane* thing you're asking me to do. *I can't sell those horses.* Not in thirty days. Not under fire-sale conditions. I can't do it, and I won't."

"If you're not up to the job of selling *my* horses, Mr. Welch, then you leave me no choice but to make other arrangements for their disposal. There *are* other possibilities, you know. To begin with, my lawyers have already ascertained that there are auction houses that can handle a mass sale of this sort."

"Auction houses! You cold, unfeeling . . ." He broke off, but his eyes flamed and his meaning was clear.

Alex had had enough. She drew herself up to her full height and met his glare head-on. "You're fired, Mr. Welch. As of right now. Forget the thirty days' notice."

Turning her back on him, head held high, spine as straight as a soldier's, she moved toward the door again. She was furious; he had made her furious. She knew it, recognized the sensation, and realized to her surprise that the hot rush of temper was the first unblunted emotion that she had felt since her father's death.

For a brief, welcome moment she felt like herself again.

His voice followed her, almost taunting in its tone. "There's twenty-two of them altogether, here and at Churchill and in Whistledown's barn. They get fed again at five o'clock. Hay and grain. Plus Toreador's on antibiotics. Feelsogood has a little crack in the bar of his hoof, and could use some ointment on it. Mama's Boy's been bleeding again, and he needs to be scoped. Plus a whole lot more. You gonna do all that, Miss Haywood? Or you think you can get somebody else in here who knows what the hell he's doing to do it? Just like that?"

Alex stopped walking and pursed her lips. He was the most obnoxious man she had ever dealt with. She didn't like him, didn't want any more to do with him, and had already derived a considerable degree of pleasure from the thought that, when she walked out of here, she never had to set eyes on him again. Yet he had a point, and as angry as she was, she wasn't fool enough to ignore it.

Gritting her teeth, she pivoted to face him. "All right, Mr. Welch. I take it back. You have your thirty days' notice again. But that's all it is. Thirty days, which you are to use to divest Whistledown Farm of its horses. Is that clear?"

She held his gaze for a long, and what she hoped was an authoritative, moment.

His lips thinned, and she thought he was going to start arguing again. But instead he nodded once, curtly. Victory, Alex thought, especially if one disregarded the clenched fists at his sides and the rigidity of his stance. She did disregard them, turning her back on him again and stalking out of the office and across the barn, conscious that he was following her every step of the way.

❦❦❦❦

"Bitch," Joe muttered furiously under his breath, stopping at the barn door and scowling after Alexandra Haywood's retreating form. His hands were clenched into fists at his sides and a pulse pounded like a kettledrum in his temples. Thirty days to dispose of twenty-two horses. Hell, he hated to part with even one, especially under conditions like these. But it didn't seem like he had much choice. Much as he hated to acknowledge the truth, she had the right to order him to sell them if she wished.

After all, they were *her* horses.

"Bitch," he said again, louder.

"Man, that woman is *fine*." Tommy came up behind him, clapping a hand down on his shoulder, his voice admiring as he watched Alexandra Haywood's shapely black leather-clad backside wiggle toward her car. Her sleek blond hair was a bright beacon against the overcast sky. "I wouldn't mind having that as *my* boss. If you're lucky, maybe she'll chase you around your desk. 'Course, you wouldn't catch me running."

Joe ignored that. Wishing he could shut the woman's

edict out as easily as he could his view of her person, he moved, stepping forward and sliding the barn door closed with a rattle and a click. Then he turned, looking around his barn with a grim expression. Well over half his income had just walked out the door, taking with it nearly every dream he had been building on for the past eight years. He couldn't quite seem to take it in.

His goal of building an internationally recognized racing stable had just been blown all to hell. And he had to deliver the coup de grâce himself by selling all the Whistledown horses. Within thirty days, yet. And merry Christmas to you, too, Miss Haywood, he thought grimly.

He would sooner open a vein.

"Holy hell, Joe, you look like a dog done mistook your leg for a tree! What's up?"

Joe took a deep, hopefully calming breath. Blind rage never helped anyone do anything except have a heart attack. He and Tommy went way back: they'd been friends since they'd been in Miss Maureen's kindergarten class together, and they knew each other well. Besides, there was no keeping this secret: news of what was going down would ricochet around Simpsonville and, indeed, the larger world of racing like a shot as soon as he started looking for potential buyers for his—*her*—horses. It was that kind of town. It was that kind of business. Everybody knew what was going on with everybody else, and there was no sense in fighting it.

"She fired me. Said she's selling the farm. Ordered me to sell the horses. Within thirty days." His voice was hard. Inside he was starting to ache. Suleimann, Toreador, Silver Wonder—God, he loved Silver Wonder! As one of the mares in foal to Storm Cat, she was worth approximately half a million dollars. He could never afford to buy her himself. . . .

Tommy's eyes widened. "You're shittin' me, right?"

"I'm not shittin' you, Tommy."

"The bitch!" There was outrage in Tommy's voice, and Joe took some small degree of comfort from hearing his own sentiments echoed so exactly. "That's hard, man. Real hard."

"Yeah." Joe grimaced. Tommy looked at him awkwardly, clearly not knowing how to express his obvious sympathy.

"You know, Joe, I don't like to question your dad's judgment—the main reason being that when it comes to horses he's usually right—but I don't think that horse he talked you into—that Victory Dance—is worth anywhere near thirty thousand. Where'd you say he found him?" Ben came walking toward them shaking his balding head. Six-one and wiry, Ben had short, mud brown hair surrounding a rapidly enlarging chrome dome, and a perpetually worried look that his friends put down to a constant fear of losing his remaining hair.

"At a claiming race at Pimlico," Joe said absently, already beginning to run through a mental Rolodex of possible buyers. If it had to be done, then he was going to do his damndest to do it right, because he wanted nothing but the best for all of his—*her*—horses. Getting them all placed properly, especially at this time of the year, was going to be a tough trick to pull out of his hat. Thanksgiving was just around the corner, and three weeks after that was Christmas. Horsemen got holiday fever just like the rest of the country.

Happy holidays to you too, Miss Haywood.

"Ben, man, Joe's been fired. She's selling Whistledown Farm. He's gotta sell all of 'em. His horses." Tommy spoke in a hushed voice, like he was announcing that Joe had terminal cancer or something.

"Don't try to BS me, Tommy." Ben was a friend from kindergarten days, too. They'd all known each other for so long that they were practically family. Which had its good points, and its bad.

"I ain't BS'ing you. It's God's honest truth."

"Yeah, Ben, it's the truth," Joe said wearily before Ben could ask him for confirmation, as he knew he was getting ready to do. Ben stopped walking and looked at Joe, concern plain on his face.

"What are you going to do?"

Joe shrugged. He was so angry he could chew nails, and hurting worse by the minute too, but he wasn't going to show it any more than he could help. "They're her horses. I guess if she says sell, I'm gonna sell."

Ben was shaking his head. "Can she just waltz in here like that and *do* that? Don't you have some kind of contract or something?"

Joe stared at Ben, arrested. In the face of Alexandra Haywood's bombshell, he'd stopped thinking clearly, apparently. Every year he signed a piece of paper sent down by a lawyer of Charles Haywood's. The first time he'd actually read it. It had last crossed his desk in September. The matter had become so routine that he had barely glanced at it before scribbling his name. But it was a contract engaging him to manage Whistledown Farm, and to act as private trainer for the Whistledown horses. A legal, binding contract that, if his memory served him correctly, ran through December of the following year.

"You know what? I do."

The three regarded each other in silence for a moment.

"So go tell Attila the Hon the news." Tommy grinned suddenly at his own joke. "Attila the Hon—H-O-N—get it? Kinda catchy, don't you think?"

Joe's answering smile was grim. "What I think is that I'm going to go have a little chat with Miss Haywood. Before she starts calling auction houses, or something."

Six

✦

By the time Alex parked the car in Whistledown's driveway and got out, she was as down in the dumps as she had ever been. She had delivered so much bad news to so many people lately that she should have been used to it, but still it bothered her. Even when the recipient was as obnoxious as Joe Welch.

Unpleasant as her interview with him had been, at least it had the virtue of being over, she reminded herself. She had assumed the mantle of leadership that her father's death had thrust upon her and done what she had to do. She should be proud of herself for handling a difficult situation—and a difficult man—with the requisite firmness. Her father would be, if he knew. But she didn't feel proud. What she felt was—tired. So very, very tired. As if she could go to bed right now and lie down and sleep for days.

As if her burst of temper had leached away every remaining bit of her strength.

What Welch didn't know was that she hated to part with Whistledown and its horses too. He'd been right: her father had loved both the farm and its animals, and if she could have she would have kept the farm going as a tribute to him. He'd looked forward to his regular biannual visits as his favorite escape from the pressures of a high-stress life. He'd even jetted in on summer weekends occasionally, stealing time from whatever else he was doing to check on the progress of a favorite horse. Whistledown was one of the few purchases he had made simply for his own pleasure, with no thought of financial gain. But there was no help for it. The farm was an expensive luxury that they could no longer afford, and it had to go.

If she'd done as her lawyers had suggested and left Joe Welch to them she could have avoided today's unpleasantness, she thought. The farm was a minor holding, after all. She could have just stayed at home in Philadelphia and concentrated on getting on with her life.

But she'd had to come. Insisting on visiting Whistledown Farm to give Joe Welch the bad news personally had been little more than a ploy to get herself here. She had ignored the advice of her friends, who had argued that the visit would be too painful, and turned down the escort of her lawyers by the simple technique of just saying no: they worked for her, after all. She had needed to come to Whistledown Farm, and she had needed to come alone. Badly. The façade of coping well that she had assumed since her father's death was starting to crack, she feared. The truth was, she was not coping well at all. She felt empty, numb, frightened, betrayed. When the matter of disposing of Whistledown Farm had been broached to her she had experienced a fierce, urgent, totally irresistible need to come to the place that her father had loved so well, the place where he had died. She needed to see where it had happened, to absorb, if she could, some sense of how and why. Otherwise, she feared she was never, ever going to be able to come to terms with his death.

Her father—a suicide? It just didn't seem possible: suicide was not in her father's character as she knew it. Which begged the question: Just how well had she known him after all?

She had thought that she had known him very well indeed. Apparently she had been wrong.

Alex took a deep breath, filling her lungs with cold damp air as she climbed the steps to Whistledown's front door. Dwelling on her loss did no good, she knew, and so she forced her thoughts in another direction. Stopping as she reached the porch, she turned back to look out over the countryside. It was beautiful even on so unlovely a day. She could turn in any direction and see acre upon acre of rolling fields. A total of exactly two houses were visible— one distant roof, and, a mere two fields to the left, the white clapboard farmhouse in which Joe Welch and his family lived. Horses fastened into scarlet blankets—scarlet and white were the Whistledown colors—dotted the fields like roving wildflowers.

The house itself had been built of massive stones decades before the Civil War. Years ago, someone had modernized the kitchen, added bathrooms, and updated the plumbing and electricity, but otherwise the house was unchanged. The original stones had long since been painted white and embellished with a double front porch boasting six soaring Corinthian columns. It looked like something straight out of *Gone with the Wind.*

The first time she'd visited had been just after her father had bought the place. She'd been fifteen, in the throes of dealing simultaneously with adolescent pudginess, rebelliousness, and a brand-new stepmother (number three, Alicia) who was a slim-as-a-reed, mean-as-a-snake former model. The family visit had lasted two interminable summertime weeks, and had included her father and her three-year-old half-sister, Neely.

By the next summer Alicia had been history, and the concept of a family visit anywhere had never been repeated.

But she remembered how excited her father had been

that summer as he'd walked her around showing off the place, and her heart ached anew.

I wish you were here with me now, she said silently to her father, and as her throat closed up she sent the thought winging skyward like a prayer.

Something cold and wet touched her face as though in response. For a moment she was startled. Glancing up, she realized that it was starting to rain. As another droplet hit her, she turned away from her memories and walked inside the house.

It was warm, she noticed thankfully as she closed the door, and the interior smelled faintly of lemon furniture polish. The red-based Oriental rug on the gleaming hard-wood floor lent a cheerful note to the vast entry hall with its cream damask wallpaper and fifteen-foot ceiling. The huge Waterford-crystal chandelier overhead provided a wash of needed light. The formal living room, cool in shades of cream and beige with only bowls of silk roses for punch, opened off the entry hall to her right, and to her left was the enormous dining room with its heavy antique furniture. Both rooms were framed by gleaming mahogany pocket doors. Before her, a wide curving staircase beckoned the way to the second floor. Behind the staircase was a swinging door that led into the kitchen.

"Well, you find Joe?" Inez bustled into the front hall from somewhere in the back of the house, her face wreathed in smiles. A onetime migrant worker who had married a local, Inez was around fifty, plump, with a round, unlined face. Today she wore red polyester slacks, a pink and red floral blouse, and flat black bedroom slippers. Alex wondered absently if that was her usual working attire. If so, it was a far cry from the black-garbed maids she had grown up with.

"Oh, yes, I found Joe," Alex said dryly, unzipping her jacket and handing it to the housekeeper.

"He is so handsome, that one." Inez accepted the jacket with a sigh. "It is such a shame he has no wife. Poor man. Poor children."

"What happened to his wife?" It was clear from Inez's tone that there was more to the story than a simple divorce.

"Ah, she was no good. She ran away, just ran away and left him with those little children. Years ago. She ran away and never came back. He is raising those three *pequeños* all alone, which is a hard thing for a man."

"Is he?" Alex felt a twinge of conscience about firing the man, impossible as he was, in the face of that news, but, she reminded herself, there was nothing she could do about it, so there was no point in feeling bad about what she could not help. There was something else she needed to talk to the housekeeper about. Although Inez came in only once a week when the house was empty, she worked as needed when any of the family was in residence. It was very possible that she had been here on that night. . . .

"Inez." Alex paused. It was hard for her to put the question into words. The images the words carried with them hurt too much. She tried again. "You were here working during my father's last visit, weren't you? Did he seem any different than usual? Sad, or—or depressed?"

Inez looked at her sorrowfully. "I have already been asked this by many people. The answer is, no ma'am. He was just as he always was, a very nice gentleman."

A very nice gentleman. Alex swallowed hard. "That last day—you were here?" Inez nodded. "There was nothing out of the ordinary? Nothing at all?"

"No, ma'am." Inez's dark eyes were distressed. "The last time I saw him, he was happy, laughing, playing cards with his guests. When I came the next morning, and heard that Joe had found him *so* . . . It was a thing that I just could not believe."

Alex focused on the one bit of new information. "Joe—Joe *Welch* found him? Found my father's body?"

"Yes. You did not know? I thought that maybe it was the reason you wished to speak to Joe."

"No." Alex shook her head. Inez knew nothing as yet about any dismissals, including her own imminent one, and Alex couldn't face telling her right at the moment. It was all just too much. Maybe she would let the lawyers handle it after all. "I didn't know. I . . ."

The phone rang, interrupting. Its summons was faint but demanding.

"You want me to get it?" Inez asked, and when Alex nodded she hurried toward the kitchen, leaving the swinging door wide open behind her. Alex could hear the murmur of her voice as she answered the phone, but paid no real attention to what was said. If Joe Welch had found her father's body, she would have to talk to him again, much as it went against the grain for her to approach him with questions. She had to know as much as she could. Knowledge provided the only consolation available to her.

"It is for you." Inez appeared in the kitchen doorway. "A Mr. Paul O'Neil."

Alex's face softened. Paul was her fiancé, and he was returning a call she'd left on his answering machine the night before. Since the funeral, he'd been so patient with her. She'd been distraught at first, then emotionally and physically numb; certainly their sex life had suffered. Actually, it had been killed stone cold dead. She was going to have to work on that when she got home, she told herself. And she'd been gone a lot, too. This past week she had spent shuttling between New York and L.A., taking care of details pertaining to her father's death. Come to think of it, she hadn't actually *seen* Paul since Thursday last. Their wedding was scheduled for the coming April 9, her twenty-eighth birthday. Of course, like everything else in her life, the plans for the ceremony were now up in the air. April seemed too soon to expect to feel the joyousness that she wanted to feel at her wedding, and the lavishness of the affair was going to have to be scaled way, way back.

"I'll take it in the library," Alex said, turning away, and Inez nodded, disappearing into the kitchen again.

Alex felt her spirits lift as she anticipated talking to Paul. She'd met him when she was scoping out the two-hundred-year-old, expertly renovated downtown Philadelphia office building in which he worked. A photographer by profession, she took pictures of interesting architecture and landscaping for coffee-table books; it wasn't a very lucrative field, but then, she'd never had to live on what she made.

Paul hadn't even known whose daughter she was until they'd dated for months. He'd asked her to marry him in September, and she had instantly said yes. A month later, her father had died and her life had fallen apart.

But in the midst of chaos, Paul had been there for her. It was good to know that he loved her, that he was someone she could count on during these dark days.

The library was a large room with an ornate vaulted ceiling. Floor-to-ceiling shelves fashioned from the wood of ash trees felled on the estate lined three walls. They were filled to overflowing with books, photographs, and other mementos. The fourth wall had been painted a soft celery green and was dominated by a large fireplace with a graceful, white-painted Adam mantel. Over the fireplace, between tall, vividly colored china parrots that graced either side of the mantel, hung a portrait of her latest stepmother, the beautiful Mercedes, her long black hair shining with blue highlights as it streamed over a pink silk Versace ball gown.

Multiple portraits of Charles Haywood's five previous wives had been kept in storage in a Philadelphia warehouse, as Alex had already discovered. She supposed that each time her father divorced and remarried, he replaced portraits of his previous spouse with those of the new one in every residence he owned. Which was rather humorous, if one thought about it. In years to come, when the shock of her father's death had eased, Alex thought she might be able to remember, and laugh.

For now, though, even the twinge of amusement she felt was accompanied by pain. Suppressing a sigh, she sat down in the big leather chair behind the polished walnut desk. A yellow legal pad, mercifully free of any of her father's handwriting, and a silver ballpoint pen lay on the desk. Instant images of her father sitting in that same chair behind that same desk talking on the phone while he scribbled notes on the legal pad crowded into her mind's eye. She could picture him as clearly as if the scene were unfolding before her.

Ah, Daddy. Why?

But giving in to the pain did not ease it, as she had already learned. She forced thoughts of her father away, then determinedly picked up the phone.

"Paul?"

"Alex! Is that you?"

"Were you expecting somebody else?" Her voice was light, teasing. At the sound of his voice he instantly came into focus in her mind's eye: immaculately groomed tobacco brown hair brushed straight back from an aesthete's bony face; bright hazel eyes, long blade of a nose, thin, well-defined lips; tall, whipcord lean, handsome, intense; a well-groomed, well-educated, sophisticated man with whom she was madly in love. Even talking to him over the phone was a pleasure. Only when her body began to relax did she realize how tense her muscles had been. Smiling, she swiveled the chair around so that she could gaze out the pair of tall, silk-festooned windows at the rain that was now falling in gentle sprinkles, and leaned back. "Oh, Paul, it's so good to hear your voice! Are you at home? I wish I was there with you!"

"Actually, I'm out of town today. Alex, um, I have something that I need to tell you."

It struck Alex that he sounded odd. Nervous, almost. Paul, the most self-confident person she had ever met, had never in her experience of him been nervous. Her eyes widened, and her hand tightened around the receiver.

"Is something wrong?" she asked. Even before he answered, she sensed that more bad news was winging her way.

"I hate breaking it to you over the phone like this. God, you're never around anymore, are you? So I guess it's your own fault."

"What are you talking about?" It was a struggle to keep her voice steady.

There was a brief pause.

"Look, I got married last night," Paul said heavily. "Ah, Alex, I'm sorry, but it just wasn't working out between us, and you know it as well as I do. I . . ."

"You—got—married—last—night?" Alex interrupted disbelievingly, spacing each word as she absorbed what felt like a body blow.

"Yes, well, I, uh . . ."

Before he could continue, Alex cut him off. "You got *married* last night? But—you couldn't have. We're engaged. You and I. The wedding's all planned for April. I'm wearing your ring." She looked stupidly down at the huge, exquisite, marquise-cut diamond that adorned her left hand.

"You can keep the ring," Paul said, his voice eager. "Tara wouldn't want it, I'm sure, and anyway if she does I'll buy her another one. The thing is, I . . ."

"Tara? Tara Gould?" Tara Gould was the only daughter of one of the wealthiest men in Pennsylvania. Come to think of it, Paul had been working on a commission for her father all through the autumn. And Tara had been around many times when Alex had been with Paul, looking over blueprints, appearing at cocktail parties and dinners, dropping things off at Paul's office. Obviously she had been around many more times when Alex *hadn't* been with Paul. A thin, brown little thing, Tara had been easy for Alex to dismiss. "You married *Tara Gould?* Last night?"

It was impossible. He couldn't have. It had to be a joke—but even as the thought ran through her mind, Alex knew that it *wasn't* a joke, that he was telling the truth, that he had really done this unbelievable thing to her, to them. . . .

"It happened really fast." Paul's tone was more defensive than apologetic. "With you gone, and she was here, and one thing led to another, and, well . . ."

"She has lots of money, which I no longer do, and her father has lots of influence, while mine is at the center of a scandal, besides being dead," Alex said bitterly, knowing as she said it that she had the situation summed up in a nutshell. To marry Tara Gould like this, Paul could only have been interested in money and a helping hand up the political ladder all along. At the knowledge, Alex felt as if her lungs were being squeezed so tightly that she could scarcely breathe.

"Now, Alex, that's not fair." Paul's voice was soft and coaxing. In the past, she had loved it when he'd talked to her in that tone. Now it just made the sense of betrayal that much worse.

She was losing—no, had lost—Paul too. Dear Lord, how was she going to bear another loss?

"I hope you and Tara will be very happy," Alex said, holding on to her dignity by the skin of her teeth while she fought to keep her voice from shaking. Shock had held the worst of the pain at bay, but now it was wearing off and she was starting to feel the sharp, cold agony of it like a knife twisting in her heart.

"You know I'll always love you." It was his coaxing voice again. "It's just that . . ."

"Good-bye, Paul," Alex said. Before he could reply, she lifted the receiver from her ear, swung around in the chair, and set it back in its cradle. For a moment she simply sat there staring at the telephone, and at her hands, both of which now held the receiver in place as if to keep it from rearing up and attacking her. She was gripping the cream-colored plastic so tightly that her knuckles showed white. Her engagement ring glowed with a life of its own as her finger moved: the huge diamond sparkled and winked as if mocking her pain.

Tara was probably with Paul right now, mocking her as brazenly as the diamond.

"You son of a bitch!" Alex said, voice low, her breathing suddenly harsh and ragged as she snatched at the ring and dragged it off her hand. "You cheater! You no-good, dirty rotten *liar!*"

Gasping as she fought back a sudden rush of scalding tears, she hurled the ring away from her as hard as she could.

"Whoa, now," a male voice said. Unbelievably, without the least warning, Joe Welch appeared in the library's open doorway just in time to field the ring that seemed to be aimed straight at his face. With a quick movement, he dodged, grabbed it out of the air, and stood there frowning at her.

Seven

♣

What are *you* doing here?" Alex demanded, struggling to control the ragged breathing that threatened to turn into open sobs at any second. She glared at him. Although her vision was slightly blurred from incipient tears, his tall form in the bright blue jacket was impossible to mistake. "This is *not* a good time for me."

"I can see that." His voice was dry.

Instead of exercising a modicum of tact and going away, he walked on into the room and right up to the desk. One large brown hand pressed flat against the desktop as he leaned over it and held out her ring to her between his thumb and forefinger. The ring looked small and delicate in his big hand; the diamond flashed again, mocking her.

"Drop something?"

She drew a deep, steadying breath. Hell would freeze over before she would cry in front of this man.

"I didn't drop it. I *threw* it," she said with venom, taking the ring from him. Opening the desk drawer, she dropped the ring inside and closed the drawer with an audible snap before looking up to meet his eyes with near loathing in her own. "And I would appreciate it if you'd leave. As I said, this is not a good time for me."

"Have a fight with your boyfriend?" He straightened away from the desk and crossed his arms over his chest, regarding her as if she were an insect on a pin.

"My *fiancé* just called to tell me that he married someone else last night." Her voice was brittle. Why she admitted such a thing to him she didn't know. It was certainly none of his business, and he was certainly not one of her biggest fans. Additionally, it wasn't like her to confide her troubles in a stranger. But she'd had so many shocks over the last few weeks that, for the moment at least, she was no longer—quite—in control of herself. She was off-balance, like an acrobat teetering wildly on a high wire.

"Poor baby." He sounded the reverse of sympathetic.

Anger stung her, and her spine stiffened. She glared at him. "Look, just go away, would you?"

"So you can sit here and bawl your eyes out?"

"I am *not* going to . . ." She broke off. Her vision had cleared enough to allow her to see past the jacket to the expression on his face. He was looking her over critically, his eyes narrowed so that the crow's-feet around them were visible, and his mouth was set in a hard, straight line. Moisture gleamed faintly on his close-cropped black hair. His skin was very tan, as though he spent a great deal of time outdoors, and roughened by the heavy growth of five-o'clock shadow that darkened his jaw. The sheer size of the man seemed to shrink the room. Unwillingly, she registered his blatantly masculine appeal, and rejected it. As the saying went, pretty is as pretty does, which left this man looking like a warthog. "How did you get in here, anyway? Did you even knock? Or is it the custom around here for people to just barge into other people's houses without an invitation?"

"Inez let me in. And yes, I did knock. Go ahead and cry if you want to. I can wait."

The hateful man was watching her as if he really did expect her to burst into tears before his eyes. Her chin came up a notch, and she took a deep, steadying breath.

"All right, Mr. Welch, since you don't have the good manners to go away when you're asked to, let's get this over with: Why are you here?"

He was studying her with more attention than she welcomed, given the fact that her eyes still felt raw and kind of tingly and were, she suspected, red around the rims. With her hair pulled back and the high collar of her black turtleneck framing her features, she felt uncomfortably exposed.

"If he broke the news to you over the phone just now, he's not worth crying over, believe me."

"I have no intention of discussing my private life with you. I wouldn't have said as much as I did if you hadn't barged in here and caught me by surprise." The tears had receded now, and she was embarrassed to think that he had seen signs of them. Ordinarily, she never cried. It was something she prided herself on. From a girlhood spent first with a procession of indifferent nannies and then at a series of impersonal boarding schools, she had learned that crying never fixed anything. All it did was give one red eyes and a stuffy nose. Besides, her father had hated weepy women. He had divorced two wives because, he said, they were forever bursting into tears when he did something they didn't like.

At the thought of her father pain stirred anew. She never cried—but she had cried a river for him.

"I'm not interested in your private life, Miss Haywood. What I am interested in is Whistledown Farm."

Alex frowned direly. Looking up at him was making her neck stiff, but if she stood she feared her knees might give way. She needed to be alone, needed time to assess the damage Paul had inflicted on her and paper over the fresh rent it had made in her already lacerated heart. If it killed her, the picture she presented to the world was not going to be one of caterwauling defeat. She would hold her head high and keep putting one foot in front of the other until things got better or until the end of time, whichever came first.

At this point, she was about ready to put her money on the end of time.

"If you're here to try to talk me into changing my mind," she said, "don't bother. What I said earlier stands."

His gaze assessed her. His jaw tightened, and his eyes grew bright and hard.

"'Fraid not, Princess. I have a contract."

Alex gave a brittle laugh. "This is getting annoying, Mr. Welch. Exactly what part of *you're fired* don't you understand?"

"That's precisely my point. You can't fire me. Like I said, I have a contract. You know, one of those legal instruments between a party of the first part and a party of the second part? You can't just give me thirty days' notice and tell me to sell all the horses and then shove off." There was a hint of triumph in his voice. "It doesn't work that way."

Alex stared at him. Gritting her teeth, she mentally counted to ten.

"Go away," she said, slowly and distinctly.

"Are you hearing what I'm telling you?" His voice was rough, impatient, as he totally disregarded her words. His gaze was hard on her face. "I have a contract allowing me to manage Whistledown Farm as I see fit that runs through December of next year. That means, to begin with, that there is not going to be any fire-sale of the horses."

Why would this man not simply give up? He was looking at her as if he held all four aces in a hand of poker. The thing to do was to keep her own cool, spell the situation out to him in terms he could understand, and then maybe he would finally leave her in peace.

"Where is this contract? Can I see it?"

"It's in my office. It's legally valid, believe me. *Your* lawyers drew it up." There was the faintest hint of mockery in his tone.

Alex's patience stretched nearly to the breaking point. "So you have a contract. Well, good for you! Tell me, Mr. Welch, did you ever hear the expression, you can't get blood from a stone?"

His eyebrows knit, and he regarded her suspiciously. "A time or two. What about it?"

"My father's estate is the stone. In other words, if you still don't get it, there is no money. If your contract is valid—which I am going to leave up to my lawyers to determine because at this point I really just don't care one way or the other—the estate may be able to come to some arrangement with you about the salary you're owed. Or maybe not, depending upon the finances involved. But either way, there is simply no money to be spared for the continued operation of Whistledown Farm. Everything has to be closed down, contract or no contract. My father's estate will be lucky to escape bankruptcy."

"Don't give me that. Your father is—was—one of the richest men in the world."

"*Was* being the operative word. Some of his investments were high-risk. They went bad. When the news of his death got out, the value of his company plummeted. Then everything else he owned went down the toilet after the company stock. There is nothing, or at least very little, left. Almost everything my father owned is being sold." She managed to say it with cool matter-of-factness, revealing none of the shame and disbelief and fear with which she still faced the news.

He was staring at her as if she'd suddenly sprouted horns. "Is that the truth?"

"Cross my heart." Her reply was flippant. She was proud of that. Never let them see you bleed. It was one of her father's axioms.

Another pang of grief assaulted her.

"Is that why he . . . no." Welch stopped himself before he could finish, looking slightly uncomfortable for the first time since she had met him.

"Why my father killed himself?" Amazing how she could so coolly say these things that were tearing her up inside, Alex thought with dispassion.

"That's what I was going to say, yes." The man no longer looked uncomfortable. He looked insolent instead.

"There's no reason for you not to call a spade a spade, after all, is there, Mr. Welch? To answer your question—the one you almost asked but didn't—I don't know. He had made some bad investments, but if he hadn't died he might have been able to recover. Our own company's stock was still strong. I don't know why he did it. We may never know."

"Like I said before, I'm sorry for your loss." There was no softness in his voice or expression.

"You found his body, didn't you?" The question was abrupt. Her hands curled around the smooth leather arms of the chair for support.

The lines around his eyes deepened as he met her gaze, and his mouth tightened.

"Yeah, I did."

"Tell me about it." The demand came out of its own volition. Breathe, she reminded herself. Breathe. That she disliked this man had no bearing on anything. Her need to know about the last chapter of her father's life overrode all else.

He hesitated before replying. "What do you want to know?"

"Anything. Everything. The details."

He shook his head. "What for? There's no point in getting yourself all upset."

"No point in getting myself all upset?" Her laugh was devoid of mirth. "No point in *getting myself all upset?* Upset is not the word for what I am. I am devastated, to put it mildly. And I have been ever since I learned of my father's death. Nothing you say can make me feel worse, believe me. You think I came all the way out here to the boonies just to fire you? No. To tell you the truth, I don't give a flip if you're fired, or hired, or have a contract, or don't have a contract; you can duke that out with the lawyers until you all turn blue in the face. I'm here because I need to be where my father was, to know what he was doing, what he was *feeling*, the night he—died." She paused, took a breath. "And you can help me, if you would. Please." It went against the grain to plead with this man, but she was hungry, starving, for every last scrap of information about what had taken place.

He looked at her without speaking for a moment, his blue eyes suddenly almost dark. Then he nodded once.

"I'll tell you what I know," he said. "It's not all that much."

Without waiting for an invitation, he snagged the back of one of the pair of small Chinese Chippendale armchairs positioned by the fireplace, swung it over in front of the desk backward, and sat down. His worn jeans straddled the fragile green silk seat while her eyes widened reflexively at the sheer sacrilege of treating valuable antique furniture so cavalierly. Seeming unaware of her visceral dismay, he folded his arms along the back of the chair, leaned forward, and regarded her grimly.

"All right, so here goes: I found him around one A.M. He

was in the barn, the barn here at Whistledown, sitting with his back against the wall. I touched him and he slumped over. I checked him, felt for a pulse. He was already dead."

"What were you doing in the barn so late at night?" Again she had to remind herself to keep breathing. The picture his words conjured up made her feel sick.

"I was checking on the horses." He paused, then continued almost reluctantly. "I'd been asleep, but something woke me up. Looking back, I think I may have heard the shot that killed him."

"Oh, my God." Alex felt the blood leaching from her face. Unable to keep up appearances any longer, she leaned her head against the rolled back of the chair and deliberately drew in great gulps of air. "Oh God. Oh God."

"Damn it, I knew this wasn't a good idea." He stood up abruptly, swinging the chair out of his way, and came around behind the desk so that he towered over her. His expression was harsh. "You're not going to faint on me, are you?"

"No, I'm not," she said, willing the words to be true. If she had been in the presence of someone who displayed an ounce of sympathy, she might have done exactly that. But in front of him? No way. He was scowling down at her, his thick black brows almost meeting over the bridge of his nose. She gathered herself together to meet his gaze head-on.

"Good." The single word was curt.

"I'm sorry." She was breathing normally by sheer force of will, hoping she didn't look as limp as she felt. He still towered over her; she kept her head tilted back against the seat so that it was less exhausting to look up at him. "I just—get sick whenever I think of him—what he did. I can't believe it. I keep asking myself why. Why?" There was anguish she couldn't prevent in the question.

"He'd been drinking." He said it as though he was offering her, and her father, an excuse.

"What makes you think that?" Her gaze sharpened on his face.

"Because . . ." He hesitated, then shook his head. "Look, Miss Haywood, enough, okay? I'm no sadist. I don't believe in torturing helpless animals, small children, or bereaved women. If you want any more information, you're going to have to get it from another source."

"I want to know why you think my father had been drinking when he died." Her voice was fierce. "My father didn't drink. He is—was—a teetotaler."

"The odor of whiskey was so strong around his body that I could smell it clear across the barn." His rebuttal was almost brutal.

"Not many people knew it, but my father was a recovering alcoholic. He'd been on the wagon for years. At least ten years, without so much as a glass of wine. He was so proud of that." Her voice faltered. She gritted her teeth, and her chin came up. "I refuse to accept that he was drinking the night he died."

He was silent for a moment, just looking at her without speaking. Then he said, quietly, heavily, "Drunks fall off the wagon all the time."

Her mouth opened as her breath expelled with an audible hiss. Her gaze fixed on his while she battled to draw air back into her lungs. She felt as if she'd been flattened, as if she'd suddenly been reduced to two dimensions in a three-dimensional world. Was that the explanation she'd been seeking? Something so sordid, so simple? *Drunks fall off the wagon all the time.* No. She didn't believe it. She refused to believe it.

"I'm sorry," he offered again. This time he almost sounded as if he meant it.

At that moment they were interrupted by someone shouting Alex's name.

Eight

✢

"Alex! Alex, are you here?"

Recognizing the voice, Alex jumped up from behind the desk and hurried toward the front hall from whence the shout had come. Even as she reached the library door, her little sister came into view. At fifteen, Neely was not quite as tall as Alex but a little curvier, with thick, straight golden blond hair that fell almost to her waist. The top section had been pulled back from her face and secured by a black scrunchy into a high ponytail that bounced on top of her head with each energetic step. Her youthfully round, naturally very pretty face had been vamped to the max by the addition of oodles of black mascara and sparkling purple eye shadow. The jarring combination completely overpowered the soft gray blue of her eyes. Her cheeks were striped with a brownish blush in an obvious attempt to create cheekbones where none yet existed, and her lips were shiny with pale pink lipstick. She was dressed in the latest retro hippie chic of artfully faded, embroidered jeans and a matching denim jacket heavily fringed with beads that allowed just glimpses of a hot pink T-shirt beneath. Spike-heeled black leather mules were on her feet, beaded chandelier earrings swung from her ears, and as Neely reached out both hands to embrace her sister, Alex saw that her fingernails had been painted sky blue with minuscule daisies at the tips.

"Neely!" Alex enfolded her little sister in a hug, breathing in clouds of floral-scented perfume, surprised by how glad she was to see the girl. Despite the havoc she routinely wreaked, Neely was the person she loved best in the world. Alex had not realized how lonely she'd been feeling until Neely appeared.

"Surprise!" Neely stepped back and spread her arms wide, grinning. Looking at her sister, Alex felt the first twinges of misgiving.

"This isn't a holiday weekend. You didn't leave school without permission again, did you?" Alex asked anxiously. "You know they said they'd expel you if you did."

Neely dropped her arms, stopped smiling, and made a face. "I hope they do. I hate that place. It's bor-*ing.*"

"Oh, no." Alex closed her eyes, understanding from her reply that her sister had, indeed, done just what she feared. Neely had not wanted to go back to her exclusive boarding school after the funeral anyway, but Alex had insisted. With both her sister's parents now dead—Neely's mother had died along with her second husband in the crash of his private plane ten years before—Alex was now her fifteen-year-old half-sister's legal guardian. But in practice, she had been Neely's de facto parent for years. With their father continually preoccupied with business and a succession of wives, it had become the norm for Neely to spend summers and school vacations with Alex. But just because Alex was now legally entitled to tell Neely what to do didn't mean Neely had to listen. In fact, Neely rarely listened. Alex loved her little sister dearly, but there was no denying that the girl was both spoiled and headstrong.

"Try pretending that you're glad to see me, why don't you?"

"I *am* glad to see you. Of course I'm glad to see you. But . . ."

Without waiting for Alex to finish, Neely marched past her into the library and paused inside the door, her attention obviously arrested by something that had just come into view. Following her, looking over her shoulder, Alex saw that Welch, having restored the chair he had desecrated to its accustomed spot beside the fireplace, was standing beside it facing the doorway. Neely was openly looking him over, and as she did so his gaze slid over Neely in turn. He looked unfazed by both Neely's open inspection and her ridiculous getup. Of course, Alex remembered, he had a teen of his own. That had probably inured him to anything the species could throw at him.

"Who're you?" Neely's question was just this side of insolent.

Alex sighed under her breath. She wasn't up to this.

"Joe Welch. Who're you?" His mouth twisted slightly as he responded to bluntness with bluntness.

"Cornelia Haywood. Neely, actually. Are you a friend of my sister?" Her cutely rounded figure still blocking the doorway, Neely assumed a provocative pose with one hand on her hip and her head cocked to the side. Alex put a gentle hand on her sister's waist to move her aside as she tried to edge past.

Welch shook his head. "I manage this farm for your family."

Alex squeezed through the opening just in time to catch the disappointed look on Neely's face. "Oh. You're an employee."

"That's right."

The arrogant man probably deserved to be insulted,

Alex thought, but she was embarrassed by her sister's lack of manners anyway.

"I'll be on my way." Welch glanced at Alex as he began moving toward the door.

"I'll walk you out." The look she sent him was pregnant with meaning. She wasn't finished with him yet, but she didn't mean to have any conversation dealing with their father's death in front of Neely. Neely's relationship with their dad had been very different from her own. His divorce from Neely's mother had been so acrimonious that the bad feelings left in its wake had spilled over to include their daughter. Consequently, he had had very little time for Neely. Neely resented his neglect and had never made any bones about telling him so during the infrequent times when they were together. That had made for a contentiousness between them that, Alex believed, made the trauma of his death even worse for Neely than it was for her. At least there'd been no angry words left hanging between Alex and her father at the time of his death. Although Neely, like Alex, had learned over the years to protect her wounds from view, Alex knew that she was grieving deeply.

"There's no need. I know my way."

"I want to. Neely, I'll be right back."

"Don't hurry on my account." Neely moved on into the room with a suggestive smile at her sister. Alex ignored the silent innuendo and followed Welch from the room. He was walking fast, as if he was in a hurry to get away.

"Mr. Welch." She caught up with him in the front hallway and stopped him by curling a hand around his upper arm.

He turned, looking down at her with a gathering frown. They were standing in front of the tall, gold-framed mirror that graced the wall opposite the staircase. A chance look at their reflection showed Alex that they were a study in contrasts. Even with her heels on, she did not quite reach his nose. He was all hard, dark strength, while she looked slender, fragile, feminine.

"What is it now?" He made no effort to conceal his impatience to be gone.

"I want to finish our conversation. About my father." Her hand slid away from his arm. Her voice was determined. "Not now, because I don't want my sister to overhear. But maybe later today. Or tomorrow."

He was silent for a moment. Then he shook his head. "I told you, if you want any more information like that you're going to have to get it somewhere else. Not from me."

Then he simply turned and walked away. Alex could do no more than glare impotently after him as the door banged shut behind him.

Rude, impossible man . . .

"At least there's one bright spot to this place," Neely observed, coming up behind her. "The hired help's sex on a stick."

"He's way too old for you." Effectively distracted, Alex transferred her frowning gaze to her sister, who was in the process of scooping a denim backpack up off the hall floor. "And you were rude to him, by the way."

"I like older men," Neely said, totally disregarding the rebuke. Backpack in hand, she headed toward the library again, glancing back at Alex over her shoulder. "Actually, I like all men. If they're hotties, that is. And that one definitely is a hottie."

Alex started to reply when her attention was caught by something that glinted on Neely's nose as she turned her head. Eyes widening, Alex realized that a tiny diamond stud protruded from the side of her sister's left nostril.

"You've had your nose pierced!" Alex squeaked just as

they reached the library. It wasn't precisely what she'd meant to say, but she was so surprised that the words just popped out of her mouth.

"Don't bitch," Neely said, dropping her backpack on the floor and crossing the room to settle on one of the few modern pieces of furniture, a plumply upholstered love seat covered in pale rose chintz.

"Don't swear," Alex, recovering from the shock, countered in the same tone, heading for the desk. First things first.

"Who are you calling?" Neely sat up straight as Alex picked up the phone.

"Your school." Alex's voice was grim.

Neely subsided with a grimace.

Mrs. Stanton, the headmistress, was forthright: "I'm very sorry to have to add to your troubles at such a sad time, Miss Haywood, but we can't have Cornelia back."

The words, although not entirely unexpected, were a blow. Alex took a deep breath, and cast her sister a narrow-eyed look. Neely stuck out her tongue at her unrepentantly. "Oh, Mrs. Stanton, you can't mean that. Since our father died, she hasn't been herself. . . ."

"Indeed, she *has* been herself, and that's the problem," Mrs. Stanton broke in firmly. "Believe me, I have great appreciation for Cornelia's good points—and they are many—but she is just too disruptive for us to be able to keep her at Pomfret any longer. I feel we've been more than patient with her, but I have to draw the line somewhere, and I'm afraid it's here, with her running away for the third time in less than two years."

Alex was silent for a moment. Even before their father's death, Neely had been in trouble almost constantly in the year and a half she'd attended Pomfret. She'd been caught smoking (both cigarettes and pot), drinking, sneaking out at night, and smuggling a boy into her room, all on multiple occasions. She had surfed forbidden Internet chat rooms, made and received unauthorized phone calls, and stayed out past curfew so often that she was no longer permitted to go into the city on the weekends. Alex was fully aware of Neely's full, less-than-stellar record.

But there were reasons for Neely's behavior, Alex protested silently. Not that anybody but herself seemed to recognize them, or care.

"Is there nothing I can do to persuade you to give her one more chance?" Alex asked, already knowing that there was not. Mrs. Stanton was a nice enough woman, but she was fed up with Neely and Alex knew it. Actually, Alex couldn't much blame her. Neely on a roll was enough to try the patience of a saint.

"I'm afraid not."

Alex sighed, defeated. "Mrs. Stanton, I appreciate your patience with Neely. I know she's been a little difficult."

"Yes, well, some girls are." Mrs. Stanton's voice softened slightly. "She's not a bad girl, Miss Haywood, just unsuited for Pomfret. If you wish to enroll her somewhere else, I'm sure we will do all we can to help you. Just let me know."

"Thank you, Mrs. Stanton," Alex said, and ended the conversation.

When the phone clicked down, Alex closed her eyes briefly, her hand still resting on the receiver. Talk about your bad days—what was she going to do with Neely now? Try to enroll her somewhere else, she guessed—but where? And would there be enough money to pay the tuition? One tiny bright spot in their financial landscape had been that Neely's fees had already been paid for the full school year, but now—did Pomfret give refunds? This was a problem she didn't need, on top of everything else. It was, however, hers to deal with. Just as Neely was hers to deal with.

Alex opened her eyes and frowned at her sister. "For your information, you've been expelled."

"Yay," Neely said negligently.

"Good attitude." Alex came around the desk and sat down opposite her sister on the love seat's twin. The pair was set at right angles in the far corner, with tall windows behind each.

"I try." Neely's glance at her was mocking.

"So now what do we do?"

Neely shrugged.

Alex waited. When it became clear that nothing more was forthcoming, she mentally reviewed her options. From earliest childhood, Neely had frequently put her in mind of the proverbial horse you could lead to water but couldn't make drink. Challenging her head-on had always been a mistake. It inevitably led to her doing just the opposite of what was wanted.

Anyway, there was no fixing what had happened with Pomfret. So what was the point of scolding about it? It would do nothing but put her at odds with her sister. And right now, they needed each other. They were all they had.

So maybe she wasn't a stern enough guardian, Alex thought. Maybe Neely deserved to be yelled at, even punished. (What, by taking her makeup away? Now there was a thought.) With all the trauma they'd both been through recently, Alex just couldn't bring herself to do either. Whether it was the proper course of action or not, she was going to take the high road, and get both of them past this relatively minor crisis as easily as she could.

Alex sighed. "Did I mention that you can be a real pain in the butt, sister? Fine. We'll deal with the situation. We'll start looking for another school first thing Monday morning. By the way, Mrs. Stanton very kindly said she'd help get you in somewhere else. She also said you have lots of good qualities."

"Old goat," Neely muttered, unimpressed. The phone rang. Neely jumped as if she'd been shot and grabbed her sister's wrist when Alex stood up to answer it.

"Don't!" Neely said sharply.

Alex stared at her. The phone stopped ringing. She presumed Inez had picked it up.

"What's up with you?" Alex asked. Neely had never, ever, grabbed her wrist like that, or jumped when the phone rang for that matter, unless she was expecting a call from her boyfriend of the moment and was in a rush to answer before anyone else could, which wasn't likely to be the case today. Alex felt a tingle of renewed apprehension. If Neely didn't want her to answer the phone, there must be a good reason—like something that Neely didn't want her to hear. Something bad, something in addition to the fact that Neely had been expelled from school, which she would have thought, in Neely's case, was just about as bad as things could get. But maybe not. Alex felt her stomach tighten as she contemplated the possibilities.

"Alex." Neely, brave, strong, ever-cocky Neely, sounded almost nervous. She stood up, and, instead of releasing Alex's wrist, took both her hands in hers. Alex's eyes widened with alarm. Whatever was coming must be as bad as it could be. Her hands tightened on Neely's.

"Oh, God, please don't tell me you're pregnant," she breathed. Short of her sister's imminent death, that was the worst thing she could think of.

"What?" Neely looked at first taken aback, then indignant. "No, of course I'm not pregnant! Do I look stupid to you?"

"Thank God." Alex took a deep breath, and felt her heart slow to nearly normal rhythm. She squeezed her sister's hands. "Whatever it is you're getting ready to tell me, just please spit it out. Nothing you've done could be as bad as the things I'm imagining."

"Nothing *I've* done . . . This isn't about me. It's about you."

"Me?" Alex stared at her sister. Neely looked uncomfortable. Her fingers entwined with Alex's, and clung.

"I've got really bad news." Neely wet her lips with the tip of her tongue before continuing. "Paul married Tara Gould last night."

Neely winced, and looked as if she was bracing herself for a catastrophic response. When Alex didn't immediately say anything, she hurried into speech again as though trying to forestall the inevitable.

"Her cousin—Carole Segal—goes to Pomfret too, and she got a call last night from her mother, who'd gotten a call from her brother, who is Tara's father, saying that Tara had gone off and married Paul O'Neil and they were all so happy and there was going to be a big reception next weekend at the Philadelphia Country Club. Carole's going to it. Can you believe that?" Then Neely's voice softened. "I'm so *sorry*, Alex."

"Cornelia Haywood, did you leave your school without permission, getting yourself expelled in the process, just to fly down here and tell me that?"

Neely nodded unhappily. "I didn't want you to hear it from one of your gossipy friends, or anybody like that."

Alex shook her head, then pulled her sister into her arms and gave her a big hug. Neely hugged her tightly back.

"Please don't be sad," Neely begged as they clung together. "I never liked Paul anyway. He's a jerk."

"He is, isn't he?" Alex pulled back from the hug and smiled wryly at her sister. "A complete and total jerk. I'm better off without him. I've been thinking that ever since he called and told me what he'd done about half an hour ago."

"What?" Neely looked, and sounded, aghast. "You *knew*? You mean I've gotten into all this trouble and come all this way and gone through all this hell worrying about how to break it to you for nothing? That's the total pits!"

Alex smiled wryly. "No, actually, that's the sweetest thing I've ever heard of in my life. Even if you are occasionally a pain in the butt, I'm glad you're my sister, Neely Haywood."

"Yeah, well, I'm glad you're my sister too," Neely muttered, still sounding aggrieved as she rested her forehead against Alex's. For a moment they stood that way, arms around each other, foreheads touching. Then Alex stepped back, smiled, and shook her head.

"We're a great pair. You've been expelled and I've been jilted. Now what do we do?"

Nine

✤

The predator had had his eye on the dog for two days. It was a small dog, not much bigger than a cat really, and it was an ugly thing, part pit bull and part who-knew-what. Except for a single black patch on its coat, it was white and hairless-looking, with a stubby tail and a wide pink mouth that constantly threatened to drool. Every time he stepped outside, the dog was there, although it would slink out of sight as soon as he appeared.

"Come here, dog," he said late in the afternoon of the second day, following it out to its hiding place, then dropping to one knee and snapping his fingers at it. Cowering under a parked car, the dog looked at him without obeying. "Come here."

"Lookin' to get yourself a pet?"

The predator glanced around to find that he was being observed. He knew the speaker, just as he knew everyone hereabouts.

"Thinkin' about it," he said amiably, and waved as the speaker got into his car and drove away.

Leaving the dog where it was for the time being, he stood up and went back to work. But not long after twilight he came outside again, this time bearing a slice of pizza on a paper plate. A blustery wind promised rain later. The parking lot was full, although since everybody who'd come in the parked cars was inside there was no one else to be seen. Looking around, he thought for a moment that the dog had finally gone. But no, there it was, a pale shadow slinking around the corner to hide under the deep purple overhang of a bush. He walked toward it and set the paper plate on the ground where the dog couldn't help but both see and smell it.

"Come here, dog," he said again, crouching beside the plate and snapping his fingers. "Come here."

This time the dog came crawling out. While it devoured the pizza, he petted it. He loved dogs, had loved them from the earliest days of his childhood. They had been among his first, and favorite, toys.

"Good dog," he crooned. "Good dog."

Then he went back inside.

Later, much later, when nearly all the cars were gone, he came out again. This time he carried a paper plate with a hamburger patty in one hand, and a makeshift leash in the other. It was raining now, and except for the lights in the building behind him it was so dark that he could barely see halfway across the parking lot. He was wearing a hooded raincoat, but the hamburger presented something of a problem: it would be drenched before he could find the dog and offer it to him. Would the dog come out of whatever hiding place it had chosen for itself for a soggy piece of meat?

Could he even find the dog in the darkness? He could always wait until tomorrow. And if the dog was gone in the morning, hey, such was fate.

But he really wanted to find the dog tonight.

In the end, just as he was getting ready to turn and go back inside without ever having set foot in the rain, he spied the dog. It was huddled in plain sight against the building, lit by the security lights, protected from the cascades of falling water by an overhanging eave.

The predator smiled, and, taking care not to get the paper plate with the hamburger wet, walked along the building toward the dog.

"Here, dog," he said softly as he approached. The dog looked at him, appeared to remember him as its benefactor from earlier in the evening, and wagged its tail.

Getting down on one knee, he set the paper plate on the ground.

"Here, dog," he said again.

The dog looked at the glistening brown circle of meat, at him, and approached, head down, tail low and wagging gently from side to side.

"Good dog." He patted the animal when it was close enough, and then, as it devoured the meat in two quick gulps, slid the makeshift leash—which was really a rope that he had tied into a slip-knotted noose at one end, with enough left over to serve as a lead—over its head.

The dog made no effort to get away.

"Good dog," he said again, pleased. He patted the animal and stood up. "Come."

He had half expected the dog to resist, but it didn't, following him willingly as he skirted the building, staying under the protection of the eaves for as long as he could. His SUV was parked in the rear lot. The dog even followed him out into the rain without resistance, and when he opened the rear door of the vehicle jumped inside as docilely as one could wish.

The predator rewarded it with a pat on the head.

"Good dog," he said again, and closed the door.

Sliding in behind the wheel, he brushed rain from the surface of his coat, decided it was useless to worry about getting water stains on his leather seats, and turned the ignition. He switched on the lights, engaged the transmission, and set out. It would take only about fifteen minutes to reach his destination, and he knew the way as well as he knew the way from his bed to the bathroom.

Lulled by the rush of the tires over the pavement and the rhythmic swish of the windshield wipers, the dog had curled up on the rear seat and settled down to nap, secure in its new position as a claimed possession, he thought. From the accepting way it had responded to both leash and car, he guessed that the animal probably had been someone's pet, either lost or abandoned by the roadside. People were bad about abandoning pets out in the country, where they apparently expected some kindhearted farmer to give the forsaken creatures a home.

Human beings were, at heart, an intrinsically stupid species. Or intrinsically cruel, which amounted to much the same thing in the end.

Only one vehicle passed him en route, an eighteen-wheeler driving far too fast for the conditions. It nearly blew him off the road as it went by, and it splashed water all over his windshield. Those big trucks had no business off the expressway, he thought disapprovingly, and speculated that this one must be looking for gas or food. If so, the driver was out of luck. Just about everything hereabouts closed up shop around ten.

Reaching his destination, he pulled off the road and bumped through the woods and down a hill. There he parked where he always did, at the edge of Bob Toler's cornfield. Removing a flashlight from the glove compartment, he got out. The dog was ready for him, standing eagerly on the seat as he opened the rear door. It jumped out without resistance even though the sky was, by now, pouring rain. Thunder crashed and lightning zigzagged overhead, lighting up the thick mass of tall, post-harvest cornstalks for an instant so that they looked like an audience of pale, slender ghosts.

Ghosts—he didn't believe in them. But if ghosts existed, they might well be standing there, waiting silently for him to add to their numbers.

The idea amused him, and he was smiling faintly as he splashed across the shallow creek toward the perpendicular rock bank on the other side, the dog close on his heels. The bank was fifteen feet high in this particular spot, and heavily covered with vegetation that had grown undisturbed, except for his occasional visits, for years. Reaching the place he sought, still standing ankle-deep in water, he carefully lifted aside the heavy curtain of vines that hung over the bank. Beneath the vines, perhaps some three feet off the ground, was a hole in the rock that looked like it had once been an animal's lair. It was, in reality, the mouth of a rather unique cave. He had discovered it as a child, and had made use of it ever since. Of course, since he'd grown older and bigger, fitting into the doorway to his subterranean world had become more difficult. But he could still do it if he slithered inside headfirst then scooted on his belly until the passage widened. The dog offered no resistance as he picked it up and set it inside the opening, and then wriggled in himself. It was dark as a grave in the passage, but he saw no particular reason to turn on his flashlight yet. He was as familiar with this route as he was his own bed.

Pushing the dog before him, he traversed the twelve or so feet that the passage retained the dimensions of a large animal's burrow with practiced ease. Then, abruptly, he was there, wriggling through the hole after the dog and standing up with some care. He had cracked his head on the low ceiling more than once. The dog, clearly uncertain in this new setting, pressed nervously against his legs as he turned on the flashlight.

"Good dog," he praised the animal, pleased that it trusted him enough to turn to him for protection. Holding on to the rope although the dog seemed perfectly willing to follow him without it, ducking his head, he walked along the ancient, stone-paved tunnel that had once been used to smuggle slaves to safety as part of the Underground Railroad. Shortly he came to an iron door. Although the door was well over a hundred years old, the padlock that secured it was new. The key was one of many on the key ring he always carried. Unlocking the door, he pulled it shut behind him as he passed on into a taller, earthen chamber. With relief, he stretched to his full height. Keeping his head low for so long occasionally gave him a crick in the neck.

"Come on," he said to the dog, which wagged its tail. Heading for a wooden door, he pulled it open and led the dog into another room in which the floor, ceiling, and all four walls were made of large, hand-carved stones. This room was as old as the tunnel, and as forgotten by everyone but him. Years ago, he had turned it into his own private playroom.

"Hello, Cassandra," he said genially to the girl who awaited him there, sitting naked on the side of the cot he had so thoughtfully provided for his guests. Lank-haired and dull-eyed, she didn't even bother to jump to her feet at his entrance anymore. She just stared at him dully through the iron bars of her cage.

"I've brought you a pet," he said, smiling at her as he turned on the battery-powered camper's lantern that he kept on the table in the part of the room that was separate from the cell. The glow from the lantern cast his shadow on the wall, and the shadow reflected the truth of him with surprising accuracy: it looked sinister, which he emphatically did not in real life. He was pleased with the image, which included the little bowlegged beast at his feet and the rope which connected them. The light did not quite reach the corners, but there was enough illumination to do what he needed to do.

Glancing reflexively around, he saw that everything was just as he had left it. His big leather recliner, his TV, his remote control, his collection of videotapes, the photo gallery of his guests. They were all there, pictured in life, death, and every stage in between, affixed to wooden strips that he had secured to the walls. He had recorded the metamorphosis of each of them, from the first of his victims to Eric, Cassandra's erstwhile boyfriend, who was the last, except for the collection of pictures of Cassandra which was not quite finished. Her portfolio began with the picture he had snapped on the night he had brought her to this room. She was beautiful in that picture, wide-eyed with fright but smiling bravely at the camera because he had ordered it. Soon he would take the last shot in her series: the look on her face as death claimed her. It might not be as conventionally pretty as the first, but it would be more fascinating. The difference in the way people died intrigued him. Some prayed, some did not. Some kept their eyes closed, others looked death in the face. All of them, every single one, screamed their lungs out at the end. Death was such a pure thing, so cleansing. He didn't know why everyone seemed to fear it so.

He did not. When it came, he would welcome it. But he was not ready to welcome it yet.

"Here, dog," he said to the dog, who was looking up at him with near-worshipful brown eyes. He led the animal closer to the wall, picked up one end of an iron chain that hung from a ring set into the stone, and wrapped that around the dog's neck, working with it until it was secure, then padlocking it in place. The dog hunkered down on its belly, not liking to be chained, but made no effort to escape.

Knowing what was coming—after all, she had seen what had happened to Eric—Cassandra started to cry, dry heaving sobs that sounded like they hurt.

"Don't you like your pet?" he said to her reproachfully. He tugged on the chain once, twice, just to make sure the dog could not get loose, then, as he caught the animal's eye, patted him on the head again.

"Good dog," he crooned, moving away to the storage cabinet where he kept his supplies. The dog strained after him, already his loyal friend. Removing a can of kerosene and a box of fireplace matches, he retraced his steps until he stood just out of the dog's reach. It looked adoringly at him.

Cassandra's sobs were abating. Looking over at her, he saw that she had her eyes tightly closed.

"Open your eyes," he ordered, his voice suddenly harsh. "Open your eyes and watch, or I'll do it to you instead."

Her eyes opened. He smiled, satisfied, and squirted almost the entire contents of the can over the dog. The scent of kerosene was so strong that he wrinkled his nose against it. The dog looked confused, cowering as the strong-smelling liquid soaked into its coat, uttering one soft little whimper and looking up at him beseechingly.

After making sure that Cassandra was still watching, he took a step back, struck a match, and tossed it at the dog. The flame touched the kerosene and ignited with a soft *whoosh*.

The screaming dog sounded almost human as it went up like a torch.

"Good dog," he said one last time, smiling as he watched the tethered animal leap and run in circles and finally collapse writhing on the floor as it fought desperately, futilely, to escape the flames.

✦ ✦ ✦ ✦

Meanwhile, Alex and Neely spent a pleasant afternoon and evening together. They talked, explored the house, raided the refrigerator for cold cuts for dinner and watched TV in the cozy den that opened off the living room. Having Neely with her made all the difference, Alex discovered. Her sister's lively and irreverent companionship was both cheering and a balm for her wounded heart. Although she was worried about Neely's school situation, she nevertheless was more glad than she could say for her sister's presence.

Every time thoughts of Paul's betrayal threatened to intrude, Alex determinedly pushed them away, but the pain was impossible to banish entirely. Add that to her ever-present grief over her father, and this could have been one of the worst nights of her life.

Thanks to Neely, it was not.

Even without the shock of losing Paul, she wouldn't have liked to be alone tonight, she mused, a book lying forgotten on her lap as she watched her enthralled sister watching *Party of Five*. Funny, when she'd made her plans to come to Whistledown on her own she had never considered what being alone in this big, strange house at night might feel like. Now that Neely was with her, she realized just how unnerving the echoing emptiness of the high-ceilinged, large-roomed space might have been had her sister not been here to share it. Their father had spent the last days and nights of his life here; he had died here. His presence was everywhere. When she was quiet, like now, she could feel it, and it disturbed her. If not for Neely, she probably would have ended up going to a hotel. Simpsonville was too small to have one, but Shelbyville did, she remembered from previous visits.

The last time she'd been here was during the summer right after she had graduated from college. She'd been twenty-one, and at her father's invitation she had joined him for a weekend at Whistledown, where he had flown in to attend Keeneland's July Selected Yearling Sale. They had rarely spent much time together on their own—it seemed like he always had a wife or girlfriend in tow—and she had been pleased and touched when he had told her that this time it would be just the two of them. What he had really wanted to do, of course, was talk to her about her future. Specifically, about her joining Haywood Harley Nichols with an eye to one day possibly taking over the firm. When the proposal was put to her, she had wanted no part of it, and she and her father had ended up quarreling fiercely. She'd left the day after she arrived without ever attending the horse sale.

Looking back, her chest ached at the memory. Oh, Daddy, she thought. If I'd come to work for you, would things have turned out differently? I could have, so easily. I should have. . . .

Tears crowded her eyes, and she blinked them away frantically. There was no point in making Neely feel bad, too. Anyway, wishing that she had made a different choice that day was useless. What was done was done.

A storm blew in about eleven, dumping what sounded like torrents of rain on the roof. Thunder rolled, lightning cracked across the sky like a whip, and the wind blew. Neely went to bed first, in the bedroom suite next to Alex's. Both automatically chose the rooms that had been theirs on previous visits. Having taken one of the sleeping pills that her doctor had prescribed to combat the insomnia she had suffered since her father's death, Alex was dead to the world by twelve. The storm raged, the old house creaked, the heating system kicked in with a soft hum. None of that woke her.

But something did. Something roused her from a sleep so sound that she'd been the next thing to comatose. One second she was practically unconscious, and the next she was awake, with the creepy feeling that something unpleasant had just brushed across her cheek. Her eyes blinked open, and she stared up into darkness so intense that she could see nothing at all. Briefly she was disoriented. It took a moment to remember where she was, and why.

Instinct kept her silent, and motionless, as she took stock.

The soft floral scent that surrounded her came from the fabric softener Inez had used on the sheets, she realized. She was lying on her right side with her face all but buried in the too-soft pillow, which was why the smell seemed so strong. The rattling sound was rain pelting the windowpanes. The cool air that slid across her face was a draft from the old and not particularly well fitting window. Surely it was that which had brushed her cheek as she awoke.

But there was another sound besides the rain, softer, closer at hand. It came from the foot of the antique, ornately carved walnut bed.

Alex lay unmoving, staring blindly into the impenetrable darkness that shrouded her like a blanket as she listened with all her might. Her heart began to speed up; her mouth grew dry. She was no longer in any doubt as to what she was hearing: the deep, steady rasp of someone, or some*thing*, in the room with her, breathing.

Ten

❦

The hair rose on the back of Alex's neck. She lay as if frozen in place. Whoever or whatever it was that waited at the foot of her bed was motionless, too, doing nothing more than *breathing*.

Oh, God, what should she do?

Her pulse raced. Her muscles stiffened. Her fight-or-flight impulse kicked into high gear, but she forced herself to remain as she was. Until she could come up with a more productive alternative, her best bet was to pretend to be still asleep.

The breathing continued unabated: in, out; in, out. Heavy. Raspy. The sound grew so loud, at least to her ears, that it drowned out everything else, even the frightened drumming of her heart, even the raging storm outside. Neely? Could it possibly be Neely standing there at the foot of her bed, for some unfathomable reason just standing silent and motionless in the dark watching her sleep?

No way. Not possible. First of all, Neely had never breathed like that in her life. Second, she would have announced her presence, loudly and unmistakably, by calling her sister's name or poking her or even, if she was scared, jumping into Alex's bed with her. Silent watching was not Neely's style.

She and Neely were alone in the house.

So what possibilities did that leave? A burglar? Alex's blood ran cold at the thought. A—ghost? Her blood went from cold to icy.

She had been dreaming of her father. Vague wisps of memory floated through her mind like drifts of fog. Whistledown was the scene of his violent death. From the very first moment that she had understood what had happened to him, she had thought that whatever else he did he would never voluntarily leave them, his family, without a word. Was this breathing some sort of ghostly visitation? Some attempt on his part to contact her from beyond?

She had never believed in ghosts—until, possibly, now.

Even as the thought formed in her mind, the breathing seemed to move, seemed to be coming from a new location. Alex could still hear the rhythmic inhalations and exhalations plainly, but they were growing ever fainter as they seemed to move farther and farther away. Whoever or whatever it was, was heading toward her open bedroom door. The realization came in a flash.

She could see nothing, absolutely nothing, not so much as the pillow on which she lay, but she knew that she was awake, that she was not dreaming, that she was not imagining this. It was real. It was happening.

Her terror overwhelmed in an instant by the fierce need to *know*, Alex sat bolt upright and groped for the switch to the bedside lamp. It was one of those lamps with the switch built into the cord. She located the cord with her fingers, followed it a few inches below the level of the bedside table, and found the switch, all in a matter of a few seconds.

Click. The sound was audible. The breathing seemed to pause in its rhythm, but nothing else changed. The light did not come on. *Click. Click.* She tried it again and again, almost frantically. Still the light did not come on—and the breathing kept moving away. It came lighter and faster now, she thought, and seemed to be retreating at some speed.

She couldn't let the breather get away without finding out who or what it was. Even confronting a burglar was preferable to not knowing.

Daddy, is that you? A foolish thought, she knew, but still . . .

Alex kicked back the covers and rolled out of bed. Bare feet silent on the smooth wool of the Oriental rug that covered the hardwood floor, guiding herself through the cave-like darkness by moving, hands flung out, from bedpost to bedpost and then groping until she found the wall, she followed the sound.

The breathing was less audible now. The steady in, out, in, out, was growing fainter as it moved away from her, into the narrow hall off which all the bedrooms branched.

Alex paused for a moment by her bedroom door to feel for the switch to the overhead light. The plaster wall felt cool and smooth to her searching fingers. A draft of chilly air caressed her feet and ankles beneath the lace hem of her cream silk nightgown. The drumming of the rain nearly overwhelmed the sound of the breathing; she would not have heard it at all now if she had not known it was there. She found the switch, turned it on—and nothing. No light.

She could no longer hear the breathing, try though she might. Holding her own breath, she strained to hear it again. So strong was her need to identify the sound that she was not even afraid any longer. She had to find out who or what it was. She *had to know.*

If it was her father, or not.

She stepped out into the hallway, arms outstretched to

find the wall, blind as a rock—and heard the breathing again. It was much softer now. Turning sharply toward the sound, she tripped over something and stumbled forward. Her flailing hands brushed a resilient, cloth-covered surface and grabbed at it in an instinctive effort to save herself from falling. Her hands closed on loose folds of cloth— and then something slammed hard into the back of her head. For an instant she saw stars, and then the world went black.

The next thing she knew, she lay sprawled on her stomach on the wool runner that ran down the middle of the hall. The musty smell of the carpet filled her nose. The wool was faintly coarse beneath her fingertips. The darkness seemed to swim around her. Besides the pain in her head, she was vaguely conscious of stinging knees and palms. She groaned.

"Alex?" Neely called. From the sound of her voice, Neely was in the hallway, too, just a few feet ahead of Alex. If she was coming from her bedroom, as she should be, that was right. The suites, which consisted of a bedroom, sitting room, and bath, were side by side at the north end of the hall.

"Be careful," Alex managed thickly, sitting up and pressing a hand to the back of her head. "I think there's someone in the house."

The darkness heaved and rolled around her like a stormy sea, but she did not pass out. The back of her head stung and throbbed as she touched it, and a warm stickiness told her that she was bleeding. What had happened? Had she fallen and hit her head? Vaguely she remembered stumbling forward, but what had occurred after that was a blur.

"What?" It was clear that Neely had either not heard or not understood. As her sister spoke, Alex heard a faint clicking sound, and realized that Neely was trying without success to turn on the hall light. "Alex, did you fall? Are you hurt?"

"I fell, but I'm okay. I think the electricity must be out," Alex managed. Her voice was a little stronger. "Neely, did you hear me? I think there's someone in the house."

Alex struggled onto her knees. Her head throbbed and swam. She was not strictly okay, as she had told Neely, but there was no time to go into it now. Neely was beside her then, kneeling, her hands reaching out to touch her through the darkness. "What do you mean, you think someone's in the house?"

Alex debated telling her the other option. Either someone was in the house or their father's ghost was trying to make contact. But of course that last was nonsense. It had to be. On calmer reflection, she realized that whatever— whoever—had been in her bedroom, it could not have been a ghost.

After all, even if ghosts existed, which in the daylight and in her right mind she was pretty confident they did not, they wouldn't be breathing, now would they? Because if they were breathing, then they wouldn't be ghosts. It was simple logic. If she had been thinking clearly in the first moments after she had awoken, she would have realized it then.

Which brought Alex to the inescapable conclusion: a living, breathing human being had been in her bedroom, *and might very well still be in the house.*

"Neely," she said urgently, gripping her sister's flannel-clad arm. "Someone was just in my bedroom. I woke up and chased them out into the hall. I think they might still be in the house."

"What?" Neely gasped.

"Shhh!" Of course, they'd made so much noise up to

this point that being quiet now was sort of like shutting the barn door after the horse was out, but the urge to whisper was strong. Her cell phone was in her purse downstairs; she had forgotten to plug it in for a recharge, so even if she could get to it, it probably wouldn't work. But there was a telephone by her bed, Alex remembered as she tried despite her aching head to review their options. The thing for them to do was go back to her bedroom, lock the door, and call the police. Did they even have 911 service here? Maybe she could just dial the operator. . . .

"Are you kidding?" Neely's voice was a hiss.

"No." Alex struggled to get to her feet, and Neely grasped her arm to help. The darkness swam again as she made it upright, but there was no help for it. She and Neely had to move. If someone *was* in the house, they were too vulnerable out there in the hall. "We've got to call the police. There's a phone in my bedroom."

"Oh shit!" Neely's whisper sounded scared.

"Don't swear," Alex whispered back automatically. With Neely grasping Alex's arm to provide support, they groped their way back to Alex's bedroom as fast, and as quietly, as they could. Alex's head pounded like a three-year-old with a hammer and she had a feeling she would have been seeing double if she could have seen anything at all.

"Lock the door," Alex said as they made it into her bedroom. While Neely did as she was told, Alex felt her way to the bed. With the door locked she felt marginally safer, but only marginally. The total darkness was unnerving by itself. Add to that the sounds of the storm outside, and the near certainty that someone—some*one*—was in the house, and she would have been a basket case if it had not been for Neely. But she had to be brave for Neely, who was only a kid, after all.

The telephone was on the table beside the lamp. By

pressing one leg against the mattress, Alex was able to find the table easily enough. Her hand skimmed the surface of the table—lamp, book, clock, *phone*. Fumbling with the receiver, she picked it up. There was no dial tone.

"Alex, do you smell smoke?" Neely's voice was small and scared. It sounded as if she was making her way around the bed toward Alex.

Pressing buttons by touch—it was so dark she couldn't even see them, much less read the numbers—Alex tried in vain to get the phone to work. At Neely's words, she stopped and sniffed. Even so small an act as wrinkling her nose made the pain in her head go from bad to worse. She closed her eyes, then almost immediately opened them again. Closing her eyes hurt, too.

There was a smell, faint but unmistakable. Sort of like—rubber burning.

"I smell *something*." Alex gave up and put down the receiver, then lifted her hand to her head. She was definitely bleeding, and there was a growing lump that was large and tender to the touch. Probing it, she winced. "The phone's dead."

"What do we do now?" Neely sounded very young suddenly, and very frightened.

"I think we should get out of the house." Something *was* burning, she decided as she felt along the bedside table for the box of tissues she had seen there. The acrid smell was unmistakable. Could the house be on fire? The possibility could not be ignored. Burglar or no burglar, she didn't think it was a smart idea for them just to sit there in her locked bedroom and wait to find out.

"I'm scared." Neely's voice was wobbly.

"Me too." Alex found the box of tissues, pulled a handful free, and pressed the wad to the back of her head. The injury ached and throbbed as she applied as much gentle pressure as she could bear. She didn't want to tell Neely that her head was bleeding. There was nothing Neely could do about it, and there was no point in scaring her sister more than she was already.

"Do you think the house is on fire?" Neely asked next.

"Maybe."

If they could just get to one of the cars . . . But the key to the Mercedes was on a hook in the kitchen, and the car itself, like the others, was in the detached garage some distance behind the house. She had parked it there herself, hours earlier.

She didn't want to chance winding her way through the pitch-dark house to the kitchen. Nor did she want to make a run for the isolated garage.

"The man who was here today—Joe Welch, the farm manager—lives just down the hill. If we go down the main staircase and out the front door, it'll only take us a few minutes to reach his house."

"But it's raining buckets out there—and what if someone's in the house just waiting for us to come out?" Neely objected, her hushed voice shaking. "In *Scream* . . ."

"I don't want to hear it," Alex interrupted. Neely loved horror movies. Alex couldn't watch them. On the few occasions when Neely had managed to drag her older sister to one, Alex sat with her eyes closed almost the entire time. If something horrible did happen when Alex chanced to be looking, she invariably shrieked like a banshee and hid her face in her hands, much to Neely's embarrassed disgust. "It'll only take us a couple of minutes to get out the front door. All we have to do is go down the main staircase and we're out."

"But in *Scream* . . ."

"This is real life, not a horror movie," Alex said firmly. She didn't even want to think about the possibility that whoever had been in her bedroom might be waiting for them out there in the dark.

The smell of burning was growing stronger. It was stupid to take chances. They had to get out of the house. Alex thought fast. If they were going to run across a cold, swampy field, shoes would be good. Her bedroom slippers had rubber soles, and were elastic enough to fit Neely, who wore a size larger than she did. Feeling with her foot, Alex located them beside the bed where she had kicked them off earlier. She scooped up the slippers and thrust them at Neely.

"Put these on."

Having unpacked the few things she had brought with her earlier, Alex knew exactly where her one pair of flat shoes, bronze Gucci loafers, were: positioned neatly on the shoe rack just inside the door of the big walk-in closet.

"Where are you going?" Neely sounded on the verge of panic as Alex moved away from her.

"To get my shoes." They both spoke in hushed voices. Feeling her way along the dresser, Alex made it to the closet. Finding the smooth brass knob by touch, she turned it, opened the door, reached inside, and retrieved her shoes from the wire rack on the inside of the door. Sliding her feet into the soft leather flats, she groped her way back to the bed.

"Alex . . ."

"I'm right here."

Alex snatched the top layer, a hand-pieced antique quilt, from the bed and thrust it toward Neely, the movement clumsy because she couldn't see.

"Wrap this around yourself, and let's go," Alex said, as Neely fumblingly took it from her.

Grabbing the wool blanket that lay under the quilt, Alex draped it over her own shoulders and felt for her sister again. Hands locked together, they headed toward the bedroom door.

Just as Alex's outstretched hand made contact with the raised wooden panels she was seeking, Neely suddenly pulled back. "Oh, God, Alex, in *Friday the Thirteenth* . . ."

"If you say one more word about another stupid horror movie I'll murder you myself," Alex hissed fiercely over her shoulder, giving Neely's hand a sharp yank. "Now come on. Don't talk until we get outside. *And whatever happens, stay with me.*"

"No shit." Neely's tone was fervent. Her hand in Alex's was cold. Alex didn't even bother to protest her language. Her own heart pounded in tandem with the throbbing pain in her head. Her stomach churned. Her mouth was dry. Anyone—any*thing* could be waiting for them in the dark beyond the bedroom door.

Unlocking the deadbolt as quietly as she could, unable to prevent a click that sounded as loud as a gunshot to her ears, Alex turned the knob.

Eleven

✢

J oe lay on his back with his hands folded behind his head, staring up at the shadowy white ceiling over his bed, wide awake although it was long after he was usually out like a light. Outside rain fell in sheets. All last summer Shelby County had endured the century's worst drought: creeks had baked dry, crops had roasted in the fields, trees had lost their leaves. Now, when it was too late to do any good, it looked like they were getting a deluge of biblical proportions. He only hoped the roof didn't spring a leak.

He could get up, go downstairs, have something to eat. Watching TV was not an option: about twenty minutes ago the electricity had gone out, as it frequently did when there was a storm. But he refused to concede defeat. Insomnia was not going to get the best of him. After Laura had taken off, leaving him in the lurch with three little kids, a pile of debts, and blasted-to-smithereens career aspirations, he hadn't been able to sleep for years. Finally, finally, he'd conquered his demons, steered himself to a good place in his life, and been able to sleep again.

But today Alexandra Haywood had blown his comfortable life out of the water once more.

His salary for managing Whistledown Farm accounted

for almost half his income. Plus it came with benefits—
health and dental insurance that he'd had to pay for, but at a
greatly reduced rate because he'd technically been an
employee of Haywood's company. All that was a lot to lose in
one blow. Then there were the horses—losing them was
almost worse than losing the job. If it wasn't for the effect the
loss of income would have on his kids, it would be worse.

He had a contract, all right, but he wasn't stupid: sometimes a contract wasn't worth the paper it was printed on.
All that contract was going to do was buy him a little time.
He could tell Alexandra Haywood and whoever else he
had to that he meant to hold them to what the piece of
paper said, and even threaten to bring a lawsuit against
them if necessary. If he was lucky he might get a few extra
weeks or months, and some kind of financial settlement
on account of the contract being breached. But no matter
what he did, if the estate was in the kind of financial trouble Alexandra Haywood claimed—and he didn't think she
was lying—sooner or later the Whistledown horses and
the farm itself were going to be sold.

That being the inescapable reality of the situation, he
might as well face it, and start making plans.

The first thing to do would be to get the horses settled
as advantageously as he could. Each posed a different set
of problems, from the most expensive—that would be
Deputy Dreamer, a feisty two-year-old out of Mr. Pros-
pector—to the least. Twelve-year-old Suleimann, who'd
never placed better than third in his racing career, was
worth maybe a thousand dollars.

He was going to have to buy Suleimann himself. A
thousand dollars he could afford. Silver Wonder at around
half a million? In his dreams. Unless, maybe, he could pull
together a group of investors and work out some kind of
deal.

What were the chances of that?

As far as his personal finances were concerned, the bottom line was that he was going to have to come up with another source of income. He could board more horses than he already did—without the Whistledown horses, there would be plenty of extra stalls in his barn. He could look for another farm to manage, but all the local ones that needed managers had them, as far as he knew. Instead of training privately, as he had been doing for Haywood, he could open a public stable and train for a variety of owners. But building a lucrative public stable took time, and to do right by the horses and their owners would mean traveling a lot. Traveling a lot was something he would do only as a last resort, because there were the kids to think about.

In his considered opinion, the boys especially needed him home almost more as teenagers than they had as little kids.

He could always get a job at the Budd plant, the local industry giant that manufactured machine parts. Or at Ford in Louisville. The pay at either was good. The benefits were good.

Joe's mouth twisted. At nineteen he'd been full of plans to become a hotshot horse trainer, convinced that he had what it took to be one of the best, one of the elite. He had dreamed of winning all the big ones, the Derby, the Breeders' Cup, maybe even the Triple Crown. But then along had come Laura and the kids and the whole disaster that had been his married life. Eventually, when it had come down to choosing between making sure his kids were taken care of and chasing his dreams, his kids had won. He'd thought he had found an acceptable compromise when he'd gone to work for Charles Haywood: a steady paycheck along with the challenge of building a first-class stable on someone else's dime. Now, at thirty-seven, he was reaping what he had sown: the stable he'd worked so hard to put together was being taken away from him because it was not, in actuality, his own, and he was reduced to thinking about taking a job in a factory to support his kids.

He should have seen it coming from the moment he had found Haywood's body. He guessed he *had* seen it coming, although he hadn't wanted to face it. When Alexandra Haywood had shown up so unexpectedly today, he had known as soon as he set eyes on her that her unprecedented appearance at Whistledown boded nothing good.

Exactly what part of you're fired *don't you understand?* she'd asked mockingly.

His immediate reaction had been to think, You smug little bitch.

The kicker was that he'd felt sorry for her at Haywood's funeral, which he had flown to Philadelphia to attend. He had respected his employer, and liked him too. They had both wanted the same thing: to build Whistledown Farm into one of the premier racing stables in the country. During the two months a year Haywood had generally stayed at Whistledown, they had spent a lot of time together, owner and trainer, talking about horses, talking about the farm. Haywood had mentioned his older daughter often, sharing an anecdote about something or other that she had done, bragging on her brains, her beauty. One day, he'd always said, one day when she had grown up a little and gotten all the liberal-arts nonsense college had put into her head out of her system, she would come to work for him, and then he would train her to take over the reins of Haywood Harley Nichols; that's how smart she was.

Joe had let the daughter stories go in one ear and out

the other without paying much attention to them, chalking them up to a father's natural partiality for his child. Thus he had been a little surprised, on first setting eyes on her at her father's funeral, to find that Alexandra Haywood was indeed as lovely as her father had claimed. Blond and slender in her fitted black suit, beautiful in a fine-boned, touch-me-not kind of way, she had caught his eye as she'd walked to the front pew with her stepmother and sister after the rest of the mourners had been seated.

He hadn't been positive of her identity until the reception following the service, but he'd guessed that she could only be Charles Haywood's beloved Alex. He had watched her off and on throughout the service. It had been obvious that she was grief-stricken. Her face had been as white and set as marble as she sat between her sister and a thin, dark-haired man in an expensive suit who'd held her hand— probably the fiancé who'd dumped her today. She had listened to the black-robed Episcopal priest who conducted the service, the florid-faced man who delivered the eulogy, and the angel-voiced choir without once changing expression, although silent tears had coursed down her cheeks. Later, at the reception in Haywood's big stone mansion with its marble floors and huge flower-filled rooms, he had hung around until he had a chance to express his condolences to her, although he'd felt as out of place as a fish in a tree. There'd been fancy people he didn't know, fancy food he didn't like—smoked salmon and caviar on little triangles of toast came to mind—and, for entertainment, a tasteful pianist and Haywood's young and beautiful widow, who periodically came through the rooms thanking everyone for coming. Joe had conversed with a few guests, sampled the food, expressed his condolences to the widow, and kept his eye out for Haywood's older daughter. Finally she'd appeared, her eyes red-rimmed, her lips pressed tightly together as if she was determined not to cry. He'd gone up to her, introduced himself, shaken the hand she'd held out to him, and expressed his sorrow for her loss and his admiration for her father.

And yet it had been obvious, when she had shown up at his barn today, that she didn't even remember meeting him. Well, he didn't hold that against her. He was no stranger to grief himself, and knew the tricks it could play on one's mind.

Angry as he'd been at being fired, he had, reluctantly, felt sorry for her again as she'd begged him for the details of finding her father's body. It was clear that Haywood's death had hit her hard. He supposed that years of taking care of everybody and everything had made him instinctively sympathetic toward women and children. In trying to counteract that impulse, which in this situation could do him nothing but harm if it caused him to abandon his determination to hang on at Whistledown for as long as he could, he'd been maybe blunter than he should have been. When she had grown visibly distressed he had cursed himself silently for giving in to her demands at all. In the end, when she'd persisted, he'd had to remind himself that Alexandra Haywood wasn't his problem, and just walk away.

He had enough problems of his own without taking on hers.

He'd invested himself in Whistledown Farm in a major way, and now the dream was being yanked out from under him like a rug from beneath the feet of a character in an un-funny cartoon.

That was what was bothering him so, he decided. It was not the loss of the job, the paycheck, and everything that went with it, although all those were pretty important too. It was the loss of the dream.

So here he was, at thirty-seven, faced with starting all over again.

God, it was depressing to think about.

Then he wouldn't think about it. He refused. Not tonight. Tomorrow would be soon enough to start making plans for the future.

Joe rolled onto his stomach, punched his pillow with more force than the reshaping of it called for, and tried again to go to sleep.

✥ ✥ ✥ ✥

"God, I'm freezing! Hurry up, Alex!"

The roar of the driving rain muffled Neely's words so that Alex could barely understand them. Wind-propelled sheets of water pounded the ground. The smell of wet mud rose from the saturated earth like mist. The mud itself churned around her feet with every step, sucking at her shoes, making each step an effort more taxing than trying to run in deep, soft sand. The night was dark, lit only by all-too-frequent flashes of lightning. Her fear of being chased was receding—even a homicidal maniac would think twice about venturing out in this downpour—but a shadow of it remained nonetheless.

Glancing up, her eyes shielded from the worst of the deluge by the blanket that now covered her like a hooded cloak with a fat rolled brim, Alex saw the dark, quilt-shrouded figure that was Neely swing a leg over the top of the four-board black fence which she herself had just reached. This was the second fence they'd had to climb. Neely, in flannel pajamas, had an easier time of it than did she in her long nightgown.

Had she really thought that it would be a simple matter to run down to the farm manager's house for help?

Her knees were threatening to turn to jelly at any minute and her injured head ached badly. The good thing about the icy rain was that it had long since numbed the stinging of the cut on her crown. The bad thing was that she was soaked to the skin and frozen to her very marrow, so numb with cold that she doubted that she would feel it if she accidentally drove a nail through her hand.

Neely gained the ground on the other side of the fence and stopped, waiting for her. Huddled in the now-drenched quilt, her face a pale oval in the darkness as it turned toward Alex, she was barely visible through the silvery sheets of falling water.

"Go on without me!" Alex shouted to be heard. The downpour was so loud that she was afraid her voice wouldn't carry, but her sister must have understood, because she turned and vanished into the storm. For a moment, just a moment, Alex allowed herself to rest. Bowing her head against the rain, she leaned on the fence, trying to catch her breath. The rain drove through the already soaked blanket, pouring down her body with as little hindrance as if she'd been standing there naked. Deliberately she thought about what she was running from—the sound of breathing, the smell of burning, someone in the house who was possibly, at this very moment, giving chase—to give herself the strength to go on.

Thunder boomed. Lightning snaked across the sky, then with a bang as loud as an explosion hit frighteningly close. Galvanized, she moved. Yanking one foot free of the muddy quagmire, Alex hitched her nightgown up to her thighs, struggled to adjust the blanket, and climbed the fence. The boards were rough and splintery beneath her hands, and slippery with streaming water. Her feet in their leather-soled shoes kept slipping off the narrow edges. The rain was falling so hard that it hurt when it hit the bare skin of her legs. Glancing up as she swung a leg over the top, she saw that Welch's white-painted farmhouse was faintly visible on the rise just ahead. Only a little bit farther . . .

Alex guessed that Neely was already slipping and sloshing over the last remaining piece of ground: the farmhouse's front yard.

Then she fell.

It was so sudden, so surprising, that she didn't even have time to cry out. Her foot slipped and suddenly she was hurtling downward to land with jarring force on her back in the mud. Her head hit something hard, and for the second time that night she saw stars. For a moment she simply lay where she had landed, too stunned to move, at the mercy of the driving rain. The blanket had caught on something and been pulled from her as she went down; it now hung from the fence like a flag of surrender.

The rain stung her skin like thousands of icy bee stings. Her breasts, which had been protected by the blanket, were painfully exposed. She rolled onto her stomach to shelter as much of her body as she could, and took stock.

She'd hit her head on the fence post nearest her, she realized as she glanced around. Two blows to the head in one night were too much for her system to cope with. She couldn't even begin to get on her feet again right away. She was dizzy, shaken. The darkness seemed to tilt and sway around her. The raindrops danced and shimmied as they hit the waterlogged surface of the ground and bounced off. Telling herself that it was just for an instant, she closed her eyes, and rested her head on her folded arms.

A rhythmic sucking sound that rapidly increased in volume caused her to glance up again what could have been seconds or minutes later. Groggily she realized that she was still lying in the icy puddle of mud and water in which she had fallen, her back pelted by even colder rain. Her skin was numb; her arms—all of her body that she could see in her present position—looked corpse-white against the soaked earth. The smell of damp turf was everywhere, as overpowering as cheap perfume. Shielding her eyes with one hand, she focused with some difficulty on a man's approaching boots. She identified them as the source of the sucking sound just as they splashed to a stop inches from her face. Even through the silvery veil of water she could see that they were huge, muddy. . . .

Terror goosed her numbed senses as memory returned. There'd been someone in her bedroom, in the house. . . .

She scrambled to her knees, heart pounding as she looked up through the curtains of rain at the tall dark form looming so menacingly over her.

"What the hell do you think you're doing, going swimming in a mud puddle?" Laced with equal parts anger and annoyance, it was a roar capable of being heard over the storm. Conversely, it filled Alex with relief. Instead of the homicidal maniac she had half expected, Welch stood in front of her, obnoxious and unpleasant as ever but a safe haven nonetheless. Water cascaded over him as brutally as if someone were standing above him with a hose pointed right at the top of his head and turned on full blast.

"I fell," she replied even as he reached down, grasping her upper arms with ungentle fingers and hauling her to her feet. Her knees quivered a protest, her head swam, and Alex sagged against him, clutching the wet flannel of his shirt in both hands, grateful to have something to lean on. Her head tipped forward instinctively to protect her face from the rain and her forehead ended up resting against the bony notch at the base of his neck. His shirt was only partially buttoned, she discovered. As she turned her head she could feel the crisp texture of his chest hair beneath her cheek. He smelled faintly of strong soap and wet cloth. Washed by the rain, his skin was cold to the touch. But the muscles beneath were reassuringly firm, and he felt big and solid and strong enough to take on all comers. Alex hadn't realized just how scared she had been until the fear left her. Welch might dislike her, but he would keep her safe. "There was someone in the house. . . ."

"Save it!" They were shouting at each other, or at least he was shouting. Her voice sounded far weaker to her own ears and she doubted that he could understand a word she said. Before she realized what he meant to do he moved, one arm coming around her shoulders and the other sliding beneath her knees, scooping her up in his arms. Turning with her, carrying her as easily as if she weighed no more than a child, he headed for his house, his long strides eating up the ground, his head and shoulders hunched protectively over her to, she thought, shield her from the rain as best he could. A little embarrassed to accept such a rescue, Alex nevertheless surrendered to necessity and clung, wrapping her arms around his neck.

Twelve

✣

People crowded the open doorway. The darkness revealed no more of them than shadowy shapes and pale, watching faces as Welch carried her with swift efficiency up the steps to the covered porch. Just getting out of the reach of the stinging pellets of rain felt wonderful. Alex sagged with relief in Welch's arms. A bright beam of light played over her; at least one of the clustered group held a flashlight. Glancing down, Alex was suddenly conscious of the sodden nightgown she wore. The thin wet silk clung to her body like milky cling-wrap. Her nipples, hard and puckered with cold, were plainly visible through the cloth; so, too, was every other inch of her anatomy. If it had not been for the darkness, she would have been indecent.

"Keep the light pointed down," Welch said to whoever was holding it, earning her undying gratitude as the beam dropped away. The group fell back before them as he carried her inside the house. Her head, feeling too heavy now for her neck to support it, rested against his broad shoulder. She was freezing cold, light-headed, nauseated. If he had not come for her, she was not sure that she would have been able to get up off the ground and make it to the safety of the house on her own.

She owed him one.

"Alex, are you all right?" It was Neely, pushing past the others to lay a hand on her sister's arm. Neely's teeth were chattering; her words were punctuated by tiny clattering sounds. Alex was so cold that she could barely feel Neely's almost equally cold fingers. "What happened? I thought you were right behind me."

"I slipped and fell climbing over the fence. I'm all right. Just cold." Her voice was weaker than normal and her teeth chattered audibly too. The warmth of the house enveloped her like an embrace, but it was not enough: she was shivering violently in Welch's arms. He was holding her close to his chest still, as he had to protect her from the rain. Her body pressed against his almost greedily. Her breasts and belly and thighs had turned in toward him like a flower turns toward the sun, seeking to absorb some of the heat that their contact generated. But with Neely's gaze on them, and the others looking at them too, she suddenly awakened to the embarrassment potential of her position. She stirred in his arms, asking without words to be put down. He obliged, but one arm still curved around her waist to provide support. The arm was dripping wet, hard with muscle, and welcome.

Alex's head swam alarmingly as her shoes touched the floor amid a torrent of water that poured rather than dripped off both of them. Her knees threatened to buckle, and she swayed. Grabbing handfuls of soaking wet shirt for support, she leaned heavily against Welch as the closest solid object.

"Okay?" he asked.

Before she could answer, the flashlight beam hit Alex full in the face. She winced, shutting her eyes. His arm tightened around her, pulling her fully against him, as one of his hands lifted to block the light from her face.

"Josh, I told you to keep that thing pointed down." Welch's voice was sharp.

"Sorry." It was a young male voice. Alex remembered the scalped teenager from the barn, and deduced that the people clustered around them were Welch's children, plus Neely. Something furry brushed against her ankles. Shifting her feet, startled, she glanced down to discover a small, fat dog sniffing around her shoes.

"She fell in the house, too. Maybe she's really hurt." Neely was close on Alex's other side, talking worriedly to Welch. Alex turned her head. Her cheek rested against the cold wet flannel covering Welch's chest. She could hear the steady beat of his heart. Neely was deep in shadow, although the multiple flashlight beams now swooping hither and yon allowed Alex a fleeting glimpse of wet hair straggling down on either side of her sister's wide-eyed, rain-washed face.

"You guys have more than one flashlight, right?" Welch asked the assembled group.

"We've got three." The speaker was another young male, taller and older sounding than the first.

"Give me one."

A flashlight changed hands, its beam flashing across the ceiling as Welch took possession from one of his sons. Then, to Alex's surprise, he scooped her up into his arms again without a word and started walking away with her into the dark interior of the house.

"There's no need . . . ," she protested, grabbing on to his neck for dear life. Being swept up so suddenly made her dizzy. She broke off without finishing, her head dropping out of necessity to rest against his shoulder until the world had a chance to settle down around her. Whatever his faults, the man was strong as an ox, she thought, and she found that suddenly very comforting.

"I think there is," he said, as if his opinion was the only one that mattered. Ordinarily such cool self-assurance would have annoyed her, but under the circumstances she was willing to permit her opinion to be disregarded. He carried her up the stairs into the utter blackness that was the second floor, issuing orders over his shoulder all the way. "Eli, get those camping lanterns out from under the sink. Josh, go round up some extra towels. Look in the dryer, I put a load in before we went to bed. Jen, you show Neely to your guys' bathroom. Make sure they have a lantern in there, Eli, and bring a lantern and some towels to my bedroom."

A chorus of assents followed them up the stairs. Alex was surprised not to hear the kind of crisp *yessirs* that normally were accompanied by military salutes.

Welch turned left at the top, walking briskly along a narrow corridor. His heavy boots made squelching sounds with every step, and Alex was reminded that he was just as wet and probably just as cold as she was.

Autocratic as he undoubtedly was, he *had* come to her rescue at the expense of his own comfort, and she appreciated that.

"Is your telephone working?" Her teeth chattered. She could not stop shivering. The faint warmth generated by her contact with his body and the greater warmth of the house did nothing to ease her bone-deep chill. Despite her physical discomfort, though, the situation she had left behind at Whistledown required immediate attention. "You need to call the fire department. And the police as well. Neely and I smelled smoke, and—and there was someone in the house."

"So your sister said when she came banging on the door." Welch sounded unimpressed as he turned into a doorway at the end of the hall, crossed a bedroom, and entered a white-tiled bathroom. By the light of the bobbing flashlight she saw that it was compact, with utilitarian fixtures and a large, glass-enclosed shower stall instead of a tub. "Okay, hold on. I'm going to put you down."

He set her on her feet again, keeping a careful arm around her waist as he put the flashlight down on the back of the toilet tank, positioning it next to a box of tissues so that it wouldn't roll. Thus situated, the small light provided an adequate degree of illumination, although the corners of the room and the ceiling remained shadowy and dark. Water dripped with an audible patter from her body and his to form a muddy puddle on the floor. He was dressed in the same red and gray plaid shirt he had worn earlier, plus jeans and boots, she saw. All were soaked, and his shirt and boots were caked with mud. She was in an equally sorry state. Long streaks of mud discolored her nightgown and smeared her arms and probably her face as well. Her shoes were mud-caked too. The nightgown itself was plastered against her breasts and stomach and wrapped around her legs, revealing every intimate detail of her slender body: her B-cup breasts with their cold-hardened nipples, her belly button, the dark triangle between her thighs. Mortified by her near nakedness, she instinctively turned away to keep him from getting a full frontal view.

"Steady, now," he said, for all the world as if she were a fidgety horse. His hand rode her hipbone as she moved. It was a big hand, long fingered and warm enough now to be felt through the almost nonexistent barrier of the wet silk. His fingertips dug lightly into her flesh.

"I'm okay." But she wasn't. Moving so quickly had been a mistake, she discovered. She felt dizzy and sick, and her knees threatened to give way. She staggered slightly as she took another step away from him. His arm contracted, reeling her in like a fish, pulling her against him. Head spinning, giving up the effort to stand alone for the moment, she subsided once more against his wide chest.

"Looks like it." His voice was dry. Holding her securely against him with one arm, he reached out with the other to turn on the taps of the shower.

"You need to call the fire department," Alex insisted into his shirtfront. His body heat was reasserting itself even through his clammy clothes, and she pressed close instinctively while convulsive shivers continued to rack her body. The promise implicit in the rushing hot water no more than inches away was tantalizing. "And the police."

"The phone line's down," he said, holding his free hand beneath the spray, apparently to check the temperature. "After we get you and your sister squared away, I'll go up and take a look around the house. If Whistledown's really burning, at this point a few more minutes won't make much difference one way or the other. And if there's somebody in the house, I'm perfectly capable of handling it on my own."

She didn't doubt it.

"You don't have a cell phone?" she asked as he withdrew his hand from the water, closed the shower door, and then reached behind him to push the bathroom door shut as well. Steam billowed up from the base of the shower, clouding the glass walls. Alex watched almost longingly.

"The reception's spotty out here. No point." He glanced down at her. His black hair glistened wet and sleek as a seal's hide, throwing the hard planes and angles of his face into prominence. His forehead was high, his nose straight and not overlarge, his mouth firm and unsmiling, his jaw square. His skin was very tan, and his cheeks and chin were dark with stubble. His eyes looked almost the color of water in the uncertain light. Mud streaked one cheek and the side of his nose. He was far bigger than she, both taller and broader, and his body was hard and warm against hers. To her astonishment she felt a tiny tingling awareness of him as a man awaken deep inside her, and her eyes widened fractionally on his face.

"Something wrong?" he asked, frowning down at her.

"No," she managed.

"Okay, let's get you warmed up." If Welch was also experiencing a sexual awakening, he gave no sign of it. He reached down, scooping her up into his arms again as if she had no say in the matter at all, which she supposed that at this point she didn't. Then, with him still fully dressed and her rather less so in her saturated nightgown and mud-caked loafers, he stepped into the shower with her. Hot water cascaded over both of them, blessedly welcome. Pools of brown water swirled down the drain as mud was sluiced from their bodies. Still shivering, Alex tightened her arms around his neck, turned her face up to the spray, and shut her eyes, trying at the same time to shut out the sudden unexpected attraction she felt for him.

It had to be a purely physiological response to being in such close proximity to an attractive male, she told herself. The good news was, it meant that her senses, frozen by the shock of her father's death, were beginning to thaw. The bad news was, they were being indiscriminate about when and with whom they did it. If it had only happened earlier, if she had not kept Paul out of her bed for the last few horrible weeks, maybe he wouldn't have turned to Tara Gould. . . .

Stop that, she ordered herself fiercely. She refused to think of Paul ever again. He was as lost to her as her father, and, in retrospect, far, far less beloved.

"Warmer?" Welch spoke almost in her ear. She refused

to open her eyes. Being held in strong masculine arms against a strong masculine chest made it hard enough to forget that sensual tingle; seeing a strong masculine face so close to her own would make it just that much harder.

"Mm-hmm."

Her limbs prickled as they warmed up, particularly her poor frozen legs, which felt like they were being stabbed with dozens of tiny needles. Curling her toes in silent protest, she wriggled uncomfortably. Apparently mistaking her movement for a request to be put down, he lowered the arm beneath her knees, allowing her to slide down his body until her feet hit the floor. The friction of her body against his was unexpectedly erotic. Her eyes popped open, and her lips parted in surprise. His face was far too close for her peace of mind, she discovered. His head was bent over hers, once again protecting her from the full force of the deluge. His eyes as they met hers appeared darker than they had before, and Alex realized that his pupils had enlarged until they almost swallowed up the light irises. The mud was gradually disappearing from his cheek and nose as water sluiced down his face. If she had cared to do so, she could have counted every individual whisker in his unshaven chin.

"You've got mud on your face," he said, cupping her chin in his hand as he rubbed at her cheek with his thumb. It was a surprisingly intimate gesture. Too intimate, she thought, for her peace of mind, and pulled her chin free.

"So do you." Her voice was husky. She glanced away from him in pure self-defense. She did not like the reaction her body was having to him, and she certainly did not want him to know about it.

"The difference is, I'm used to mud."

"What makes you think I'm not?" She looked at him

again, unable to help herself. His gaze moved over her face, and one corner of his mouth twisted up wryly.

"Call it a hunch," he said, gripping her waist again and turning her so that the hot water streamed down her spine.

Defending herself against her body's natural responses was difficult under the circumstances, Alex discovered. She did not think she could stand up without his support, and under the circumstances his support required lots of physical contact. She could feel the firm grip of his hands on her waist. They were big and strong, possessive almost. Her hands remained linked behind his neck. Her arms were draped over the hard muscle and solid bone of his shoulders. Her body was plastered to his. Her breasts, naked except for the almost nonexistent veil of wet silk, pressed tightly against the soaked flannel covering his chest. Although she was warm now, her nipples remained hard and puckered, sensitized by their close contact with his body. The realization that she was getting well and truly turned on by him unnerved her. It had been so many weeks since she had felt anything, much less anything sexual, that she was alarmed by the renaissance of her own senses, especially since it was happening courtesy of this particular man.

Wasn't this the same rude, impossible man who had been so difficult to deal with just a few hours earlier? How could he possibly be affecting her so?

"Hang on," he said, and let go of her waist to reach for the soap in the dish built into the white-tiled wall. Picking up the green-speckled bar, he worked it into a lather. The smell was spicy, pungent, a stronger version of the faint scent she had noticed about him earlier—Irish Spring? she wondered.

"Close your eyes," he directed, interrupting her

thoughts. When she obeyed, he ran his soapy hands over her face, his fingertips lightly brushing over her cheekbones, down the bridge of her nose and around her mouth to her chin. They were faintly callused, and his palms were large and square, the hands of a man accustomed to working with them for a living. The smell of the soap was stronger than ever. The sound of the shower reminded her of the driving rain outside. Only this onslaught of water was hot and welcome—like his touch. She found herself breathless suddenly as she imagined his hands in other places, busy at other things.

"Tilt your face up."

She did, and he turned with her so that the water poured over her face and upper body, rinsing away the soap. Then he moved again so that his back took the brunt of the spray, and returned the soap to the dish. Blinking away the droplets that still ran down her face, she opened her eyes and watched as he washed his own face now, scrubbing both soapy hands over it, then tilted his head back so that the suds were rinsed away. Fascinated, she stared at the strong brown column of his throat, at the hard line of his jaw, at the firm, well-shaped mouth and the black crescents of his lashes that lay against tanned, unshaven cheeks.

There was nothing to stop her from pressing her mouth to his throat, unbuttoning his shirt and running her hands over his chest, delving inside his jeans. . . . Stop! she told herself frantically, horrified at the direction of her thoughts. Of course, she had no intention of doing any of those things, or indeed anything sexual with him at all, but the desire was there, as powerful as any she had ever felt.

Why now? Why him? The questions swirled through her mind even as she registered various sensations with an almost guilty pleasure. Her nipples tingled as the hard wall of his chest rubbed against them. She could feel the flexing of his muscles every time he moved. Her body with its covering of wet silk slithered against the wet flannel of his shirt and the hard denim of his jeans; unable to help herself, she gave in to the urge to get closer to him yet and pressed her pelvis discreetly against his muscled thigh. The sensation produced by her nearly naked body pushing against his clothed one was indescribable. Heat shot through her body. Her pulse quickened. Her loins clenched. The intense physicality of her reaction stunned her. He was reacting, too. Against her stomach she could feel the surging bulge in the front of his jeans, growing unmistakably hard. His head snapped upright, and their eyes met and held. His were narrowed and faintly wary, as though his reaction was as much of a surprise to him as hers was to her.

Thirteen

✦

His eyes remained locked with hers as his hands closed over her hipbones. He shifted positions slightly, his jeans-clad thigh pushing deliberately now against the juncture of hers. He was looking down at her, unsmiling, his gaze sliding from her eyes to her mouth. Her lips parted in response to the smoldering quality of that look. Her insides quivered and quaked.

Then his eyes flickered, his mouth compressed, and he used his tightened grip on her hipbones to edge her away from him, putting a few millimeters of space between their lower bodies.

"You've got mud in your hair, too," he said, his voice devoid of inflection. As Alex registered that he didn't mean to follow through on the supercharged atmosphere that had sprung up between them, he maneuvered her so that the full force of the water pounded down directly on top of her head, presumably to remove the mud of which he spoke. The water hit the cut in her crown; her head seemed to explode with pain, and she yelped in agonized surprise. Immediately all thoughts of a sexual nature were forgotten as she jerked her head out of harm's way.

"What?" He was frowning down at her.

"My head. There's a cut." The burning pain was enough

to get her mind off his body, for which she was thankful. She had been so cold, and so wet, and so shaken up, that she had almost forgotten about the original injury to her head. Now it was reminding her of its existence with a vengeance.

"How'd you cut your head?" He turned with her so that his back was to the spray again and her head was completely shielded from the water by his upper body.

"I told you, there was someone in my bedroom when I woke up. I chased whoever it was into the hall, and—and I think they hit me over the head with something. It knocked me out for a few minutes. When I came to, they were gone and my head was bleeding."

"And you're just now getting around to mentioning it?" He sounded exasperated. "Show me."

Alex obediently tilted her head forward, careful to keep the injury out of the stream of water, and swept her dripping hair out of the way with one hand so that he could see the approximate location of the wound. The whole crown of her head throbbed and burned. Until now, she guessed, the site must have been pretty much numb from the cold.

"See?"

He let out a near-silent whistle. "No wonder you're having trouble standing up."

His fingers gently probed the area, and she winced.

"You've got a nasty cut, right on top of a lump the size of a golf ball." He withdrew his hand. Dropping her hair back into place, Alex looked up to meet his gaze. "Are you telling me that someone attacked you inside the house?" There was the faintest hint of skepticism in his tone.

Alex bristled. "What I'm telling you is, there was somebody in my bedroom. Whoever it was, was standing at the foot of my bed when I woke up. I distinctly heard them breathing, in and out, really loud, like this." She demonstrated. "I chased the breathing out into the hall, and—and I stumbled, and got hit over the head. I think whoever it was hit me, but I can't be sure. I might have hit my head on something. It was dark; the lights were out. I couldn't see anything."

He said nothing more for a moment, frowning slightly as he seemed to mull over her words. Tired of looking up at him, Alex gave in to weakness and closed her eyes, resting her cheek on his chest. The hot water had warmed her nicely, but in exchange she now had to endure stabbing, burning pain. She didn't know which was worse, hurting or feeling frozen. She did know that the explosion of pain in her head had taken the edge off her nascent sexual interest in Welch. It had not, however, undermined her growing feeling that she could rely on him. Given the events of earlier in the day—she had fired the man, after all, and he hadn't reacted too kindly to it—she was a little surprised to discover that she was perfectly willing to let him deal with the present situation as he saw fit. At least, she would be if she were convinced that he appreciated the facts of what she was telling him.

She opened her eyes. "Believe me, I didn't just imagine the whole thing." Her voice was tart.

"You didn't imagine getting hit over the head, that's for sure." He sounded thoughtful.

Her eyes narrowed. "I didn't imagine the rest of it, either."

"I never said you did."

"You implied it."

"I didn't mean to." His voice was soothing as his gaze met hers. "Look, we'll get to the bottom of it, okay? First things first. I know your head hurts, but I think we need to rinse that cut off before we do anything else. Like I said, there's mud in your hair. Think you can stand it?"

The memory of the stinging pain that had accompanied the injury's last encounter with running water was almost enough to make her say no. But she knew he was right, and so she grimaced, giving a barely perceptible nod.

"Good girl." His hands were in her hair, gently separating the long strands, exposing her lacerated scalp. Alex buried her face in his chest, closing her eyes and tightening her arms around his neck in wincing anticipation of what would come next.

"Here we go," he said, and turned with her so that her head was once again exposed to the full force of the shower spray. The pain was sharp and immediate, but not as explosive as before because she was expecting it. Alex bit her lip to keep from crying out as hot water poured over the tender wound.

"All done." He shifted position again so that her head was once again out of the reach of the spray. His arms wrapped tightly around her, supporting her as her knees threatened to buckle.

A loud banging on the bathroom door startled them both.

"Hey, Dad, I'm putting a lantern and a bunch of towels on your bed," a boy's voice called through the door.

"Thanks, Eli," Joe called back. When he looked down at Alex there was a wry twist to his mouth.

"I think that's our cue," he said, and scooped her up, stepping out of the shower with her. Even the warm moist air of the bathroom was cooler than the steamy atmosphere of the shower, and Alex immediately regretted the loss of so much welcome heat. She shivered, not convulsively like before but just a little, a natural response to the change in temperature. Water poured from them in streams, mixing with the muddy water that was already on the floor until the entire area was awash.

"Think you can sit on the toilet for a minute without keeling over?"

"Yes." The pain in her head was no longer quite so acute, but it was definitely there and, in addition, she felt weak and nauseated. Still, as long as her knees didn't have to support her weight she was pretty sure she wouldn't just collapse.

Welch deposited her on the toilet's closed lid, hanging on to her shoulders for the moment or so it took to satisfy himself that she wasn't going to topple over sideways. She bent forward when he let her go, resting her elbows on her knees and her head in her hands. Closing her eyes, she took deep, steadying breaths, determined not to let the head injury get the best of her. He hesitated, and she felt his gaze on her.

"I'm okay," she said without looking up.

He made a dubious sound, but she heard him moving away from her, heard the bathroom door open, and felt a draft of cool air. She shivered again, all too conscious of the fact that she was soaking wet and almost naked and vulnerable to every small drop in temperature, or, for that matter, passing glance. Fortunately, for the moment her posture preserved her modesty, and anyway, as far as Welch was concerned, she wasn't sure that she had much modesty left to preserve. To his credit, he didn't seem inclined to take advantage of her vulnerability, which she supposed she should count as a point in his favor.

Seconds later he was back, draping a towel over her bent head and tucking the dripping strands of her hair up in it before wrapping another towel, longer and thicker than the first, around her shoulders. Light, which she presumed came from the lantern his son had left in the bedroom, glimmered through the open bathroom door, brightening the surroundings a little.

The deep breaths had helped to steady her. So, too, did sheer determination. He began blotting the moisture from the ends of her hair, then pressed a handful of towel firmly against the cut, presumably to stop the bleeding. Alex winced and grabbed his hands to stop him, but managed not to cry out.

"I can do it," she said, opening her eyes and sitting up so that her back rested against the cool china tank, thereby moving her head out of his reach. To prove her point, she pressed the towel down over the injury and held it, although with far less enthusiasm than he had used.

After watching for a moment, Welch shrugged and stepped away from her. Alex pressed the towel to her head for a moment longer and then took stock. She didn't think she was bleeding all that badly, and, anyway, applying direct pressure hurt. But a quick examination of the white terry-cloth showed that it was already stained with blood, and her fingers gingerly probing the wound came away sticky and dark. Folding the towel into a pad, she positioned it over the cut. Then, bending forward, she carefully wrapped the second towel turban-fashion around her head to hold the makeshift bandage in place. Straightening, she glanced his way again just in time to see him take hold of the dripping edges of his shirt with both hands. Without bothering to unbutton the saturated flannel, he dragged the shirt up over his head. As quickly as that she found herself staring at a naked masculine chest that was sexy enough to make her almost forget the pain in her head.

"What are you doing?" she asked with careful politeness as he dropped the soaked shirt to the floor with a soft plop. Her gaze moved over him without her being able to help it. Clearly he was no stranger to either physical work or regular workouts, or both. His shoulders were massive; his upper arms bulged. His pectorals were sharply defined and his abdomen was flat and ridged with muscle. His waist and hips were narrow compared with the corded width of his shoulders, and the center of his chest was covered with a thick mat of curling black hair.

How had Neely described him? Sex on a stick? Her little sister didn't know the half of it.

"Stripping off," he said as if doing so in front of her was the most natural thing in the world. "I'm kind of wet, in case you haven't noticed. Here."

He tossed her another towel, one of several he had carried back into the bathroom with him and tucked into the chrome bar that was the towel rack. It was big enough to cover her like a small cape. Wrapping it around her shoulders and clutching it closed with both hands, Alex said nothing more. But she could not help but watch as, balancing on first one foot and then the other, he pulled off his now rinsed clean boots and dropped them to the floor too. Her eyes widened in semi-shocked anticipation as she waited for his only remaining garment, his jeans, to follow. Instead he stopped with his thumbs hooked in his waistband, and looked at her.

"Your turn," he said.

"What?" His meaning did not register, probably because his words were not the foremost thing on her mind. She could not seem to keep herself from looking at him. Indeed, in the tight confines of the bathroom there was really no place else to look. He stood scarcely more than an arm's length away, close enough so that she could see the dark indentation of his navel peeking over his waistband, close enough where she could see individual drops of water glistening on his shoulders and snaking down

through the wedge of hair on his chest. Of their own volition, her gaze slid down the front of his jeans.

The wet denim and uncertain light made it impossible
to be sure of anything, but she thought that he was as
aware of her as she was of him. Embarrassed to think he
might realize where she was looking, Alex glanced up hur-
riedly to find that his gaze was on her face.

"See this towel?" He pulled a bright orange beach towel
from the bar and held it up for her inspection. When Alex
nodded, he continued: "I'm going to give it to you, and I
want you to take off your nightgown and wrap it around
yourself. Think you can do that without doing yourself an
injury?"

Attracted to him or not, that was going too far, Alex
thought. She was not going to just take off her nightgown
and sit there stark naked in front of him. Her mind
refused, no matter how her body might quicken at the
prospect.

"Not with you standing there," she said positively.

He grinned, a crooked and charming grin that made
her blink. It was the first time she had ever seen him
smile, and the sheer masculine appeal of it was startling.

He was really a mouthwateringly attractive man.

"I was going to turn off the flashlight first. What'd you
think?"

"Oh. Good idea." Of course. He'd been anything but
lecherous so far. In fact, he'd been more gentlemanly than
most men would have been under the circumstances. For
a few minutes there in the shower, he could have done just
about anything to her that he wanted. With her enthusias-
tic cooperation, honesty forced her to add.

And he had known it, and refrained. It was kind of
embarrassing, now that she thought about it. And kind of
exciting, too.

He moved toward her, handed her the towel, then reached behind her for the flashlight.

"For God's sake, tell me if you need help," he said, and turned off the light.

The sudden darkness was as absolute as if she'd been plunged into an unlit subway tunnel. Fumbling because she couldn't see, she kicked off her shoes, then pushed the ruined nightgown down her body, careful to balance herself by holding on to the tank as she lifted her bottom up just enough to get the garment all the way off. Her skin was wet and slippery, and for a moment she feared she might really slip off the toilet seat as she sat back down again. She was shivering, and her head throbbed as she dried herself with the towel that had been draped around her shoulders, but the pain was less than it had been. The worst thing was the weakness in her limbs, and the transient dizziness she experienced whenever she moved.

"Doing okay?" he asked, his voice echoing through the small bathroom as if it were a cave.

"Yes," she replied hastily, in case he should get the idea that she needed help and turn the flashlight back on.

Without her sight, her other senses became more acute. He was close, as he'd promised. She could hear him, hear the rustle and slurp of wet jeans that told her he must be removing his clothes too. She could smell him, the sharp scent of soap overlaying a warm musky smell that spoke silently of man. She could feel him, feel the invisible weight of his presence nearby.

After drying off, she wrapped herself sarong style in the beach towel, tucked the ends between her breasts, and tried not to imagine him, naked, doing the same thing less than three feet away.

Fourteen

✤

D ecent?" Welch asked.
   "Yes."
   The flashlight clicked on. He was standing in the
middle of the bathroom with a forest green towel hitched
around his hips and another towel, this one solid white,
slung around his neck. He had obviously towel-dried his
hair, which was tousled and black as a crow's wing in the
uncertain light. The white towel contrasted nicely with the
wedge of hair on his chest and the swarthiness of his skin.
The green towel covered him from belly button to knees.
Below it his calves were hard with muscle and fuzzed with
dark hair. His feet were bare.

His gaze flicked over her, too. Alex knew what she
must look like: pale and too slender, with narrow shoulders, long, elegant limbs and a fine-boned, delicate-
featured face. Clad only in the orange beach towel with
another towel, a blue-striped one, wrapped around her
head, without makeup, hair, or clothes to hide behind, she
felt vulnerable and just a little ill at ease. She had never
before questioned whether or not a man, looking at her,
would find her attractive; now, suddenly, in the wake of
Paul's defection, she found herself doing just that.

Which begged the question: Did she want Welch to

find her attractive? The answer came almost instantaneously: Yes, she did.

At least as attractive as she found him. For her pride's sake, if nothing else.

"Come on," he said, and moved toward her, his feet making splashing sounds as he dodged the discarded garments that formed small islands in the mini-lake they had created on the floor. He bent over her, picking her up as casually as if it was something he did every day. She was getting almost used to being scooped up without warning, but this time when he lifted her into his arms she found herself pressed against a hard chest that was softened only slightly by a crisp cushion of black hair, her arms curled over broad bronzed shoulders that were heavy with muscle, her hands locked behind a strong brown neck.

His body was warm. His skin was smooth and just faintly damp and smelled of their recent shower. His chest hair tickled her everywhere it touched.

Her senses reeled.

Alex sucked in her breath slowly, trying not to be obvious about her instant, instinctive response to being held against so much bare masculine flesh. Whatever else this trip to Whistledown had or had not done, she thought with a glimmering of amusement, it had certainly restored her libido to working order. With a vengeance.

If only she weren't having all these lustful thoughts too late, and for the wrong man. If she'd spiced things up with Paul—but she was not going to think of Paul, ever again.

"You're going to have to wear some of my clothes, unless you want to go to the hospital in that towel."

Having carried her into the bedroom, Welch set her down on the king-sized bed as he spoke. The covers had been flung aside, the sheets were mussed, and the pillows were lumpy and misshapen. Obviously it was his bed, and he had been sleeping in it earlier. Trying not to dwell on that, Alex released his neck with some reluctance, scooted back against the headboard, and stuffed the abused-looking pillows behind her back.

"I don't need to go to the hospital."

He had already turned away, moving toward the chest against the opposite wall. Like most of the rest of the furniture—bed, bookcase stuffed with paperbacks, a pair of nightstands, and a green-upholstered armchair with a floor lamp beside it—it was of sturdy oak, plain in design. The bedroom itself was small, painted a soothing sand color, and except for the mussed bed meticulously neat.

"Oh, yes, you do. You need stitches. I can sew up a horse in an emergency, but I think you'd rather have a doctor sew up your head. You could probably use an X-ray, too." He glanced at her over his shoulder. His broad bare back gleamed faintly in the soft glow of the lantern, which sat atop the chest. Farther down, his butt in the loosely draped towel looked small and tight. She noticed its charms with objective interest even while she frowned at its possessor.

"You know, I appreciate everything you've done up to this point, but I'm the one who'll decide when I need to go to the hospital and when I don't. And I don't." She hated hospitals. The last time she'd been inside one had been when she'd been nine and had gotten slammed in the head by a hockey stick at boarding school. Her skull had been fractured, and they'd had to do surgery. Her parents hadn't shown up for three days. They'd been divorced by then, and her mother had been unreachable, on one of her innumerable vacations with one of her innumerable boyfriends. Her father had been on a drunken bender; he'd owned up to it years later, after he'd sobered up. She could still remember being afraid

she'd die, and then, as the teachers had kept coming by
to check on her, having her embarrassment because her
parents didn't come grow until it outweighed her fear.
She had felt unloved, and unwanted, and embarrassed
because she was unloved and unwanted. The experience
had given her an aversion to hospitals that had remained
with her ever since.

"I disagree." His tone was mild. He opened a drawer,
rummaged around, and withdrew some garments—charcoal gray sweatpants, a lighter gray sweatshirt, and a pair
of tube socks, she saw at a glance—which he tossed onto
the bed beside her. "And around here what I say goes."
Then, in a lighter vein, "Sorry, but my wardrobe doesn't
run to women's underwear."

"You work for *me,*" she reminded him, ignoring that last
as she watched him cross to the closet opposite the bed,
slide open the door, and pull more clothing from the
depths. "I think that means that what *I* say goes."

"You fired me, remember? That kind of takes the edge
off your authority, in my book." Clothes in hand, he
headed toward the bathroom.

"What I remember is giving you thirty days' notice,
which you refused to accept. At least until the end of that
thirty days, you still work for me. Which makes *me* the
boss."

"Yeah, well, the signature on my paycheck reads
Whistledown Farm Inc., not Alexandra Haywood, last
time I looked. Not that it matters, anyway. I'm going into
the bathroom to get dressed now. If you need help getting
into those sweats, just wait till I get back, and I'll be glad to
oblige."

With that not so lightly veiled threat, he disappeared
into the bathroom, pulling the door shut behind him. Alex
glared at the closed door. Maybe he was right, and maybe

she did need to go to the hospital. Her aversion wasn't so strong that she would deliberately harm herself to keep from going. But she didn't like him just telling her what she was going to do. She'd been making her own decisions for a long time now, and she liked it that way.

His cool assumption of authority was infuriating.

Nevertheless, she struggled into the clothes, and only then fully appreciated his aside on the lack of women's underwear. The laundered-to-softness sweats felt awkward against her bare skin, but that was the least of her concerns. She'd seen enough of how he operated by this time to have little doubt that he would put the clothes on her by force if he had to. And to allow that to happen would be to sacrifice her dignity.

A brisk knock on the bathroom door just as she was gingerly removing the towel from around her head and checking her makeshift pad for blood warned her that he was about to emerge. Dropping the bloodstained white towel over the side of the bed as hastily as if it had burned her, she snatched up the blue and white towel and began, rather gingerly, to towel-dry her hair. When she didn't answer, he opened the door and came out anyway. A single glance showed him that she had done as he'd said.

"Good girl," he said. Once again sitting propped up against the headboard, now rubbing the wet strands of her hair with the towel as if the cut were the farthest thing from her mind, Alex glowered at him. Dressed now, in jeans and the navy sweatshirt, he looked almost cheerful. Which was quite a stretch, in her experience of him.

"I was cold," she said with bite, dropping the damp towel over the side of the bed to hide the other one, with its visible bloodstains. She had on no underclothes, his sweats were miles too big, her hair would be frizzing out like dandelion fluff as soon as it dried, and, most maddening of all, her head ached and pounded and swam. Maybe he was right, maybe she did need to go to the hospital and get herself checked out, but she wasn't about to give him the satisfaction of admitting any such thing. His self-satisfied expression as he came around the foot of the bed already made her want to throw something at him. If she had it to do over again, she would still be sitting there in the towel and would dare him to do something about it.

His expression goaded her into adding, "Don't think I got dressed because I'm going to the hospital, because I'm not."

He stopped at the side of the bed, cast a single, keen-eyed glance at her crown, and handed her a folded washcloth. "Press this down on the cut until we get there," he said.

"Did you not hear what I said?" Her voice was sharp. Her hand closed into a fist around the washcloth, which she had accepted without thought.

He stood for a moment, arms crossed over his chest, looking down at her with a contemplative expression on his face. "Are you always this much trouble, or am I just getting lucky here?"

"Look, Mr. Welch, all I need is a . . ." She was going to say *a couple of aspirin,* but she got no further because, just like that, he scooped her out of the bed into his arms.

"If you're going to argue with me the rest of the night, you might as well call me Joe while you're doing it."

"Listen, damn it, *Joe,* I'm not going!" His name came easily to her lips. Indeed, it was hard to think of the man as *Mr. Welch* when she'd practically melted all over him in the shower. But instead of wrapping her arms around his neck, she pushed at his shoulder. "Put me down!"

"Fine." He set her on her feet so abruptly that the room

spun. "Show me that you don't need to go to the hospital. Go on, show me. Walk across the room."

The arm that had been around her waist was withdrawn, although he stayed close behind her. Alex blinked as the floor seemed to tilt. Determined to show him, she lifted her chin and took a step, followed by another. Then her knees quivered, and she staggered. He caught her as she groped instinctively toward the bed for support, swinging her up in his arms again.

"Still feel like arguing?"

"Okay, so maybe I do need to go to the hospital," she muttered resentfully, one arm sliding around his neck. Her other hand still held the washcloth; surrendering, she pressed it against the cut, lifted it, looked at the blood staining it, and winced. He glanced at her, one corner of his mouth twisting up in a wry smile.

"You think?"

Alex's head fell back against his shoulder in a silent gesture of defeat. Holding the washcloth to her throbbing head, she was so dizzy that she could have been riding a carnival tilt-a-whirl as he carried her downstairs.

"Alex! Is something wrong?" Clad in a yellow terrycloth bathrobe over what looked like a pair of boys' pajamas, her curly hair as unruly as Alex felt her own straighter locks were starting to be, Neely jumped up and hurried toward them as Joe carried her into the lamp-lit kitchen. Neely had been sitting at the big rectangular table with Joe's three kids: a prepubescent girl with boyishly cut brown hair wearing white, waffle-weave long johns; the scalped-looking boy in jeans and a white T-shirt; and another, older boy, also in jeans with a flannel shirt, who looked like a younger, leaner, long-haired version of Joe himself. They broke off what had been an animated conversation as their father entered with his burden. All of them stared curiously at Alex. Even the dog emerged from beneath the table to take a good look.

"I'm taking your sister to the hospital for stitches," Joe said to Neely before Alex could answer.

"Stitches!" Neely exclaimed as Joe walked past her to deposit Alex in the chair she had vacated. Alex clung to his neck for an instant as her head cleared. Her weakness was not lost on Joe.

"Don't fall over," he whispered in her ear with a hint of mockery, then stepped away. His place was immediately taken by Neely, who hovered over her, her eyes wide with alarm as she took in the washcloth Alex was pressing against her head.

"I cut my head when I fell down. No big deal." Alex was determined to downplay the extent of her injury as she reassured her anxious-looking sister. Neely had suffered so many losses in her life that she was far more sensitive than most teenagers to the fact that a loved one could be snatched away from her at any moment without warning, and Alex knew that. Unconvinced, Neely moved around behind her.

"Let me see."

Alex lifted the washcloth.

"Oh, Alex!"

"That bad, huh?" Alex asked ruefully, reapplying the washcloth to the wound.

"A couple of stitches and she'll be fine." Joe was back, wearing a dark green rain poncho that reached halfway down his thighs and dropping a huge trench coat that from the size of it could only be his own around Alex's shoulders. As she slid her arms into the sleeves, he crouched in front of her. Looking down at him, she registered that his broad shoulders looked massive in the enveloping poncho, and the lamplight picked up blue highlights in his black hair.

"Put your feet in here," he said. Then, glancing around, "Eli, find me an umbrella, would you?"

Here meant a pair of rubber boots, too small to be his. One of the boys', maybe? Alex did as he told her, sliding her feet into the shanks. The boots went on easily. Standing, bundling the trench coat around her like a blanket, he picked her up again. Having accepted the inevitable, she held the washcloth to her head with one hand and curled an arm around his neck, feeling more than a little self-conscious under the interested gazes of four children.

"These are my kids, by the way. Jenny, Eli, and you remember Josh," he said, nodding at each in turn. Then, to them, "We'll be at the hospital if you need me. This is probably going to take a while, so you guys might as well go on back to bed." He looked at Neely. "There's an extra bed in Jen's room. You can sleep in there, if you want. Your sister can have my bed when we get back, and I'll sleep on the couch. Unless you're planning to go back up to Whistledown for what's left of the night."

Alex and Neely exchanged glances, and both simultaneously shook their heads. Their recent terrifying experience within its walls had definitely robbed Whistledown of some of its charm.

"It's probably burned down by now anyway," Alex muttered for his ears alone as he turned and headed for the back door.

"Nah," he said. "We'd see the flames from here." He nodded at the uncurtained windows. Beyond them, the night was black.

"Alex, do you want me to come with you?" Neely trailed them anxiously.

Looking over Joe's shoulder, Alex managed a smile for her sister. "In that getup? No way. Stay here and go to bed."

"Dad, here's an umbrella." The oldest boy, Eli, passed an unopened umbrella to Joe.

"Thanks. You're baby-sitting."

"Yeah, I know."

"He's not baby-sitting *me*. I'm almost as old as he is." Josh, who had materialized on his father's other side, sounded surly.

"He's baby-sitting Jen. In fact, you both are." Joe said it in a quelling tone. Then someone—Eli, Alex guessed—opened the back door. Cold, gusty air laden with moisture and the rushing sound of falling rain swirled around them as Joe stepped onto the small back stoop. It was, fortunately, covered, which gave him time to get the umbrella positioned over their heads before braving the monsoon.

"I'll hold it," Alex volunteered, as he seemed to be having a little difficulty managing to hang on to both her and the umbrella. He passed her the umbrella without comment. Hastily tucking the washcloth into a pocket of the coat, she held the umbrella in a precarious, one-handed grip over both their heads while rain pounded the taut nylon like pellets on a kettledrum and the wind tried to tear it away from her altogether. With her in his arms, he ran nimbly down the back steps toward the vehicle parked in the driveway below. Rain pelted her legs below the knees, and her feet. If it had not been for the water-repellent properties of the coat and boots, she would have been soaked. Tiny windblown droplets struck her face, icy cold. A narrow rectangle of light from the door vanished abruptly as it closed behind them. Darkness wrapped around them like a blanket.

Fifteen

⚜

"They'll lock the door, won't they?" Alex raised her voice to be heard over the rain as Joe tipped her onto her feet beside the car, which was some kind of dark-colored SUV. Being back outside in the storm reminded her of how afraid she'd been until he'd shown up to rescue her. Opening the door and then all but thrusting her inside, he didn't answer. Alex waited until he was sliding into the driver's seat beside her, tossing the dripping umbrella into the back and slamming his own door, before repeating the question.

"One of them probably will, but I wouldn't worry about it either way: there's no crime around here to speak of." He started the car, turned on the lights, windshield wipers, and defrost, and put the engine into reverse. The head-lights revealed shiny curtains of falling rain. The rumble of thunder overhead all but blocked out the sound of the wheels crunching down the gravel driveway. It was cold inside the vehicle, but sheltered from the rain, and surprisingly cozy.

"Oh, really? Let me remind you, there was someone in my bedroom tonight!" Alex's voice was tart. Her head rested back against the leather seat, and she was once more pressing the washcloth to the wound.

"Sure you didn't dream it?"

"I'm sure I didn't dream getting hit over the head!"

"No, you didn't dream that."

They reached the road, and he glanced at her as he backed out and then put the car into drive. The faint glow from the instrument panel was the only illumination, making it difficult to discern more than his general outline. Alex hoped that he could see better than she could; except for the twin beams of light bouncing off the driving rain, the night around them was black as the inside of a coal mine.

"Head hurt much?" He glanced her way as he spoke.

"Some."

"You know, the chances of somebody breaking into Whistledown are pretty remote, especially on a night like this. Even criminals like to stay dry."

"If you can think of another expla—"

She broke off as a flash of lightning split the sky. They had almost reached Whistledown's driveway. At the top of the hill, the house was lit up suddenly as if caught in a camera's flash. *A dark form on the second-story porch stood out clearly against the white stone.* A human form. A man.

Alex's eyes went huge. Her pulse raced. She sat bolt upright in the seat, riveted, gaping, as the lightning faded away and night dropped over the house once more like a magician's scarf.

"Look! Did you see . . . ? Someone's on the porch! There's a man on the upstairs porch!" She grabbed at his arm, pointing.

The SUV veered sharply to the right, then recovered as Joe slammed on the brake and pulled his arm free.

"Damn it, Alex, don't you know better than to grab someone's arm when they're driving?"

Alex didn't even register that, or his use of her name.

Her gaze was still fixed on the house. There had been someone on the porch. She was sure of it. She glanced at him almost wildly.

"Did you see him? He must have been the one who was in my bedroom—the one who hit me! He's still in the house! We've got to get the police!"

He was looking at her narrow-eyed. "You really think you saw someone?"

"Yes! On the second-floor porch! I'm sure of it!"

"You are more trouble than anyone I ever met," he growled under his breath, and put his foot on the accelerator. Seconds later he was turning the SUV up Whistledown's driveway.

"What are you doing?" As they swooshed up the rain-washed asphalt her surprised gaze swung from the house to him.

"I'm going to take five minutes and check this out."

"You can't! We need the police! He might have a gun, or . . ."

"I doubt it," he said dryly.

"You think I'm *imagining* this?" Alex's voice was shrill with outrage.

"I think that, if you'd use just an ounce of common sense, you'd see that what you're suggesting is almost impossible. This isn't Philadelphia, you know: distances are pretty far out here. You've got to ask yourself, if there's someone in the house, where did he come from? How did he get here? I don't see a car, do you? Did he walk? From where? Simpsonville? It's a good five miles away, and Simpsonville's the nearest town. For God's sake, Alex, use your brain: it's been raining cats and dogs all night. Even wanna-be rapists have enough sense not to walk for miles in the pouring rain!"

They reached the top of the driveway, and he parked

the car at the foot of the stone walk that led to Whistle-down's front door. With the lights still on and the engine still running, he leaned over and opened the glove compartment. Horrified, Alex watched as he withdrew a standard-size black flashlight. As far as weapons went, if he got close enough to club someone over the head with it, it might raise a pretty good bump.

"Oh, no!" she said, grasping the back of the seat as she slewed around to look at him. A wave of dizziness assaulted her at the sudden movement, but she ignored it. "Don't do this! Please don't do this! Let's go get the police! This is really stupid. I . . ."

But he was already opening the door. The interior light flicked on, allowing her to see the determined expression on his face. She supposed her appalled one was equally apparent to him. Their eyes met.

"Lock the doors and sit tight. I'll be back as quick as I can. If you need me, honk the horn."

"Oh, Joe, *please* . . ." she moaned.

He slammed the door behind him, and was gone, swallowed up by the night.

Alex hit the button that locked all the doors, then huddled in her seat, her gaze searching for him in vain. She was clutching the bloody washcloth in one hand, she discovered, and pressed it once again to her oozing head. The falling rain seemed suddenly very loud. It was a steady rushing sound, much like the roar of traffic on a busy highway. The headlights were twin swords of yellow slicing through the darkness directly ahead. The rain looked like dozens of falling icicles as it passed through the light. She debated turning off the lights, but the thought of sitting all alone in the darkness dissuaded her. Anyway, what would be the point? If the intruder had remained on the upstairs porch, he had certainly seen them coming up the driveway, and if he had stayed around to watch he would even have seen them park. But of course he hadn't stayed around. If he had any sense at all, he would have left the house when he saw them approach, and was very likely outside right now. He could be right beside the car . . .

The skin on the nape of Alex's neck prickled as she glanced swiftly around. She could see nothing outside the windows except the rain falling through the twin shafts of light. She could hear nothing over the rain and the hum of the engine, either. She was alone with the darkness and relentless rain, effectively deaf and blind, her only defense against anyone who might choose to attack her the locked doors of the car.

Oh, God, if he had a hammer or something similar, he could smash right through the window.

Alex scrambled over into the driver's seat, ignoring the resultant pain in her head and her subsequent dizziness, the better to have access to both the horn and the gear shift. Thunder crashed; if she was attacked now, Joe wouldn't hear the window smash, wouldn't hear the horn sound. Would she have time to slam the car into reverse and drive away?

Lightning forked toward the horizon. Glancing swiftly around, Alex saw nothing except translucent sheets of falling rain on every side.

A few minutes later, a sharp rap on the driver's-side window made her jump straight up in the air. Looking to her left, she saw a dark form, big but otherwise indeterminate as to shape, looming beside the car. Joe? Oh, please let it be Joe, she prayed, peering through the glass. Another rap, a glimpse of knuckles, and then a face looking in at her. She caught her breath instinctively, then recognized him.

Joe. Thank God.

She unlocked the door. Immediately he pulled it open, and a swirl of cold damp air hit her. Shivering, she clambered back over the console as he got in, then collapsed in the passenger seat, feeling shaky as a bowl of gelatin.

"Miss me?" he asked with the merest suggestion of a smile, after one look at what, from the feel of it, was her chalk-white face. Water ran from his poncho in streams to puddle on the floor. He had flipped back his hood. His hair was dry, but his face was glistening wet.

"Oh, God," was her heartfelt reply as he leaned over to restore the flashlight to the glove box. "Did you . . . ? Was there . . . ?"

He reversed down the driveway. "There was no one in the house. There was no sign that anyone—any stranger—had been in the house. There was no sign of any fire anywhere. The front door was unlocked—I presume you left it that way?"

"Yes, but . . ."

He held up a hand to stop her. "Let me finish." Reaching the road, he put the car into drive and headed in the direction in which they'd originally been traveling. "The back door was locked. I checked the upstairs porch. Not only was no one up there, but the door that opens onto it was locked from the inside. The bedroom doors were open, all of them—and a bronze statue of a woman about as tall as my forearm is long lay in the middle of the floor in the upstairs hall. I figure that's what hit you."

"He must have used it . . ."

"Alex, honey, there are two bronze statues, a pair, that stand on wooden brackets on either side of the mirror in the upstairs hall. If you tripped over the rug and fell forward, don't you think it's just possible that you knocked the statue off its perch and it clobbered you with no help from anyone at all?"

Alex stared at him. That drawled *honey*, coupled with the faintly patronizing note on which he finished up, told her that he had consigned the night's events to a combination of accident and imagination.

"I am not nuts and I am not given to hysterical imaginings," she said firmly. "Even if the statue fell on its own and hit me, what about the breathing that woke me up? And who was that on the upstairs porch just now?"

"Are you sure you saw anyone?" His voice was gentle. They had reached the highway by this time, and he turned left, accelerating along the deserted stretch of two-lane road to the accompaniment of the steady swish-swish of the windshield wipers. "You've had a pretty rough day today, haven't you?"

That was the understatement of the year. Alex's head throbbed as if giving its own answer, and getting hit over the head wasn't even the worst of it. She'd had to fire the man beside her, who hadn't even had the decency to stay fired; her fiancé had announced that he had married another woman; her sister had been expelled from school; and an intruder had been in her bedroom, waking her from a sound sleep. It didn't get much better than that, she thought wryly. Making a face, she winced at the resultant pain, and pressed the washcloth more firmly to her head.

"So what's your point?" Her response was truculent. They were reaching civilization: Alex could tell because of the glowing neon signs they passed. First, a Wal-Mart on the left, then, on the right, next to each other, a Thornton's Gas Station and a motel called the Dixie Inn. Finally, a barrage of streetlights; clearly the town had electricity, even if the outlying areas did not. Or perhaps the electricity had been restored everywhere by now.

"Only that there was no one in the house when I checked it." He smiled at her with a flash of genuine humor. "Now, don't get mad. I'm perfectly willing to admit that whoever it was could have hidden from me, or run out the back door, locking it behind them of course, while I came in the front. Or something."

"Oh, shut up," she said irritably, as his point went home. But she wasn't mistaken about the man on the upstairs porch: she had seen him clearly. And she hadn't dreamed up the breathing, either.

Had she?

There were only three possible explanations: some combination of the sleeping pill, stress, and possibly even, in the case of the man on the porch, the blow to her head, had caused her to suffer hallucinations; a real live intruder had been in her bedroom and, later, on the porch; or something paranormal was happening here, and what she had seen and heard was not of this earth.

"Joe," she said hesitantly. "Do you believe in—ghosts?"

"Ah," he said, and glanced at her. "Are we talking about your father's ghost here?"

"Sounds pretty stupid, doesn't it?" It even sounded stupid to her own ears, when expressed aloud in so many words.

"Not really." He glanced at her again. "My mother and sister were killed together in a car accident when I was twenty." His voice was as matter-of-fact as if he were talking about the weather. He was looking straight ahead now, his attention on the road. The classic lines of his profile were illuminated by the rain-blurred glow of the streetlights. Only a slight twist at the corner of his mouth indicated that the subject might be painful for him. "For months after they died, I dreamed about them. They would come into my room almost every night, sometimes my mother, sometimes my sister Carol, sometimes both of them together, and they would talk to me, tell me that they were all right, that I shouldn't grieve for them. Dream or not, it was one of the most real experiences I've ever had. Finally, I guess I got more able to handle their loss and they stopped coming. Looking back, I think it was my mind trying to come to terms with their deaths. I also think it's a pretty universal experience."

"Oh, Joe," she said softly, touched that he would share something so personal with her. "I'm so sorry."

He glanced at her. "It was a lot of years ago. I've been okay with it for a long time now. But I know how the first weeks and months after someone you love dies feel. Believe me, I'm the last person in the world to laugh at your ghost."

He pulled off the road into a parking lot. "Here we are."

Glancing around, Alex saw a glowing sign that said TRI-COUNTY HOSPITAL. Tall lights in the parking lot revealed the dark shape of a one-story building. Joe drove under a concrete carport at the far side and stopped the car. The sudden cessation of rain was startling. Security lights revealed that the building was of yellow brick, with double, steel-framed glass doors opening into a well-lit interior. A sign above the doors read EMERGENCY ROOM.

"Let's get you fixed up," he said, getting out of the car. By the time he reached her door, she had it open and was swinging her legs out. Disdaining her efforts to try one more time to make it on her own two feet, he gathered her up in his arms and strode into the emergency room with her.

Sixteen

✦

The next morning, Alex awoke slowly, stretching and turning over in bed without opening her eyes. For those first few seconds she felt vaguely anxious—she had been sitting in the library at Whistledown talking to her father over the telephone, and he had been trying to tell her something important. But static had kept her from hearing him clearly, and then the line had gone dead. Even as she frowned at the recollection, meaning to call him back as soon as she was up, reality came crashing in. The now familiar sorrow settled atop her like a thick eiderdown quilt, smothering her, weighing her down. Her father was dead. Her interrupted conversation with him had been nothing more than a dream. She would never talk to her father in life again.

Yesterday, Paul had married another woman.

Oh, God, it was too much. How was she going to survive?

She lay there for a moment, wishing vainly that she could just go back to sleep. Getting up and facing the world required too much effort: her limbs felt too heavy to move. Emotional pain paralyzed her, as it had for the past five weeks. But she knew now, knew from bitter experience, that she *could* move, *could* function. Could survive.

Just breathe, she told herself as a first step. Breathe: In, out. In, out.

Just as someone had been breathing in her bedroom last night. The same someone she'd seen standing on the upstairs porch later? A real someone, an imagined someone, or—a ghost?

At the memory her eyes popped open, and she rolled onto her back. The sudden movement caused her head to brush the headboard, and brought pain of the physical variety with it. Arggh, that hurt! She winced, gingerly probing the place where three stitches held her scalp together.

At least, according to the doctor who had examined her X-ray, she hadn't suffered a concussion.

Sunlight filtered in through the lightly curtained window at the far end of the room. Obviously it had quit raining, and from the angle of the light she had slept a long time. She was lying in Joe's bed. At the realization, a small tingle started in her loins and radiated out along her nerve endings. Too bad he wasn't in it with her, she thought, toes curling at the prospect. As a cure for what ailed her, sleeping with Joe probably wouldn't do the trick. But it was good to know that her sex drive was becoming functional again. Maybe she would get over this heartbreak one day after all.

Joe had promised her that she would. The trick, he'd told her as they'd waited together for the doctor to put stitches in her head, was to just keep putting one foot in front of the other until she discovered that she had walked right out of the shadows into the sunlight again.

It would happen, he said.

Thinking of Joe, Alex smiled to herself. Yesterday's rude, impossible man had morphed overnight into a sexy shoulder to lean on. He'd taken care of her with brisk efficiency even over her protests, listened to her talk about ghosts without laughing (Paul would have called the nearest psychiatrist), stayed with her through the ordeal in the hospital, and even carried her upstairs when they got back and tucked her into his bed.

All without asking for a thing in return.

Paul would never have taken care of her like that. Paul never did anything without expecting a return. Every thoughtful gesture he'd ever made toward her, from the first time he'd taken her to dinner, had been with an eye toward a payoff, usually sex. Anyway, he certainly wouldn't have been able to lug her around all night like Joe had. He didn't have Joe's physical strength.

So take that, Alex said to her mental image of Paul, and sat up, moving cautiously to see how her head reacted to being vertical. The stitches tugged at her scalp and she had a slight headache, but besides that she felt relatively normal. Certainly far better than she had last night.

The question was, could she stand up without falling on her face? The matter was becoming increasingly urgent. Swinging her legs over the side of the bed, she put her feet on the floor and, holding on to the nightstand for support, maneuvered herself upright. For a moment she stood still, testing to see if her knees would support her. Then she took one cautious step followed by another, until she made it all the way into the bathroom. When she flipped the light switch, it failed to work. From that she deduced that either the electricity was still out, or the bulb needed replacing.

The clothes and towels that had been on the floor the night before were gone, and the floor had been wiped clean. Only a pair of the oversized towels that Joe had tucked by their corners into the towel rack was left. Remembering what Joe had looked like clad in just such a towel brought on another of those sexy little tingles, and Alex reveled in the feeling.

Slowly, slowly, she was coming back alive.

Stripping off the T-shirt she'd slept in—it was Joe's, given to her by him after they'd gotten back from the hospital, and it reached halfway down her thighs—she took a quick shower, taking care not to get her hair wet. Finishing, wrapping herself in a towel, Alex overcame her qualms about respecting Joe's privacy and opened the medicine cabinet to look for, at the bare minimum, aspirin and moisturizer. She came up empty on both counts. Shaving cream, a razor and blades, deodorant, toothpaste, mouthwash, dental floss: that was the sum total of the contents of his medicine cabinet. In the ceramic holder built into the wall above the sink hung a green toothbrush. A cheap plastic hairbrush lay on the back of the toilet.

Clearly, Alex thought, surveying her meager choices, a man occupied the premises alone. Picking up the hairbrush, she gingerly started to brush out her tangled hair.

"Alex?" It was Neely. Alex stuck her head out of the bathroom door, surprised to discover that her sister was dressed in jeans and a clingy pink turtleneck sweater, both of which were clearly hers.

"Here. Where'd you get the clothes?"

"Joe drove me up to Whistledown. I brought you some, too." She held up a bulging plastic grocery bag as evidence, then put it on the foot of the bed and perched beside it as Alex walked into the bedroom.

"Great. Thanks." Alex started rummaging through the bag.

"How are you feeling?" Neely looked her over critically. She and both of Joe's sons had been awake when they'd gotten back from the hospital, sitting on the floor around the living-room coffee table playing cards by lamplight, apparently on the best of terms. The little girl, Jenny, had been curled up on the couch fast asleep. Neely and the boys had heard a quick outline of Joe's search of the house and seen and exclaimed over Alex's stitches before Joe herded all of them off to bed.

Alex had said nothing to Neely about the figure she had seen on Whistledown's porch. Although she was still convinced that she had seen *something*, she was no longer sure exactly what: man, ghost, or figment of a grief-stricken mind. Whatever the truth of the matter was, she saw no point in worrying Neely with it.

"Better. You don't have any aspirin on you, do you?"

Neely shook her head regretfully. "'Fraid not. I could go ask Joe for some."

"I'll ask him myself when I go downstairs." The bag yielded slim khaki slacks, a black cashmere twin set, undergarments, her black high-heeled boots, and her purse, with its travel-wise stash of cosmetic necessities—including a small tin of aspirin. "Blessings on you, sister," Alex said, retrieving and holding up the tin, then turned back to the bathroom to swallow the pills with a handful of water.

"So, what do you think about the Welches?" Neely asked in an elaborately casual tone as Alex returned to the bedroom and started to dress.

Alex's antenna immediately went up. "Are we talking about one in particular?"

Her sister made a face at her. "Eli."

"Cute." Alex's voice was muffled as she pulled the crewneck over her head with special care so as not to hit her stitches. Emerging, she picked up the khakis. "What do you think?"

"I think he's even more of a hottie than Joe. Eli's kind of shy, which I think is sweet. I wonder if he's a virgin?"

Zipping up her slacks, Alex shot her sister a look. "Too bad we're not going to be here long enough for you to find out."

Neely grinned tantalizingly at her. "Oh, I don't know. . . ."

"Lunch," a boy's voice yelled up the stairs.

"That's Josh," Neely said, jumping up. "Since the electricity's out, Joe went to Kentucky Fried Chicken. Come on, I'm starved." She headed out the door, then stopped and looked back. "Oh. Do you need help getting down the stairs? I can wait. Or I can go get Joe."

Alex shook her head. The idea of having Joe carry her again was tempting, but . . . "I'm fine."

Flashing her a naughty grin that told Alex that her sister had at least an inkling of what she was thinking, Neely disappeared.

Except for a headache, which the aspirin should take care of once it kicked in, and a rather generalized feeling of lethargy, she *was* fine, Alex discovered as she quickly applied cosmetics and brushed her hair into a smooth ponytail, which she secured with a silver barrette at her nape. Then, taking care to hold on to the handrail, she headed downstairs. The scent of food greeted her. As Alex inhaled, she was surprised to find that it actually smelled—good. She hadn't enjoyed the taste or smell of food since her father's death. She ate because she knew she had to, and for no other reason. Her sleep had been affected the same way: she forced herself to do it because she knew she needed to. Ergo, the sleeping pills.

"Hey. Good morning." Joe appeared when she was halfway down the stairs, pausing at the foot to look up at her. A quick glance told her that he was dressed in sneakers, jeans, and a navy-and-gray plaid flannel shirt that hung with the ease of well-loved old clothes from his broad shoulders. He had shaved, she saw, and without stubble to obscure the clean lines of his jaw and chin he was handsome enough to make her eyes widen. He grinned at her, and the effect was dazzling. "Or rather, good afternoon. I thought you might need some help."

She returned his smile with one of her own. It was amazing what the sight of him did to her, she thought. This time yesterday, he had been the enemy. Now, he was a friend; no, she corrected herself, not a friend exactly. She had lots of friends, and none of them affected her quite the way he did. "Thanks, but I'm much better. At least I can stand up. What time is it, anyway?"

"Almost one o'clock. You hungry?"

"A little." She was surprised to find that she wasn't lying. Reaching the bottom stair, she found her head on a level with his, and was reminded once again of how tall he was. "Thanks for all you did last night, by the way."

"My pleasure." He met her gaze, and for a moment Alex thought she saw a flicker of her own awareness in his eyes.

"Hey, Dad, if you don't hurry up we're going to start without you," a boy's voice called from the kitchen.

"Coming," Joe called back. Then, to Alex, "Come on, or there won't be anything left."

At his gesture, Alex preceded him down the hall to the kitchen. She was conscious of him behind her every step of the way. At first glance the kitchen seemed to be packed with people. A sixty-something man with solid white hair, tall and wiry in build and dressed in well-pressed khakis with a blue dress shirt tucked into them, carried two platters loaded with chicken pieces toward the table. Behind him came Jenny in yellow oven mitts bearing a big bowl of mashed potatoes. Josh followed with a casserole dish loaded with ears of corn. Neely—her sister Neely, whose aversion to any kind of domestic chore was legendary—was standing at the counter filling tall glasses with ice from a large plastic bag of commercial cubes that someone had put in the sink. Ferrying the ice-filled glasses to the table was Eli, which explained a lot. Like Neely, all of Joe's kids wore jeans. Eli wore a football jersey over a white T-shirt, and with his long black hair pulled back into a ponytail looked studly enough to enrapture any teenage girl, much less one as susceptible to the opposite sex as Neely. Josh wore a flannel shirt and a frown. Jenny's oversized sweater had clearly once belonged to either or both of her brothers.

"Well, what do you know! Looks like she's up!" The older man was the first to see Alex as she paused in the doorway, and his eyes ran over her in quick appraisal even as he smiled a welcome at her. Neely acknowledged her with a glance and the Welch kids all murmured some version of *hi*. Behind her, Joe put a gentle hand on the small of her back, urging her on into the kitchen. The older man put the platters on the table and came toward her. "Good to meet you, Miss Haywood. I've heard a lot about you this morning. I'm Cary Welch."

"My dad," Joe put in, and out of the corner of her eye Alex saw him give his father a quelling look. Alex wondered just what Cary Welch had heard—and if Joe had been his source.

"Please call me Alex." Alex held out her hand to Joe's father. His hand was warm, with strong thin fingers.

"Well, Alex, I hear you all had some excitement up at Whistledown last night." He looked at Alex with a twinkle in his eyes. She saw that they were blue, the same light, lady-killing shade as Joe's and his sons'. Jenny's eyes were different, a soft shade of brown that almost matched her hair.

"A little," Alex answered.

"Yeah, it was great. We ended up staying up so late we

didn't have to go to church this morning," Eli said, carrying the last of the glasses to the table.

"What're you talking about? You love going to church and you know it." Grinning, Joe gave his son a playful smack on the side of the head as Eli walked past him.

"About like I love going to the dentist," Eli muttered, setting the glasses down.

"I bet Heather was upset that you weren't there," Jenny put in teasingly, separating cans of Coke from a plastic six-pack holder and setting them down beside the glasses.

"Who's Heather?" Neely asked, oh-so-casually.

"Eli's girlfriend. He's in lo-o-ove," Josh chimed in.

"Shut up, twerp." Eli glowered at Josh.

Joe intervened. "Okay, gang, let's eat. Alex, you can sit over there by your sister."

There was general hubbub as everyone took his or her seat. The Welches said grace, Alex discovered to her mild surprise. Somehow, she wouldn't have expected Joe to be a stickler about such things as Sunday church attendance and prayer before meals, but it was clear that he took his responsibilities as father of this crew seriously. Apparently it was Josh's turn to do the honors. When his family turned expectant faces on him, he grimaced and cast a quick, almost embarrassed look at Neely before complying.

"Good food, good drink, good God, let's eat! Amen."

"Josh!" Joe said on a note of warning, giving him a narrow-eyed look.

Josh's cheeks turned pink, and he cast another glance at Neely. "Oh, all right, then. *Thank you for what we are about to receive. Amen.*"

"Better," Joe said, and general conversation ensued as the food was passed and everyone began to eat. Fast food was not generally a favorite of hers, but the chicken was surprisingly good and Alex was surprised to find that she was actually able to consume a small portion of everything and enjoy what she ate.

"Can we ride your ATV now?" Neely asked Eli when the meal was over.

Eli glanced at his father.

"Sure," Joe replied to the unspoken question. "As soon as your chores are done."

"What chores?" Neely asked.

Eli grimaced. "I load the dishwasher. Josh clears, Jen scrapes. Usually, Dad cooks." A grin dawned. "Ruffles eats the scraps. Grandpa gets to do whatever he wants."

"You'll get to do whatever you want too, when you're as old as I am," Cary Welch retorted as they all rose from the table. He looked at his son. "Well, Joe, I think I'm going to mosey on out and check on Victory Dance. If you need me for anything, I'll be in the barn."

Joe nodded, and glanced at Alex. "You want to go take a look around Whistledown now?"

"Sure." On her feet now with one hand resting on the back of the chair she had just vacated, Alex glanced at Neely. Her sister, who had surely never done such a thing in her life, was helping Jenny scrape plates. Wonders would never cease. "Neely, I'm going up to Whistledown now."

Neely waved an airy hand over her shoulder. "Have fun."

"You need a coat," Joe said as they headed toward the back door. Before Alex could reply he snagged a garment off the coatrack by the back door and dropped it over her shoulders. It was an ancient green army jacket, and, she discovered as she buttoned herself into it, it was big enough for her to swim in. She guessed it belonged to Joe. He shrugged into the blue parka he'd worn when she had first set eyes on him. Alex was reminded again of the grim man she'd first met, and smiled to herself, thinking, What a difference a day makes.

The sun was shining brightly, Alex saw as she stepped out onto the small stoop, but evidence of last night's storm was everywhere. Puddles as big as ponds stood in the yard and the fields, shining almost gaily in the sunlight, and limbs littered the ground. Narrow streams ran through mini-canyons of reddish brown clay that bisected the flattened grass. More mud had washed over the black asphalt of the driveway, and lay now in a thin layer, drying in the sun. The air was crisp and cold, and the smell of wet earth was strong.

"You have any objection to riding in a pickup truck?" Joe asked as he stopped beside her. Alex looked where he nodded to discover a battered blue truck parked in front of the shed he apparently used for storage. As the SUV he'd driven the night before (it was a dark green Chevy Blazer, Alex saw by daylight) was parked beside the truck, she assumed that there was a reason for his preference for the truck.

"Why would I?" she said, giving him a narrow-eyed look. "I like pickup trucks."

"Oh, yeah?" He grinned as his eyes swept her face. "Well, I like debutante balls, too. Come on, then, Princess. I want to drop some feed off by my barn while we're out and about."

Seventeen

☘

"I have to ask you something," Alex said as she followed Joe into his barn. He carried a hundred-pound sack of sweet feed on his shoulder as easily as if it had been a loaf of bread. No wonder the man hadn't had any trouble carrying her around! He must heft loads like this every day.

He lifted his eyebrows at her questioningly. They were black and thick, like his hair.

"Where did you *get* this?" She tugged on the sleeve nearest her.

The skin around his eyes crinkled as he smiled. "What, my coat? Don't you like it?"

"It's—um—bright. And a very unusual shade of blue." It also added bulk to a torso that she had already discovered was very nicely muscled on its own.

They were inside the barn now. The distinctive smells of hay and horse reached her nostrils. The overhead light was on, and a glance told Alex that Cary Welch was down at the far end, leading a horse out of its stall.

"It's UK blue. UK being the University of Kentucky Wildcats. This is my spirit coat." His eyes danced as he opened the door to a small room just past his office, and raised his voice almost to a yell. "Now, Pop down there is a U of L fan."

Cary Welch looked around, then waved a dismissive hand at them. "Wait till game time, and we'll see who wins."

Joe laughed, and moved inside what Alex saw was a storage room to deposit the sack of feed on the ground.

"I take it you're talking about a basketball game," Alex said dryly.

"University of Kentucky versus the University of Louisville. A classic basketball rivalry. The big game's this Saturday." He emerged from the storage room and closed the door, carefully latching it behind him, and glanced down at her. "I'd tell you to catch it on TV, but you'll be back home by then and I doubt they'll carry it in Philadelphia."

"Yeah." The thought of going home gave Alex a pang, and instantly she knew why. This thing with Joe—this awareness, this sexual vibration—was not going to have a chance to develop. Tomorrow she'd be on an airplane, probably never to see him again.

"Hey, Joe, come here a minute. I want you to look at Vicky's hoof," Cary called.

Joe headed toward where his father stood with the horse, and Alex fell into step beside him. Most of the stalls were empty, and Alex assumed the horses had been turned out for the day. Her heels sank into the thick carpet of neatly raked sawdust. Her ankles wobbled, and she instinctively clutched at Joe's arm for support. He looked down at her with a faint smile.

"High heels and barns don't mix," he said.

"Tell me about it."

Then they reached Cary and the horse. The big red thoroughbred was the same tall, skinny, neglected-looking creature she had championed yesterday, and he looked no better today. His liquid brown eyes gazed into hers with what she could swear was recognition. He snorted gently, and nudged her upper arm with his head. She patted him.

"Here, give him this," Joe said, passing over a cellophane-wrapped peppermint candy. Alex unwrapped it and offered it on her palm to the horse, who picked it up with soft lips and chewed with obvious satisfaction. Ignored by the men now, Alex murmured to him and spent a few minutes rubbing his big head while the scent of peppermint filled the air. Meanwhile, Joe and his father passed his right front hoof back and forth, poking and prodding at it while they discussed the merits of various treatments for whatever the problem was.

"What do you think of him, Alex?" Cary asked when the two men were finished, and Victory Dance was once again standing on all four legs.

"He looks like he could use a few square meals and a regimen of vitamins to me," Alex said. "Or at least a couple dozen more peppermints."

Joe laughed, and Cary shook his head at her. "Young lady, this is a champion. You mark my words. Don't laugh, son. If I'm wrong about this, I'll never make another prediction again for the rest of my life."

"The funny thing about it is, he knows horses, and he's not wrong about them too often," Joe said as Cary led Victory Dance away and he and Alex were walking out of the barn toward the truck again. The gravel outside was as bad for high heels as the sawdust within, and Alex curled a hand around his elbow without even thinking about it. "That's why I bought him in spite of the way he looks. He belongs to me, by the way, not Whistledown Farm."

There was a slight crispness to that last that told Alex that the situation with Whistledown still rankled.

"I'm really sorry about yesterday," she said, glancing up at him. They had reached the truck by this time, and her hand slid away from his elbow as he opened the passenger-side door for her. "About being the bearer of bad tidings, I mean. Believe me, this whole situation isn't easy for me, either."

His mouth, which had compressed when he said that about owning the horse, relaxed into a wry half-smile. "No, I don't guess it is."

She climbed up into the truck, and he slammed her door, then came around the hood and got in beside her.

"So tell me about yourself," he said, starting the engine and turning the truck around. Alex grabbed on to the door as the vehicle lurched. "What was it like to grow up filthy rich?"

"Not as much fun as you might think." Alex rested her head back against the blue vinyl seat and turned her eyes toward him. "I had a lot of toys when I was little, a lot of clothes when I grew older, lessons for everything under the sun. Tennis, golf, skiing, piano, dance—you name it, I probably had lessons in it. We owned a lot of big houses, with lots of servants, and once I was old enough I could basically travel anywhere I wanted to go. But you know, you can only own so many things, and you can only go so many places. After a while, none of it really seems to matter that much. Or at least, I don't think it matters. I've never *not* been rich. I don't think it's going to be so bad, but I don't know."

"You get used to it." Joe gave a grunt of laughter as the truck bumped up onto the road. "Did you go to school?"

"Of course I went to school. Boarding schools, actually. Shipley, the Pensionat de la Chassotte in Switzerland, and Le Rosey. Rich kids always go to boarding school. It gets them out of the way."

Joe's glance was keen. "Where is your mother? Is she still alive?"

Alex nodded. "She's done even better than my father: she's on her *seventh* husband. She's living in Australia now. We don't have a great deal of contact, although she will call occasionally. Number one, she can't abide the idea of having a grown daughter. It makes her feel old. Number two, she can't abide Neely. Although, to be quite accurate, it's not Neely per se that she can't abide. She's never so much as set eyes on her. It's the *idea* of Neely."

"How so?"

"My mother was my father's second wife. Neely's mother was his third wife. My mother blames Neely's mother for stealing her husband from her, even at this late date. She doesn't seem to realize that if it wasn't Neely's mother, it would have been someone else. My father was into young and beautiful women. Once they were no longer young and beautiful, then his attitude was *off with their heads*. Well, metaphorically speaking, of course."

Joe looked at her curiously. "So who did you stay with during summers and Christmas vacation and times like that? Your father or your mother?"

"Both. Neither. Sometimes I'd go home with friends. Or I would stay at one or the other of our houses, but my parents were generally not there when I was. They'd be off doing their thing, and I'd do my thing. There was always staff to look after me, of course."

"Sounds kind of lonely."

"Actually, it wasn't. I liked being on my own. Then when Neely came along, I would always spend vacations wherever she was. Her mother died when she was six, so I've been the closest thing she's had to one ever since. None of my father's subsequent wives were interested in taking on the job. Several of them had children of their own, and the ones who didn't, well, let's just say they weren't particularly motherly types."

"I've seen your current stepmother. I have to admit, I can't picture her being motherly towards Neely or anyone."

Alex smiled a little. "No, being a mother is not much in Mercedes' line, I'm afraid. Not that I dislike her. I don't. We get along very well, when we're together. Neely's a different story. If you push Neely, she pushes back twice as hard, and Mercedes can't seem to get that through her head. She and Neely don't get on."

"So what do you do? Now that you're all grown up and out of school? Or do rich girls do anything at all?"

Alex blinked. "Are you *trying* to be insulting?"

Joe laughed. "Sorry. My experience of billionaires' daughters is limited."

She sent him a narrow-eyed look. "I'm a photographer. A very good photographer, if I do say so myself. You know those big picture books people have lying around on their coffee tables? I take the pictures. It doesn't pay all that well, but that's never been a concern before."

"I suppose your ex-fiancé was rolling in dough too?" They had reached the driveway that led to Whistledown, and Joe headed up it.

Alex sniffed derisively. Surprisingly, the mention of Paul barely hurt. She was getting over him faster than she would ever have thought was possible—and she knew the reason. A sexual attraction to another man was a powerful palliative. "Suffice it to say that his new wife is the daughter of a very rich man. He's successful in what he does, but he doesn't have any real money. Or at least, he didn't. Now that he's married to Tara Gould, he does. Actually, finding out about Paul was probably the best thing to come out of all this. I wouldn't like to be married for my money."

He gave her a crooked smile. "There's no reason why you should be. You're a beautiful woman. Intelligent. Charming. A little bossy, but maybe that's just me."

Alex laughed. "Thank you. I think."

Whistledown was in front of them, and Alex couldn't help looking up at the upstairs porch as Joe stopped the truck. Involuntarily she shivered. There—right there, between the two tall windows on the right—was where she had seen the man. Today there was nothing there. She could see clear through the railing to the white-painted stone.

"Ready?" He was already getting out of the truck. Alex climbed out too, without waiting for him to come around and open her door. She lagged a little behind as they headed up the front walk. Last night's terror was too fresh a memory to be so easily discarded.

"I've checked the place over with a fine-tooth comb, by myself and with your sister, and as far as I can tell not a thing's out of place." Joe's voice interrupted her musings. He had opened the door and was waiting for her to precede him into the house.

For a moment longer Alex hung back, her sense of dread as solid a barrier as a wall would have been. But then she glanced at Joe. He was big and strong and utterly reliable. She totally trusted in his ability to deal with whatever they might encounter. At the very least, he would keep her safe. With that thought firmly in mind, she walked past him into the house.

Without electricity, the interior was dark and faintly eerie even on so bright a day. The heavy curtains, which were still drawn from the night before, were responsible for that, of course, Alex told herself stoutly. The faint aroma of rose potpourri wafted beneath her nostrils. The house seemed almost too quiet, as if it waited for something. For her? The thought popped into her head of its own volition, and Alex shivered again. She had to bite her lip to keep from protesting as Joe shut the door behind them.

For a moment the house seemed to close in around her. The sudden gloom seemed alive with shadows that seemed to hang back in the corners like silent wraiths.

"Let's get some light in here." Joe broke the spell by striding into the living room and opening the curtains. Alex, trailing him (no way was she letting him out of her sight), gave a sigh of relief. With sunlight pouring in, the atmosphere no longer seemed so ominous. She followed Joe through the downstairs as he opened curtains in each room.

When they reached the kitchen, Alex stood for a moment glancing around. Since her father had bought the house, the kitchen had been outfitted with malachite green granite countertops and hand-painted Smallbone cabinets, which gave the room an old-fashioned look. The floor was paved with bricks waxed to a dull luster, and the walls were heavy wood paneling painted a soft green. It was a beautiful room, just as all the rooms at Whistledown were beautiful. At least, Alex thought, they were beautiful on the outside. She still had that sense of some kind of repellent undercurrent running beneath.

"Ready to go upstairs?" Joe was standing beside the small door to one side of the kitchen that opened onto the narrow back staircase. At the thought of going upstairs, Alex's sense of dread increased. But she reminded herself, again, that with Joe accompanying her there was nothing to fear.

"I guess." Her obvious lack of enthusiasm made him smile. He was waiting for her by the door, and she reluctantly walked past him and began to climb.

"I don't know, but it seems to me that if you really thought there was somebody who had no business being here in this house last night, maybe getting out of bed and chasing him wasn't the smartest thing you ever did." There was a faintly trenchant note to the drawled observation. Alex, already halfway up the steep stairs, cast him a look over her shoulder. Although he was two steps behind her, the top of his black head was about level with her chin, and his shoulders, hugely wide in the Michelin-man coat, seemed to fill the passage. His eyes glinted up at her in the dim light of the windowless stairwell. His solid presence was so comforting that she was willing to let his intimation of her foolishness pass.

"It probably wasn't," she admitted, gaining the second floor and walking slowly along the hallway with him right behind her. "But I thought . . ." Her voice trailed off as she looked around.

"You thought . . . ?"

"It might be my father."

"Ah." The wealth of understanding in his voice made her send him a quick, glimmering smile.

Everything was just as it had been the previous day—the soft cream walls, the elaborate white-painted doorjambs surrounding polished mahogany doors, the red Oriental runner on the dark wood floor, the console table, flanked by twin Duncan Phyfe chairs, with the elaborate hanging tapestry over it. Above the chairs were two small gilt shelves, set at eye level, and on the shelves were, as Joe had said, matching bronze statues of some mythical goddesses. Somebody, Joe probably, or maybe Neely, had returned the fallen statue to its perch. Mentally Alex reviewed the seconds before she was hit. She had tripped—she remembered that—and a glance confirmed that it could have been on the carpet, which ended in an elaborate white fringe just outside her bedroom doorway. She had stumbled forward, and put her hand on cloth—the tapestry? It was possible. Reaching out to touch the tapestry to see if the feel of it matched what she remembered, she frowned. Was the tapestry thicker and oilier than she recalled the cloth being? She thought so, but her memory of the few seconds when she had been actually falling was hazy. Was it possible that, by grabbing the tapestry, she had knocked the statue down on her own head?

Remembering the blow, her stomach grew queasy, and her poor stitched scalp seemed to throb. Just being in the hallway again brought the whole thing back to her. She could almost hear the sound of the breathing: In, out. In, out. . . .

"For God's sake, don't hyperventilate," Joe said, grabbing her upper arms and turning her around so that she faced him, pulling her out of the memory. Alex looked up at him, realizing that she had been unconsciously mimicking the breathing she had heard. Thank God for Joe, she thought, meeting his gaze. He was making this whole terrible business much easier. His eyes darkened as their gazes clung, and his hands tightened around her arms.

A sudden sound startled them both. It wasn't a loud sound, more of a muffled thump, but in a supposedly empty house there shouldn't have been any sound of that sort at all. Alex stiffened as an icy finger of foreboding ran along her spine, and turned her head sharply in the direction from whence the sound had come. Her hands came up to clutch Joe's forearms, her nails digging into the puffy rolls of nylon in a death grip.

"What was that?" she hissed.

"Wait here." Joe's hands dropped away from her arms and he pulled free of her grip as he started to walk past her. "I'll check it out."

While leaving her alone in this hall, prey to God knew what?

"Not in this life!" She grabbed the big, warm hand closest to her as he passed and held on tight. Memories of the night before replayed themselves in her mind as she followed him down the hall. This time there was no room for any doubt. There was something—some*body*—in the house. She'd been right all along.

Her heart speeded up at the realization.

Thump. The sound was coming from her bedroom. Trailing a step or so behind him, Alex clung tightly to Joe's hand as they approached the partly open door. Her breathing was ragged, and she had to deliberately remind herself to keep it under control.

"Maybe we should just leave, and go get the police." She whispered the suggestion without much hope of having it attended to.

"*Shh.*" Joe stopped, and with an outstretched hand swung the door of the bedroom open the rest of the way. The creak of the door made Alex wince, and surely would have alerted anyone in the room—but the room was deserted. Alex saw that at a glance. The only possible hiding places were under the bed, or behind the closed door of the closet.

Thump. Alex's eyes widened. The sound *was* coming from the closet. Joe freed his hand with a quick tug, gave her a quick, meaningful frown that said as plainly as words *stay here,* and crossed the room in four long strides, leaving Alex to break into a cold sweat as she watched. If a real, live human being was in that closet, he might just have a real, live gun...

Eighteen

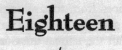

If a gun-toting housebreaker emerged, she would run. She would scream. She would call 911.

The phone was out.

Joe jerked the closet door open, looked inside—and an enormous orange tabby cat came strolling out past his feet.

For a moment Alex simply stared at it. Joe, from his expression initially as surprised as she, burst into laughter, and bent to scoop the furry behemoth up in his arms. It was a sleek and extremely well-fed-looking cat that must have weighed in the neighborhood of twenty pounds.

"Meet Hannibal," he said, stroking the cat's fur as he carried it toward her. "How he got in that closet I don't know, but he seems mighty glad to see us."

"Hannibal?" Alex repeated doubtfully. It seemed like a strange name for a cat.

"He's a mouser," Joe explained with a twinkle. "Good at it, too. You know, Hannibal the Cannibal?"

"Oh. Funny."

Tail twitching, the cat looked up at Alex through slitted green eyes. Its purr was loud enough to be heard downstairs. In between purrs it paused for breath—deep, audible breaths.

"Where did he come from?" Clearly she remembered retrieving her shoes from that selfsame closet the night before. She had shut the door afterward, she was pretty sure. Had *she* shut the animal in? Good God, could the breathing have come from him? Had she been chasing a *cat* when she fell, and had the animal somehow doubled back in the confusion and taken refuge in the closet?

Not for anything was she mentioning the possibility to Joe. Talk about feeling like a fool. . . .

"He's Whistledown's resident cat. Usually he stays in the barn. Somehow he must have gotten into the house."

Alex patted the animal's head a trifle gingerly—she'd never been allowed to have pets, and wasn't quite trustful of domestic animals—and glanced up to meet Joe's eyes. His wide grin was, she thought, at her expense. She only hoped he wasn't having the same thought she was.

But of course he was.

"A little too solid for a ghost, but he'd make a fantastic burglar—if you had a tuna sandwich stashed away," Joe said thoughtfully.

"Oh, shut up. And anyway, even if, by some remote possibility, he *is* the source of the breathing I heard, what about the man on the porch? A cat doesn't explain that."

"No," Joe said, "it doesn't." But a grin continued to lurk around his mouth just the same as he put the cat down. Hannibal, tail waving in the air, stalked away. "Come on, let's go check out the porch."

The upstairs porch was deserted. There was nothing on it, no rocking chairs, no swing, no hanging plants. Nothing that could have perhaps cast a shadow or been transformed by darkness and imagination into the figure of a man. Alex walked to the rail where she had seen the figure and stood for a moment, looking out over the driveway and the front lawn and the road.

From here, she had a clear view all the way to Joe's house and beyond. . . .

Thoughtfully, she turned, leaning against the rail as she studied the wall of the house directly behind her. It was the same shade as the rest of the stone: no fading, no cracks, nothing. Frowning, she looked down at the gray-painted boards of the floor.

"What, no ectoplasm?" Joe asked. He was standing a few feet away, one shoulder propped against the stone wall, his arms crossed over his chest as he regarded her with a faint smile.

"I saw something," Alex said stubbornly. Then honesty forced her to add, "I think."

"That's okay, honey, I know where you're coming from." Despite the lurking smile, his voice was warmly sympathetic. "He used to talk about you, you know."

Alex glanced at him quickly. "My father? To you?"

"Yeah. All the time, whenever he was here. We would be talking horses, and then, somehow, he'd always get going on his daughter. To tell you the truth, after a while I got kind of tired of hearing about Princess Alex. At least, that's what I started calling you in my mind. He would go on and on about you, how beautiful you were, how smart, how you were going to run his company one day. It got so bad that whenever your name came up I'd pretty much tune him out."

"Oh, Daddy," Alex said with a catch in her voice, a wobbly little smile hovering on her lips. "He wanted me to come to work for him, you know. We were always fighting about that. I feel so bad about turning him down. . . ." Her voice faltered.

"No guilt, now. He was proud of you for doing what you wanted to do. He always said his little girl had balls."

That sounded so like something her father would say that Alex was surprised into a laugh.

"Oh, Joe." Alex walked toward him, stopping only a foot or so away. He straightened away from the wall, and his hands came up, automatically she thought, to grip her waist. Resting her hands on his upper arms, Alex looked up at him, her eyes dark with pain. His gaze met hers, inscrutably. "Will you show me where you found him? Please? Please?"

A quarter of an hour and much persuasion later, Alex stared down at the spot where Joe had found her father's body. They were inside Whistledown's barn. Although she, personally, was so cold she was shivering, the interior of the barn was warm, and smelled of hay. Dust motes danced in the sunbeams that slanted down through the glass sides of the twin cupolas overhead. The horses had been turned out earlier, so except for a single lost sparrow perched on a rafter she and Joe were alone. Alex stood silently, her arms crossed over her chest to conserve body heat, as Joe talked. There was no physical reminder, no blood, no imprint on the spot where Charles Haywood had died, but despite the deliberately sparse description Joe gave her Alex could picture the scene all too clearly, and the picture in her mind made her feel ill.

"He didn't drink anymore," she said again, protesting one of the many parts of the story she found hard to understand. "He knew he was an alcoholic, and he had beaten it. He hadn't had a drink for ten years."

"Alcoholics fall off the wagon all the time," Joe said, as he had once before. Only this time his voice was matter-of-fact. "I know from personal experience. Pop's an alcoholic too. He's promised to reform so many times I've lost count. I don't think it's going to happen in my lifetime."

"Oh, God." They looked at each other in mutual understanding. Then Alex burst out, "I don't believe it. Daddy might—just might, mind you—have started drinking again because of all this stuff that was going on, but he wouldn't kill himself. He just wouldn't do it."

She looked down at the ground again, and then, without even being aware that she meant to do it, she sank to her knees in the soft sawdust. One hand went out to flatten on the place where he had lain in death. Her father—for years he had been larger than life to her, an all-powerful figure like the Wizard of Oz. But the man behind the curtain—what had *he* been like? Had she known him as well as she thought? She saw now that many of her life choices had been made because she was rebelling against being nothing more than billionaire Charles Haywood's daughter. The college she had chosen, Fordham, was not one of the elite institutions he had wanted for her. Her career, photography, he had regarded with disdain. Briefly she wondered if Paul had been part of that syndrome, too. Her father had not liked Paul. . . .

Back in the days before her father's death, when his lifetime, and hers, had seemed limitless, Alex had always thought that one day she and her father would be granted the gift of time to spend together, real time, hours and days and weeks and months. When he was old, perhaps, he would slow down and stop traveling so much, and there would be room in his life for something besides young wives and the running of his business. Maybe, she'd thought, when she had babies of her own, he would make up for never having been there for her by being a doting grandfather to her children. He would love—would have loved—a grandson. . . .

It was this, this hypothetical son of hers that her father would never see, that brought tears welling into Alex's eyes and spilling down her cheeks. She crouched there in the sawdust with her hand on the place where her father's lifeblood had soaked into the ground, and wept for him, for the man he had been, for the man she had always wished he was, for the man he might still one day have become. Whatever his shortcomings, she had loved him.

He had been her father.

Unable to help herself, she cried for him with great gulping sobs that she couldn't seem to control no matter how hard she tried, with torrents of tears that rained from her eyes to mark the spot where he had died.

"All right, come on." An arm came around her waist, warm and strong. Barely aware of who the arm belonged to, Alex followed its lead blindly, allowing herself to be pulled to her feet, to take comfort from the fact that another human being was with her, holding her. She leaned against a warm solid wall and cried until there were no more tears left.

"Oh, God, I'm sorry," she managed between deep shuddering breaths as sanity returned. She was leaning against Joe, her head tucked beneath his chin, weeping into the front of his ugly Michelin-man coat, a handful of silky nylon fabric clutched tightly in each fist. His arms were wrapped around her, and his breath stirred her hair as he murmured things like *shh* and *it's okay*. "Until this happened, I never cried."

"Feel free to cry all you want." His voice was a low murmur in her ear. Alex was suddenly grateful to him, grateful for his kindness and strength and for his sheer physical presence that had given her refuge. Someone to lean on— that was what she needed in this, her hour of weakness. Always she had been the strong one; now she needed someone else's strength. Joe had strength to spare. "Everybody needs to cry sometimes."

"It doesn't do any good. Crying never cured anything. It won't bring my father back." She gulped and sniffled without looking up, and clung to his coat with both hands.

"No, it won't do that. But it might make you feel better."

I don't want to feel better. Alex didn't say it aloud, but the sudden flash of insight was so patently true that it was like a shout inside her head. To feel better would be to be disloyal to her father. To feel better would be to start to let him go.

"He was only sixty-four. Even if he knew the company was going down the tubes, even if he knew he'd have to declare bankruptcy, that he would kill himself just doesn't make any sense. That's what I can't get past: Why? Why?"

"I don't have any answers for you there."

She was still cradled against him, Alex realized, and realized, too, that being in his arms felt like the most natural thing in the world. She sighed, a deep and shuddering sigh that acknowledged the futility of asking questions with no answers, and looked up at him.

"Thank you," she said, her fingers smoothing the damp place her tears had made on his coat.

"For . . . ?" The question was polite. His arms around her were warm and strong. Viewed at an angle, his jaw was square and, although she knew he had shaved just that morning, already darkening with five o'clock shadow. The plane of the cheek nearest her was brown and smooth. His nose was straight, his eyelashes and brows were thick and black, his forehead was high. His eyes as she looked into them were the color of the ocean where it nears the beach. He was handsome, sexy, and wonderfully comforting to be with, because he knew firsthand what she was going through.

"For being so kind to me—to us—to Neely and me—especially after . . ." Her voice trailed off guiltily.

"After you fired me, you mean?" There was the merest hint of humor in his voice, though his eyes were grave as they moved over her face.

Alex nodded.

"Don't worry about it. I've been fired before. I'll survive."

"Have you? When?" She felt drained, almost drowsy, in the aftermath of so much emotion. The warmth of his body surrounded her. His drawling speech was soothing, like a lullaby. She knew she should move out of his arms now, but oh, how she wanted to stay right where she was for just a moment or two more. She wanted the comfort of physical contact. She wanted to listen to the deep slow cadences of his voice.

"I'll tell you about it some other time, maybe. Come on, let's go back to the house." His voice had taken on the faintest suggestion of a husky note, and as Alex frowned up at him his hands closed on her waist and he moved her bodily away from him.

"You okay?" he asked, meaning could she stand unassisted, and when she nodded he let go of her altogether. Surreptitiously she rubbed the sleeve of her coat across her still-damp eyes. Joe's hands were in his pockets as, side by side, they walked back through the bright, crisp afternoon to the house. Small branches and leaves and lime green bumpy balls that he told her were called hedge apples littered the ground, the residue of last night's storm. The faintest hint of woodsmoke tinged the air. A flock of geese flew overhead in classic V formation, honking madly. In the distance, past the black-fenced fields of horses, past Joe's house and barn, two squat red ATVs could be seen charging toward the trees on the horizon. Neely was riding with Eli and perhaps Josh and Jenny were with them as well, Alex surmised. Neely at least was probably having the time of her life. Closer at hand, Cary was leaning on a fence just beyond Joe's barn, watching Victory Dance as he grazed alone in a small, fenced paddock.

"When are you leaving, you and your sister?" Joe asked as they reached the house.

Unpleasantly reminded that she *would* be leaving, Alex

frowned. The reason the thought was unpleasant, she realized, was that it meant that she would be leaving him. She
would never have a chance to find out what he was like in
bed. . . .

"Tomorrow. A little after noon. Neely will be going with
me, of course. We'll have to work something out about her
ticket, but I'm sure it won't be a problem." She was climbing the stairs to the narrow porch that ran the length of the
back of the house as she spoke, and he was behind her.

"I'll drive you to the airport."

"Thank you." She gained the porch and looked back at
him. A damp spot the size of a saucer was still visible on
the front of his coat from her tears.

"You're welcome." His voice was dry. His expression
was unreadable.

Alex opened the back door and went through a small
utility room into the kitchen. He followed her, closing the
door behind him. The house was quiet, hushed, and shadowy, but no longer forbidding. Or maybe she was just too
distracted by Joe's proximity to notice.

His boots were loud on the brick pavers. He paused
just inside the door, watching her.

"Sit down, why don't you?" She waved a hand at the
pair of barstools that were pulled up to the center island.
"Can I get you something to drink?" Crossing to the refrigerator, she opened it and looked inside. Without electricity, the interior was dark, with a dank smell. "I don't trust
the milk, but there's Diet Coke. Or orange juice."

"Water's fine." Unzipping his coat, he sat on one of the
barstools.

"Do you suppose they'll get the electricity turned back
on soon?" Alex asked as she got a glass from the cabinet
and filled it at the sink.

Joe shrugged. "Who knows? There are only a few people on our line, so they usually get to us last. That's one of the drawbacks about living in the country. If it's still out by tonight, you and your sister are welcome to stay over with us."

"That's very kind of you." Alex handed him the glass.

"Oh, kind is my middle name."

Was there sarcasm in his voice? His hand was curled around the glass, but he wasn't drinking. As she looked at him he smiled, a wry, faintly self-mocking smile, and took a sip of water. His gaze met hers over the top of the glass, and something in his eyes—a darkness, a kind of veiled heat—made her pulse rate increase.

He was as aware of her as she was of him, she thought, but it was becoming increasingly obvious that he didn't mean to do anything about it.

Right there and then, Alex made up her mind. She'd always heard that the things one most regretted in life were the things that one didn't do.

His eyes narrowed as he watched her walk around the end of the counter toward him, and he turned slightly on the stool so that he was facing her as she approached. She didn't stop walking until her thighs almost touched his bent knees. Their eyes were nearly on a level, and the heat in his was no longer quite so veiled. The glass of water sat forgotten on the counter beside his outstretched hand.

"Joe," she said huskily, resting her hands on his broad shoulders. His mouth was long and sensitive and beautiful. She couldn't stop looking at it.

"Hmm?" His hand on the counter closed into a fist.

Her gaze lifted and locked with his. For a moment they simply stared at each other while the air seemed to sizzle between them. Then she leaned forward and kissed that beautiful mouth.

Nineteen

✦

S he kissed him gently, experimentally, her lips mold-
ing his with tender care, her head tilted to one side,
her hands resting lightly on the wide expanse of his
shoulders.

He made a slight, harsh sound. Then his tongue was in
her mouth as his hands closed on either side of her waist,
pulling her into the cradle of his spread legs. His tongue
was hot, with a faint spicy taste, and his lips were hard as
they slanted across hers, taking control. Alex thought that
she would melt at the sheer heat of the kiss. Her arms
wrapped around his neck. Quivers started at the base of
her spine to race along her nerve endings. Her tongue met
his, touched it, caressed it. His hands slid down from her
waist to move up under her too-big coat and cup her
behind. With her coat rucked up around her waist, he
pulled her against him. She felt the size and hardness of
him pressing against that part of her that already ached
and wept for him. His hands squeezed her bottom, kneading, pulling her closer yet against the unmistakable evidence of his desire, and Alex went weak at the knees. He
was kissing her like a man who was starving for the taste
of her mouth.

Desperate for air, she freed her mouth from his and

took a great, shuddering breath. Then she bent her head, pressing a string of kisses along the unshaven line of his jaw until she gently captured his earlobe in her teeth.

"Wait a minute." His hands were on her hipbones now, pushing her a little away from him. His voice was hoarse and faintly breathless, and his expression was both hungry and wary as he pulled his head back to look at her. "What is this?"

"A kiss?" she offered huskily, her gaze sliding once again to his mouth.

"Just a kiss?" His jaw was clenched, she saw, and his hands were holding on to her hipbones so hard they hurt.

"It can be anything you want it to be," she whispered, her eyes bright with promise as she lifted her gaze to his. She was so hot for him she was melting inside, and tomorrow they said good-bye. Why shouldn't she take what she wanted? When she had been so devoid of wanting anything for such a long time?

His eyes turned suddenly dark, dangerous, as he sucked in his breath.

"I want a lot."

"So do I."

He pulled her back toward him, slowly, nestling her between his legs. Her hands slid from his shoulders to link behind his neck. For a moment they just looked at each other. Then he kissed her again, drawing her tongue into his mouth, sucking on it. His mouth was hot, and wet, and devastating.

Alex shivered, wrapped her arms around his neck, and kissed him back. She pressed her body against his, reveling in the feel of him against her, in the sheer magnificent size of him, in the hard evidence of his desire. His hands on her bottom pressed her closer yet. The heat and pressure of his body radiated to her through his jeans. She felt herself turning liquid with wanting, and moved sensuously against him. Undulating tremors of arousal raced down her thighs.

Alex stroked the warm skin at the nape of his neck. She ran her fingers through his short crisp hair. His puffy blue coat was preventing her from getting as close to him as she wanted. Her own coat was in the way too.

She pulled her mouth from his. His eyes opened, smoldering and heavy-lidded as they met hers. With his gaze following her every move, she began to slowly unbutton her coat. When she was finished, she slid out of it, letting it drop to the floor at her feet. The soft sound it made as it hit echoed through the quiet house.

"Don't stop there." He smiled faintly at her, but his eyes were ablaze.

"Your turn." She tugged at his sleeve. Removing his hands from her bottom, he shrugged out of the coat. It fell with a heavy slithering sound. She stayed where she was, her pelvis pressed deliberately against the hard mound in his jeans, her hands running over the firm muscles of his chest through his flannel shirt.

"You're beautiful," he said, his voice thick. Then he caught her by the waist and leaned forward to press his open mouth to her breast.

For a moment Alex stood unmoving. The moist heat of his mouth took a moment to penetrate the soft cashmere of her sweater and the thin silk of her bra. When it did her nipple instantly hardened and she gasped. Her hands moved to clasp the back of his head.

Her eyes closed. She stood there while he suckled her through her clothes, holding him against her, her toes curling in her boots at the sheer exquisite pleasure of it. When he shifted his attention to her other breast, though, she pulled away from him and stepped back.

"Come back here," he said, again with the faint smile and burning eyes, and reached for her.

She shook her head at him. "Wait."

With his eyes on her, she took off her expensive black cardigan, let it drop to the floor, and stood before him for a moment in her sleeveless black crewneck and slim khaki slacks. Then she pulled her sweater free at the waist and lifted it over her head before letting it, too, drop.

Her bra was a flimsy creation of white silk and lace, and her breasts filled the cups out nicely without being overly large. Her nipples, hardened by his attentions, pressed wantonly against round wet circles where his mouth had been. As he looked at her, a dark flush rose to stain his cheekbones and his breathing suspended.

"Pretty," he said. "You going to take that off for me, too?"

Again she shook her head. "I'll let you."

He drew in his breath with an audible sound and stood up so abruptly that the barstool scooted backward. This time, when he reached for her, she went into his arms, loving the feel of his solid muscles beneath the soft flannel shirt, loving the hard strength of the arms around her, loving the sheer size of him and the way he kissed and how her body throbbed and burned for him. . . .

Even when things were good with Paul, she had never wanted him like this.

Joe stopped kissing her abruptly, his eyes glittering, his jaw set, and said, "Let's take this upstairs."

Then he swept her up in his arms and started walking with her, through the kitchen door into the front hall, up the wide staircase and along the narrow upstairs hall to her bedroom, all without so much as breaking a sweat. Alex clung to his neck, pressing short sweet kisses along the faintly rough underside of his jaw, tickling the already-

proved-sensitive lobe of his ear with her tongue. Shoulder-
ing through the door, he pushed it closed behind them
with a foot and looked down at her.

"I want you. God, I want you." His voice was thick.

"So take me."

He made a sound that was a cross between a groan and
a growl and put her down on the bed. The covers were
pulled back, and the sheets bore the same floral scent that
she remembered from last night. But before the images of
fear and flight could intrude he was coming down on top
of her, fully clothed and heavy as a body bag full of wet
cement, pressing her down into the mattress and kissing
her with a torrid hunger that turned her brain to Jell-O
and her body to fire.

There was no room in her thoughts for anything but
him, and how he was making her feel.

He kissed her mouth, her neck, her shoulders, her ears.
The slight roughness of his jaw rasped against her soft skin.
His hands found her breasts, caressing them through her
bra, running his thumbs over her nipples. Then his mouth
followed his hands, and he suckled her through the fragile
silk. Her still fully clothed legs parted for him instinctively,
and he settled himself between them, rocking against her,
his body a solid ridge of granite as it both teased and
promised. Then he shifted his weight so that he was lying
alongside her, and slid a hand beneath the nape of her neck
to position her mouth for his. His other hand was scalding
hot as it slid along her rib cage and over her stomach to the
fastening of her slacks. He freed the button, then eased the
zipper down. The slight sound it made was, she thought,
the most erotic thing she had ever heard.

He was still kissing her, long, slow kisses that made her
head reel, as his hand delved inside her zipper, crept over
her stomach, then slid beneath the lace-trimmed edge of

her panties. His palm was flat against her stomach, his fingers gentle as they found and caressed the triangle of curls between her thighs. Then he pushed his fingers deeper, down between her legs, touching the most sensitive part of her, making her quiver and gasp into his mouth.

Just when she thought she couldn't stand it anymore, when the sheer pleasure of it was making her loins contract and her thighs tremble, his hand slid lower yet, finding the opening that wept for him and wedging two fingers inside. His hand moved, in and out, in a steady, tantalizing rhythm, at the same time as he moved his thumb against the quivering nub nearby. Alex writhed desperately beneath that knowing hand, tugging at his shirt but too mindless with mounting desire to even so much as locate the buttons that held it together, wanting him naked and inside her more than she had ever wanted anything in her life.

Without warning his mouth lifted from hers, and his hand was withdrawn from her panties. Alex's eyes blinked open, to find that he was propped on one elbow looking down at her. His eyes were so bright they looked feverish, and his skin was flushed. His gaze moved from her eyes, which she knew were heavy-lidded with desire, to her mouth, which was soft and wet from his kisses, down along her body, which was half-naked and open to his touch and quivering with desire for him, before returning once again to meet her eyes.

"Please," she whispered, because she was burning for him, hotter than she could ever remember being, and quaking with need. If he did not take her soon she would die. . . .

"Please what?" His voice was thick and low. His hand found her breast, flattening over it. She was still wearing her bra. The thin damp silk did nothing to protect her sensitized nipple. The heat and pressure of his hand rubbing back and forth over her breast made her squirm. She watched the hungry, beseeching movement of her own hips with a heated fascination.

"Make love to me." Just hearing herself say the words made her quiver. She was no prude, and no virgin either, but she had inhibitions just like any other normal woman and a good measure of pride, too, and she had never, ever thought that she would beg a man she scarcely knew to have sex with her.

But then, she had never, ever thought that she could want a man she scarcely knew like this.

"First you have to take off your bra for me."

Hands trembling, she complied, sitting up and reaching around behind her back to undo the clasp, mesmerized by the knowledge that he was watching her every move. When the straps slid down her arms, baring her, his gaze was on her breasts, and, looking down, she tried to see herself through his eyes: her breasts were the size of oranges, round and firm, silky smooth and pale as milk and tipped with strawberry-pink nipples that were puckered and hard with arousal.

He looked at her breasts without touching her, then rolled off the side of the bed and came to his feet to stand towering over her as she sat in the middle of the bed. His gaze never left her as he swept the tangled covers from the bed, leaving only the fitted bottom sheet.

"Now take off your pants."

"Joe. . . ." It was a husky plea. She wanted him so badly, and he was making her wait. . . .

"Do it."

Alex did, first fumbling with her boots, pulling them off one by one and dropping them over the side of the bed, then sliding her slacks down her legs. The knowledge that he was watching her undress, telling her to undress, was so erotic that she was trembling. She dropped her khakis to the floor, and looked up to find his gaze moving hotly all over her body, which was clad in nothing now but her tiny white bikini panties.

"Now those."

Her lips parted as she fought to breathe. Then, slowly, she slid her fingers beneath the scraps of lace that rode her hipbones and eased them down her hips to reveal the ash-brown curls that he had caressed but not seen, then pushed the panties down her legs and, finally, took them off.

Naked now, sitting in the middle of the bed, she looked up at him. He was taking off his own clothes, his movements fast, jerky, his eyes glittering with passion, his jaw hard. He pulled off his boots, then, disdaining buttons, he pulled his shirt over his head, leaving her to admire the splendor of his wide, black-furred chest and broad, line-backer's shoulders as he unzipped his pants and pushed them and his plain white jockey shorts down his legs, then kicked them aside. For an instant more he stood over her, mouthwateringly handsome, all black hair and bronzed skin and hard muscles, the evidence of his desire for her huge and swollen and jutting out at a straight, ninety-degree angle from his body.

Then he came down beside her. She lay back, gasping, trembling with passion, her eyes closing tight as he moved on top of her.

He was hot, heavy. The weight and friction of his body on her breasts and stomach and thighs were just what she craved. Her legs parted instantly, instinctively, to allow him to settle between them. She arched her hips up off the mattress in anticipation, needing him to take her now. . . .

But he didn't. He caught her wrists, pulling her arms

straight up over her head and holding them there, pinned to the mattress. He lowered his head, his mouth closing over a pebble-hard nipple, tugging it into his mouth, rubbing it with the rough wet surface of his tongue.

Alex moaned. His mouth moved to her other breast, repeating the exquisite torture. She moaned again.

She could feel his body with every nerve ending she possessed. His legs were hard and hot and abrasive between her trembling thighs; his chest and stomach were hard and hot and abrasive too as they moved against her breasts and belly and the slight protuberance of her femininity. The enormous, scalding-hot part of him she ached for just barely touched her between her legs.

He was doing this deliberately, she thought, toying with her, tantalizing her, until he had her panting for him, melting like superheated plastic for him.

He had her pinned down so that she could scarcely move. She writhed beneath him, arching up off the mattress, pleading with him without words.

He lifted his head from her breasts.

"Alex. Look at me."

She did, opening her eyes to meet his gaze.

"Tell me what you want."

"You." It was a mere breath of sound.

His eyes were so dark they were almost obsidian. His mouth was slightly open as he drew in air with short, harsh, breaths. Tiny beads of sweat had popped out on his brow.

"Me? Where?"

Her body moved in instinctive answer, shifting beneath him, pleading without words. But still he held back, his shaft pulsing and burning as it just barely prodded the hot moist folds of her flesh.

"Where?" The question was insistent.

She gasped. "Inside—me."

"Ah." It was a low, guttural sound. Slowly, slowly, slowly, he began to push inside her, thick and hard and hot, filling her to capacity, stretching her. . . .

She cried out.

Twenty

✦

Later, much later, Alex stirred. She was lying back to front against a warm male body, his arm hard and possessive around her waist, his chest rising and falling against her back, his breathing regular in her ear. She was drowsy, lethargic. Her mind might not be quite awake yet, but her body felt soft and totally sated, and she knew, in some vague way, that she had just been well and truly fucked.

Her movement must have awakened him, because he stirred too. The hand that had been resting heavily across her stomach now slid up to cup her breast.

Alex smiled without opening her eyes.

"Oh, Paul," she said huskily. "Paul, darling, that was *so* good."

The hand caressing her breast stilled. The arm lying across her rib cage went rigid. The body behind her stiffened.

Alex's eyes popped open as she realized what she had done.

"Oh, God," she said, rolling onto her back. He was still lying on his side, but he raised himself up as she watched, supporting his upper torso on a brawny bent arm. Their gazes met. Wide, horrified blue eyes looked into narrowed aqua ones.

"Wrong guy," he said, and levered himself off the bed.

Alex sat up, supremely conscious of her nakedness as his eyes raked her. "Oh, Joe, I'm sorry! It's just—I was half asleep and . . ."

"No problem. Glad to fill in." His tone was hard and clipped. He was already pulling on his clothes, first his jockey shorts and then his jeans. . . .

She watched him with consternation, almost babbling in an effort to make things right. "Joe, it was just a slip of the tongue, I swear. I'm so used to being with Paul—when I woke up next to a man I just naturally assumed—but like I said, it was so good. The sex, I mean. I feel so much better now."

He pulled his flannel shirt over his head, thrust his arms through the sleeves, bent to pick up his boots, and looked at her. His eyes were flinty, his mouth a thin straight line.

"Honey, next time you feel like indulging in a little sex therapy, leave me out of it, okay?"

"Jo-oe!" She almost wailed his name as he turned on his heel and stalked through the door.

"I'll wait for you in the kitchen," he said over his shoulder, and disappeared from view.

For a moment Alex sat where she was, stunned, while the events of the last couple of hours replayed themselves in her mind. They had made love a total of three times. After he had brought her to a shattering climax the first time, he had given her only a few minutes to recover before turning onto his back and pulling her on top of him. At his direction she'd ridden him while he'd looked and played. She hadn't thought she could come again so soon, but he knew just where to touch her and what to do, and she had, crying out at the end and collapsing on top of him. Finally, when she'd been lying on her stomach, exhausted and just about to fall asleep, he had wrapped an arm around her waist and pulled her up onto her hands and knees and entered her from behind. His thrusts had been slow and deep, and in between he had kissed the back of her neck and run his tongue along her spine and nibbled on her bottom. Her climax had been spectacular, and afterwards she had just died, tumbling fathoms deep asleep, for how long she couldn't say, but with disastrous results.

It had been the best sex of her life, too.

Oh, God, now she had to go find him and tell him so. Men were so sensitive.

Making a face, Alex got up, gathered up her clothes—she had left her twin set in the kitchen, she remembered with just the teeniest niggle of embarrassment—dropped them in the mesh bag she was using as a hamper, and took a quick shower. Operating in the dark bathroom was tricky, but she was sweaty and covered with his body hair and juices, and she just couldn't stand herself. The shower, which was on the cool side as the water in the tank was, apparently, gradually losing its heat, took no more than three minutes. It took only slightly more than that to don fresh clothes from her suitcase—soft gray corduroy slacks, a white sweater, and her boots—and brush out her hair, wincing only a little as she smoothed the area around the stitches. Smoothing gloss over her lips with a fingertip, she headed downstairs.

He was in the kitchen, as he had said, leaning against the far counter, his expression meditative rather than angry as he sipped a Diet Coke.

She smiled contritely as soon as she saw him and walked across the kitchen to plant a kiss on his cheek. He suffered the kiss but did not respond, slanting a look at her that told her she still had a considerable amount of fence mending to do.

"Joe," she said plaintively, a hand on his arm. "I'm sorry."

"No apology needed." His face and voice were impassive. His body language was relaxed even as he moved away from her and stood in front of the sink, pouring the remaining contents of his can down the drain. But his eyes as they met hers were wintry.

Alex gave a wry little laugh. "That's obvious. You're being ridiculous, you know. Saying Paul's name like that— it was just an accident."

"The kind of thing that could happen to anybody, in fact." He crushed the empty can in one hand.

"I meant the other part of what I said, though—the sex was good. Great really." She smiled at him coaxingly. "The best I've ever had."

"Yeah, it was good for me, too." He moved, throwing the can in the trash. "Come on, I'll take you back to the house. It'll be dark in an hour and I've got some work I need to do."

"If you're going to be crabby, I'm not going anywhere with you." The threat was half playful.

"Fine by me. Stay up here in the dark for as long as you like. If you think you see a ghost, you can always run screaming down the hill again."

Alex's eyes narrowed at him. "You know, that was uncalled for."

"Hey, Princess, truth hurts."

Alex felt her temper begin to heat. "If you want to talk about truth, let's talk about a man who's so ego-sensitive that he gets his feelings all bruised over a perfectly innocent slip of the tongue."

He smiled at her, a quick stretching of his lips that was

utterly devoid of humor. "Or we could talk about a woman with so many lovers, she can't keep their names straight."

Alex's jaw dropped. "You know, I'm really not going anywhere with you."

"Like I said, fine by me." He turned and headed toward the door, then stopped when he reached it, stood stock-still for a moment, and pivoted to face her. "You don't even have a damned flashlight. Get whatever you and your sister need for the night together, and be quick about it. I'm not leaving you up here."

Alex met his gaze with a glittering one of her own. "You know, I don't know where you get off thinking you can give me orders."

"You liked me giving you orders earlier." His tone made it perfectly clear which orders he was referring to. Her face crimsoned as she heard them again in her mind: *take off your bra; take off your pants; now those.*

"Get out of my house!"

"Get your things together."

"Like hell I will!"

"Fine, don't." He came toward her. Knowing what he was about to do—he was a fine one for picking her up and carting her off—Alex turned tail and ran. The bedrooms all had doors that locked. . . .

He was close behind her, his boots loud on the brick pavers and then muffled as he chased her through the front hall. Casting a single hunted look over her shoulder, Alex managed to beat him to the stairs and was halfway up when, without warning, the front door opened.

Joe had just reached the foot of the stairs. He, and she, froze in their tracks as Neely bounced into the hall, followed by Eli.

"There you are," Neely said, spying Alex, while Eli, after a single quick look at Alex, focused on Joe.

"When you were late seeing to the horses, I thought I better come check on you," Eli said.

Joe had let go of the banister and turned to face the new arrivals, his posture carefully casual. Now he managed a smile for his son.

"What, did you think I got lost? Miss Haywood here was just getting a few things together so that she and her sister could spend the night at our house again, since the electricity doesn't look like it's coming back on."

"Oh, yay," Neely said, looking at Eli.

"Actually, I thought we'd go to a hotel." Alex addressed this to Neely, then directed a glittering look at Joe. "I wouldn't dream of imposing on your hospitality for a second night."

"A hotel?" Joe sounded like he was on the verge of letting loose with a derisive hoot. "'Fraid we're fresh out of five-star establishments hereabouts."

"I saw a hotel on the way to the hospital last night." It was all Alex could do to keep her voice relatively pleasant, and a smile pasted on her lips.

"You did?" For a moment he looked at a loss. Then genuine amusement lit his eyes. "Oh, you mean the Dixie Inn."

"That's right."

"By all means, if you don't want to impose, you should certainly spend tonight at the Dixie Inn."

"But Dad . . ." Eli protested under his breath.

"Alex, I really don't want to go to a hotel." Neely's voice was louder.

"Too bad. Because that's what we're going to do." Alex shot Neely a killer look.

"Actually, that's probably a pretty good idea, now that I come to think about it. The Dixie Inn has electricity, and this is a school night." Joe's voice was bland.

"Dad . . ." Eli groaned.

"Alex . . ." Neely wailed.

"Hey, that's the end of the discussion," Joe said. Eli, being his son and, Alex thought, thus long inured to taking orders, shut up. What was surprising was that Neely, after a single thoughtful glance at first her sister and then Joe, was silent too.

꩜ ꩜ ꩜ ꩜

About an hour later, Alex and Neely were driving in the white Mercedes down U.S. 60 toward Shelbyville and the Dixie Inn. It was shortly after six o'clock, and night had fallen. Only a single car passed them going the other way. Alex flipped the headlights on high, the better to see through the darkness. At least, she thought, it wasn't raining.

"So how was he?" Neely asked as she fiddled with the radio dials, trying to find an acceptable station.

Alex shot her sister a quick, wary glance.

"What?"

Neely grinned at her.

"I said, how was he?"

Alex tried, with, she hoped, some success, to keep her face perfectly blank. "I don't know what you're talking about."

"Come off it, sister. Daddy Studmuffin. You did him. I can tell."

"Neely . . ." Alex got a mental grip. "I don't know what you're talking about," she said again, firmly.

"Fine. Don't tell me. But if you're going to hold out, I won't tell you about Eli."

This time the look Alex sent her sister was truly appalled. "Neely—you didn't."

Neely laughed.

Alex was still trying to figure out whether her sister was teasing—she was horribly afraid she was not—as they pulled into the Dixie Inn. It was a one-story building, Alex saw with a glance, that could more properly be described as a motel rather than a hotel. It was long and low and U-shaped, built around a rectangular courtyard that served as the parking lot. Alex remembered Joe's amusement at the idea that she and Neely would spend the night here, and braced herself for less than stellar accommodations. At one end was a glassed-in restaurant that also functioned, apparently, as the motel's reception area. It was toward this that they headed.

"If I were you, I'd let my hair loose before we go in here," Neely said seriously as they walked under the yellow security lights. The rooms were still being cleaned, apparently. A Mexican-looking woman in a tired gray uniform pushed a white laundry cart along the paved inner sidewalk in front of the rooms. A man with a push broom swept debris from the parking lot.

"Why?" Alex asked as they reached the door. Through the heavy glass she could see a man in a white shirt sitting behind the reception desk.

"'Cause you've got a hickey." Neely touched a spot right under Alex's ear. "Right here."

Eyes widening, Alex clapped a hand to the spot. It was an automatic reaction. Obviously it was too late to hide. . . .

Neely laughed. "Gotcha. So you did do Daddy Studmuffin. I knew you did."

Alex's hand dropped as she glared at her sister. "Neely, you little brat," she said with some venom, and pulled open the door.

Her sister was still laughing as she followed her inside the Dixie Inn.

Twenty-one

❦

It was nearly midnight, and Joe was seated at his kitchen table, paying bills by lantern light. He'd been to bed, but it hadn't taken. Tired as he was—and he was so tired his eyeballs felt grainy—he couldn't sleep.

He knew the reason, of course: Alexandra Haywood. Charles Haywood's little princess had been all her father had ever claimed, and lots more that Joe was sure Daddy had never even thought about.

The sex had been mind-blowing. For her, too. He'd known it, even before she'd told him so.

The best sex I've ever had. He could still hear her voice saying it. The memory made him hard.

Damn it to hell.

What, exactly, was his problem? he asked himself for what must have been the dozenth time. He'd just had the mother of all sex sessions with the most desirable woman he'd run across in some time. He wasn't all bent out of shape just because, post-coitus, she'd called him by her lout of an ex-fiancé's name. No. He wasn't that childish. Or that jealous-natured.

But he was, definitely, bent out of shape. He'd been irritable with the kids, which he always tried his damndest not to be. He'd been impatient with the horses. He'd growled at his father. He'd been unable to sleep.

Which all added up to a major funk. And the cause of it was Alex. He knew it, and knew precisely why, too, even if he hated to face the truth.

She'd gotten under his skin.

From the moment he'd first laid eyes on her, at Charles Haywood's funeral, he'd been struck by her beauty. Then she'd marched up to his barn, and her boss-lady manner had raised his hackles even before she'd gotten around to firing him. Later, at Whistledown, he'd felt sorry for her.

If it had ended there, that would have been fine. He would have acknowledged feeling a certain degree of attraction for a beautiful, bitchy woman presently kind of down on her luck, and left it at that.

Then, of course, she'd had to come running to him with her tales of burglars and ghosts, and his control over events had gone downhill from there.

He'd wanted her in his bed from about midway through that ill-advised shower. It had been clear that she was willing, no, wanting, too. But he'd been careful to keep his distance, careful not to do anything he was sure to regret. Even earlier today, when she'd cried all over him in Whistledown's barn, he'd been strictly hands-off, for which he'd been ready to award himself a medal. And he would have continued to keep his hands to himself, too, because he had known that in the long run it was better that way.

But then she had kissed him, and at the sweet, hot touch of her mouth all his calm good judgment had been blown straight to hell.

Wasn't there a saying about the way to a man's heart being through his stomach? Well, whoever had thought that one up was dead wrong. The way to a man's heart was through his dick, and anyone who didn't know that didn't know crap about men.

She was beautiful in just the way he liked, slim with high, firm breasts that were as real as the nose on her face. He liked blondes, and her hair was silvery, and if that wasn't her natural shade it was close to it. The evidence was the ash-brown down of her pubic hair. He liked sassy women, too, women who weren't afraid to look him in the eye when necessary and tell him to go take a long walk off a short pier.

Most of all, he liked women who liked men, and weren't afraid to show it in bed.

On that last count, she met the gold standard.

She'd made him so hot that he'd taken her three times and still been ready to do it again. Until she had called him by her last lover's name, that is.

Even now, he was having trouble concentrating on his work because he could not get the image of her naked out of his head.

Naked and begging, to be precise.

Spread-eagled beneath him and squirming like a worm on a hook and begging him to come in.

Where do you want it?

Inside me.

Fuck. No, not fuck. Shit, damn, something else. Anything else. He was now so hard that he was physically uncomfortable, and he still couldn't seem to keep the damned woman out of his head.

Naked.

Begging.

Stop it, he ordered himself fiercely. If he wasn't careful, Princess Alex would have him panting after her like a lapdog, and that just wasn't going to happen, not if he could help it, and he could. Falling that hard for another woman was the last thing he ever meant to do. Especially a woman who was basically using him to get over another man, who was in town for a limited amount of time, and who was his boss's daughter, or boss, or however the hell you wanted to look at it, to complicate the situation.

He had panted that way after a female once, lusting with all the force of a boy's first wild passion. He'd lusted his way right into falling in love. And that, of course, was how the whole damned nightmare that had been his marriage had begun. He'd been crazy for Laura, his boyhood sweetheart, his wife, the mother of his kids; Laura, who had slept with everything in pants before, during, and after their marriage, who'd boozed and drugged and partied until booze and drugs and partying had meant more to her than he and the children ever had; Laura, who'd left him and the kids so many times that he had lost count before she had finally taken off for good; Laura, who'd first broken his heart, then left it encased in a hard shell that he was determined no woman was ever going to crack open again.

Not that he had sworn off sex: he hadn't. Or women, either. Unfortunately, women were necessary for the kind of sex he liked. But the women he saw knew up front that if they wanted to keep seeing him, they had to keep it light.

Getting hot and heavy with another woman was not part of his game plan. He liked things just the way they were, with his kids and his horses taking center stage and women and sex on the side.

So his black mood was his own fault, Joe knew. He'd caved to unholy temptation, taken what he wanted, and now he was paying the price.

At least she was leaving tomorrow. In all likelihood, he would never see her again.

That was a good thing, he told himself. And refused to consider why it made him feel so bad.

"Dad?" The voice from the doorway made him start almost guiltily and look around, even though it was as familiar to him as his own: Eli. Joe watched as his tall son, who looked enough like him to be his much-younger, hipper clone, padded barefoot across the floor toward him, rubbing his eyes with both fists. From the time he was a toddler, Eli had always rubbed his eyes that way upon first waking up. The memory brought a half-smile to Joe's lips.

"What are you doing up? It's after midnight, and you've got school tomorrow." His voice was gruff. He was still a little ticked at Eli for putting the ATVs away covered with mud. The fact that, ordinarily, such a transgression would have earned his son no more than a mild *clean 'em up tomorrow* was not lost on him, but he'd been too grumpy to remind himself of that when he'd yelled at Eli earlier.

"Is everything okay?" Eli stopped beside him, laying a hand on his shoulder and squinting down at the checkbook in front of him and the bills and notices scattered across the tabletop. Eli's long hair flopped over his face, and he tucked it back behind one ear with a long-fingered hand.

It struck Joe that his kid was rapidly turning into a man.

"What do you mean, is everything okay? Sure everything is okay." He looked up at Eli with a frown. His son could not know about his turmoil over Alex—God help him if the boy did. A father's sex life was something that no kid, even if he was almost a man, needed to be privy to.

"Neely told me about you losing your job at Whistledown. She said her sister came down here to tell you."

"Oh." For a moment Joe said nothing more, simply

staring up at his son as he tried to think how to reply to that. "Well, yeah, Miss Haywood did say something along those lines."

Eli's expression turned earnest. "If things are going to be tight, I could get a job and help out. I'm old enough. I'm sixteen."

"Eli." For a moment Joe felt like standing up and giving the kid a hug, but that was not really the kind of thing he did, not since Eli had started getting so big. He settled for patting the hand on his shoulder. "You don't need to get a job. Everything's going to be fine. Yes, I'm probably going to lose the job at Whistledown, because the Haywoods are having financial problems. But it won't be for a while, because I have a contract that runs through a certain date. And in the meantime I'm going to take steps to make sure that we don't lose any income when it happens. Believe me, there's nothing for you to worry about, so go back to bed."

"What about you?"

"What? What about me?"

"Are you coming to bed?" Eli gave him a fleeting, teasing grin. "You're getting kind of old, you know. Old men need their sleep."

Joe made a sound that was partway between a snort and a laugh. "Eli, if I wanted a mother hen I'd move your grandpa in. Yes, son, I am coming to bed. Just as soon as I finish up here. Now go on. I'm fine, everything's fine. Go to bed."

Eli finally went. But Joe stayed up for a long time, unable to sleep.

Unable to get Alex, naked and begging, out of his head.

Twenty-two

✦

T he sound of laughter made him prick up his ears. The predator glanced around and saw, under the yellow security lights, not one but two beautiful blondes. They were getting ready to enter the building, and he was almost dazzled by his good fortune.

Two beautiful blondes, right here at ground zero. God, he thought, had surely smiled.

Maybe, just maybe, if God was in a really good mood and the stars were aligned just right and all that crap, he could keep one or both of these girls. He was getting tired of Cassandra anyway. She didn't laugh anymore. She didn't cry anymore, or even act scared anymore. She wasn't much more fun than one of those life-size blow-up dolls with a vagina, which, incidentally, he had tried when he was younger and found unsatisfactory. Time to think about replacing her.

If these girls filled the bill, he could replace Cassandra tonight. Send her up to join her Eric in a blaze of glory while his new playmates watched. Showing them right off the bat what would happen if they weren't good girls was always best. After that kind of demonstration, they never gave him any trouble. In fact, they were usually almost pathetically eager to do exactly what he said.

But, as it turned out, God was in a playful mood, as He sometimes was. As soon as he learned the identity of the blond beauties, the predator realized that. Alexandra and Cornelia Haywood. If that wasn't some kind of cosmic joke at his expense, he didn't know what was.

He'd been in their house last night. Of course, when he'd finished topping his evening off with Cassandra and climbed up out of the subterranean depths for a quick shower, he hadn't even known that the house was occupied. Subtle clues—well, not so subtle, really, a purse in the kitchen—had tipped him off to the presence of at least one woman, and he'd gone to investigate.

He was an opportunist, after all. If God handed him a woman on a plate, who was he to say no?

He'd hit paydirt with the first bedroom he'd entered. A quick flash of the pen-sized flashlight he routinely carried, and he'd realized that he was looking down at a slender young blonde. She was fast asleep, the covers drawn up over her shoulders, her face turned to one side, her skin all white and creamy. Then, because he simply couldn't resist the urge, he'd reached out and touched her cheek just to see if her skin felt as soft as it looked. It did, but touching her was a mistake, because she stirred. He'd turned the flashlight off, and not a moment too soon. She'd awakened—he'd known by the change in her breathing—and then she lay there in the dark for a moment, wondering why, he imagined.

He'd been tempted, really tempted, just to zap her there and then and take her down to join Cassandra, but he had resisted. He didn't know who she was, but he figured that she had to be somehow related to the Haywoods, and to be related to the Haywoods meant that she was probably rich and well connected. To steal a girl from her bed was to invite a search of the premises; to steal a rich and well-connected girl from her bed was to invite a truly massive search of the premises.

Now, he was confident that the entrance to his secret place was well concealed. No one had ever found it in all these years. But to intentionally bring scads of law-enforcement types right into what he liked to think of as the very heart of darkness would be plain stupid. And whatever else he was, he wasn't stupid.

So he had decided, reluctantly, that he must let the girl be. He'd been standing at the foot of the bed, regretting his decision but on the verge of leaving, when she had sat up abruptly and tried to turn on the light.

Click. He'd heard it clearly. *Click. Click.*

Good thing for her the light hadn't worked. If it had, if she had seen him, he would have had no choice but to take her.

In a way, he almost regretted that the electricity had been out. If she had seen him, he would have taken it as a sign that she was meant to be his.

As it was, he had left the room, quickly, and, he'd thought, silently. But she had followed him. Such courage! Such stupidity! She had followed him, and almost caught him, too, as he had pressed himself against the wall of the hall, expecting her to pass on by.

But she had tripped, stumbling into him and grabbing at his shirt to save herself, and in that split second he had hit her over the head with one of the bronze statues that graced the hall. If he'd had his wits about him he would have used his taser, but everything happened so fast, and it was in his back pants pocket, buttoned in. The statue, though clumsy, had been at hand. He'd seen it on the wall scores of times, and had almost knocked it off himself when he'd taken refuge beside it.

Then he had fled the house, promising himself that, if

she was still there in a couple of days, he would call again.

Not to touch, this time. And not to take. Just to look.

He liked to look. Looking was almost, though not quite, as fun as taking. The sights he had seen over the years—well, if he ever chose to write a book, it would be a humdinger. He could call it *What the Bad Man Saw,* or something like that.

Now here she was, served up to him again. He had recognized her as soon as he had learned who, exactly, was checking in.

Taking her was not an option. The disappearance of Charles Haywood's daughter so close on the heels of his unfortunate death would bring the kind of attention to the area that he could do without.

He would have to content himself with watching her.

But watching was fun, too. He always liked to watch. Of course, his view of the proceedings was rather restricted, given the exigencies of the situation, but still they'd put on quite a show, she and her sister, once they were in their nice, safe, private motel room.

Each one of them had stripped naked, and showered, and dried herself very, very thoroughly, before putting on pretty nighties and getting into bed.

By the time they'd turned out the lights, ending his viewing pleasure, he'd been so aroused that he had decided to visit Cassandra again.

Twenty-three

✦

A knock on the door of the motel room surprised Alex the next morning. It was not quite nine o'clock, and she'd been up for just long enough to take a shower and get dressed. This morning she'd washed her hair—very carefully—although the doctor who'd put in the stitches had advised her to wait three days. But to someone who was in the habit of washing her hair daily, three days was an eternity, and Alex simply hadn't been able to wait any longer.

She was, consequently, blowing her hair dry when the knock came. Neely was still in the shower, so she had no choice but to put down the hair dryer and brush and answer the door herself.

Frowning, tossing her still slightly damp hair back from her face and expecting the maid, she pulled the door open.

There on the threshold stood Joe, his hand raised to knock again.

For a moment they simply stared at each other. He was frowning slightly, and the morning sun was behind him flooding the landscape with light, so that his face was in shadow. In that instant she took in all kinds of details about him: his height, which, since she hadn't put her shoes on yet, put the top of her head about on a level with his chin; the breadth of his shoulders and the easy grace of the rest of his hard athlete's physique in a red flannel shirt and jeans; the utter blackness of his hair; and his hard, handsome face. He was looking at her too, his gaze running down her body in a single, comprehensive glance. Alex knew what he saw: a slim body in a snug navy turtleneck and gray slacks; long blond hair falling loose and straight around her shoulders; a fine-featured, high-cheekboned face, with blue eyes made more intense by the color of her sweater.

In that instant, that same instant in which she was registering all those details, she was so glad to see him that her heart gave a little leap.

Then she remembered why she wasn't glad to see him, and she, too, frowned.

Their gazes met. Alex saw a quick, fierce flare of heat in his eyes, and she was alarmed to discover that that was all it took to spark an answering flame deep inside her body. It was a purely physical reaction to the memory of what they had done together in bed, and it annoyed her so much that her frown deepened into a scowl. But by then he was glancing beyond her into the small, musty room, at the pair of twin beds with their ancient mattresses and the white and gold, fifties-era fake French Provincial furniture. The heat was gone and his frown had changed into a slight, mocking smile by the time he looked at her again.

"Enjoy the accommodations, Princess?"

"Did you want something?" Alex asked coldly.

"Nah. I just happened to be in the neighborhood. . . ."

"Fine," Alex snapped, and started to close the door in his face.

"Don't be childish," he chided, stopping her from closing the door by laying his big hand flat against the flimsy wooden panel. He was able to hold the door open with ridiculous ease despite her best efforts. When his mocking smile widened into a full-fledged, goat-getting grin, she had to remind herself forcefully that the ultimate in childishness would be to give in to her impulse to kick him as hard as she could in the shin.

"If we're going to talk about being childish . . ." Alex began, only to be interrupted by Neely's voice calling from the bathroom.

"Alex! Do you have a hair dryer?"

Before Alex could answer, Neely walked into the bedroom, fortunately wrapped in a towel. But it was a skimpy white hotel towel, and it covered her—barely—only from her armpits to the tops of her thighs.

"Oh. Hi, Joe." Neely stopped short when she saw Joe, but instead of retreating she came toward him, apparently not the least bit concerned about her state of undress. Joe's gaze flicked over her, Alex saw, and he looked suddenly rather grim.

"Hello, Neely." His voice wasn't encouraging.

"Is Eli with you?" Neely asked, clearly not bothered by his tone as she looked past Joe to the parking lot, which, surprisingly, was pretty well filled.

"Eli's in school." Joe's voice implied that Neely should be there, too.

"Oh. Too bad." Neely made a face, then smiled at Joe again. "Well, I'll let you and sister talk." She glanced at Alex. "I'll be in the bathroom drying my hair. Not that you'll need me, of course."

She walked over and picked up the hair dryer from where Alex had left it on the shabby dresser, waved an airy good-bye, and then sauntered toward the bathroom, long slim legs flashing to the point of near indecency as she moved.

"Modesty isn't your sister's strong suit, is it?" Joe asked

after she was gone. "You really ought to tell her that it's not a good idea to go swanning around half naked in front of strange men."

Alex sighed. "Telling Neely not to do something is like waving a red flag in front of a bull. If I did, she'd probably come out without a stitch on the next time."

Joe looked disapproving. "You don't have much control over her, do you?"

"No, I don't. Not that it's any of your business."

"You're right, it's not. Thank God." He reached for an envelope, which had been folded and stuck in the pocket of his shirt, and held it out to her. "Federal Express delivered this this morning. It's for you. I didn't know if you were coming back by Whistledown before you took off, so I brought it out."

Alex took it. "Oh. Thank you." She looked down at the envelope in some surprise, and frowned. "It's been opened."

He shrugged. "Sue—the girl who works part-time in the office—said it came with some packages for the farm and she didn't realize who it was addressed to until it was too late. It's from your lawyer, by the way. She says that it's very important that you call her before you head back to Philadelphia."

"You read it!" Alex looked up at him accusingly.

"Yeah, I did. Actually, Sue read it first. That's when she realized it was addressed to you."

"Why would Andrea . . ." Her voice trailed off. Andrea Scoppolone was a close friend who also happened to be her lawyer. Actually, she was one of the phalanx of lawyers who'd been dealing with the estate, a junior one admittedly, but since Alex had known her for years Andrea was the one Alex preferred to speak to whenever possible. "Oh. The phone's out."

"Yep. It was still out when I left, by the way. So if you want to call your lawyer, you'd better do it from here."

"Yes." Alex cast a distracted look over her shoulder. If something was urgent enough for Andrea to send her a FedEx message to call, it couldn't be anything good. "I don't want Neely to overhear."

Joe glanced at the closed bathroom door too, then looked down at her again. "Homer—he owns this place— has a phone in his office I'm sure he'll let you use. Tell your sister we're going to step down to the restaurant for some breakfast."

"Okay." Alex took a deep, steadying breath and let go of the door, crossing to the bathroom and knocking. "Neely, I'm going down to the restaurant with Joe."

"Have fun." Neely's voice came clearly through the thin panel. It was loaded with innuendo, but Alex scarcely noticed.

It was only a few steps from their room to the motel office, which was located inside the restaurant. Joe was greeted by name by two gray-uniformed maids and a burly handyman on the way, and exchanged laughing comments on the weather and other mundane matters.

As they entered the restaurant, warmth and the smell of cooking food greeted them. Sun poured in through the jalousied windows of what had once been a glassed-in sunporch. The wooden counter to Alex's left held an old-fashioned cash register and a clear plastic bowl of wrapped peppermints. On the front of the counter hung a sign that read WELCOME TO THE DIXIE INN. Beside that were smaller stick-on emblems of various credit cards that the restaurant accepted. There was no one behind the counter at the moment, although voices and laughter from the interior rooms indicated that the restaurant had its fair share of patrons.

Joe brought his hand down on a small silver bell on the countertop. The resulting jarring *ding* made Alex wince. However, it had near instantaneous results. A plump, gray-haired woman in a pink uniform appeared.

"Joe!" she said delightedly, hurrying toward them. "Here for breakfast?"

"Maybe in a minute," Joe said easily. "Right now, I'd appreciate it if this lady could use the phone in Homer's office. Ours is out."

"Oh, gosh, still?" The woman looked at Alex expectantly.

"It's a long-distance call. I'll put it on my calling card," Alex said. The woman waved a dismissive hand.

Joe made the introductions. "Alex, meet Mabel Waters. Mabel, Alex Haywood."

"Oh, a Haywood from Whistledown, right? For a minute there, I thought you had yourself a new girl." Mabel grinned at Joe, then looked at Alex again. "Sure, honey, you go ahead and use the phone. Joe'll show you where it is."

"Thanks, Mabel." Joe was already ushering Alex behind the counter through a door that opened into a small, wood-paneled office. Alex noticed nothing but the black telephone on the desk. The more she thought about receiving a FedEx message from Andrea, the more nervous she grew.

It could not mean anything good.

"I'm so glad you got my message!" Andrea exclaimed when Alex got her on the phone. "First off, I heard about Paul! That snake! That louse! That bitch Tara Gould! Are you devastated? Tell me you're not!"

"I'm not," Alex assured her, and it was true. Joe was in the office with her, his shoulders propped against the wall near the closed door while she sat behind the desk. When he had asked if she wanted him to leave while she talked, she had shaken her head. If there was a new crisis, she might need moral support, and despite their current mutual antagonism she knew she could count on him to help her in any way he could. Her glance at him as Andrea mentioned Paul was strictly involuntary. He was a major part of the reason why Paul's defection had ceased to be more than a tiny, fading sting, she knew.

Great sex kind of tended to eclipse the glow of so-so sex, Alex had discovered.

"I'm glad. Alex, I'm sorry, but I've got more bad news."

"I guessed that. What is it now?" Her voice was resigned.

"We were contacted by a source at the newspaper. For the next few weeks they're going to be running a series that they're calling 'The Fall of the House of Haywood.' It's all about your father and his business, and—and what happened to him, and it. Alex, here's the toughest part: they're alleging he bribed public officials in several states to get the necessary permits to do business there. Our informant said that the DA's office is investigating, and we've confirmed that with people we know over there."

"Oh, no!" Alex felt her stomach lurch. "Andrea, it's not true! Is it?"

"I don't know. All I know is that the paper's going with the story, and the DA's office is taking it seriously. Alex, you don't want to be here when this hits the fan. The firm's gotten five calls from reporters just this morning asking for comments, and the story hasn't even been published yet. They'll be going after the human interest angle, too: you know, the billionaire's beautiful daughter, and how she's bearing up, that sort of thing. There are photographers hanging around your father's house, and we've alerted Mercedes, who is already packing up to go spend some time with friends in London. My suggestion to you is this: Why don't you stay where you are for a little while? You're well out of it down there."

Stay at Whistledown? Alex looked at Joe. He was unsmiling as he met her gaze. "For how long, do you think?"

"I don't know. A few weeks? The series starts Wednesday, and we were told that it would run for a week, so I should think that by, say, the first of December you'll be old news. Of course, the DA's investigation is ongoing, but that could last for a while. It'll happen pretty much under the radar unless a grand jury is convened, or charges are filed against someone. Then you'll probably want to lay low again, but that shouldn't happen any time soon."

Three weeks. Three weeks to do—what? Take a break from her real life, maybe. Spend more time coming to terms with her father's loss in the place where he died. Let the gossip about Paul die down. Explore this thing she had going with Joe?

That last was the deciding factor, although she hated to admit it, even to herself. "I guess I could."

"Listen, I hate to keep piling it on, but that brings me to another bit of bad news: If this charge holds up, the estate could be subject to any number of sanctions, including civil or criminal fines."

"Oh, God." Alex glanced up at Joe, who was frowning as he met her gaze. Obviously he had heard enough to understand that the news was not good.

"Well, worst-case scenario, at least you and Neely've still got your trust funds," Andrea said in a bracing tone. "Even if you can't touch them until you turn forty, they're still there and they're secure. And the estate will continue to pay your expenses until it's settled, of course. Oh, by the way, did you give the guy down there notice?"

Funny to think that she had flown out of Philadelphia two days ago to do just that. Alex glanced at *the guy* again. She had thought it would be simple: just walk in, do the dirty deed, walk out again, do what she needed to do at Whistledown, and get on with her life.

What she hadn't counted on was Joe.

"Actually, he's being a little difficult. He says he's got a contract," Alex said, meeting his gaze. His eyes narrowed at her.

"Damn right I'm being difficult," he said, divining the subject of their conversation and straightening away from the wall. "Let me talk to . . ."

Meanwhile, Andrea was saying in her ear. "Oh, God, is he there with you? Well, Mark's in charge of . . ."

"Stop!" Alex said, to Joe, who was moving toward her with the clear intent of taking the receiver from her, and Andrea, who was equally clearly getting ready to impart some information for her to pass on to Joe. "I don't want to be in the middle of this. Joe, you need to talk to Mark Hanigan. Andrea, tell Mark that Joe Welch will be contacting him shortly."

Joe stopped, thrust his hands in the front pockets of his jeans, and looked at her measuringly. Andrea trilled with delight.

"Joe? Is he cute? From the way you talk to him, he must be. . . ."

Alex interrupted before her friend could get going. "Andrea, there's one more thing. When I looked over my father's autopsy report, I don't remember seeing anything about a blood alcohol level. I'm sure I would have noticed if anything like that had been in there. Could you check on that and let me know, please?"

"Sure." Andrea's voice was filled with compassion. She knew that Alex was having a hard time accepting that her father was a suicide. "I'll have somebody get right on it."

"Thanks." Alex smiled, although, of course, Andrea couldn't see. "If there's nothing else, I really have to go. This is a borrowed phone."

"No, that's it. Sorry it had to be bad news. I'll keep checking in. And I'll let you know about the blood alcohol thing as soon as I find out."

They said good-bye, and Alex hung up.

Joe was still standing in the middle of the room looking at her. His eyebrows lifted questioningly.

Alex sighed, her anger at him forgotten under the exigencies of the moment. "The bottom line is, you better start looking for another job."

His expression softened as his gaze swept over her face. "That bad, huh? Come on, let me buy you breakfast and you can tell me what she said."

Twenty-four

✤

Alex, meet Homer Gibson. Homer here is the owner and chief chef, and he cooks up the meanest sausage gravy and biscuits you've ever eaten in your life. If you're thinking eggs, he makes some pretty fair eggs, too. Every bigwig who passes through this area stops in at the Dixie Inn for breakfast."

What Alex was thinking was that she didn't feel like eating anything, much less something as revolting as sausage gravy and biscuits, but she had let Joe talk her into breakfast—he had pointed out with perfect truth that, with the electricity still off, there was nothing fit to eat at Whistledown—and she smiled politely and shook hands as Joe introduced her. Gibson led them to a table in one of the small dining rooms. He was half a head shorter than Joe, bald and stocky, with a florid round face and a beaming smile. A white chef's apron was tied around his middle over a white dress shirt and black pants. Various other diners were scattered throughout the converted house's four downstairs rooms, most of whom could be seen sitting at their respective tables through the open doors that connected one room to another. All of them appeared to know Joe, and either waved or called out to him as he passed.

"Hey, Joe!"

"You all ready for the game Saturday? UK, baby!"

"I saw Eli hit a three four times in practice last week. You tell that boy I said he's gettin' good!"

"Sue got that invoice ready for me yet?"

Joe replied to their greetings and various remarks with answering waves and a laughing word or two, but kept on walking. Alex guessed that, living in a town like this, you learned early on that if you stopped to talk to everyone you knew every time you saw them, you wouldn't have time to do much else.

When they reached their table, a four-top with a clear plastic sheet over a white tablecloth, Homer pulled out her chair and put a menu on the table in front of her. Alex thanked him with a smile and sat down. The table was positioned in front of a large, multi-paned window over-looking a garden area that featured a currently leafless elm and an empty concrete birdbath.

"I heard you were just at Whistledown for the one weekend?" Homer's intonation made it a question. Alex's faint surprise that he knew even that much about her comings and goings must have been apparent in her expression, because Joe chuckled as he sat down opposite her.

"Everybody knows everybody else's business around here," he told her. "Nothing's sacred, believe me."

"Isn't that the truth? We're all the nosiest bunch you'll ever meet," Homer agreed, while Mabel appeared with two glasses of water and stood to one side with her pad and pencil ready, nodding.

"We—my sister and I—will probably be staying a little longer than that, maybe a week or two."

"You're here in the rainy season," Homer said, shaking his head at her. "You really oughta see this place in the spring. Or the summer. The summer's somethin' to see around here, too."

"I've been here in the summer. You're right, it's beautiful." When she'd quarreled with her father. The thought brought a now-familiar ache with it.

"Well, I'll let you all get on with what you came here for. It was nice making your acquaintance, Miss Haywood. Mabel here will take your order when you're ready. Joe, I'm cookin' up that bean soup you like today, and corn bread, if you want to come back for lunch." Homer turned away with a wave, heading toward the back of the house where, presumably, the kitchen was housed.

"Sounds good. I might have to do it, if my electricity doesn't come back on," Joe called after him. "See ya, Homer."

"Want me to give you all a few minutes, Joe?" Mabel asked.

Joe looked inquiringly at Alex. Having scanned the brief menu while Joe and Homer were talking, she was ready to order, and said so.

"I'll have toast and coffee, please."

Joe looked at her like he wanted to comment on her order. He didn't, switching his attention to Mabel instead.

"You want your usual?" she asked.

"Yeah, thanks, Mabel."

Mabel nodded and left.

Joe took a sip of water and looked at Alex. "Want to tell me all about it?"

Alex smiled at him a little wryly. "What are you, my father confessor?"

"Something like that."

She told him the whole story. By the time she was finished, their food had arrived, and Joe was tucking into a breakfast of scrambled eggs and sausages with gravy and hash browns and toast with enthusiasm. She watched him eat with some fascination. He was a big man, but that was a lot of food.

"So they think he bribed some public officials, huh?" he asked.

Alex nodded. The knot in her stomach that had formed on hearing of the latest scandal involving her family was beginning to ease. She didn't know whether to attribute it to the slice of toast and jam she was nibbling, or to the fact that she had shared her troubles with Joe.

She suspected it was the latter.

"You know, whether he did or didn't, it doesn't have anything to do with you."

Alex looked at him in surprise. "Of course it does. He's my father."

He gave her a level look. "He's dead, Alex. You need to start letting him go."

She put down her slice of toast, suddenly no longer even slightly hungry. "Easy for you to say."

"No, it's not easy for me to say. But it's what you need to do. Look at you: you've lost, what, ten pounds since he died? I saw you at the funeral, remember." This was in response to her surprised look. His gaze touched on the still largely intact plate of toast. "You're not eating. Are you sleeping?"

Alex hesitated. Then she admitted, "If I remember to take my sleeping pill."

The look he gave her told her what he thought of that. "Do you think he'd want you to grieve this way? He loved you, remember. He'd want you to be strong, to take care of yourself, to have a good life."

A lump formed in her throat. "I know he would, but . . ."

He met her gaze and apparently realized that he'd said as much as she could stand to hear, because his expression changed from serious to something less intense as he looked down at her plate significantly. "You can start by eating that damned toast. It's been driving me crazy, watching you nibble a crust here and nibble a crust there. Eat a piece, for God's sake."

The lump in her throat receded as Alex looked over at his plate in turn. "If I ate as much as you, I'd get fat."

"Honey, you have a long way to go before you have to worry about getting fat."

Hearing him call her honey in that slow drawl of his brought up all kinds of memories that she didn't want to think about at the moment. Her eyes met his, and she knew from the expression in them that he was remembering the same thing.

"Can I get you all some more coffee, Joe?" Mabel was back, with a pot of coffee. Joe nodded, and she refilled both their cups before leaving.

"How's your head, anyway?"

"Okay. If I take aspirin. The stitches pull a little bit, but there's no real pain."

"When do they come out?"

"Friday. I was going to see my doctor at home, but . . ." Alex's voice trailed off.

"So you'll see a doctor here instead. Carl Allen's good."

"Is he a friend of yours?"

"Yeah."

"Everybody around here is a friend of yours, it seems."

"Hey, I was born here, raised here, went to high school here. I was gone for nine years, then I came back. That was about ten years ago. I've been here ever since. Of course I know everybody."

Alex looked at him curiously. "What did you do in California?"

"Worked as an assistant trainer for a guy named Ted

Gray. Ever heard of him?" Alex shook her head. "Well, he's a big-time trainer. You *should* have heard of him. He was a great guy to learn from."

"So why'd you leave him?"

He smiled just enough to make his crow's-feet apparent. "Remember me telling you that I'd been fired before? Well, he was the guy who fired me."

"Why?" Alex couldn't imagine that Joe would be anything other than an exemplary worker. Even on their admittedly brief acquaintance, she had been impressed by his utter competence. He was hardworking, disciplined, responsible, intelligent, the kind of man upon whom one could completely rely.

Joe grimaced. "We—Gray's team—were at Santa Anita, and an emergency came up for me at home. It was on the eve of the Santa Anita Derby, and we were pretty heavy into prepping about eight horses, sleeping there at the track and everything. When I told Gray I had to go, he said if I left before the race was over he'd fire me. I left, and he sure enough did."

"What was the emergency back home?" Alex was fascinated.

Joe looked at her and hesitated. Alex had the feeling he was debating answering. "Laura—my wife—had taken off and left the kids. Just left 'em alone in the house for more than a day. Eli was four, Josh was two. A friend of Laura's who'd come by looking for her found them, and called me. Laura was nowhere around. I had to go."

"Oh, my God!" Alex was shocked. "Had something happened to her?"

He shook his head. His voice hardened, and his eyes as they met hers levelly were cold with remembered bitterness. "Nope. She wanted to party, is all. Laura always wanted to party. Nothing was ever allowed to stand in the way of that."

"So is that when you divorced her?" Alex remembered Inez telling her that Joe's wife had just up and left him with all three children. But he'd only mentioned there being two at that time.

His expression warmed into a slightly rueful half-smile. "That's when she left me the first time. She was gone for three weeks. After that, she pretty much took off whenever she felt like it, but we didn't actually divorce until after we'd moved back here and Jenny was born."

"Have you only been married once?"

"Once was plenty, believe me."

He sipped at his coffee. "Okay, so let's hear about you: tell me how you became a photographer. Do they teach that in those fancy boarding schools you went to?"

It was obvious that the change of subject was a very deliberate effort on his part to get the focus off his personal life. Alex didn't blame him. That wasn't exactly a heartwarming story to have to tell.

"I told you I took a lot of lessons. When I showed an interest in photography one summer when I was a teenager, Daddy heard about it through the servant grapevine and hired the best professionals he could find to teach me. I've been doing it ever since, and getting paid for it—all right, not much, but something—since I graduated from college." She took a sip of coffee. No matter what Joe said, she couldn't bring herself to eat more toast. She knew it would sit like a brick in her stomach. "What about you? Did you go to college?"

Joe's mouth crooked into a half-smile. "Yep. UK. University of Kentucky."

"Why am I not surprised? What did you major in?"

"Equine management. What about you?"

"Classical studies."

"Oh, now that's practical."

Alex frowned at him. "It's as practical as equine management."

"Hey, I got a job."

"Hey, I didn't have to."

Neely appeared just then, dressed in a denim jacket over a teeny denim mini, and walked toward their table, slipping into a chair.

"You started without me," she said.

"Can I get you something?" Mabel appeared, casting a disapproving glance at the diamond stud in Neely's nose. Joe performed the introductions, and Neely ordered. Alex waited until the waitress was gone before she told Neely the highlights—or rather the lowlights—of her conversation with Andrea.

"Does that mean we really get to stay here a couple more weeks?" Neely asked with enthusiasm when Alex had finished. Alex knew her sister was thinking of Eli, and hoped Joe hadn't realized the same thing. She wasn't sure what Joe would think about Neely "doing"—if indeed she was telling the truth—his son, and she didn't want to find out.

"It means that *I* am going to stay here a few more weeks. We have to get *you* back in school."

Neely looked at her. "I'm not leaving you here all by yourself. If you're staying, I'm staying too."

"Neely, you can't. You *have* to go to school. You can't possibly sit out three weeks or so. You'd have to repeat this entire school year."

Mabel returned with Neely's order. Neely took a bite of the cheese omelet, and glanced at Joe.

"Where does Eli go to school?"

"Right up the road. Shelby County High School."

Neely looked at Alex in triumph. "I could go there."

"For three weeks? Get real."

Neely looked stubborn, and Alex thought, Uh-oh.

"You can't make me go to any school I don't want to go to. If you send me to another boarding school before I'm ready, I'll just run away."

"Neely . . ." Alex felt helpless, and, acutely conscious of Joe as an audience to the exchange, embarrassed as well. The hideous thing about it was, she knew Neely well enough to know that it was no idle threat. Neely was perfectly capable of doing just as she said.

"You're not my mother, Alex. You're just my sister. So don't try to run my life, okay?"

Joe, taking another sip of coffee, looked sardonic.

"Neely!" Alex glared at her sister, more out of mortification that Joe should witness her behavior than true anger because of it. This was vintage Neely all the way, and she had grown pretty much inured to it over the years.

"You're just trying to get rid of me! All my life, that's all anyone's ever wanted to do: get rid of me! Off to boarding school, off to camp, off here, off there, all the time! I'm surprised my mother didn't just have an abortion and be done with it!"

Glaring at Alex, throwing her fork down on her plate with a clatter, Neely sprang up from the table and practically ran from the restaurant.

Mabel and half the patrons in the place turned to watch her go.

Twenty-five

❦

W hen Alex would have gotten up and followed Neely, Joe stopped her with a hand on her wrist.

"Stay put and finish your coffee. If you go running after her when she pulls a stunt like that, you're just teaching her that that's the way to get your attention." Joe's voice was quiet.

"What do you know about it?" Alex felt both sorry for Neely and angry at her too. Sorry because she knew that there was some truth in her sister's accusations about everybody, all her life, trying to be rid of her, and angry for exposing such private family dysfunction to Joe and everyone else in the place.

"I have three kids, remember, two of them teenagers. You pick up a few pointers along the way."

"Oh, yeah? So how would you handle Neely's little outburst, pray tell?"

Joe looked at her thoughtfully. "I'd tell her that if she ever did it again I'd blister her ass until she couldn't sit."

Alex was horrified, and he grinned at her expression. "All right, so I wouldn't really do it. But in her case, I sure as hell would make the threat."

"That might work for you. Unfortunately, I'm not quite as physically intimidating as you are, and I don't think it's going to work for me. Do you have any other suggestions that don't involve violence?"

"Just sit here drinking your coffee. Ignoring undesirable behavior takes longer, but it works in the end." He took another sip of his coffee as if to demonstrate. "By the way, you might want to rethink letting her stay here with you. How comfortable are you going to be living up at Whistledown all alone?"

Alex hadn't thought of that. So far, every time she'd walked inside the house she'd gotten a major case of the creeps.

"I wouldn't keep Neely with me for that reason. That's not fair to her. I'll be fine by myself." She had to suppress a shiver at the thought.

He smiled crookedly at her. "You can always come running down the hill if you get scared."

Their gazes met, and Alex felt the strength of the sexual pull between them. The last time she'd run down the hill to him for help, she'd ended up in his shower, and, later, his bed. If she ever got a chance to do them over again, those experiences would, she thought, end very differently. Next time she wouldn't keep her hands to herself. And neither, she thought, would he.

"Can I get you any more coffee, Joe?" Mabel approached them again, this time carefully not looking at Alex. The deliberate avoidance of eye contact signaled embarrassment, Alex knew, and she once again felt the mortification of Neely's behavior.

"Just the check, Mabel," Joe said. He paid the bill and followed Alex out the door.

Neely was standing beside a public telephone box on the opposite side of the parking lot, her hair glinting gold in the bright sunlight, talking to the burly handyman who'd spoken to Joe earlier. Alex headed toward her. Joe was behind her. This was one time, Alex thought, when she could have done without his presence.

Neely, seeing their approach, scowled. The man turned at her expression and, spotting Joe, waved.

"Hey, Benny."

"Hey, Joe. Is this little lady with you? I thought she might be needing some help."

"I am *not* with him," Neely said icily.

Alex gave an inner groan. The handyman looked alarmed at the signs of imminent discord.

"Uh, sorry, just trying to help. See ya, Joe," he said, and took himself off.

"Who are you calling?" Alex asked with some trepidation. When Neely got in one of her snits, there was no telling what she might do.

"I called Shelby County High School and asked what you had to do to go to school there."

Alex groaned out loud.

"They said all you had to do was live in the district. If Eli does, then I must too."

"Neely . . ." Alex began, feeling helpless.

"If you send me to a school I don't want to go to, I'll just get myself kicked out. And there's nothing you can do to stop me!"

At the expression on Joe's face as he looked at her sister, Alex knew that it was all he could do not to put into practice the recommendation he had made in the restaurant. On the verge of tears now, Neely was glaring at her, Joe was looking from one to the other of them with a disapproving gaze, and finally Alex had had enough.

"Fine!" she snapped, returning her sister's glare. "Just fine! If you want to stay here and go to school, you've got it! And if you end up having to repeat a grade, you can damned well blame yourself! Now get your stuff out of the room, your butt in the car, and let's go get you enrolled in school, okay?"

✛ ✛ ✛ ✛

It was late afternoon by the time Alex got back to Whistledown. She was alone. Joe's blue pickup truck, with Eli at the wheel and a gang of kids inside, had rolled past the driveway heading toward the farmhouse just as Alex and Neely had gotten out of the car. From the window of the truck, Eli had yelled at Neely to come on over. Without so much as a glance at Alex for permission, Neely had sped down the hill. It seemed not to have occurred to Neely that, in the aftermath of her outburst in front of Joe, he might not be exactly eager to welcome her into his home.

They had parted ways at the Dixie Inn. At Alex's request, Joe had shown them where the high school was, driving ahead of them in his car. Then he had gone on about his business, leaving Alex to get Neely enrolled. The process was relatively simple, involving a few phone calls and some faxed papers, and Neely started school tomorrow. To Alex's relief, once at the school her sister had been on her best behavior—she tended to be on good behavior when she got her own way—but Alex still felt drained by the whole unsettling day as she walked inside the house. To have to stay at Whistledown for three weeks—the thought sent a shiver down her spine. The only thing that made the prospect bearable was Joe.

It hadn't been twenty-four hours since he had rocked her world in bed, and already she was anticipating, with great pleasure, getting him there again. Surely he'd put her slip of the tongue behind him by now. He had seemed over it. . . .

The mere act of opening the front door and stepping inside the vast, empty house made her nervous. To her enormous relief, the chandelier in the front hall was ablaze, indicating the electricity was back on at last. Alex left it on as she closed the door behind her, and turned the lights on in every room she passed as well, despite the fact that it was still broad daylight out. There was nothing to be afraid of, she told herself stoutly. Last night had been the result of an unfortunate set of circumstances. Monsoons and power outages and lightning strikes and hard-breathing cats were not likely to occur in conjunction again any time soon.

Speaking of hard-breathing cats, Hannibal, tail twitching, appeared from the direction of the library as she headed toward the kitchen. She was carrying a bag of groceries she had picked up in Shelbyville, and the faint rattle of the brown paper bag might, she thought, have been what had drawn him. She eyed him askance, and gave him a wide berth as she walked through the swinging door. He followed her, his big body amazingly silent as he padded after her on the proverbial little, or in his case big, cat feet.

Could it possibly have been this cat that she had chased into the dark of the upstairs hall two nights ago? Foolish as it made her feel, it seemed the most likely answer.

The preferred answer.

"Go away," she said to Hannibal when she reached the kitchen and he was still behind her. He ignored her, jumping onto the counter and from there to the top of the refrigerator, where he sat and watched as she kicked off her shoes and, in her stockinged feet, started to put the groceries away. His rapt attention made her uncomfortable; she was reminded of Edgar Allan Poe's poem "The Raven," the part where he wrote that the creature *perched upon my chamber door, perched and sat, and nothing more.* Any second now, she expected to hear the odious cat croak *Nevermore*.

For a moment she toyed with the idea of picking him up and bodily removing him from the room, but a long look at the sheer size of him dissuaded her. He was one big feline, and looked as if he could be unpleasant if crossed.

"So, did you get her enrolled?" The voice, seemingly coming out of nowhere, made her jump a foot straight up in the air before she recognized it. She almost dropped the eggs. Recovering, she put the eggs on the appropriate refrigerator shelf and headed toward the small utility room, from whence the voice had seemed to come.

Still in his red flannel shirt and jeans, Joe was in there, hunkered down, doing something that involved plastic-sheathed electrical wiring, a roll of which he seemed to be connecting to the back door.

"What are you doing?" she asked him, crossing her arms over her chest. It was a surprise to find him in the house—apparently he had a key—but a pleasant one. The last bit of her nervousness disappeared.

He glanced over his shoulder at her. "Installing a security system." He picked up the drill that lay beside him and applied it to the doorjamb, raising his voice to be heard over it. "Every window and outside door in the house is hooked into it. This is the last one. You won't have to worry about any real live human being getting in here."

The relief Alex felt upon hearing that was palpable. She realized in that instant that somewhere in the back of her mind she was convinced that a real, live human being was what she had grabbed at in the hall. The feel of the surface underlying the cloth had not been hard and slick, like a wall; it had been warm and resilient, like a human body.

Alex felt a cold chill run down her spine at the memory.

"Joe." He was using the drill again, and she had to raise her voice. He glanced around at her. "Thank you."

His response was a quick grin, and then he was back to using his drill. Alex returned to the kitchen to finish putting up her groceries, the sound of the power tool a comforting background buzz.

She was just putting the last items—plastic bags of prepared salad and fresh mushrooms from the grocery's salad bar—into the refrigerator when he emerged from the utility room.

"Been to the grocery already?" he asked as she closed the refrigerator and began to smooth and fold the brown paper bag.

"We have to eat," she said.

He eyed her. "Can you even cook?" He put his drill and the thick coil of remaining wire down on the counter.

"Of course I can cook." Honesty compelled her to add with the merest glimmer of a smile, "Well, some. Omelets and hard-boiled eggs and tuna salad, things like that."

"I just bet you're great at peanut butter sandwiches, too," Joe said with a straight face.

"You're right, I am."

"You want me to call Inez, and tell her to come in every day while you're here?"

Alex looked at him thoughtfully. "I'm not helpless, you know. I can run a vacuum cleaner and load the dishwasher and dust the furniture. I can even do my own laundry if it really becomes necessary. You know, put the clothes in the machine, add detergent, close the lid, turn it on?"

Joe laughed. "Was I being insulting again? Sorry. I don't have a clue how billionaires' daughters live."

"In the real world, just like everybody else," Alex said, her smile a little whimsical. With amusement lighting up his eyes and a grin playing around his mouth, he was so handsome that just looking at him was a pleasure. He was standing near the barstools, and vivid memories of him sitting on one as they kissed flashed into her head. She had taken off her top for him. . . .

She had three weeks to while away, before returning to her real life again. Three weeks that she could spend with Joe.

There was no point in wasting a single, precious day.

She put the bag that she had smoothed down on the countertop and moved toward him.

"Joe," she said, stopping right in front of him and smiling up into his eyes. "I really, really appreciate you putting in that security system for me. It's going to make all the difference in the world about how safe I feel here."

"It's not going to help in the case of cats or ghosts," he warned, looking down at her with a smile of his own and darkening eyes.

"Cats or ghosts I can handle. Real, live burglars are what give me heart palpitations. Thank you." Placing a hand flat on his flannel-covered chest, she rose up on tiptoe to press a quick, soft kiss to his mouth. He let her kiss him. His lips hardened and parted beneath hers and his eyes flamed. But when she pulled her mouth from his and sank down flat-footed again he made no move to prolong the kiss or pull her back into his arms.

"My pleasure," he said.

Clearly he was still smarting from her having called him by the wrong name. Well, if she could forgive and forget the insulting things he had said to her afterward he could forgive and forget that. In fact, she meant to make sure that he did.

"I also appreciate you bringing that message from Andrea over to the inn this morning. So thank you again." Her hands moved to his shoulders as she rose up to kiss his mouth.

This time she put a little tongue into it, and this time

his hands came up to grip her waist and she had the pleasure of being—almost—kissed back. A tilt of his head, a
quick, hard pressure of his lips, a glide of his tongue, and
then he was lifting his head, breaking off contact.

She smiled to herself, and sank down again.

"No problem." His voice sounded just a little thick, and
his fingers bit into her waist. She kept her hands where
they were, resting on his wide shoulders, smiled into his
eyes, and leaned forward, so that her breasts just brushed
his chest.

"And you were kind to listen to my problems this
morning. I know this whole thing has created problems
for you, too. So thank you for that."

This time, when she rose up on her tiptoes, she slid her
arms around his neck and kissed him with all the slow,
sweet provocation of which she was capable.

Twenty-six

✤

For just a moment he remained basically unresponsive, letting her kiss him, making her do all the work. Then he made a slight, harsh sound, and suddenly he was kissing her back as if he were ravenous for the taste of her mouth, as if he could never get enough of it. His mouth slanted over hers, hot and wet and demanding, and his arms wrapped around to pull her tightly against him. He was already hard, and Alex's heart began to pound at the realization. She wanted him. . . .

He turned with her in what was almost a dance step so that the small of her back was pressed against the unyielding edge of the center island counter, and then his hands were on her bottom, cupping it, stroking over it, squeezing it, kneading the round cheeks. She moaned, clinging to him, pressing her swelling breasts against the solid wall of his chest, remembering how he had kissed her bottom before. . . .

He lifted her, sitting her down again on the countertop as his hands slid down the backs of her thighs and he parted her legs and positioned himself between them. A hot, deep longing sprang up inside her as he pressed the steely bulge in his jeans against the apex of her spread thighs. She was on fire for him already, wet for him already. The question swirled clear as crystal through her sex-befuddled mind: What was there about this man that made her so needy for him, so greedy for him?

"Joe." She moaned his name into his mouth—no possible way could she ever mistake him for anyone else again, because nobody else had ever, ever, made her feel like this—and started to wrap her legs around his waist.

She wanted him to take her, right here, right now, with her sitting on the kitchen counter under the bright fluorescent light. She wanted him naked and loving her until she was wild with it, mindless with it, crying out for it. . . .

Begging for it.

God, she wanted him.

He broke off the kiss without warning, pulling his mouth from hers, his hands moving around behind his back to clamp on her ankles before she could lock them around his waist, opening her legs, stepping back away from her. He caught her wrists, pulling her arms down from around his neck, and held them for a minute while his eyes, which were narrowed and glittering with passion, locked on to hers and his breath came in short, harsh bursts.

"Joe!" she protested. His hands tightened around her wrists, his eyes blazed, and for a moment she thought he was coming back to her. But then he let go of her altogether, stepping back out of her reach, leaning back against the cabinets behind him while his eyes burned over her and his mouth clamped into a hard, straight line.

"Joe," she said again, holding out her arms to him.

"Alex." His voice was rough-edged, guttural. He ran his fingers quickly through his short black hair as if in frustration, then closed his hands around the edge of the counter against which he leaned, his fingers tightening until his knuckles showed white. "Alex. Look. You're a beautiful, sexy woman. I want you so bad right now that I'm hurting with it. But I'll be damned if I'm going to provide you with three weeks' worth of stud service to help you work your ex-boyfriend out of your system."

Alex's mouth fell open. She didn't believe what she was hearing. "What?"

"You heard me."

"That's ludicrous." She was still sitting on the counter; she pulled her knees up to her chest, wrapping her arms around them, and stared at him over them. "This has nothing to do with Paul!"

"Honey, it has everything to do with Paul. You're on the rebound right now and you're looking for something to assuage the pain. I know. I've been there. Sleeping around after a bad breakup is a natural instinct, I think. But I don't feel like being the cure for your disease."

"Joe. . . ." Alex stopped short as it occurred to her that she was, literally, pleading with this man to make love to her. Where was her pride? With every other man she'd ever known, she had been the object of desire, the one to be chased and cajoled and persuaded, if possible, into a date, a relationship, bed. Even Paul had had to work hard to get her. He'd courted her with flowers and dinner dates and funny messages and phone calls. . . .

With Joe, much as it embarrassed her to realize it, she'd done all the chasing. Every single bit.

The realization stopped her cold. Her backbone stiffened, her chin came up, and her dignity returned.

"You may be right," she said coolly. "Of course, you may be wrong, too. We'll never know, though, because it'll be a cold day in a hot place before I sleep with you again."

Mouth compressing, eyes hard, he looked at her silently for a moment. Then he straightened away from the counter and picked up his drill.

"The code number for the security system is the same as the first four digits of the phone number: three-seven-three-oh. The box is in the utility room. Make sure you turn it on before you go to bed. Want me to show you how to operate it?"

Alex shook her head. Pride kept her chin up. Anger made her eyes sparkle.

"I know how to operate a security system."

"All right then. If you need anything, call me down at the house. I'll be up here before you've hung up the phone."

➤✦➤✦

Neely returned just about the time Alex was starting to think that she was going to have to call down to Joe's house to request that she come home. Security system or not, the thought of being alone in the house after dark spooked her, and the sun was beginning to set. Loath to do that—the very idea of having to do it made her mad—she was relieved when Neely came banging in through the back door just as the last orange rays of the sunset sank behind the horizon. As Alex was standing in the kitchen in front of the open refrigerator door contemplating which of its contents could best be made into a meal—cooking was emphatically not her strong suit, and she couldn't summon up the tiniest pang of hunger anyway—she had only to turn her head to witness her sister's entrance via the utility room.

"Alex, I'm back!" Neely yelled, then with her next breath started talking a mile a minute over her shoulder to Eli and two other teens, a boy and a girl, who followed her into the kitchen. Seeing Eli made Alex instantly think of Joe, and thinking of Joe was not what she wanted to do at the moment. Or any other moment for as long as she lived, for that matter.

"Hi, Miss Haywood," Eli offered, glancing at her over Neely's head.

There was no point in taking her anger at the father out on the son. Alex summoned a smile as she closed the refrigerator door.

"Hi, Eli," she said, adding, "You can call me Alex, you know. I'm not that old."

His crooked answering grin reminded her so much of Joe's that it was all Alex could do not to turn away.

"Yeah, well, Dad's a stickler on manners," he said. "He'd get mad if I called you Alex."

"If he gets mad, tell him . . ." Alex's voice was silky, and it was all she could do to change what she had been going to say to the mild, ". . . that I said you could."

"Eli's going to drive me to school," Neely said. Alex got her first good look at her sister as she moved into the middle of the kitchen, and her eyes widened. Quarter-sized splotches of dried mud covered Neely from head to toe. Her hair, teased by the wind into massive disorder, stood up around her head like the seeds of a blond dandelion. More mud, so thick it obscured the leather, caked her thick-soled sneakers. The teens with her were in no better shape. At least, Alex thought, the brick floor was easy to clean.

"Good God, what have you been doing? Making mud pies?"

Neely flashed her a withering look.

"Riding ATVs." Eli's voice sounded like Joe's too.

"It was great," Neely said. "We went through the creek. Oh, yeah, this is Heather Isaacson and David Saunders."

"Hi," Alex said. They echoed the greeting.

"Oh, cool, a cat. Where'd it come from?" Having spied

Hannibal, who was on the floor lapping milk that Alex had been cozened into pouring for him from a bowl, Neely dropped to her knees and ran a hand down his furry spine. Hannibal responded by arching his back appreciatively even while continuing to inhale the milk.

"His name's Hannibal. Apparently he lives here," Alex replied, then turned her attention to Neely's companions. One thing she had learned was that it was better to know Neely's friends than not to know them. She was subject to fewer surprises that way. "Do you go to Shelby County High?"

"Yeah."

Alex engaged them in small talk for a minute. It seemed that the trio were just dropping Neely off prior to going home themselves.

"See you at school tomorrow," Heather said sweetly to Neely as they prepared to leave, and linked her arm rather ostentatiously with Eli's. Eli immediately looked self-conscious, and he never so much as glanced down at the girl on his arm. Of course, Alex remembered now. Hadn't a Heather been mentioned in the context of Eli's girlfriend? This must be she. Clearly she was staking her claim for Neely to see.

However, Neely seemed to be taking her existence in stride, Alex was relieved to discover.

"Yeah, see you there," Neely said, and smiled.

The visitors headed for the door.

"Oh, Dad said to give you this." Apparently just remembering, Eli turned back to Alex and handed her the plastic grocery bag that he carried in one hand. "It's your clothes and things from the other night, and one of the long-range walkie-talkies we use to keep in touch when we're working on the farm. Dad said to tell you that if you take it upstairs with you, you can contact him anytime during the night, just like an intercom. If you should need to, that is. Even if the phones go out."

"Thanks, Eli." Alex smiled at the boy, accepted the bag without looking inside it, and set it on the nearest counter-top with something of a thump. She would be calling Joe over an intercom approximately as soon as she would be sleeping with him again, which was to say, never. Eli gave her a heartbreakingly beautiful smile in return—shades of Joe again—and turned back to his friends, lifting a hand in farewell as he did so.

"Yo, Neely. Pick you up at seven-twenty. Good-bye, Miss Haywood. I mean Alex."

"Is he the most gorgeous thing you've ever seen, or what?" Neely demanded rapturously of Alex after her friends were gone.

Not quite was Alex's immediate mental response, which made her mad, because the exception she'd been thinking of was Joe, of course.

"You know, I kind of think Eli might already have a girl-friend," Alex pointed out without directly replying.

"You mean Heather?" Neely opened the refrigerator and grabbed a can of Diet Coke. "I'm not worried about her. She's a virgin. She doesn't put out."

"Neely . . ." Alex was horrified. "You're only fifteen. Eli's not much older. You're not really doing anything with him, are you? Truth?"

Neely laughed as she popped the top on the can. "When you tell me the truth about Daddy Studmuffin, I'll tell you the truth about Eli. I've got to go wash some of this mud off. I'll be back."

Alex wasn't sure how Joe felt about his teenage son hav-ing sex in general, but she certainly didn't want to be around if he should discover Eli having sex with Neely.

"Oh, by the way," Neely's voice floated back to her

from the powder room. "I'm thinking about having my tongue pierced. I've heard that you can give incredible blow jobs if you've got one of those metal studs in your tongue."

Alex shuddered inwardly. Then, knowing—hoping?— Neely had said that last just to be shocking, she didn't reply.

Ignore, Joe had said. Ignore, ignore.

It was full dark outside by this time, with the soft purple light of a late fall twilight having faded away, and in contrast the kitchen was brightly warm and brightly lit. With Hannibal stretched out purring on a kitchen counter—Alex had tried without success to shoo him down, but she was more intimidated by him than he was by her—the scene was warmly domestic. When Neely returned to the kitchen, Alex headed off all conversation about Eli and tongue studs by asking her what she wanted for supper.

"We can have tuna sandwiches, or I can make an omelet," she added.

"Your omelets suck," Neely said succinctly, perching on a barstool and resting her chin in her hand. Traitorously rewarding Hannibal for his insubordination, she began to stroke his fur. "Why don't we just order pizza?"

"They have pizza delivery way out here?" Surprised, Alex looked around from the refrigerator, the contents of which she was once again perusing, and took a moment to scowl at the smug-looking cat who seemed to be smiling at her before switching her attention back to Neely. "What makes you think so?"

"Eli said that's what they're having for dinner. He said his dad's grumpy, and doesn't feel like cooking tonight."

So Joe was grumpy, was he? That was an interesting bit of news.

"Pizza it is, then." Closing the refrigerator door, Alex found a phone book and, after a little difficulty locating the proper store, managed to order food. When she put down the phone, Neely was looking at her pensively, one hand resting on Hannibal's fur, the other propping her chin.

Twenty-seven

✦

W hat?" Alex asked, knowing that look of Neely's of old.

"Alex, do you think Daddy felt anything? I mean, when he shot himself? Do you think it hurt?"

Alex winced, and her stomach started to knot. "Oh, God, Neely. I don't know. I don't think so. It would have been so fast. Instantaneous, almost."

"The night he died I had this weird dream."

"What kind of dream?"

"I dreamed he called me on the phone at school and told me he loved me. I couldn't see him, but I could hear his voice on the phone. It was so real, Alex, that when they woke me up and told me he was dead I didn't believe them at first. I said he couldn't be dead, because I'd just been talking to him on the phone."

Alex stared at her sister as an icy finger ran down her spine. When she spoke, the words came slowly. "I had a dream about him calling me on the phone, too. When we were at Joe's house the other night. Only I couldn't understand what he was trying to say."

For a moment they simply looked at each other.

"You want to know the really weird thing?" Neely asked.

Alex wasn't sure she did. She could feel the knot of grief forming in her stomach again. "What?"

"The next night, after he died, after I'd flown home, the phone in my room kept ringing all night long. For real, I mean. I wasn't asleep. I'd pick it up, and there'd be no one there. Just this kind of echoing silence. It must have happened four or five times. I finally took the phone off the hook, but I never did go to sleep."

"It was probably a crank caller," Alex managed. "Someone who knew Daddy had died."

"Or do you think maybe he's trying to contact us?" Neely asked in a small voice. "Like from beyond the grave?"

Alex could feel goose bumps rising on her skin.

"Oh, Neely, you watch too many horror movies," she said with some asperity, trying to shake off the disturbing image. She had wondered that, too, but of course the dreams that they were both having were probably some standard manifestation of grief, and not a netherworldly version of *Contact*. Joe said he had had them too. . . .

Alex told Neely that, trying her best to sound calmly rational, and leaving out the part about Joe.

"The thing is," Neely said, clearly not fully convinced by Alex's careful explanation, "that if Daddy were going to call me right after he died like that, that might be the reason. To tell me he loved me, I mean. He never once said it while he was alive."

At the look on her sister's face, Alex's heart broke for her. Here, of course, was the explanation for all Neely's bad behavior. Her sister had lacked a parent's love.

"He did love you," Alex said. "He just wasn't good at showing it, that's all."

"He showed you." Neely's voice was suddenly stark. "It was never any secret that he thought you were God's gift to the universe. It was always Alex this and Alex that. He never even wanted me around."

"Neely. . . ." Alex was appalled. Neely's words were the exact truth, but all these years she had hoped that somehow her sister hadn't noticed.

"Oh, don't worry, I don't blame you," Neely said, sounding suddenly bored as she slid off the barstool. "You're wonderful, everybody knows that. Not to change the subject, but what do you think I ought to wear to school tomorrow? I didn't bring much with me: we'll have to get the gorgon to send my clothes."

"Neely, you're wonderful, too," Alex said fiercely, ignoring the blatant attempt to change the subject.

"Yeah, yeah," Neely said with a dismissive wave, already on her way out of the room.

Staring after her sister, Alex felt the sudden prick of tears sting her eyes. She had loved her father, but there was no denying that he had been a neglectful parent, and his total lack of interest in his younger daughter had obviously hurt Neely deeply. In a physical sense, he had never been there for Alex, either, but, as she had gotten older at least, she had known that he loved her.

Her impulse was to go after Neely and talk this thing through, but she knew her sister: for her, for now, the conversation was over. She'd revealed as much of her heart as she could bear to reveal.

At that moment the doorbell rang. Glad of a diversion, Alex went to answer it, Hannibal trailing at her heels. It was the pizza. Alex paid, and carried the warm, fragrant box into the den, which was the coziest room downstairs and, in addition, boasted a large-screen TV. They watched TV as they ate, or at least Neely ate and Alex nibbled, and the subject of their father didn't come up again.

They stayed up late, and Alex realized, without either of

them saying a word about it, that they were both trying to avoid going upstairs to bed for as long as they could. Finally they could put it off no longer. The eleven o'clock newscast signed off, and they were both so tired that they were yawning.

"Did you figure out what you're going to wear tomorrow?" Alex asked, trying for a light note as they climbed the stairs. Neely was carrying Hannibal in her arms, obviously intending to sleep with the cat. Alex was envious. At least her sister wouldn't have to go to bed in this spooky old house all alone.

Neely shrugged. "Jeans, I guess. With my tie-dyed purple T-shirt and my jean jacket. I thought I might take the diamond out of my nose and replace it with one of those long purple feather earrings I usually wear with the purple top. What do you think? Fashion statement or fashion victim?"

Alex almost shuddered at the idea of Neely going to a new, small-town, public high school with a purple feather dangling from her nose.

"Fashion victim," she said. Then, tentatively, as they reached the upstairs hall, "Are you nervous about starting a new school tomorrow?"

Neely shook her head. "I know a couple of the kids now, and I'm friends with the hottest guy in school, so it should be okay."

"How do you know Eli's the hottest guy in school?" Alex asked, having no difficulty figuring out who Neely meant.

Neely grinned wickedly. "Heather told me so, while we were watching the guys ride ATVs. Hey, he's star of the basketball team and the cutest guy in school. She also told me that he is strictly her property, so I should just keep my horny little hands off. I think she and I are going to be best friends—*not.*"

"Oh, Neely," Alex said, half amused, half despairing. The image of the two girls resorting to smiling, backstabbing warfare over Eli was almost funny. Poor kid, did he have any idea what he was in for?

"Night," Neely said, and went into her room, closing the door. Alex heard the click of the deadbolt, and realized that, whether she showed it or not, Neely was nervous about going to sleep tonight too.

Oh, God, Alex thought as she walked on toward her bedroom, if only she were at home in Philadelphia, in her own distinctly nonthreatening brick town house, getting ready to climb into her own comfortable bed! But of course, she reminded herself, if she were back in Philadelphia, she would be alone. Paul, with whom she had shared the house, lived elsewhere now; and Neely would be off again in boarding school. Her friends might visit, and even stay a night or two if they thought she needed comforting, but they all had lives of their own, and problems of their own. There might be reporters outside, maybe photographers too, if what Andrea had told her was accurate.

And there would not be an arrogant, infuriating, impossibly sexy man living down the hill.

But she refused to think of Joe.

When she imagined going home to Philadelphia, she was picturing the home that had existed six weeks ago, before her father's death, before Paul's defection, she reminded herself. A quiet, serene home that she had purchased just last year, where she had been happy, going out to lunch with friends, developing her pictures, and spending the evenings and nights with Paul.

That home was gone forever. It was in the past. When she went back to Philadelphia, the house would still be there, but the life she had lived in it would be utterly changed. Her father was gone, and Paul was gone. The money was gone. She was left, and she would have to build a whole new life for herself out of the broken pieces of the old.

In the meantime, she was here at Whistledown, for good or for ill.

On that thought, Alex entered her bedroom and looked around with some trepidation. She had checked it that afternoon while waiting for Neely to get home, having remembered that the last time she'd been in the room the bed had been left in something of a mess. But to her surprise, the bed had been neatly made. She could only conclude that Joe had remembered and had erased the evidence of their encounter after she and Neely had gone to the Dixie Inn. Earlier, when she'd entered the room in broad daylight, thoughts of Joe and the things they had done together on her bed had superseded all else.

Now, however, it was different. The hushed silence of the house seemed almost—portentous. Thoughts that seemed foolish by daylight did not seem so impossible now that the sky outside was inky black, and stars blinked down at her through the parted curtains. On either side of the bed was a long, many-paned window with glass so old that it distorted images seen through it, so that the stars and moon took on a watery indistinctness that made them seem as ominously foreboding as the house. Alex crossed the room quickly, pulling the curtains closed to shut them out

Oh, God, she was afraid. She acknowledged that to herself, hoping that naming the emotion would help her to let it go. But she still couldn't get the memory of waking to the sound of breathing out of her head. Thank God for the security system, she thought—and her sleeping pills. . . .

Taking one, she washed it down with water from the sink in her bathroom, then took a shower and brushed her teeth. Putting on her nightgown, she came back into the bedroom, pulled back the covers to reveal fresh sheets, and prepared to climb into bed.

She almost wished she had the thrice-damned cat. At least Neely wasn't alone.

Of course, if she had her druthers, she would rather have Joe. . . .

It was then that she remembered the walkie-talkie. She had left it, along with the bag of her belongings, on the kitchen counter. The idea of traipsing back through the dark, deserted house was not appealing, but the idea of having something happen in the night again and being unable to summon help was even less so.

Alex took a deep breath, and, turning on lights as she went, headed back downstairs. When she reached the kitchen, she practically snatched the bag off the counter and scurried back to her room, leaving the lights on behind her. It was ridiculous, she knew, but the house felt safer to her when the lights were on. When they were off, the darkness seemed to breathe. . . .

Alex shuddered at the thought. Reaching her bedroom, locking the door securely behind her, she reminded herself that tonight there was an activated security system and a locked bedroom door between her and anyone who might wish to harm her. The house was well lit. Her room was bathed in a warm yellow glow from the small twin brass lamps on either side of the bed.

Putting the plastic bag down on the dresser, she delved inside, beneath the fuzzy blanket and the silk of her nightgown, both of which had been laundered, for the walkie-talkie, which rested in one of her (cleaned) shoes. Picking it up, she examined it. It was a little bigger than her hand and made of bright yellow plastic with rounded corners.

As she turned it over static crackled from it suddenly, and an irate voice spoke.

"Alex?" Joe's voice was so distinct and unexpected that she jumped.

"Joe?"

"You got a problem up there?"

Alex stared at the toylike object in her hand. "N-no. Why would you think that?"

"The house is lit up like a damned Christmas tree. It was almost completely dark a few minutes ago."

"How do you know?"

"I can see it through the window."

"You can?" The thought was both unsettling and reassuring.

"Yep. So what gives?"

"I went downstairs to get something, and I turned on the lights."

"You downstairs now?"

"No, I'm back upstairs." Too late, Alex realized that she could have lied. He couldn't see *her,* after all.

"You left the lights on."

"I know."

"Oh." There was a pause. "You scared?"

"No," she lied without hesitation this time.

He chuckled. Alex made a face at the walkie-talkie.

"You remember to turn the security system on?"

Duh, Alex almost said. Like she would forget something like that. Instead she very carelessly replied, "Yes."

"You got the house all locked up?"

Duh again. "Yes."

"Then you're as safe as the gold in Fort Knox."

Alex was glad he thought so. Too bad she didn't feel that way.

"How does this thing work, anyway?" she asked, turning the walkie-talkie over again.

"It's simple. I've got my unit on. You turn your unit on, and you can talk to me. You don't have to do anything else. If you need me, just sing out."

"Where *are* you?"

"In bed. Trying to sleep. The unit's beside my bed. That's so I can hear you in the night."

Alex began to smile. "Like a baby monitor."

"You got it."

"And I'm the baby."

"You said it, Princess, not me. You gonna leave the lights on all night?"

"Why do you ask?"

"So that the next time I look out the window, I'll know what to look for. Dark house, I check on you. Lit house, I don't. Or vice versa."

"I'm leaving the lights on." Alex was almost embarrassed to admit it, but he had a point. Lights were another good signaling device.

Joe chuckled again. "It's your electric bill. Well, if you don't need me for anything, I'm going to sleep. Good night."

"Good night," Alex said softly. Then she set the walkie-talkie down on the bedside table and climbed into bed, snuggling in beneath the covers—and leaving on the light. The pill was starting to take effect, she realized, because she was beginning to feel drowsy. In a few more minutes, she knew from experience, she would be asleep.

The wonderful thing was, she realized, she no longer felt afraid. Being able to talk to Joe over the walkie-talkie was almost as good as having him in the room with her.

Almost, but not quite.

"Joe?" She basically just wanted to make sure the thing still worked in its new position.

"Hmmm?"

"Nothing. G'night."

"Good night."

She felt surprisingly safe, and warm—and groggy. Her lids drooped, then closed. Only as she was falling asleep did she remember that she was angry at him. Really angry. Never-darken-my-door-again angry.

Oh, well, she thought. She could be angry again in the daylight. All hostilities were suspended for the night.

Twenty-eight

✤

That's it, Joe thought, flopping onto his stomach and putting his pillow over his head, pressing the soft sides down against his ears with both arms. No way was he going to be able to sleep now.

He could hear the little sounds she made as she slept.

The soft inhalations of her breathing. The rustle of the bedclothes when she moved. And, just seconds ago, a tiny moan.

Man had never before invented such torture. And to think he'd done it to himself.

Who would have guessed?

The sad thing was, he was hard as a brick, horny as a goat, hot as a jalapeño pepper—and he didn't have to be. In the kitchen, she'd been all over him. God, she'd felt so damned good—too good. Like she belonged in his arms. A perfect fit, custom-made.

The kind of lady-in-the-living-room, whore-in-the-bedroom woman he'd been looking for for most of his life.

It was precisely this thought, which had occurred just as she'd started to wrap her beautiful long legs around his waist, that had made him pull back.

Spend three weeks bedding her, and he wasn't going

to be able to let her go. He knew that as well as he knew the sun would come up in the morning.

Only she would go. Her life was elsewhere, and his was here.

She'd be cured of her disease, but he might never get over his.

She sighed, long and deep. The sound was as audible as if she were lying beside him. His reaction was instant and excruciating.

Jesus, this was sad. Sadder than a teenager in the throes of first love. Sadder than Eli on the phone till all hours with this Heather girl.

He, a grown man of thirty-seven, had a boner the size of the Washington monument just from listening to a woman breathe.

That was it. All over. If he lay here listening to her any longer, he was going to forget every intelligent piece of advice he'd ever given himself, climb the hill, use his key, turn off the blasted security system, and crawl into her bed.

She would welcome him, he knew.

The thought of the welcome he would receive made him grit his teeth. He swung his legs over the side of the bed and stood up. Of course, standing up he could see, through the window with the curtains he'd deliberately left open, the bright blaze that was Whistledown up the hill.

She'd said she wasn't scared.

Yeah, right. Just like he wasn't horny.

He was 99.9 percent sure that she was as safe in that house as he was in his own. The security system was designed to take care of the one-tenth of one percent of doubt that he had left.

Grabbing his jeans from the chair where he had left

them, he put them on and headed for the kitchen. Without bothering to turn on the light, he poured himself a glass of milk and stood, leaning against the counter in the dark, drinking it. Milk was supposed to promote sleep, he had heard.

Alex had told him that she was taking sleeping pills.

No wonder she had gone out like a light. He only wished he could.

He took a last gulp of milk, set the glass down on the counter—and heard the unmistakable sound of a key being inserted into his back door.

It was a soft, stealthy sound. The click of the lock yielding was a little louder, but not much. Then the door opened.

Joe leaned against the counter, crossed his arms over his chest, and waited.

Unlike Alex, he wasn't worried about a burglar. There just wasn't that kind of crime in Paradise County. He had a pretty good idea of exactly who was going to be sneaking into his kitchen in the middle of the night.

The kitchen door closed as carefully as it had opened. The lock clicked. Joe reached out a long arm and flipped a switch.

Eli stood blinking at him in the sudden burst of bright light like a deer caught in the headlights.

"Well, hello, son," Joe said amiably, noting at a glance that Eli was fully dressed in jeans, sneakers, and a zipped-up army jacket. This was not a kid who had just stepped out on the back porch for a breath of air. The last time Joe had seen him, about two hours previously, he'd been wearing jockeys and a T-shirt as he walked from the bathroom to his bedroom.

"Hey, Dad." If the guilty half-smile that accompanied

that was any indication, Eli had definitely been up to no good.

"Mind telling me where you've been?"

Eli shrugged, and started unzipping his coat. "Out."

"You know, I kind of guessed that. Out where?"

Eli's eyes met his. "Just out."

For Eli, that was outright defiance. Joe straightened away from the counter and walked toward the boy. His son watched him warily. The unzipped coat hung from surprisingly broad shoulders, and Joe realized with a pang that in a few more years the kid would be as big as he was.

When he got close enough, Joe inhaled. Nothing too obvious, but a good, long drawing-in of breath.

Eli's eyes narrowed at him. "I haven't been drinking, if that's what you're smelling me for," he said. "And I haven't been doing drugs, either."

"Fair enough," Joe said, relaxing a little. Eli stood only a couple of feet away from him, glowering at him now, a little sullen. Joe almost smiled at him before he could stop himself. There were only three things that could draw a sixteen-year-old boy from his bed in the middle of the night. The first two had just been ruled out.

And he would have heard a car coming back in the driveway, so the identity of Eli's partner in crime was pretty much a given, too.

"Did you go in or did she come out?" he asked pleasantly.

Eli's eyes widened on his face. "Who?"

"Come off it, kid," Joe said, sitting on the corner of the kitchen table and giving Eli a derisive look. "You know very well who. Neely Haywood."

At the expression on Eli's face Joe almost smiled again. Astonishment was written there plain as anything. If he'd said *how'd you know* out loud he couldn't have made it any clearer.

"She came out." The admission was grudging. At Joe's assessing look, Eli blushed all the way up to his hairline and started taking off his coat to give him an excuse to look somewhere else.

"All we did was talk," Eli said defensively.

Joe almost said *yeah, right* but didn't.

"She says you're sleeping with her sister."

Talk about a good offense being the best defense. Joe had to fight to keep his face impassive. His sex life was not something he meant to discuss with his son.

"You've got a ten o'clock curfew on school nights." The offense thing worked both ways.

Eli looked pained. A curfew violation was pretty generally cause for a grounding. "C'mon, Dad. I just went up the hill."

Joe looked at him for a minute. "All right. Go to bed. Don't go creeping out of the house in the middle of the night again, understand? Next time I catch you at it, I *will* ground you."

"Yeah, okay." Eli looked relieved. Hanging his coat up on the coatrack, he headed for the kitchen door. Then he looked over his shoulder at Joe, who was putting the milk away, and grinned.

"Hey, Dad, about Miss Haywood: She's totally hot. Way to go," he said cheekily, and disappeared into the hall before Joe could reply.

Joe had unkind thoughts about Neely all the way back upstairs. Entering his bedroom, he glanced out the window at Whistledown: still ablaze. Had the spoiled little witch remembered to turn the security system back on? he wondered. There was no way to check. Telling Alex that her menace of a sister was creeping around outside at night was probably a waste of time, because it was clear that Alex had no control over her whatsoever, but he would tell her anyway. As for Eli, he'd had a talk with him about safe sex years ago. Other than that, and the curfew violation, he wasn't too concerned. The boy was almost seventeen, after all.

Joe took off his jeans, dropped into bed, and cocked an ear at the monitor. Alex was up, moving around. He could hear the soft footfalls as she crossed the floor, then the slight creak of an opening door. Must be going to the bathroom, he thought as he turned onto his stomach and kicked the bottom of his covers free of the mattress in an effort to get comfortable. A moment later he heard her sigh, and he realized that she was back in bed.

The sound of her breathing filled the room.

He almost said something to her, but then realized that starting a conversation with her now was probably not the smartest move he could make. If she said something on the order of *come up and see me sometime* he was liable to take her up on it.

Besides, she sounded like she was already asleep again. The tenor of her breathing had totally changed.

It was soft and even, just like it had been when he'd been listening to her before.

And he was responding in exactly the same way.

Here we go again, Joe thought. He rolled onto his back, threw his pillow on the floor, linked his hands behind his head and stared up at the ceiling in frustration. If he was as pragmatic as he liked to imagine, he would just reach over and turn the damned unit off. End of problem. Hel-*lo* Mr. Sandman. But he couldn't do that either. Because she might wake up and be scared. Because she might call out his name. Because she was trusting him to be there for her. And he was going to come through.

Coming through was, he thought glumly, one of his specialties. He'd been coming through for people all his life.

Much good had it ever done him.

Twenty-nine

✦

The night belonged to the predator. In the natural order of things, it always had, and it always would. Owls hunted over moonlit fields, soaring silently on great outstretched wings, dropping without warning to snatch up unwary mice as they scampered about their business. Coyotes roamed the dark wooded bottomland down by the creek, trotting along until they came upon a calf or a goat or a young deer unprotected, and then accelerating with fierce howls of pleasure to bring down the hapless victim.

Like God, predators giveth, and predators taketh away, he mused. They decided which creatures lived and which creatures died. They chose among potential victims, picking the ones that would provide the sustenance they needed while still keeping in mind their own vulnerabilities. It would never do for a predator to choose as prey one who might endanger him.

Taking Alexandra Haywood would endanger him. The predator reminded himself of that quite forcefully as he stood in her bedroom, his gaze sliding over her sleeping form. She was beautiful, so blond and fresh, and tonight she'd left the lights on, so he had a wonderful view of her from her silvery hair to the teeny, curling vulnerability of her smallest toes.

He'd pulled the covers down, gently, so gently, to get a better look.

She lay on her stomach, her arms beneath her pillow, her face turned toward the nightstand. Her hair trailed away from her like a platinum banner, bright against the soft blue sheet. Her body was veiled by a nightgown, a pretty floral on a white background, of some shiny soft material that looked like silk. It was rucked up around her thighs. One long, slender leg was bent at the knee, curving across the mattress. The other was quite straight.

Her ass was small but shapely, and would be, he thought, firm to the touch.

But he had not come here tonight to touch. He was, in effect, a window-shopper. Look but don't buy. Not tonight.

He knew what was concealed from him, and knowing made just looking more exciting and harder at the same time. Watching her last night as she had gotten naked for him had given him a gnawing hunger for her. The sister had been cute, but this one was succulent. He had a gnawing hunger to taste her flesh.

But he couldn't, he reminded himself. No, no. Bad boy.

If he took her tonight, they would be looking for her tomorrow. The search would be massive, perhaps even massive enough to uncover his lair.

But he wanted to take her. He could hardly resist. Looking was all well and good, but it was not, after all, enough. Not when the taking would be so easy. All he had to do was touch her with his taser, and carry her away.

She would be his.

If he did it tonight, he could have the double pleasure of taking her, and letting Cassandra go—up in flames.

He smiled at his little joke. When he was ready to rid himself of Cassandra—and it would be soon now, soon—that's what he would tell her.

"Come out of your cage, darling. I'm going to let you go."

He'd add the "up in flames" part when she was shackled to the wall and he was dribbling the kerosene over her.

But Cassandra was dull as dishwater nowadays, and he doubted she would even get the joke.

It would be interesting to see how Alexandra—ah, he was already calling her Alexandra, see how fond he was becoming of her?—would react to her predecessor's turning into French toast before her eyes.

She sighed in her sleep, and her lips parted. Her eyelids moved, as if she were dreaming. Did she know he was there, on some unconscious level? he wondered.

He hoped that she did.

His hand hovered over her cheek. He remembered how soft her skin had been, before. He wanted to feel it again.

If he took her away with him, he could feel every inch of her skin.

He could run his finger over her cheek. Right now. It would be the test. The last time he had touched her, she had awoken. This time, if she awoke, he would consider it a sign that he should take her.

That he was her destiny.

Or that she was his.

The thought gave him pause, and he frowned and drew his hand, which hovered over her face, index finger extended, back.

He was not so greedy, his passions were not so uncontrolled, that he would satisfy them at risk to himself.

Was he?

The temptation was almost irresistible, but in the end he made himself cover her up again and turn away.

His strength of will was stronger than his desire, he congratulated himself.

At least, for tonight.

Thirty

✦

Hannibal was crouched on the end of Alex's bed when she opened her eyes. Just crouched there staring at her with the wide, unblinking gaze of an owl. He looked like he had been sitting that way for hours, or centuries.

"Shoo!" she said, shaking the covers to dislodge him. He didn't budge, but he did blink, and his tail twitched.

She was too exhausted to fight with him. It occurred to her that she was able to see him so well because her bed was in a pool of light. She'd left the lamp on, of course, and now the light from it seemed so bright that it was hurting her eyes. No wonder she'd awakened in the middle of the night. She reached for the lamp, meaning to turn it off so that she could get back to sleep. . . .

The alarm clock on the bedside table went off. Startled, Alex grabbed for it, almost knocking over the lamp in her haste. Shutting the alarm off, she groaned. It was 6:45 A.M., and she felt like she had been asleep for about two hours. Her head ached, and her mouth felt like she'd been chewing on cotton balls. She wanted to do nothing more than curl back up in bed and pull the covers over her head.

She had dreamed of her father again last night. The

memory came back in a rush. This time she'd been standing in the middle of a bright, sunlit meadow, and he'd been walking to meet her. She'd been smiling, happy to see him, but then he'd started running toward her and yelling and waving his arms, and she had realized that he had been trying to frighten something away. She'd had the sense that whatever it was was behind her, looming near, but she'd been too scared to turn around and look. . . .

"Alex?" The voice that came over the walkie-talkie sounded decidedly grouchy. Breaking into her reverie right when it did, it made her jump.

"Good morning, Joe," she said, recovering. It was daylight, and her tone was frosty.

"Your sister was outside with my son about two A.M. I just thought you ought to know."

"Oh, God. How do you know?"

"I was in the kitchen when Eli came sneaking in."

"And did you blister his ass?" She remembered his prescription for Neely, and asked the question mockingly.

"I told him not to do it again."

"Tough disciplinarian, aren't you? You talk the talk, but you don't walk the walk."

"Your sister needs straightening out. My son doesn't."

"Your son was out there, too!"

"I'm not just talking about last night, and you know it. By the way, she told Eli that I was sleeping with you. What did you do, give her a play-by-play?"

"No, of course I didn't. . . . You know something, I don't like your tone."

"Oh, that just makes me want to cry."

"I don't have to listen to this," Alex said, seething, and took great satisfaction in turning the unit off.

Now as grouchy as Joe had sounded, she took a shower, pulled on her black leather pants with a long-sleeved white T-shirt—she was going to have to have Andrea send someone over to the house and pack up some more clothes for her if she was going to stay here for three weeks—and headed downstairs, beating a fist on Neely's door as she passed it. Hannibal padded at her heels. It was only when she opened the refrigerator door to pour the complaining feline some milk that it occurred to her to wonder how he had gotten into her bedroom.

Her door had been locked. She was certain he hadn't been in there when she'd gone to bed the night before. Neely had carried him into her room. Alex could picture the scene clearly. She knew she wasn't mistaken about that.

Neely had gone out to meet Eli. Hannibal could have gotten out of Neely's room then. But that didn't explain how he had gotten into her room.

"Did you sneak out to meet Eli after I went to bed last night?" Alex asked Neely without preamble when her sister came trudging down the stairs. Dressed in the outfit she had described last night without, thankfully, the addition of the purple feather, Neely looked anything but bright-eyed and bushy-tailed this morning.

Alex never thought she'd be glad to see the diamond stud.

"So what if I did? And how'd you know, anyway?" Neely yawned hugely and poured herself a glass of orange juice.

"Joe told me. He also said you told Eli I'd been sleeping with him."

Neely took a sip of juice and made a face at the taste. "Was it confidential information? Sorry, I didn't know."

"Damn it, Neely. . . ." Alex gritted her teeth. "You had no business going out in the middle of the night, and you had no business talking to anyone about my sex life. Which you are just speculating about, by the way!"

"Oh, yeah, right, like it isn't true."

Alex glared at her sister, then abandoned the argument in favor of a burning question.

"Do you know how Hannibal got in my room last night?"

Neely looked surprised. "How would I know? Actually, I thought he slept with me."

"He was on my bed when I woke up."

"Was he? I wonder how he managed that?" Neely took another sip of juice.

"I don't know. But he was there."

"Cool. A cat who can materialize and dematerialize at will."

The muffled sound of a horn tooting in the driveway interrupted.

"Shit," Neely said, taking one last swallow of orange juice and setting the glass down. "That's Eli. Gotta go. By the way, I decided to forget the tongue stud. Eli thinks au naturel is just fine."

"Oh God," Alex muttered as Neely sauntered from the room and, a moment later, went banging out the front door. With Joe around, this thing Neely had for Eli was definitely not good. Grimacing, she made a pot of coffee and pondered the mystery of the dematerializing cat. Hannibal, who wasn't talking, watched her and purred.

Could he possibly have gotten into her room when she had gone downstairs to get the walkie-talkie? Only if he'd been let out of Neely's room by then. But Joe had said Neely had been outside around two. She'd gone down for the walkie-talkie far earlier than that.

But still, that did provide a window of opportunity when he could have crept in, and maybe hidden under her bed. If Neely, for some reason, had let him out of her room.

Until Hannibal learned to talk, that was probably the best explanation she was going to come up with, Alex told herself. Something like that had to be the answer. After all, the cat could not walk through walls.

The next few days passed quickly. Visitors stopped by, mostly acquaintances of their father who had heard through the grapevine that she and Neely were staying at Whistledown, but also a steady procession of neighbors who just wanted to say hello. Alex got out and about, checking out tiny Simpsonville and the bigger town of Shelbyville, and discovering, happily, the malls and shopping that were available in the city of Louisville, only half an hour away. She talked to Andrea daily, about mundane matters such as getting additional clothes sent down and more personal issues such as Paul's marriage to Tara Gould and the reaction of their friends and social circle to the unexpected couple. Andrea also kept her updated on the circus, as she called it, surrounding the "House of Haywood" articles in the newspaper, and sent Alex copies, which she could barely bring herself to look at, much less read. The headlines were lurid, the pictures of her father painful, and the text almost libelous, in her opinion, in its depiction of what it called her father's "robber baron" style of doing business. The features on and pictures of herself and Neely and all six of her father's wives gave the story the feeling of a slightly unsavory soap opera. Didn't the reporters realize that they were writing about real people with real feelings? Alex fumed to Andrea. Andrea's reply: They don't care. Not if the story's good.

Having checked the toxicology reports that were submitted with the autopsy papers, Andrea confirmed Alex's conviction that her father had not been drinking at the time of his death. As for the smell of booze, when Alex related her conversation with Joe to Andrea, Andrea didn't know what to make of it, either.

"With all the big guns involved in investigating your father's death, I don't see how something like that could be missed. I mean, the local police might have, but the state police were involved, and the FBI, too." Andrea's voice turned doubtful. "The guy telling you that is not some kind of flake, is he?"

This description was so very far from applying to Joe that Alex smiled. "No. In fact, he's extremely reliable. If he says there was a strong smell of alcohol, there was."

"You seem awfully sure. You want me to have somebody check into it? We've still got the private investigators on the payroll. They're finishing up their final report. I could have one of them check with your source, and maybe poke around a little bit more."

"That would be great," Alex said gratefully.

"Alex." Andrea's voice was hesitant. "I know you're having trouble accepting that your father—did what he did, but you realize that the only other option is that somebody else killed him? In other words, murder? That's been pretty conclusively ruled out, I think. There was residue from a recently fired gun on his right hand, and the gun itself was there beside him."

"I know all that, Andrea. But the smell of alcohol—it bothers me. Why would there be a smell of alcohol if Daddy hadn't been drinking?"

"And you're sure this guy isn't wrong. Oo-kay. I'll pass this on to the investigators." Andrea paused. "Wait a minute. Is this the guy you were talking to when you called me Monday? Joe something-or-other? The farm manager down there?"

"That's him."

"Oh-ho! Mark's been talking to him. He says he's quite a forceful guy."

From the sound of that, Joe had been giving Mark grief. "Yeah, I'd say that's a pretty good description of him. What's he been hassling Mark about?"

"Actually, he's threatening to sue the estate if his contract isn't honored. Mark's looked the contract over, and he says it's valid. He's passed it on to David Rowe and the group to decide whether to just go ahead and pay the guy off or let him work out his time."

"The group" referred to the other half-dozen or so lawyers involved in settling the estate, Alex knew.

"The problem with just paying him off is that there are all these horses to consider," Alex said. "Apparently it's going to take a little time to get them settled in with new owners."

"You sound like you care." A hint of amusement crept into Andrea's voice. "This guy has got to be good-looking. Is he?"

"What makes you think that?" Alex asked defensively.

"I know you, girlfriend. You're not nearly as upset about Paul-the-creep as you should be. And you're a lot more concerned about the disposal of the Whistledown assets than you have been about the settling of any other property. Now, I ask myself, what does that add up to? There's only one answer: a hunky man."

Alex had to laugh. "All right. He's good-looking."

"Good in bed? Or don't you know that yet? Nah, you always did work fast: you know."

"Andrea!"

"Come on, 'fess up! On a scale of one to ten, give me a number."

"Eleven," Alex said, laughing. "And that's all you need to know."

"I think I'll come for a visit." Andrea's voice dropped to a sexy purr. "Or better yet, maybe I'll find an urgent need to check on the Whistledown property personally after you come home."

Alex laughed, but the thought of herself returning home and Andrea flying in to make a move on Joe did not amuse.

Which was ridiculous, of course. She had no claims on Joe, as she reminded herself daily. Their relationship, at the moment, had degenerated into deliberate and unmistakable coolness on her part and matter-of-fact courtesy on his, except at night, over the walkie-talkie, when she had come to depend on the low, deep drawl of his voice talking to her as a kind of lullaby to go to sleep by. Despite the sleeping pills, she wasn't sleeping well, and she dreamed about her father nearly every night. Knowing that Joe was there, listening, was all that got her through the night.

She was actually, for purely professional reasons, around him quite a bit during the day. A call to her publisher had produced an "on spec" assignment for a coffeetable book about horse farms of the Bluegrass, which she hoped to complete while she was in residence at Whistledown. She spent quite a bit of time in Whistledown's barn and fields, taking pictures of everything from Joe (to his annoyance) and the stablehands and grooms and exercise riders and veterinarians and various other horse-types who were in and out of the barn on a daily basis, to the horses, to the farm itself. The prospect of turning this forced sojourn into a paying assignment cheered her immeasurably. There were several more horse farms within shouting distance and even more less than an hour's drive away, and she photographed them, too. She'd brought her favorite camera with her, simply because she rarely traveled anywhere without it. After converting one of the spare bedrooms into a makeshift photographer's studio complete with bathroom as darkroom, Alex found she was able to do some serious work.

Inez came in, following the same schedule of cleaning the house two days a week that she adhered to when Whistledown was empty. Both Alex and Neely (the latter reluctantly) swept floors, ran the vacuum, and did laundry as needed. Alex even bought a cookbook with the aim of refining her cooking skills and at the same time preparing wholesome homemade dinners for the two of them that did not also pack on the pounds. The results were so positive that she and Neely wound up eating pizza every night. Neely begged to be allowed to go down the hill (that's how she referred to going to the Welches', which she did five times a day; Joe, to Alex's surprise, seemed to have no objection to her sister's visits, or at least if he did she had heard nothing about it) for supper, which Alex flatly refused to permit. Joe, Neely whined, was a good cook.

"Tough it out" was Alex's unsympathetic response. The Haywoods were not depending on the Welches any more than they had to.

One night about a week after they had settled in, just as Alex was contemplating two suspiciously pink-looking chicken breasts that she had pulled out of the oven after what she was sure was the specified time, the phone rang. Still frowning at the chicken, Alex picked up the receiver.

"Alex?" It was Joe. She had last seen him in the barn about two hours earlier. He had been showing several of the horses to a potential buyer. His expression had been rather grim, and Alex, taking pictures of the scene to his obvious but unexpressed displeasure—who owned the farm, anyway? was what the look she shot him said—had herself felt a pang at the idea of having to part with the animals, each of whom she was coming to know and appreciate as an individual.

But there was no help for it. Even Joe now admitted as much. There was no money, and the horses had to be sold. He was making the best of a bad situation, but it was obvious he didn't like it.

"Yes?" she responded, deliberately cool.

"Your pizza's on its way up." His voice was dry.

Alex frowned. "How do you know?"

"Because the delivery boy is a friend of Eli's and he stopped by here first to drop off Eli's algebra notes, which he borrowed. He tells me that he's delivered pizza to your house every night for a week."

"Good God, is there no privacy around here at all?" Alex was indignant.

"Not much. I told you. Alex, aren't you getting a little sick of pizza?"

Alex bristled. "I *like* pizza," she said defiantly. Then a thought occurred to her. "Wait a minute. I didn't order pizza yet. I'm cooking chicken breasts with rice for dinner." Her superior tone in no way reflected the sorry state of the chicken breasts that lay limply waiting for some kind of resuscitation on top of the stove.

"Yeah, I've heard about your adventures in cooking. Listen, I've made a roast with potatoes and carrots for supper. I'm getting ready to take it out of the oven. Why don't you and Neely come down and join us for supper?"

At the picture his words conjured up, Alex's stomach gave a little twitch. Was it hunger? she wondered with surprise. She'd been eating so little lately that not eating was getting to be the norm for her. Which, Alex realized, was maybe not a good thing.

The doorbell rang.

"I'll get it!" Neely sang out from the den, where she was supposedly doing her homework while watching TV.

"At a guess I'd say there's your pizza." Joe's voice was even drier than before. "Alex, come for supper. Please. Consider it a business meeting if you want to. I've got a couple of offers on some of the horses I need to talk to you about, anyway."

"Really?"

Wearing the same bell-bottomed jeans and skintight orange T-shirt that she had worn to school, Neely walked into the room carrying a pizza box. She grimaced at Alex as she set the box down on the center counter.

"I never thought I'd say this, but I'm getting really, really sick of pizza," Neely said.

"*You* ordered it," Alex retorted, not thinking to cover the mouthpiece. "*I* thought we'd have chicken breasts and rice."

"Yeah, I saw your chicken breasts and rice. That's when I ordered the pizza."

Alex thought she heard a chuckle on the other end of the phone.

Thirty-one

✦

"A" re you laughing?" Alex demanded, talking into the mouthpiece again.

"No, ma'am. Absolutely not."

"Is that Joe?" Neely lifted the lid of the pizza box. The scent of tomato sauce and garlic wafted toward Alex's nose. She shuddered.

"Alex, come to supper." Joe's tone made it part request, part order.

Alex weakened. The idea of eating pizza again made her chicken breasts look almost good by comparison. And that, given the state of the chicken, was sad.

There was also the lure of seeing Joe. . . .

"Thank you, but no," she said with dignity. They could always eat tuna-fish sandwiches.

"What does he want?" Neely asked, making gagging faces as she looked down at the cheese-topped pie.

"Alex, don't be an idiot," Joe said. His voice was crisp and oddly tender at the same time.

The undernote of tenderness did it.

"He wants us to eat dinner at his house," she said to Neely.

"Yes!" Neely pumped her fist in the air.

"I heard that," Joe said.

"All right." Alex capitulated without any real regret. "We'll be down in a few minutes. Thank you for the invitation."

"You're welcome," he said, and hung up.

"Thank goodness!" Neely slammed the lid back down on the pizza box, turned up her nose as if it were the smelliest garbage, carried it across the kitchen, lifted the lid, and dropped it into the trash can. "No more pizza!"

"Neely." Alex gave her sister a beseeching look. "While we're down there, please, pretty please, behave."

Neely grinned at her. "Oh, don't worry. I'm not stupid. I'll be a perfect little angel—as long as Daddy Studmuffin's around. Eli says he can be pretty strict, and I don't want to get Eli grounded or anything. Then what would I do for fun?"

As far as reassurances went, Alex had had better ones, but, she thought, in Neely's case she'd better take what she could get.

Five minutes later, the Mercedes pulled into Joe's driveway. It was only a little after six, but it was full dark outside. Alex and Neely got out, turning up their coat collars and ducking against a cold drizzle that had been falling steadily all day. Josh, in baggy jeans and a flannel shirt unbuttoned over a white T-shirt, opened the door to Alex's knock.

"Eli's supposed to go over to Heather's later," Josh said to Neely in a taunting undertone once they were inside. Alex, overhearing, felt a tingle of trepidation as she waited for her sister's response.

"Am I supposed to care?" Neely asked as they all stepped from the dim hall into the bright welcoming light of the kitchen.

"Eli, what do you think?" Jenny was asking doubtfully, pirouetting in front of her brother in an unflattering blue dress with a white lace Peter Pan collar.

Wearing jeans and a white football-style jersey that had *Rockets* written in script on the front, Eli was tossing salad in a clear glass bowl on the counter. He gave his sister a cursory glance. "Looks okay to me."

"I don't want to just look okay!" Jenny sounded on the verge of tears. "I want to look *hot*. Daddy, this dress isn't right!"

"Told you it made you look like Little Orphan Annie," Josh said, heading toward the refrigerator. Jenny's lower lip quivered.

Alex had to admit that, with Jenny's boyishly short hair and thin frame, the too large, too prim dress was definitely orphanlike.

"Shut up, Josh!" Joe growled. He was stirring something in a skillet on the stove, attending to the conversation over his shoulder. He sent Alex a quick, welcoming grin before turning his attention to his daughter.

That grin warmed her clear to her toes. Her frostiness melted under its impact. After all, it was difficult to be cool to a man who had invited one for dinner.

"If you don't like it we can take it back. No need to get bent out of shape here," he said soothingly. Joe was wearing jeans and an ancient gray sweatshirt. He looked very tall, very handsome, and very at home in the kitchen as he deftly whisked a spoon through whatever he was cooking.

"It won't do any good! You never get the right thing! Daddy, you don't know anything about girls' clothes!" Jenny sounded almost despairing. She stood in the center of the kitchen, her face woebegone, her hands clenched into fists by her side. "And I need it by tomorrow night!"

"Jesus Christ, Jen, you're just going to be standing there in a big group singing." Eli carried the bowl of salad to the table. "Nobody will even notice what you're wearing."

"Yes, they will! We're going to have our picture made! And all the other girls will look hot, and I won't!"

"Gingerbread, you always look beautiful," Cary put in. Dressed in rumpled khakis and a blue oxford-cloth shirt, he was standing near the microwave, which pinged as he spoke. Opening the door, he withdrew a tray of rolls and headed toward the table.

"Oh, Grandpa!" Jenny threw him an exasperated look.

"Okay, let's ask an expert," Joe said. He picked up the skillet, and deftly poured its contents—brown gravy, Alex saw—into a gravy boat. "Alex, what do you think of Jenny's dress?"

He headed toward the table with the steaming dish.

Alex hesitated. "Where are you going to wear it?" she asked Jenny directly, stalling for time.

"My choral group is going to be singing at the pep rally tomorrow night," Jenny said, looking at Neely appealingly. "I have to wear a blue dress—all the girls do—but this one makes me look like a dork. I know it does!"

"Yeah, you're right," Neely said, before Alex could find a tactful way to say that maybe that particular dress was not overly flattering. Neely had been looking Jenny over critically ever since the conversation had started. "It does look pretty bad. You could do a lot better."

Alex gave Neely a killer look as Jenny said to her father, "See!"

"It's better to tell her the truth," Neely said defensively to Alex in response to that look. "Otherwise she'll go to this thing looking like a dork."

"Alex?" Joe looked appealingly at Alex, who, with Neely's warning in mind and Jenny's beseeching eyes on her, felt obliged to tell the truth.

"She could do better, Joe," she admitted.

The look Joe gave her said *traitor.*

"Daddy, I told you!" Jenny sounded almost accusing. "You're no good at picking out girls' clothes! I need another dress!"

"We'll take it back tomorrow," Joe said, sounding harassed. "You can pick out whatever you like."

"I don't know what looks hot!" Jenny almost wailed. "*You're* supposed to know! But you don't, 'cause you're a man!"

"How about if Neely and I take you shopping tomorrow, Jenny?" Alex interposed before Joe could say anything. "I need to get some things anyway. It'd be fun to shop for a dress for you. And Neely knows what's hot, believe me."

Joe looked slightly alarmed as his gaze shot to Neely. Alex had to grin.

"That'd be great!" Jenny said, shooting a look at Neely. Suddenly she sounded almost shy as she added, looking at Alex, "If it's not too much trouble, that is."

Alex realized that Jenny was in awe of Neely, and supposed that seen through the younger girl's eyes Neely was the ultimate in cool.

"It'll be fun," Neely said. Jenny beamed, Alex smiled at Neely and Jenny both, and Joe looked relieved.

"Thank you, ladies," he said to Alex and Neely. "You've averted a crisis. Jen, run and change, and let's eat."

When Jenny returned, they all sat down. It was Jenny's turn to say grace, which she did very nicely. Food was passed around the table family style, and Alex was surprised to find herself eating almost hungrily. She sat at Joe's right hand, with Neely across the table and Josh beside her, and she felt totally at ease. Tonight being with Joe felt like being with an old friend, someone whom she had known all of her life—but with a difference. His eyes met hers, he smiled at her, his hands brushed hers as he passed the food, and she felt each smile, each glance, each touch, as a tingle of pure electricity. Looking at him, at his dark, handsome face, at his sea-blue eyes and crooked smile, she asked herself again, what was it about this man?

Conversation was general, ranging from the offers Joe had received on the horses (half a million each for two mares in foal to Storm Cat) to Jenny's science project (she was training mice to navigate a maze) to the unfairness of the algebra teacher (Eli and Neely, while not in the same class, had the same teacher, and both had done poorly on the previous day's pop quiz) to Josh's prospects for being asked to the upcoming freshman morp (*prom* backwards, held right before Christmas, and girls had to ask the boys), which he gloomily rated as not good.

"If you'd start talking to a few of the girls in your class, one of them would probably ask you," Eli advised between mouthfuls of his meal. "Girls aren't going to ask somebody who doesn't even talk to them."

"Don't you talk to girls, Josh?" Jenny asked curiously. "Why not?"

"He's shy," Eli said.

Josh turned red to his ears. "'Cause girls are stupid," he said to Jenny after shooting a quick, glowering look at Eli. "Especially fifth graders."

"Girls are not stupid!" Jenny and Neely fired back simultaneously, acknowledging each other's contribution with a quick, high-five-like exchange of glances. Then Jenny added, bristling. "Especially not fifth graders!"

"Oh, yeah?"

"Okay, guys," Joe intervened. "That's enough. Josh, Grandpa said you helped him out with Victory Dance today. What'd you think of him?"

"He's really fast," Josh said, with more enthusiasm than

Alex had yet heard from him. "He's pretty skinny, though. Grandpa says some of the greatest racehorses are like that."

"We'll make a horseman out of that boy," Cary said to Joe from his place at the foot of the table. "He's got a good feel for it."

Josh barely smiled, but his face shone with pride.

"By the way, Joe, this food is really good," Alex said. "I'm impressed."

His eyes twinkled at her. "I hear that you've been trying to cook."

"Trying's right. Know what the title of the cookbook she bought is? *Cooking for Dummies*. I'd say that pretty much sums it up," Neely chimed in with a chortle, earning a killer glare from her sister and a round of guffaws from everyone else.

"You going to the pep rally tomorrow night, Grandpa?" Jenny asked.

"Sure am, Gingerbread," Cary said cheerfully. "Think I'd miss hearing you sing? Not a chance."

"Yeah, he's even got a date," Josh said, and snickered. "With Mrs. Shelley."

"Mrs. Shelley?" Neely sounded horrified.

Eli nodded glumly. "Yup. The guidance counselor. Can you believe it?"

"What a bummer," Neely commiserated. Eli and Josh nodded in unison.

"If they do anything wrong, Mrs. Shelley tells on them," Cary said to Alex with a grin. "Keeps them on the straight and narrow."

"I don't see why you can't find some other woman to date, Grandpa," Josh said grumpily. He looked at Neely. "She even tells him our grades before *we* get them. Then he tells Dad, and it's all over."

"Only if you have bad grades," Joe said smoothly. "Try making the honor roll and experience the difference."

After supper was over, Joe insisted on driving them home in the Mercedes.

"I've got to check the horses anyway, so I'll walk home," he said, accompanying them into the house.

"It's raining," Alex protested as Neely headed for the den with a murmured *thanks for dinner* to Joe. Seconds later Alex heard the TV.

"Honey, I don't melt." They were standing beneath the glittering chandelier in the entry hall, and the water droplets on his black hair glittered like diamonds. The green army coat he wore made his shoulders look very broad, and his height meant that she had to tilt her head back to meet his gaze. His eyes were a luminous blue against his swarthy skin, and his gaze was warm and caressing on her face.

Alex's gaze slid down to his mouth. His beautiful, sensitive mouth.

He picked up her hand, held it for a moment, then smiled at her with a crooked, heart-stopping smile as he carried her hand upward and pressed the back of it against his mouth.

His lips were warm and just faintly moist. Alex could feel the heat of his breath against her skin. Still looking at her, he turned her hand over, kissing her palm. Lightning bolts of sensation burned across the surface of her skin.

Her lips parted as she drew in a deep, shaken breath.

"Thank you," he said. "For offering to help out with Jenny."

Alex leaned toward him. She wanted that beautiful mouth on hers so badly that her knees were trembling. . . .

"Alex," Neely called from the den. "Do you think we

can scare up a sleeping bag somewhere? Tomorrow night, after the pep rally, there's a lock-in."

Joe dropped her hand and stepped back.

"Good night," he said, and turned and walked out the door, closing it behind him.

Alex stared at the closed portal until Neely, calling to her again, broke the spell.

Thirty-two

❦

"Pop, you done anything lately I oughta know about?"
It was around ten the next morning. Joe had just
gotten off the phone with Tommy. The sheriff had
called, asking him to come by and see him as soon as possible. Tommy had refused to divulge what it was about
over the telephone, but his tone had been sufficiently
businesslike to alarm Joe. He'd known Tommy long
enough to know when something was up. He'd made an
appointment for ten-forty-five. Besides his kids, his dad
was the only person Joe could think of that Tommy might
need to talk to him about, and his kids were in school,
where he couldn't question them. So he'd gone in search
of his dad.

"Joe, son, this son-of-a-gun just did three-quarters of
a mile in 1:10!" Stopwatch in hand, Cary was just outside the training ring behind the barn, leaning against an
open gate that looked into the ring as Joe came up
behind him. As Victory Dance, carrying Lon Macleod, a
local semi-retired jockey who worked for them as an
exercise rider, had just galloped past the opening, Joe
had little trouble deciphering the subject of his father's
excited speech.

"Listen, Pop, Tommy asked me to stop by his office

and . . ." Joe got no further. His father turned and grabbed him by the arm.

"Joey, Joey, you're not listening to me! This is him! This is the one! This is our ticket!"

Joe sighed, barely sparing a glance for the big red horse as he cantered past the opening again, although he did raise a hand in greeting to Macleod, who was now cooling the horse out after his workout.

"Pop, I got more important things to worry about right now than that worthless piece of horseflesh you talked me into paying thirty thousand dollars for. Tommy just called and asked me to come by his office as soon as he could. Said there was something he needed to talk to me about. Now, you tell me the truth: Have you done any hit and runs or anything like that you haven't told me about lately?"

Cary looked at him in disgust. "Hell, no, I haven't! Why do you immediately have to think any bad news has to do with me? You got three kids. . . ."

"I thought about that, but they're not around to ask, so I'm asking you."

"You ever think it might be about you? No, of course not. We should all be so perfect."

"Pop . . ."

"Listen, Joey, I don't give a crap about Tommy right now. This horse here has what it takes to run with the best of them. He can fly! He can flat-out fly!"

"You swear you haven't done anything?"

"Joey, you're not listening to me!"

"Well, hell, you're not listening to me, either!"

They glared at each other, father and son, nose to nose, until Cary's eyes welled up and he glanced away suddenly. "If you aren't the spittin' image of your mama when you get mad like that, I've never seen her. Louisa always was slow to anger, but look out when she did."

"Ah, Pop. . . ." Joe's anger drained away just as quickly as it had arisen, and he draped an arm around his father's shoulders. His father had never been the same since the deaths of his wife and daughter. Even so many years later, just the mention of them could bring him to tears.

"I miss her, Joey. Her and your sister." Cary's voice was low. "Sometimes I miss them so bad."

"I miss them too, Pop." Briefly Joe tightened his arm around his father's shoulders, then let it drop. That was more emotion than the two of them usually shared, he reflected, and immediately sought to lighten the atmosphere. "So you say that bag of bones did three-quarters of a mile in 1:10? You better get that stopwatch of yours checked. Hell, it's older than I am."

"It still works as good as when it was brand-new, too. Victory Dance is our ticket, Joey! I'm telling you, he's our ticket!"

"You can tell me all about it later," Joe said, glancing down the track to see Victory Dance coming toward them again, walking this time and blowing mightily. "I gotta go see Tommy, then I've got an appointment with some bankers at one to talk about getting financing to convert our operation to a public stable. Pick Jen up, would you? I might not be back in time."

"Yeah, yeah." Cary gestured at Macleod, waving him closer. "Lon, you tell this boy of mine that I'm not senile yet: that horse can run!"

Still on Victory Dance's back, Lon nodded. "He can run, Joe."

"Great." Joe looked at his father. "Don't forget about Jenny."

"You think I'd ever forget about my little Gingerbread?" Cary was already focusing on the approaching horse and rider. "Lon, you think he's toein' out a little?"

"Yeah, but it don't seem to make no difference. . . ."

Shaking his head in exasperation, Joe walked away. His father was as fervent a believer in the eventual coming of *the one*—the great horse that would salvage his reputation, make Joe's, and change all their lives—as a new convert was in his religion. Personally, Joe hoped his father was right, but he wasn't putting any great reliance on it. In his experience, life just didn't work out like that. He put more faith in his own efforts to put together a consortium of investors to buy Silver Wonder and a couple of the other horses as the basis for his public stable.

Hard work and initiative were what he put his faith in. Not miracles. Not even miracle horses.

➴ ➴ ➴ ➴

Tommy's office was in the tiny town of Simpsonville, which consisted basically of a restaurant, a small shopping center, a few mom-and-pop stores of different persuasions, and the First Baptist Church, which, as the only two-story building in town, towered over the rest even if you didn't count the steeple. It took Joe just about ten minutes to get there. Located in the small shopping center along with a Quik-Pik, a shoe-repair shop, and Gunther's Hardware Store, Tommy's workplace was, at first glance, just another glass-fronted store. But a sign on the door said SHERIFF'S OFFICE, and inside the counter was manned by a brown-uniformed deputy in a black vinyl chair who was busy filling out paperwork.

"Hey, Joe," the balding, burly deputy, Billy Craddock, greeted him, looking up from what he was doing with a smile. In his sixties now, Billy had been deputy for as long as Joe could remember. Hell, in Joe's rambunctious teenage days Billy had hauled him in for a talking-to more than once.

"Hey, Billy. Tommy in?"

"In his office." Billy jerked his head toward the rear, and without waiting for a more explicit invitation Joe walked on back. Tommy's office was a small room with cinderblock walls painted a delicate eggshell white. The room directly opposite had been outfitted with bars on the door and a single window to serve as a holding cell in case of need. Besides the occasional rowdy drunk or belligerent teen, Joe didn't think anybody was ever put in there. If somebody had to be transferred to the Shelby County Jail in Shelbyville, either they'd sit in the office with Tommy waiting for a jail officer to come pick them up, or Tommy would drive them over himself. Simpsonville was that kind of town: friendly even to its wrongdoers.

Tommy had his feet up on his desk and his hands linked behind his head as he leaned back in his chair talking to Rob Mayhew, who was lounging (as well as one could lounge in such chairs) in the molded plastic chair in front of the desk. On the wall behind Tommy's head hung a bulletin board crammed with flyers, including a prominent black-and-white picture of the FBI's current most-wanted suspect. Tommy kept hoping that one day a criminal with that kind of star power would wander into his orbit, and he'd be the one to take him down. There were also the usual missing posters. One, with double pictures of a pretty blond college-age girl and a boy of about the same age, looked to be new, and it was tacked on top of the flotsam underneath.

"So what's up?" Joe said without preamble, walking into the room. He glanced at the other man, who was also a friend of long standing, now a lawyer. "Hey, Rob."

Tommy and Rob both looked up at him for a couple of seconds without saying anything. Tommy lowered his feet to the floor and sat up.

"Why don't you go ahead and close the door, Joe?" Tommy said.

Joe's eyes widened. "Hell, Tommy, you're starting to scare me," he said, complying. "You want to go ahead and spit it out before I have a heart attack?"

"I'm here as your lawyer, Joe," Rob said, standing and placing a hand on his shoulder. "And I'm telling you right up front that you don't have to talk to Tommy or anybody. You don't have to say a word. In fact, I'm advising you not to."

"What?" Joe stared from Tommy to Rob.

"I called him for you, Joe. I didn't think it was fair to try to talk to you without you having a lawyer. I felt like I'd be taking advantage of our friendship if I did."

Joe looked at him as if he'd grown an extra nose. "What the hell are you talking about, Tom?"

"Are you willing to talk to me?"

"Yeah. Yeah, I'm willing to talk to you. About what?"

"I want to ask you some questions. And I want to tape-record this, if you don't mind." Tommy touched a small silver tape recorder that sat on his desk. Joe hadn't noticed it before.

"Are you serious?"

"You don't have to agree to this, Joe." Rob's hand rested on his shoulder. "And I'm advising you not to."

"Yeah, I'm serious. *This* is serious. You might want to listen to your lawyer. And I'm telling you that as your friend, not as sheriff."

"Jesus Christ, Tommy, would you cut to the chase? You can tape-record me from here to Sunday if you want to. And shut up, Rob. I know I don't have to talk."

"You giving me permission to tape-record, then, Joe?"

"Yes. Hell, yes."

Tommy switched on the recorder. "I am talking to Joe

Welch, on Tuesday the seventeenth of November at approximately eleven A.M., with his permission, in the presence of his lawyer," he said, and then looked at Joe. "Joe, I want to show you something."

"If I tell you to shut up, Joe, you shut up right then," Rob said urgently. Joe silenced him with a wave.

Tommy opened his desk drawer, pulled on a pair of thin white surgical gloves, then reached down on the floor near his chair to lift a black plastic garbage bag up onto his desk. He opened the bag to reveal another black garbage bag, tattered and dirty and clearly much older than the first. A musty smell began to fill the room. Handling the second bag carefully, Tommy opened it and extracted a battered woman's purse, and the musty smell grew strong enough to make Joe grimace. The purse had once been saddle brown, but it was black in some places and moldy in others, and so flattened it looked like it had been run over multiple times by a truck.

"Recognize this?" Tommy asked, his eyes fixed on Joe's face.

Joe looked from the purse to his friend.

"Well, it sure as hell isn't mine," he said.

Rob grinned, seeming to relax a little, but Tommy did not. In fact, Tommy's seriousness was starting to annoy Joe.

"You wanna bottom-line me here? What's this about?" Joe asked impatiently.

Tommy met his gaze. "There's ID in the purse," he said. "A woman's wallet. Makeup, a hairbrush, miscellaneous other items too, but the ID's what's important. Know whose name is on it?"

"No, Tom, I don't, but I presume sometime in the next day or so you're going to tell me."

"It's Laura's, Joe. Laura, your wife."

"*What?*" Joe grabbed for the purse, but Tommy was

quicker, whisking it up and away from his hands. Joe glared at him. "Let me see."

Taking care to keep the purse out of Joe's reach, Tommy opened it and extracted a wallet, then flipped the wallet open to reveal a mottled driver's license enclosed behind a once-clear plastic shield, and two credit cards still in their slots. As he dangled it in front of Joe's face, Joe grabbed it.

"Hey!" Tommy protested. "You'll get fingerprints all over it!"

"Shouldn't matter. Everything's already been checked for prints, you said. If they need to go over the wallet again, then we'll just stipulate that any newly recovered prints are the results of this," Rob put in as Joe glared at Tommy, then looked closely at the driver's license. Laura's face looked back at him through the scratched plastic.

"It's Laura's," he confirmed, handing the wallet back to Tommy. "So what's your point?"

"What's my point?" Tommy looked at him like he was mentally defective. "Joe, where is Laura?"

"How the hell should I know? We're divorced, remember? I haven't seen or heard from her in years."

"Did you ever file a missing-persons report on her?"

Joe stared at him. "Why would I do that? First of all, I don't know that she is missing. She could be living the high life down in someplace like Mexico for all I know. Second of all, I don't want to find her. The kids and I are better off with her out of our lives, and you know it as well as I do."

"Okay, Joe, shut up now," Rob intervened.

"What? Have you guys lost your minds? So you found an old purse of Laura's! What's the big deal?"

Rob looked at Tommy. "Look, it's as plain as the nose on your face that he doesn't know anything. He's not that good an actor. Remember Cinderella?"

Cinderella had been the sixth-grade play. Chosen for the role of Prince Charming because he was the only boy then taller than the leading lady, Joe had been stricken with stage fright on opening night and had stood there in the spotlight like he'd been turned to stone, every line he'd so painstakingly memorized going out of his head forever. The girl lead—Cindy Webber (Harrison now)—had had to drag him into position and whisper his lines to him for him to parrot back before responding with her own.

It had been his first and last foray into drama, but he knew that, among his friends, former classmates, and fellow citizens, it would never be forgotten.

"Go to hell," Joe said to Rob without any particular heat.

Tommy glanced from Rob to Joe, and nodded. "You're right. He's not that good an actor. Okay, Joe, sit down and let me tell you what's happened here."

"I don't want to sit down." Joe wasn't feeling particularly happy with his old friend Tommy at the moment.

"Fine, then. Don't." Tommy glared at him. "This bag, containing Laura's purse and a pair of size eight narrow high-heeled shoes—Laura wore size eight narrow, didn't she?—was found on Bob Toler's farm this morning, washed up out of the creek. He was cleaning up his bottomland where it flooded after Saturday night's rain when he found this, and called me."

"How do you know what size shoe my ex-wife wore?" Joe fixed Tommy with a narrow-eyed stare.

"Hell, I dated her, too, Joe. Everybody at Shelby County High did. I told you so before you married her."

"Okay, guys, let's not get into ancient history here," Rob intervened hastily. "Joe, there's more. Tommy, would you just tell him?"

"A little bit farther down in the same field, Mr. Toler

found another plastic bag containing possible human remains. Bones, some hair, that kind of thing. That bag's on its way to the state crime lab now. I'll be sending this bag, with the purse and shoes, along after it. I kind of suspect the black stains on the purse may turn out to be blood."

Joe stared at Tommy as the full sense of what he was saying began to percolate through his brain. His knees felt weak suddenly, and his stomach began to churn.

"I think I will sit down," he said, pulling the chair Rob had vacated closer, and suited the action to the words.

"Told you," Tommy muttered.

"You think the remains—and the blood—are Laura's?" Joe took a deep breath.

"I'd say it's a good possibility, given that the garbage bag is identical to the one we found her purse and shoes in. Joe, there was money in that purse—a hundred thirty-two dollars. And an unused plane ticket to California for a flight that left in June 1991. That makes it seem highly unlikely that she just put her purse in a garbage bag and decided to throw it and her shoes away. When did you last see Laura?"

"Don't answer that, Joe," Rob said swiftly.

"Jesus Christ, Tommy, you brought me in here and asked me those questions because you think I killed her!" Joe shot to his feet in outrage.

"Watch your mouth, Joe." Rob's warning was urgent.

"Shut the hell up, Rob," Tommy said irritably. "Joe, I don't think you killed her. I admit, when I first started looking at this, given everything I know about your and Laura's history and how she was with the kids and everything, the thought that you *might* have killed her occurred to me. Hell, if I'd been married to her I might have killed her myself. But I can see that you don't know nuthin' about nuthin', so just get that look off your face. I'm not charging you with anything, and I don't suspect you of anything anymore either. Now I just want to know what you know, so maybe we can find out who did do this."

"*If* indeed anything was done," Rob put in. "At this point, Tommy, all you have is an old purse of Laura's with dark stains on it and a pair of shoes in a garbage bag. There's nothing criminal about throwing away a purse and shoes. The remains—if they are indeed human remains, which we don't know at this point—may have no connection to Laura at all."

"That's true," Tommy said. Then he looked at Joe again. "So when was the last time you saw Laura?"

Thirty-three

✤

"It's really hard not having a mother, you know," Jenny said seriously as she, Alex, Neely, and Neely's friend Samantha Lewis, a tall, thin girl with long, straight, caramel-colored hair, drove back toward Simpsonville. It was a bright, sunny day, warm enough so that no coats were needed. The shopping trip to Louisville had been both successful and fun. Bags full of purchases, including a lovely sky-blue dress for Jenny with long, tight sleeves, a puckered spandex top, and a short full skirt, crowded the trunk. It was now almost five o'clock, and traffic on two-lane U.S. 60 was surprisingly heavy. Alex glanced at Jenny, who was seated in the backseat with Samantha, through the rearview mirror. Jenny's soft brown eyes sparkled and her cheeks were flushed, and she looked as pretty as Alex had ever seen her.

Trust shopping to bring out the female in a girl!

"Tell me about it," said Neely, who was turned sideways in the seat so that she could talk to the occupants in back.

Jenny frowned. "Don't you have a mother either?"

Neely shook her head. "Mine died when I was little. I don't remember much about her."

"I don't remember *anything* about mine," Jenny said.

"Is she dead?" That came from Samantha, who had a

perfectly good mother. Alex knew, because she had talked to her on the phone just to make sure that the girls, as well as the rest of the students of Shelby County High, were really supposed to spend the night in the school after the pep rally. Under teacher supervision, of course. It was called a lock-in, and they did it every year, Mrs. Lewis assured her.

Not that Alex didn't trust Neely, but it was always safer to check.

"No. I don't think so. She just took off years ago and left us with Dad. They're divorced." Jenny's voice was matter-of-fact. "Divorce sucks."

"My parents were divorced," Alex put in. "It's tough, I know."

"Who did you end up with, your dad or your mom?" Jenny asked curiously.

"Actually, neither. I ended up in boarding school." Alex smiled a little ruefully. "Where I pretty much stayed until I grew up."

"Boarding school sucks," Neely chimed in, looking at Jenny. "If you look at it that way, you're pretty lucky. At least your dad wants you."

As she heard that, Alex felt a pang, and glanced sideways at her sister. But addressing that issue again would have to wait until they were alone.

Jenny and Samantha returned to Whistledown with them. Leaving the girls to amuse themselves, Alex went upstairs to take a shower, stopped by her makeshift darkroom to check on some film she had in the fixer, then headed back downstairs to the library to check the answering machine. Hannibal tailed her, waiting patiently outside the darkroom and then following her into the library. He jumped up onto the mantel and crouched there between the gaudy china parrots, staring at her.

"Shoo!" Alex tried. She could have sworn he curled his lip at her. Certainly he didn't budge.

Even Poe's fictional human counterpart in "The Raven" could not have been so cursed, Alex thought, ignoring the cat's unblinking regard as best she could. Andrea had called, and, settling down behind the desk, she reached for the phone. As she dialed, her gaze wandered around the room. She'd searched the desk, the bookshelves, even leafed through the books themselves for something, anything, that might help explain her father's state of mind in the days and hours before he died. Although her gut feeling was that he had not killed himself, there was always the possibility that she was wrong. If he had known these allegations about bribing public officials were coming, maybe he'd been pushed over the brink. Maybe he was guilty; maybe he hadn't been able to stand the idea of possibly facing trial, or even going to jail. But if he *had* turned to suicide as the only way out, surely he would have left behind a note for her, or Neely, or Mercedes, or the other principals in his company—some sort of written explanation for somebody. But no note of any sort had been found. Nothing like that had been found. *That* was what made it so impossible for her to believe. Even if he had been in extremis, he wouldn't have left them without a word.

Would he?

If some sort of message existed, she was pretty sure it would be somewhere in this room. This was the room in which he would have spent most of his time during the last days and hours of his life. But where? Where?

Andrea answered the phone just then, interrupting her thoughts.

"Are you doing all right?" Andrea asked.

"I'm fine." Amazingly enough, Alex thought, it was true. She was growing stronger by the day.

"I saw Paul at a party the other night, with Tara," Andrea said. "He didn't look all that happy. She was all over him like grass on a lawn, and he kept coming up with excuses to get away from her." Andrea giggled. "I never saw a man make so many excuses to go to the bathroom."

"I am so over Paul," Alex said. "I don't even care. Believe it or not, I hope he's happy. Well, all right, I don't actually *hope* he's happy. But it won't make me sick if he is."

They both laughed.

"Oh, good news. The last of the 'House of Haywood' articles ran today. And the mayor fired the police chief, which created a whole new scandal. Give it another week, and you should be able to come home."

"That is good news," Alex said, and immediately thought of Joe. She wasn't ready to leave just yet, she realized as she finished her conversation with Andrea and hung up. There was so much sexual chemistry between them—how could she just walk away from it? They had barely scratched the surface. . . .

Remembering last night, she smiled almost grimly to herself. Just the touch of his mouth on her hand had made her burn. Thinking of how they were in bed together was enough to make any sexual fantasy she'd ever had seem lame.

Never in her life had she wanted a man the way she wanted him. She had a feeling that the kind of physical combustion that existed between them was rare. Maybe so rare that it would never come along for her again.

She liked him too, and respected him. But more than that, he made her feel safe.

Was she just going to get on an airplane and fly away from all that?

Pondering, Alex walked into the kitchen, Hannibal trailing at her heels. Neely was sitting on one of the barstools, her elbows on the island counter, a half-eaten apple in front of her. Samantha was standing behind her, twisting thin strands of Neely's blond hair into long spirals and then spraying them with hot pink dye. Hannibal immediately jumped up on the counter and butted Neely's arm with his head, asking to be rubbed. She complied. The cat's purr sounded like a buzz saw.

"Where's Jenny?" Alex asked, glancing around before her gaze returned with some fascination to Neely's hair.

"She went home."

"What are you doing?" Alex's tone as she addressed the question to Neely was carefully neutral. If she implied any disapproval, Neely was liable to dye her whole head pink.

"Putting streaks in my hair." Neely rubbed Hannibal's ears, ratcheting up the cat's purr until it sounded like a 747.

"They're pink." Alex said it as if she thought Neely might not have noticed.

Neely grinned at her. "Pink's hot. You know you're giving us a ride to the pep rally, don't you?"

"Fine by me. What's this thing for, anyway?"

"The basketball team. There's a big game on Saturday," Samantha said, twisting and spraying. "The whole town goes, practically."

"You should come too," Neely said, adding slyly, "Joe will be there. Eli said he always goes. And Jenny's going to sing."

"I wouldn't miss seeing Jenny in her dress for the world," Alex said with perfect sincerity. And didn't add the corollary out loud: She wouldn't miss the chance to see Joe for the world, either.

By the time Alex, Neely, and Samantha got to the pep rally, it was full dark. They were late, and the high-school parking lot was packed, Alex saw as she drove in.

She drove the girls up to the gym entrance, where they got out with their sleeping bags. Then she went to park the car. It was a fine night, she saw as she got out, clear and not particularly cold, with a slight fall-scented wind that stirred her hair, which she had left loose. She was comfortably warm in a camel cashmere blazer and sweater over black pants with her black boots. Overhead the sky was a silky midnight blue sprinkled with stars that shone like tiny silver sequins. Riding low in the sky, the moon was a shy white sickle. The yells of the crowd and musical flourishes from the band could be heard clear through the brick walls of the high school all the way down to where Alex and a few other stragglers walked, and beyond.

All of a sudden the gym doors opened, and waves of people, students and adults alike, came rushing out. Within seconds Alex found herself engulfed in a flood tide of people who all seemed to be running toward the playing fields at the far end of the parking lot.

Eyes widening, Alex pressed herself close against a car bumper to keep from being swept along.

"Alex! Alex! Come on!" Galloping at the very end of a crack-the-whip-style chain of teenagers, Neely grabbed Alex's hand as the group thundered by. Forced willy-nilly into a near run by her sister's death grip on her fingers, Alex, laughing, found herself being pulled through the crowd.

"What on earth . . . ?" she gasped at Neely, struggling not to stumble. Her boots were not made for running, definitely. But she liked the length they added to her legs when she wore pants.

"We want to get on the first wagon with the team!"

"What?" This made no sense to Alex until she saw them, a lineup of big, hay-filled flatbed farm wagons at the far end of the parking lot very near to where she had parked the car. There must have been a dozen of them, all hitched to various sizes and colors of farm tractors. Several seemed to be half-filled already, and people were scrambling onto them as they reached them.

"That way! That way!"

Propelled by running teens, Alex's group broke ahead of the pack, heading toward the first wagon in line.

"It's full!" somebody farther up the line groaned as they reached it.

"Pile on! Pile on!" someone else shouted, and the kids began heaving themselves onto the wagon regardless of how full it was, clambering over earlier arrivals and flopping down in the straw.

"Neely! Here!"

Alex's hand was released as Neely was yanked up into the wagon, and for a moment she stood there, not knowing quite what to do. The wagon bed really did look full. . . .

"My sister! My sister!" Neely was reaching for Alex, and then other hands were too. Not sure what she was getting herself into, Alex nevertheless grabbed the hands that were reaching for hers, put a foot on the edge of the wagon bed, and let herself be hauled on board.

The wagon really was full, she saw as soon as she got up there. Balancing carefully, stepping over cross-legged bodies jammed together shoulder to shoulder, Alex reached the middle of the hay-filled wagon bed and looked around for someplace to sit. Neely was snuggled down between Samantha and a boy—was it Eli? It was too dark to be certain.

The only sure thing was that Neely wouldn't want her big sister sitting next to her.

Anyway, there wasn't any room. Anywhere.

"Pullin' out!" the tractor driver sang out. Alex looked wildly around once more. The wagon bed was, literally, packed. There did not appear to be any space left.

The tractor roared and the wagon lurched forward. Alex tottered dangerously in her high heels, lost her balance, toppled sideways—and felt someone on the wagon bed below her catch her by the upper arm and hipbone, anticipating her fall, controlling and guiding it.

She gave a little cry as she went down, then landed with a thud right on top of somebody.

"Oof!" The person's breath expelled as her bottom landed on something with more cushion than she would have expected—a stomach?

"I'm so sorry," Alex said, trying to maneuver herself up and off. But the hand that had rested on her hipbone slid around her waist. An arm, heavy, hard, and masculine, prevented her escape.

"You're sure heavier than you look," a voice grunted in her ear even as she swung her head around to confront her captor and demand that she be instantly released.

She recognized voice and face at almost the same instant.

"Joe!" Alex said with delight, and abandoned all thought of struggling to get free.

She was exactly where she wanted to be.

Thirty-four

✦

"Hang on for a minute and I'll get us situated." Joe's breath was warm as it feathered past her ear. He'd been eating something that gave it a faint buttery smell: popcorn? He shifted beneath her, scooting an inch or so backward, and Alex found herself sliding downward and a little to the left. When she stopped, she was sitting between Joe's bent knees on a thick layer of hay that covered the bed of the wagon. Her bottom was fitted snugly against his crotch, his arms were wrapped loosely around her waist, and her back rested against his chest. Her own knees were bent, too; with one kid's back directly in front of her and more crowding close on all sides, there was no room to stretch out her legs. Considering their company, the posture seemed very intimate, but a quick glance around assured Alex that there was, literally, no other place to sit. The wagon was crammed full. There would have been no room at all for her if Joe had not shared his space.

The wagon lurched again as they turned a corner and headed down the street in front of the school. By the yellowish light of the ornate iron streetlamps at the end of each block, Alex could see the Civil War–era houses and shops that lined the streets of Shelbyville. A glance around told her there were two other adults in the wagon. The rest, perhaps twenty-five or so in all, were teens. The basketball team appeared to be there in force. In deference to the crisp night air, they wore dark sweats with *Rockets* emblazoned across their chests in white. She saw Eli huddled at the opposite end of the wagon between Neely and Heather and had to smile. Poor boy.

While her position in Joe's arms had the potential to be embarrassing for both of them, considering that they were in full view of a wagonload of teens including Joe's son and her own sharp-eyed and big-mouthed little sister, as well as two potentially gossipy adults, a quick glance around reassured her. The kids were talking among themselves, joking and laughing, cutting up. The adults, a couple in perhaps their late forties, were chatting to each other. Nobody seemed to be paying her and Joe any attention whatsoever.

"Comfortable?" Joe asked.

Alex nodded. Actually, she could think of no place else in the world where she would rather be. Relaxing slightly, she allowed her head to rest back against his shoulder. Her cheekbone brushed his jaw as she moved. His skin was warm, and faintly prickly with five-o'clock shadow.

Not sure that he could see her nod, she said, "Yes," turning her face toward him a little more to be certain that he could hear her over the steady drone of the tractor engine and the rising and falling voices of babbling teens. A faint smell of soap reached her nostrils: Irish Spring? She inhaled the scent, hardly aware that she was doing so, and at her movement her bottom slid down an inch or so on the slippery hay. Joe's arms tightened around her waist, pulling her back up against him again, repositioning her deep within the cradle of his thighs.

The resulting jolt of electricity made Alex catch her

breath. His thighs tightened around her, presumably, she thought, to help hold her in place.

"Can't have you slip-sliding away," he said in a perfectly normal voice in her ear.

Was it possible that he wasn't feeling what she was feeling?

Alex realized that he was wearing his favorite blue Michelin-man coat. It was unzipped and she was inside it now, so that the parted sides enfolded her, curving around her like his arms—and legs. Under the coat, he wore a black or perhaps navy sweatshirt over a white T-shirt, and it was against this that her back rested. In the sideways glimpses she got of it, she could not be sure of its color. The changing light as they rolled past one streetlight after another, as well as through the relative darkness in the middle of each block, made details such as that uncertain. His bent knees, which cradled her on either side, made his legs easy to see: he was wearing jeans, with tan lace-up work boots on his feet.

"What is this, anyway? Part of the pep rally?" She had to talk, so she said the first thing that came into her head. She could not just sit there dumbly, absorbing the effects of his proximity on her body like a sponge in a puddle.

"Haven't you ever done anything like this before?" He shifted again so that his mouth was close to her ear. She could feel the brush of his lips as he spoke. Exquisitely sensitive to even such a slight touch from his mouth, the delicate outer curve of her ear seemed to tingle and burn.

Alex shook her head. "No."

"Yeah, well, I don't guess tractors and farm wagons are real big with the boarding-school crowd," he said. A husky note crept into his voice. "This is a hayride, Princess. It's taking everybody to a bonfire. We'll burn the opposing team in effigy and sing the school fight song and roast hot dogs and marshmallows and in general have a hell of a good time. And then tomorrow night, we'll play basketball."

His thigh muscles were taut and powerful. She remembered how they had looked naked, long and well defined and roughened with dark hair, as he shifted position a little and she was squeezed between them. They ended up pressing against her blazer-clad arms, which she had wrapped around her knees in a posture that sought to make the most of limited space. The effect this casual contact had on her was instant and electric: the tingling and burning spread, and burst along the way into a full-blown flame of desire.

"What is it about men and basketball, anyway?" Alex asked in a commendably lighthearted tone. "I have to admit I don't see the attraction."

Joe chuckled. The sound shook his chest and the breath that accompanied it was warm on her ear. He moved again, changing position, and the flame gained strength, shooting out fiery tendrils that crawled like an army of red ants over every inch of her skin. "Sort of like women and shopping, I imagine. By the way, thanks for taking Jenny."

"You're welcome."

"She was thrilled with that dress. She tried it on for me. I have to admit, it sure was hot." There was a teasing note in his voice now, as though he sought to deliberately lighten the atmosphere that had sprung up between them. But his arms around her waist remained firmly in place, hard and strong, holding her against him a shade more tightly, she thought, than he needed to. The heat of his body curled around her, quickening her heartbeat.

"Jenny's a sweetheart," Alex said sincerely.

"You know, I think so too."

"We all had fun: Jenny, Samantha, Neely, and me."

"Speaking of Neely," he said. "I have a bone to pick with your sister."

"Oh?" They had passed beyond the outskirts of town now, and the sky opened before them in an endless, starry expanse. On either side the fields were dark and still. The other occupants of the wagon could still be clearly heard—they were laughing and shrieking and calling back and forth to one another—but they could be seen now only as shadowy shapes, with much of the detail lost. The wagon rolled on, rocking slightly from side to side. Alex lay back in Joe's arms, inhaling the scent of hay and gasoline and man, and luxuriating in her position. She could feel the heat of his body, the steely strength of his muscles, all along her body. "What did she do?"

"She painted pink stripes in my daughter's hair."

Remembering Neely's and Samantha's occupation in the kitchen earlier, Alex was surprised out of her contemplation of her body's various responses to Joe's closeness into a giggle. She was surprised she hadn't guessed. "Oh, dear."

"Yes, oh, dear. I gather that your sister and her friend painted stripes in their hair in honor of tonight's event, and Jen wanted some too."

"Oh, my," Alex said, still smiling. "So what did you do? Give her a stern lecture on the danger of hair streaks and send her to wash them out?"

"I didn't see them until she was on her way out the door. She rode over with her choral group, and I saw her hair and her dress at the same time. It was an eye-opener, I have to admit. But I'm sure pink hair stripes are hot."

"They're called streaks, not stripes, just so you'll

know." Alex smiled up at the night sky. Stars twinkled down at her as if they shared in the joke. "And yes, they're hot."

"You haven't heard the worst of it, either. Know what else your busy little sister did?"

"What?" Alex asked with some trepidation, as his tone conjured up hideous visions of body piercings and the like.

Joe pushed her hair behind her ear. Then his mouth nuzzled right up against it as if he didn't want to be overheard. His lips were hot and his breath was moist, and the sensation tightened her loins and started a quake, rhythmic and slow, between her legs. Alex gritted her teeth, and tried to concentrate on what he was saying.

"She told Jen that if she *really* wanted to look hot, she should buy a padded bra."

That wasn't so bad. Joe, obviously, had no idea of the range of possibilities, most of them far more hideous, that Neely could have suggested. "Is that all?"

"Is that *all*? That's plenty, believe me. Know what my daughter wants me to do this weekend? Take her to the mall in Louisville to buy a padded bra." There was an undertone of only semi-amused savagery in his tone.

At the thought of Joe wandering around a suburban mall in search of a padded bra for Jenny, Alex relaxed enough to grin.

"Victoria's Secret has some very nice things," she said primly.

"*Victoria's Secret? For Jenny?* Oh, my God. . . . Quit laughing, it's not funny."

"*You're* what's funny. She's a girl, you know. Sooner or later, she's going to have to start wearing a bra."

"Yeah, but not now. And not a padded one, for God's sake. She's eleven years old, and flat as a pancake. A little girl.

And I'd like to keep her that way, thank you very much."

Glancing up at him, she saw him frown. His mouth brushed her ear again, and the quake deepened into a real hunger. Her toes curled in instinctive response.

"Joe, little girls have to grow up."

"It's getting harder, you know." His voice was suddenly almost stark. "Raising her by myself, I mean. Boys I know. A girl . . ."

"I think you're doing a great job," Alex said in a softer tone, releasing her knees to curve her arms over his where they were wrapped around her waist, "on all of them."

"Yeah, I'm a regular Mr. Mom." There was an undertone to that that made Alex turn her head and look up at him.

"Joe, is something wrong?"

Seen in profile with the glittering sky as a backdrop, he was almost sinfully handsome, she thought. She let her gaze wander over his face with what was close to being an ache of pleasure. His features were classically even. He had a high forehead, a long, straight nose, a strong chin. His eyes were shadowed by short, thick black lashes as he glanced down at her. His beautiful mouth curled in a faint, sardonic smile.

"No, not really." His arms tightened around her waist. "Tell me what you did today."

It was an obvious attempt to change the subject. Whatever was bothering him—and she was fairly sure something was—perhaps, she thought, he felt that this was not the place to talk about it. Not with, potentially, listening ears on all sides. And watching eyes as well.

His call.

"Besides expose your daughter to a world of pink hair streaks and padded bras?" She was reaching for a carefree note, and wasn't quite sure if she hit it. To her own ears the question sounded slightly forced.

"Yeah, besides that." He was smiling for real now. She could see the faint gleam of his teeth as moonlight struck them.

"I talked to Andrea today." The feel of him against her—the rise and fall of his chest as he breathed, the rasp of his chin against her cheek when he moved his head, the occasional shift of his legs—created a weakness that seemed to afflict every single muscle group she possessed.

"And what did Andrea have to say?"

"The newspaper series ended today. She said we can go home in another week. If we want to."

He went suddenly very still. The arms around her waist seemed to grow harder, heavier.

"That's good news."

"Is it?"

"Isn't it?"

She was breathing too fast, she realized suddenly. He must be aware of it, just as she was aware of the steady rhythm of his breathing. If she moved her head just a little, she could touch his jaw with her mouth. . . . It was all she could do to resist.

"It depends."

"On what?"

"On you."

He said nothing. Alex was supremely conscious of the feel of him holding her. His chest was hard against her back. The arms around her waist were solid, even possessive. His legs cradled her with their strength. She felt almost happy suddenly, and the feeling was so foreign to her after the last wrenching weeks that she immediately took stock to try to figure out why: She was breathing in the crisp November air, looking up at the cloudless night sky with its glinting stars, bathed in the soft glow of moonlight, wrapped in Joe's arms.

Ah, wrapped in Joe's arms. That was the key. Joe's arms were what had chased away the worst of her grief and pain, and made everything better. Joe's arms were what made her happy.

She didn't want to just fly away.

"Andrea was telling me about Paul."

"Oh, yeah?" The tone of that was promising. The back against which she rested stiffened, and his head lifted so that his chin no longer brushed her cheek.

"She said she didn't think he was liking his new marriage very much."

"Hmm." More promising still. That single syllable was almost a growl.

"And *I* said I didn't care. I said I was *so* over Paul."

He didn't say anything, so after a tiny pause she snuggled closer. When she continued, her voice was as soft as the wind caressing her face.

"I said there was somebody new."

"Oh, yeah?" He took a deep breath. Alex felt the rise and fall of his chest against her back, and the tensing of his arms around her waist. She slid her own arms down along the slick, puffy sleeves of his coat so that her fingers, oh, so lightly, could rest atop the warm backs of his hands.

"Yeah." She shifted a little so that she could see more of his face. His eyes met hers, silvery in the moonlight, but his expression was impossible to read. "If you want there to be."

"Alex?"

"Yes?"

"Could you do me a favor?" His voice was curiously devoid of expression.

"Like what?"

"Just sit there and don't move."

She was still looking up at him, waiting for his answer, her head thrown back against his shoulder, her lips almost brushing the underside of his jaw. She could feel a new tension in the legs that cradled her, an unusual immobility in the wide chest against her back, a hardening in the arms around her waist.

Before she could ask him why he didn't want her to move, she had her answer: his arms, almost imperceptibly at first, began to shake.

"Joe?" His name was no louder than a whisper. He wet his lips, and then his jaw tensed as his gaze slashed down to meet hers.

"Just give me a minute," he said.

Alex smiled. She had known it all along. He was as turned on by her as she was by him.

"Okay folks, hang on!" The driver called, and without further warning the wagon plunged off the road and lurched through an open farm gate into a field. Alex braced herself, and, from real necessity now, clung to Joe's arms with both hands. Distraction had accomplished what willpower had not been able to, she noticed: the tremors vanished as he planted his feet and held her tight.

In the distance a bright red glow lit up the sky. The bonfire, Alex guessed. It crackled and roared, the sounds growing louder the closer they drew. The smell of burning was strong.

"Can I move now?" she asked with husky pertness as the wagon lumbered up a hill.

"Only if you're prepared to take the consequences," Joe said, his mouth brushing her ear, deliberately this time, she thought. Instinctively she turned her face toward his—and the wagon jolted to a stop.

"Oh, I am," she said, and smiled up into his eyes.

The driver turned in his seat.

"You all can hop on out now. We're here."

Thirty-five

✤

The kids needed no second invitation. They plunged out of the wagon like lemmings over a cliff, and ran for the bonfire, which was situated in a field that was really more of a small valley. Knobby hills encircled it on three sides, and on the fourth, which was flat, there was a woods. The bonfire itself was a pyramid-shaped stack of logs piled as high as a two-story house. It was already furiously ablaze, painting the surrounding countryside and the sky above it with a flickering red glow.

"Well, that was fun, wasn't it?" asked a pleasant voice out of the darkness. Alex realized that the speaker was the woman who had ridden along with them. Alex was very aware that she was still sitting almost in Joe's lap with his arms around her waist. She tapped his uppermost arm, silently asking to be set free. The woman was getting to her feet and at the same time brushing off her clothes as she peered in Alex's and Joe's direction. The man who'd been sitting beside her was getting up too. He was no more than a shadowy figure just beyond the woman.

"It certainly was," Alex said, hoping no one else recognized the falsely cheerful note in her voice as she scrambled to her feet, aided by a boost from Joe's hands on her waist. She felt horribly self-conscious suddenly with the other woman's eyes on her, as though her thoughts had branded her with a glowing scarlet *A* that was visible to all eyes.

"Alex, have you met Patsy Whelan? Patsy, Alex Haywood." Getting to his feet behind her, Joe sounded perfectly at ease.

"Oh, I guessed who you were right off," Patsy said, as Alex stepped carefully through the hay to shake her hand. All Alex could see in the darkness was that Patsy was shorter than herself and plump, with short dark curly hair. She wore jeans, a shiny baseball jacket, and sneakers. Alex was still wondering what to make of her last comment when the woman added, "We don't get that many strangers around here."

"Patsy's the mother of Terry, our center. Like me, she and Bill there"—Joe nodded to the man behind Patsy, who was also dressed in jeans and a baseball jacket, although he was lean—"are on chaperone duty for the pep rally. That's Bill Whelan."

"Welcome, Alex," Bill said, shaking Alex's hand in turn. "Terry's told us about your pretty little sister. She's made quite a hit with the boys, it seems."

"Bill!" Patsy poked him. "No telling tales on Terry. Come on now, those kids are going to eat up everything before we get there."

"You're right." Bill Whelan jumped off the wagon and Patsy clambered down behind him by the simple expedient of sitting down on the edge and then scooting off. "You comin', Joe?"

"Yeah." Joe passed Alex and jumped down too. Alex reached the edge of the wagon bed and looked over. It was a good distance to the ground, and she was wearing high heels. She hated to follow Patsy's ungainly example and scoot off on her bottom, but . . .

Joe, who glanced back at her even as he chatted with the Whelans, saw her hesitate.

"Come on," he said, turning and holding up his arms for her. Alex looked down for a moment at his tanned, handsome face limned now with firelight, at his tall, wide-shouldered form braced to receive her, and was conscious of a sudden fierce wish that the Whelans would vanish in a puff of smoke. But they remained as they were, watching curiously as she leaned forward and put her hands on Joe's shoulders. He caught her around the waist with his hands inside her blazer so that she could feel the imprint of his fingers through the fine cashmere of her sweater. With easy strength he lifted her down to stand before him. Their eyes met. It was a second before she dropped her hands from his shoulders and stepped to the side.

"Who you think's gonna win tomorrow, the Rockets or the Bruins?" Bill Whelan asked Joe. It was apparent that the other couple expected the four of them to walk companionably down the hillside together. Joe started off with them, with Alex on his far side listening with half an ear to the conversation. She'd gone several paces before she realized that she was clinging to Joe's hand.

"We're gonna smoke 'em," Joe said with certainty.

Alex rolled her eyes. Did these men talk of nothing but basketball when they were together? Even Joe was a bore on the subject.

The conversation continued with a spirited dissection of, apparently, every basketball game that had ever been played or ever would be played. Patsy was in on it as well, while Alex said nothing, tried not to stumble over the uneven ground, and savored the fact that, even when she tried to let go, Joe still kept a tight grip on her hand.

More wagons were arriving behind them. Alex could hear the growl of tractors and the rattle of wooden wagon beds as the clumsy vehicles climbed the hill, then the sudden cessation of motion-related noise as they stopped. Shouts and shrieks of laughter and the thud of running feet replaced the previous sounds as each wagon's occupants plunged on foot toward the bonfire, engulfing Alex and the others, who were still moving at a walk, in wave after wave of celebrating teens. The good news was, the surging crowd separated them from the Whelans before they ever even reached the bottom of the hill. The bad news was, the crowd itself was impossible to escape.

"Give me an *R!*"

"*R!*"

"Give me an *O!*"

"*O!*"

"Give me a *C!*"

"*C!*"

The cheers were deafening. Instead of going directly toward the bonfire Joe skirted the growing crowd around it. Long tables had been set up at the far end of the field, Alex saw. Covered with white paper tablecloths, they held everything from raw hot dogs ready to be skewered and roasted over the fire to soft drinks and ice to a mound of Oreo cookies. Adults worked behind the tables. Most were women, although there were a few men. A line of cars and trucks was parked off to one side, which explained how the workers had beaten the first hay wagon to the field.

"Hungry?" Joe asked.

Alex realized that she hadn't eaten, but the long answer was, not for food.

"No," she said.

"Me neither."

They kept walking. Alex stumbled over a rough spot in the grass for what must have been the dozenth time. Joe's hand tightened around hers, keeping her from falling to her knees.

"Princess, do you *own* any tennis shoes?"

Knowing that he was taking a swipe at her heels, Alex smiled sweetly at him. "Why, yes, I do. I wear them when I play tennis."

"You might try breaking them out for occasions like pep rallies."

"If I had known that I'd be outside hiking through cow pastures, I might have. On second thought, combat boots seem more appropriate. Do you think that maybe you could slow down a little bit? Then my high heels might not be a problem."

He laughed, and slowed his pace marginally. "Am I walking too fast? Sorry. I'm trying to get out of the way before the whole town spots us and comes over to talk."

That goal was so in keeping with Alex's own desires that she was perfectly willing to walk as fast as he thought was necessary to accomplish it, high heels or no. "In that case, I take it back. Lead on."

"Eli's getting an award tonight, so I want to hang around and watch. And Jenny's singing. After that . . ."

"After that?" she asked when he broke off.

"After that we can do whatever we want." They had reached a spot near the woods where the shadow of the tall trees blended with the darkness of the night to offer a degree of extra privacy. The glow from the fire provided some illumination, and there were a few other people in the vicinity, but still the spot was on the edge of the crowd, and away from the back-and-forth traffic to the food tables.

"And that would be?" Alex asked, looking up at him as they stopped.

"I don't know. Maybe we could grab a hot dog or something." He grinned at her, carried her hand to his mouth in a gesture that left her melting inside, then shifted his attention to the front of the bonfire where a man with a bullhorn was shouting something that Alex could not, at the moment, understand.

The knuckle he'd kissed burned. She shivered. Joe glanced down at her.

"Cold?" he asked, his gaze moving disparagingly over her extremely chic and expensive blazer and sweater. It was clear from his expression that his opinion of her choice of clothing for the evening's event matched his opinion of her choice of shoes.

She wasn't cold, not really. Although the night had turned chilly she was burning up inside.

But she had no intention of telling him that. Yet.

"A little," she lied.

"Here." Clearly distracted by the hoopla going on in front of the bonfire—cloth dummies were being thrown on it as if it were some kind of auto-da-fé—he let go of her hand, slid out of his jacket, and dropped it over her shoulders.

As the slithery blue folds enveloped her, Alex didn't know whether to laugh or cry. Here she was, in her elegant Jil Sander outfit, her Manolo Blahnik heels sinking into the dirt of a cow pasture in the middle of nowhere, draped in the ugliest coat she had ever seen in her life, watching a bizarre ritual that she cared absolutely nothing about.

And the sad part about it was, she was actually glad to be there.

The presence of the man beside her meant she was exactly where she wanted to be.

Grasping the edges of Joe's jacket, she pulled them closer so that the jacket wouldn't slide off. It was still warm from the heat of his body, and it smelled of him. Alex inhaled, then smiled a little at her own idiocy.

"Go, Eli!" her sex-bomb hollered, cupping his hands around his mouth. Surfacing briefly, Alex realized that Eli now stood in front of the cheering crowd, accepting something that looked like a—canned ham? It didn't make much sense, but then she'd missed every word the master of ceremonies (or whatever the man with the bullhorn was called) had said. She clapped dutifully as Eli held the canned ham (surely not!) over his head like a coveted trophy, then winced as Joe let loose with a piercing wolf whistle almost in her ear.

When her ears had stopped ringing, she nudged him with an elbow.

"Tell me something," she said when he looked down at her inquiringly. "Did they just give Eli a canned ham?"

"You're not paying attention," Joe chided.

"So did they or didn't they?"

"They did. It's the annual award for showmanship on the basketball court. Meaning Eli's a ham, get it? He dribbles behind his back a lot."

"Oh, I see," Alex said. "You must be very proud."

Joe grinned.

The cheerleaders cavorted, the crowd yelled some more, and somebody tapped Alex on the shoulder. She glanced around, surprised.

"Don't tell me you're a Rockets fan?" It was the dentist, the one she had met on her never-to-be-forgotten mission to fire Joe, with a thin thirty-something brunette in tow. The woman smiled at Alex. Alex smiled back.

"Looks like it," Alex said lamely.

"Hey, Ben, they're gonna be something this year, don't you think?" Joe had looked around and discovered the newcomers.

"Goin' all the way."

"Alex, you remember Ben? This is his wife, Tracy. Their boy Steve is our sixth man."

Whatever, Alex thought, but she smiled as if she knew just what Joe was talking about. Really, if she wasn't almost dizzy with desire for the man she'd be tempted to hit him over the head. She was not standing out here up to her ankles in cow pies just to listen to him talk about basketball.

"This is Miss Haywood, Tracy," Ben said to his wife. Tracy's gaze slid from Alex's face down to Joe's coat, which Alex still clutched closed with both hands.

"I guessed," she said. Something in her tone made Alex wonder again just what, exactly, was being said about her around town. Probably, she thought, she didn't want to know.

"Alex," Alex said, letting go of one side of Joe's coat to hold out her hand.

"Tracy." They shook hands, and Ben and Tracy turned to watch the proceedings with them. A group of about thirty little girls was lining up in front of the bonfire now, and Alex realized that Jenny was getting ready to sing.

In the darkness, it was hard to differentiate one from another. Alex had to look really, really hard to find Jenny. She was in the middle row, third from the left. With the firelight playing over her, it was impossible to discern the pink streaks in her hair, or anything except the most general outline of her dress.

"See why I wasn't too worried?" Joe said in her ear, then clapped wildly as the girls finished "America the Beautiful" and launched into "My Old Kentucky Home."

When the group's performance was finished, the girls ran off. They all clapped again, and remarked on how beautiful the singing had been.

"Dad, can I have five bucks?" It was Josh, swaggering up with a group of his friends. Alex hadn't seen him previously; he and his friends must have been on a different hay wagon. Tonight he had a heavy gold chain around his neck and a ski cap pulled low over his ears. Alex had to smile, even as she glanced at Joe to see how he would react to his son's punk look. It didn't seem to bother him. He forked over some money, and the boys disappeared.

"Alex, are you hungry? 'Scuse us, guys, I think we're going to go scare up some food."

Before Alex could reply, Joe grabbed her elbow through the coat and turned her in the direction of the food tables.

"See you later!"

"Bye!"

With his friends' good-byes echoing in their ears, Alex was marched away.

"Talk about Grand Central Station," Joe muttered under his breath, skirting the tree line while heading in the general direction of the white-covered tables. Then he looked down at her.

"Hungry yet?"

"Not really."

"Good," he said, and, grabbing her hand, he pulled her into the woods.

Thirty-six

✦

U p until about forty minutes previously, if it hadn't been the worst day of his life it had been right up there in the top ten, Joe thought. It had taken a while for the ramifications of what Tommy had told him to sink in. When it did, the horror of the situation made him literally sick to his stomach; he'd had to stop and buy some Tums on the way to his next meeting. Laura's purse and shoes found, the former stained with what was possibly human blood; a garbage bag full of ashes—Laura reduced to ashes? *Laura?* Her face—her young face, full and rosy and laughing, the way she had looked back when he'd first met her—kept appearing in his mind's eye. God, as a boy and young man he had loved her madly. They'd all warned him against marrying her, his friends, his dad, his mom, and Carol. A party girl, they'd called her, and they'd been exactly right. But he'd been so sure that what he and Laura had was unlike anything anyone had ever felt before that he hadn't listened, he'd married her—and then of course he'd reaped what he had sowed. By the time he'd filed for divorce, he had hated her. Eventually he had quit hating her, just like, years earlier, he had once quit loving her. But now, long after every emotion he had ever felt for her had died stone cold dead, the thought of

Laura reduced to a garbage bag full of ashes could still make him sick.

If Laura *was* in that bag—and she couldn't be, things like that just didn't happen around here—then she sure hadn't gotten in there by herself, as Tommy had said. Somebody had put her there. Somebody had killed her, and put her body in that bag.

That meant that a murder had been committed. Someone had murdered Laura, apparently years ago. In Paradise County? No way.

He sure hadn't killed her, although as Rob had warned him the spouse was always the prime suspect, and then there was the history of his relationship with Laura, too. Everybody for miles around knew about that. Fortunately, everybody knew him, too. He didn't anticipate being charged with Laura's murder. He didn't think.

But if there had been a murder, and he hadn't done it, then who had?

The thought, when he bent it around his friends and neighbors, was mind-boggling.

But then, Laura had been wild, out of control, into men and drugs. Maybe she'd gotten into something way over her head, some drug deal or something. . . .

God, he hoped not. That would just be piling it on. More muck for the gossips to rake over when, if, it all came out.

Whatever else Laura was or had been, she remained the mother of his kids.

God, if this thing were true, if it was Laura in that bag— and he prayed to God it wasn't—he would have to tell his kids.

Wait, he'd told himself when the thought with its attendant hideous images had first occurred to him, just wait. Right now, all anybody knew was that an old pair of shoes and a purse of Laura's with unidentified stains on it had been found in a garbage bag in a field, along with another garbage bag containing bones and hair. Tommy wasn't even positively sure yet that the remains were human, let alone Laura's.

No need to jump the gun. When he knew something for sure, then he could get sick to his stomach. Then he could tell his kids.

For now, the best thing to do, the only thing to do, was try not to think about it, and wait.

About an hour and a half after his meeting with Tommy had concluded, he'd met with a conference room full of bankers and other investors in Louisville. They'd listened courteously to his plans for buying some of the Whistledown breeding stock and establishing his own racing stable. They'd gone over his business proposal with a fine-tooth comb. Then they'd bottom-lined him.

It was a good plan, a workable plan, a plan they'd be willing to back—as long as he assumed a fair portion of the risk. What that meant, in the end, was that as well as his expertise, labor, and current facilities, he was going to have to pony up about a quarter million dollars in cash.

That was like telling somebody fine, yes, sure you can marry the handsome prince—if you can squeeze your size eleven foot into this size three glass slipper.

A quarter million in cash. He didn't see how he could make that happen. If he sold everything he owned—not that it was debt-free or anything, because it wasn't—he didn't think he could realize that.

And then he and the kids would have to live while he struggled to make it work.

He'd gotten back from that meeting just in time to make a quick round of the horses, shower, change clothes, and head, with Josh, for the pep rally.

By the time he'd climbed into that hay wagon with the team, he'd been about as down as he'd ever felt in his life.

Then Alex had come aboard, and literally fallen into his lap.

And he'd found the silver lining to his gray cloud, the one bright spot in a very bad day.

Just having her in his arms had worked better than any medicine he'd ever tried. By the end of that hayride, if he hadn't forgotten all about the shocks of the day, he'd at least been able, for a while, to push them aside.

Now, as he pulled her into the woods, Alex was the only thing on his mind.

Juvenile. That was the best way to describe how he was behaving, Joe thought with a quick inner grin as he towed Alex along the nearly pitch-dark path he remembered so well that he could have followed it blindfolded. He'd been pulling girls out of pep rallies and into this woods since he was in elementary school. Lots of pep rallies, lots of girls. He knew all the good spots.

He wasn't the only one, either, judging from the flashes of movement he glimpsed under trees on both sides. Kids making out in the woods—it was a story as old as teenagers themselves.

The only problem was, he was now thirty-frigging-seven years old. And making out in the woods was a mild description for what he had in mind.

"Hey, you up there! Where's the fire?" Alex sounded amused and faintly breathless at the same time. Her voice was low and husky, just barely audible over the sounds of the party behind them and the closer rustling of the woods.

Even listening to her voice with its faint Northern accent made him hard.

"I don't know about you," he replied over his shoulder,

"but I'd just as soon get out of sight before somebody sees us and decides to come with us on our walk."

Joe slowed down all the same, in deference to her high heels, which, if truth were told, might be impractical footgear for a pep rally but were, nevertheless, sexy as hell. Actually, everything she had on was sexy as hell, from the skinny black pants that made her legs look impossibly long and shapely to the sweater that clung like a second skin to her breasts and was so soft to the touch that, in the wagon, it had been all he could do to keep his hands where they belonged. *Deliver me from temptation* should have been the theme of that hayride. Sitting there with her pressed against his privates had been the worst kind of hell—and heaven. His arms hadn't shaken like that since he was seventeen years old.

It had also taught him something: Trying to protect himself from Alex Haywood was a waste of time. He was already in about as deep as it was possible to get.

The path was too narrow to permit them to walk side by side, so she was trailing behind him, hanging on to his hand. Her hand was slender and long-fingered, with cool, soft skin. He burned when he remembered what her hands had felt like moving over him.

"Is that what we're doing? Going for a walk?" The hint of amusement in her voice almost made him walk faster again.

"Uh-huh."

"Oh. I see. Do you often walk in the woods in the pitch dark?"

"Not often, no." Actually, the last time he'd pulled a girl into these woods he'd been eighteen. After that he had graduated to making love in more private, and comfortable, surroundings.

"But you do know where you're going, right? I'd hate to

get lost in here—or walk off a cliff." She did sound a little worried, he thought, and smiled wryly to himself. Walking off a cliff was definitely not on tonight's agenda.

"I know where I'm going."

"Joe, I think I saw somebody over there under the trees." Her voice had dropped to a scared whisper.

"Hmm."

"Really." The single word, still whispered, was urgent.

"Probably just some kids."

"Why would kids be out here in the woods? All the action's up by the bonfire—oh."

That small *oh* as revelation struck made him smile again. "Yeah, oh."

He found the now badly overgrown turnoff he had been looking for, took it, and, finally, stepped around a thicket of blackberry brambles that effectively boxed off a grotto containing a picnic table, a pair of wooden park benches, and a concrete statue of a dog with a basket of flowers in its mouth from the rest of the woods. A quick glance around told him that he and Alex were alone.

Good. He would have hated to have had to run off a pair of lip-locked kids.

"Joe . . ."

Before she could complete the thought, he swung her around in front of him and backed her up against the trunk of the towering elm that kept this spot cool and dark even on the hottest, brightest summer day. His hands curved around her upper arms through the down-filled channels of his coat. He hadn't even missed the garment, and no wonder. On the wagon ride over, she'd made him so hot he would have sold his soul for a bucket of ice water to dump over his head. The way he felt right now, he might never cool down.

She was looking up at him. There was just enough

moonlight sifting down through the barren canopy of branches overhead to allow him to see the shadowy shape of her face. Delicate bones, wide blue eyes, the lushest, sexiest mouth it had ever been his pleasure to see. He slid his hand beneath the pale curtain of her hair to rest against the side of her neck. His thumb caressed the silky skin of her cheek.

She shivered beneath his touch.

"Remember what we were talking about just before we got off the hay wagon?" His voice was husky. It was, he discovered, an effort to pause long enough to talk, but there was something he needed to say.

"About Paul?" Her voice was soft, unmistakably short of breath—but still full of sass.

"About someone new in your life," he said with the merest hint of an edge. "Honey, you've got yourself a volunteer."

Then he kissed her. Her lips trembled and parted at the first touch of his, and her arms came up to wrap around his neck. His coat slid, unlamented, from her shoulders to the ground.

Her mouth was just like he remembered: warm, and wet, and incredibly sweet. God, he'd been having fantasies day and night about the taste of her mouth!

About the taste of all of her.

Thirty-seven

✢

A lex was trembling as his arms came around her, under her blazer, strong enough to crush the breath from her lungs if he chose, pulling her tight against him. His body was big and warm and hard with muscle, and she reveled in the feel of him as her breasts flattened against his chest and she wrapped her arms around his neck. One hand slid down her spine to curve over her buttocks, bringing her hard against the bulge in the front of his jeans.

She moaned, and wriggled even closer, pressing against him with unashamed need. She wanted him naked and all over her and inside her—and she didn't want to wait.

The hard arms holding her close to him began to shake.

He lifted his head then, breaking the kiss, drawing in a sharp breath.

"See what you do to me? My arms haven't shaken like this since I was a kid." His voice was a near whisper, husky, dark, and unbearably sexy.

"I like it when your arms shake."

"Oh, yeah?"

"Yeah."

With hungry urgency, she went up on tiptoe to press her lips to the warm prickly skin on the underside of his jaw. His breath caught, and then he slid both hands beneath her bottom and picked her clear up off her feet.

"Joe . . ."

"Shh."

His mouth found hers again even as he swung her around, his hands moving from the cheeks of her bottom down along her thighs until her legs, at his urging, wrapped around his waist.

He lifted his mouth from hers.

"Remember the kitchen, when you were sitting on the countertop trying to wrap your legs around my waist?" He was walking with her.

"Mm-hm." Clinging to him, she was busy kissing his neck.

"Walking away from that almost killed me."

"Your own fault."

His mouth found hers again as he set her down on the picnic table that she had just glimpsed in the seconds after he had pulled her around the briars, then bent over her until her back was against the hard cold wood. Her legs were locked around his waist, her arms around his neck. The table was bearing her weight; she could feel the small gaps between the boards through her clothes. He was leaning over her, lying almost on top of her, with the bulge in his pants grinding hard and deep against her crotch. Burning up with passion, her nails digging into the back of his neck, her hips moving in hungry answer to his thrusts, she had to pull her mouth free of his just to breathe. His mouth was scalding hot as it trailed wet kisses along her cheek and down her neck.

"What do you say we try that kitchen thing again?" he murmured in her ear.

"Oh, God, Joe." She arched against him helplessly, weak with hunger for him, absolute putty in his hands as his mouth moved down to find her breast. Her hands gripped his shoulders as he pressed his mouth against her there. Then he was pulling up her sweater and her bra, pushing them out of his way, and closing his teeth around her already pebble-hard nipple, biting her gently. She gasped at the sharp pleasure-pain of it. His hand slid down between their bodies to find the button that closed her pants. . . .

"Give me a toke, would you?"

The voice probably wouldn't have penetrated the fog Alex was lost in if it hadn't been close—and familiar. Joe must have heard it at the same time, because his head came up.

"I didn't think you smoked dope." The second voice was higher pitched, coquettish, and even more horribly familiar.

"You must be thinking about somebody else." The first voice again.

A giggle was the response.

"What the hell . . ." Joe muttered, lifting himself off her and yanking her clothes back into place. Still slightly dazed but appreciating the urgency of the situation, Alex slid off the picnic table. She was decent and standing beside Joe when the tall, shadowy figure that was Eli came into view around the blackberry bush. Behind him, holding his hand, was Neely. Eli was, unmistakably, taking a drag on a joint as he stepped into view. The red glowing tip grew brighter as he inhaled. The sickly sweet smell of marijuana wafted through the air.

"What the hell . . . !" This time Joe's voice was louder as he stared in horror at his son. Eli stopped dead, the hand holding the joint falling and the joint itself dropping to the ground.

"Oh, shit!" Neely said, and dropped something too. A

can, which rolled toward the side of the clearing. The scent of beer joined the smell of pot as the can's contents spilled out.

"Dad!" Eli's voice was a croak. He must have glanced down and seen the still burning joint, because he stepped on it, and pulled his hand from Neely's at the same time.

For an instant there was an appalled silence as adults and teens stared at each other.

"What are you *doing?*" Joe said to his son, as if he couldn't believe what he indubitably had seen. "What the *fuck* do you think you're doing?"

"Dad . . ." There was anguish in Eli's voice now.

"It was my stuff," Neely said defiantly. "All Eli did was take a drag. The beer was mine, too."

"I don't doubt it," Joe bit off, barely sparing Neely a glance. His attention was focused almost exclusively on Eli.

"Neely!" Alex groaned.

"Dad!" This was another voice, a more distant voice, calling Joe: Josh.

"All right, give me the stuff." Joe held out his hand, palm up, toward the kids. "Whatever you've got. Right now."

"Dad!" Josh's voice was closer, coming down the path, and urgent.

"Dad, I'm *sorry,*" Eli said.

"Give me the stuff." Joe's voice was low, ugly.

"Dad!" Josh was yelling.

"Here." Neely pulled something from her bag and slapped it—a Baggie with something in it, Alex saw—into Joe's palm. In the dark, Alex couldn't be sure about its contents, but she was prepared to make a guess. "It's mine, I told you. Not Eli's."

"Oh, Neely!" Alex moaned. For the moment, at least, there just didn't seem to be anything else to say.

"All right, march. Both of you. Back to the field. Damn it to hell anyway, Eli, I never would've believed . . . I said march! Josh wouldn't be looking for me if it wasn't important."

Stuffing the Baggie into his pocket, Joe caught Alex's hand, pulling her after him as he followed the silent figures of Neely and Eli from the clearing. At the last minute Alex remembered Joe's coat. It had fallen to the ground beside the elm tree. She snatched it up, clutching it in one hand as Joe stepped around the briars and out onto the path.

"Josh!" He called to his second son in response to another hail. "I'm here!"

"Dad!"

"Hang on, I'm headed your way."

Josh was waiting at the mouth of the path. He glanced at Neely and Eli as they emerged first, but then his focus was all on Joe.

"What is it?" Joe's voice was sharp. It was obvious from Josh's face that something was badly wrong.

"It's Grandpa—Dad, he's dead drunk and he's trying to drive and the sheriff's trying to stop him and . . ."

"God damn it," Joe interrupted bitterly. "Where is he?"

"Out by where the cars are parked."

"Come on. Eli, you stay with me."

"You too," Alex said to Neely.

With Josh running ahead, they crossed the field to where the line of cars was parked beside the food tables. Joe was moving so fast that Alex almost had to run to keep up. Eli and Neely, the former white as a sheet, the latter pouty-faced, kept pace at their side. Joe seemed oblivious of the fact that he was still holding her hand. Under the circumstances, nobody else seemed to notice.

There was a small crowd—perhaps three dozen people—gathered around a black pickup truck that Alex recognized as belonging to Cary.

Dropping her hand, Joe shouldered through the crowd, which, when they looked around and saw who it was, parted to let him through. The rest of the group stayed close behind him. Emerging from the semicircle of bystanders, Alex took in the scene at a glance.

Dressed in khakis and a black leather jacket, Cary lay on his stomach on the rough grass kicking and bucking and bellowing curse words for all he was worth. His hands were cuffed behind his back, and the stocky sheriff was straddling him to keep him down.

Joe's whole body seemed to vibrate with tension as he approached them.

"What the hell is this?" Joe demanded. Cary bucked and yelled harder. The sheriff seemed to be having a hard time holding him down. "Damn it, Tommy, get off him!"

"He friggin' punched me in the face, Joe!" From his position astride the struggling Cary, the sheriff looked up at Joe, an aggrieved expression on his face. There was a big red mark on one cheek along with a small cut that oozed blood at the corner of his mouth. "He's drunk as a polecat, and he was gonna get in his truck and drive home. I took his friggin' keys." The sheriff held up a set of keys. Joe took them from him, and stuck them in the front pocket of his jeans—the same pocket, Alex recalled, that held the Baggie.

"Damn it to hell and back! Get off him, Tommy. I'll take care of him."

"I oughta arrest him."

"Yeah, I know. Here, get off. He'll be sorry in the morning."

"You tell him that if he punches me again, I will arrest

him, your father or not." The sheriff climbed off his unwilling bronco. Cary immediately rocked onto his side, and from there to his knees.

"You can't tell me I can't drive my own truck! Little snot-nosed punk! I've known you since you was in diapers, and . . ."

Joe reached down, grabbed the back of his father's motorcycle-style jacket, and hauled him to his feet. Seeing Joe glaring at him, Cary faltered for an instant, but then he recovered himself and went on to describe the sheriff in terms so profane that they made Alex blink.

"Damn it, Joe . . ." the sheriff began.

"Shut up, Pop," Joe said grimly, giving his father a shake. "Just shut up. Tommy, take the cuffs off him."

"But, Joe . . ."

"Do it, would you please? Then I'll take him home."

"Damn all, I oughta put him in jail." But the sheriff unlocked the handcuffs all the same, then sprang back out of the way. Which was a good thing. Cary came up swinging. Joe grabbed his father, whirled him around, locked his arms around his chest from behind and wrestled him toward the truck.

"God damn it, you're no damned son of mine! Let me go, you . . ."

"Joe, you can't drive with him like that. I'll drive, and you hold on to the belligerent so-and-so so's he don't do me no harm." Sounding disgusted, the sheriff followed Joe and his father toward the truck. Eli, Josh, Alex, and Neely trailed them too. Eli, looking white and miserable, kept his eyes on Joe. Alex, who was still clutching Joe's coat, glared at Neely, who looked sullen.

Cary was still ranting: "You get in the truck with me, you slimy little sheriff bastard, and I'll knock your damned teeth out! I'll . . ."

"Dad, I'll drive," Eli said to Joe over his grandfather's bellowed invective, his voice low and shaken. Still grappling with his father, Joe looked around at his tall son, whose expression was both anguished and embarrassed, and shook his head.

"I don't want you to drive, Eli. I want you to get yourself in your truck and get yourself home."

"Dad, I can't. I . . ."

"What do you mean, you can't?" Joe's voice was low and furious. "If you know what's good for you, you'd best be home when I walk through the door."

"My truck's at school, and you know the wagons won't head back until about three A.M. Dad, if I miss the lock-in, Coach will want to know why, and—and he'll kick me off the team if he finds out."

Anguish was in Eli's voice.

"God damn it, Joey, you let me go!" This was Cary, kicking at the side of the truck as he tried to break free of Joe's arms.

"Eli, damn it . . ." Joe said to his son, trying to hold on to his father at the same time. "All right. We'll deal with this tomorrow. You stay for the lock-in, and do what you're supposed to do, and get yourself home early. And if I were you, I wouldn't make any plans for quite a while."

"Dad, I'm so sorry." Eli looked it, too. Josh stood close to his brother, frowning as he tried to understand what was happening.

"We'll talk about it at home tomorrow."

"Let me drive, Joe," Alex offered quietly, as Joe opened the pickup door with one hand and manhandled his struggling father into the passenger seat. It was obvious that he was going to need help getting Cary home, and the sheriff, who was watching the proceedings from a little distance now, was not a good candidate.

Joe met her gaze. "Fine. Thanks." He fished the keys from his pocket and handed them to her. Then his glance swung to Eli. "You heard what I said. Tomorrow early."

Eli nodded miserably. On her way around the truck, Alex stopped beside Neely.

"You and I will deal with this tomorrow, too," Alex said under her breath, and for once meant every word. "And if you cause any more trouble tonight, or if we can't come to some kind of understanding about future behavior tomorrow, you'll be heading off to boarding school by dark. I swear to God you will."

Thirty-eight

✤

T he predator was whistling as he worked. He was having a really good day. He'd had an epiphany last night. Instead of spending maybe ten minutes at a time in Alexandra's bedroom, he had thought of a way to have her nearly full-time without taking any of the risks associated with her actually going missing.

He was at Whistledown, in her bedroom, installing tiny video cameras in the ceiling over her bed, and in the ceiling in her bathroom. When he was finished, he would have his own private television station: all Alexandra, all the time.

She and her sister were at the pep rally, which would go on until the wee hours of the morning. He knew, because he had been there himself and seen them there. The whole town was there, just as it always was, including Whistledown's next-door neighbor Joe and his family.

So being in the house at such an early hour—ten P.M.—really wasn't a risk at all.

Nobody was around except the damned cat.

It had been watching him. For a moment, earlier, as he had worked, he had felt like something was behind him. The sensation had been so strong, and so eerie, that he had whirled around, moving faster than he had moved in some time.

To find that the big orange tabby cat that seemed to haunt this place was staring up at him from the doorway, its eyes wide and unblinking as it took in his every move.

He hated the cat. He'd seen it here at Whistledown before. It always seemed to appear out of nowhere, to follow him around, and no matter how he tried he—could—never—catch—it.

He tried again, and came up short again, panting, as the animal darted under Alexandra's bed.

One day, he promised himself, one day he would make a crispy critter out of that cat.

In the meantime, he would enjoy himself watching Alexandra, he promised himself. *Every move you make, every breath you take.* . . . He discovered that that was the tune he was whistling as he installed the last tiny component in the last tiny hole he had drilled, and broke off, grinning broadly.

He was nothing if not a witty and amusing man.

When he was finished, he stood for a moment, admiring his handiwork with satisfaction: a hole no bigger than a pinprick over the bed. Another the same size in the bathroom.

Alexandra would never see them, never suspect that he was watching as she changed clothes, watching as she showered, watching as she slept. . . .

The idea excited him so much that he decided to drop in and visit Cassandra before he left.

Although she was not, really not, what he had a taste for tonight. Her dry, unresponsive body was about as toothsome as overcooked steak compared to Alexandra's silken curves. . . .

Oh, well, he told himself philosophically. And grinned again as he found himself humming *love the one you're with.*

Thirty-nine

✤

I'm really sorry, Eli," Neely said humbly. They were in Eli's pickup truck barreling down dark, near-deserted U.S. 60 toward Whistledown. It was about fifteen minutes after Eli's dad and his grandpa and Alex had taken off to take the old drunk home. If she and Eli hurried, she thought, she just might be able to make it up to her room and get the stash of dope out of there before anybody found it. Because of course they'd search—she'd been through this before at boarding school. Every time they caught you doping, or drinking, they always searched your room to try to find your stash. In her room at Whistledown she had pot and lots of other stuff—speed, mostly, to help her keep her weight down, and poppers and some reds to chill with—and if Alex found it she would shit bricks. She would also probably send her to some, like, military boarding school for the rest of her life. If anybody else found it— for instance, say, Eli's studmuffin of a dad—they'd probably call the cops. So she had, like, this brief window of opportunity to remove it and save her ass.

All she had to do was nip into the house, run up to her room, grab the stuff, and she was out of there. Five minutes, max, she'd promised Eli, pleading with him to take her, explaining to him what was at risk.

The only problem was, as he pointed out, his truck was at the school, and neither of them had a way to get from the pep rally to the school. That had been easily solved when, in the middle of their argument, Neely had spied a girl, Cinda Hawkins from English class, whom she knew getting into a car with an older boy who'd dropped by specifically to pick her up. No problem, Cinda had said when Neely had run over and begged a ride for her and Eli just as far as the school. Cinda had obviously assumed that Neely and Eli were, like her, planning to duck out of the lock-in.

Eli had been really quiet all the way to school, and Neely guessed he was worried about his dad being mad. She felt a little guilty about that. Eli wouldn't have been smoking that joint—not at the pep rally, anyway—if she hadn't brought the stuff with her. He smoked a little ordinarily, but not much, and he didn't drink. She could understand why, now that she'd seen his grandpa totally smashed.

Alcoholism was kind of like a family weakness. It ran in her family, too, even though everybody kept it real quiet. Years ago, her dad had been a drunk just like Eli's grandpa. She didn't remember much about it—she'd never been around him much—but she'd heard tales, from the servants and others.

Maybe that was why she liked beer so much, she mused. Maybe she was, like, going to develop into an alcoholic, too. When her dad was alive, she'd used to kind of hope that she would. At least then he would have to deal with her, would have to do something about his unwanted daughter with the disease he'd passed down to her.

Or maybe he still wouldn't care.

"I don't think this is a good idea, Neels," Eli protested uneasily even as he floored it down the road. "My dad is mad enough already. If he catches us sneaking around Whistledown when I'm supposed to be at the pep rally . . . *God.* I don't want to be there."

"He won't catch us," Neely promised. "You can cut the lights, and I swear I'll be so fast. Eli, if I don't go get that stuff out of my room, Alex will search or your dad will search or they'll call the *cops* and they'll search, and they'll find it. I'll be *toast*. If they bring the cops into it, I might even have to go to jail."

"You're too young to go to jail," Eli said sourly. "Detention center, maybe."

"Like that's a big improvement."

"What if they're in the house?" Eli asked uneasily. "God, I don't want to run into my dad. He's never going to get over this as it is."

"If they're in the house, we won't go in. Besides, they won't be. They have to take your grandpa home, and stay with him until he's settled down. That's bound to take a little while. They won't be at Whistledown yet—we've got a little time."

"Shit, Neely. I can't believe I'm doing this." Eli sounded so miserable that Neely looked at him curiously.

"Is your dad, like, going to beat you up or something over this?" From the way Joe had looked, she could imagine that happening very easily. Never having had a relationship with hers, she wasn't quite sure how a father would react to something like this. From the look on Eli's dad's face, his response was going to be something bad.

Eli shot her a disgusted look. "No, he's not going to beat me up. He's going to ground me for the rest of my life, probably, and take the keys to my truck and make me work my ass off around the property and God knows what else. And he's going to say that I let him down. And I have. It's always been Josh he worried about doing something like this, never me. He trusts—trusted—me."

Eli ended on what was almost a forlorn note.

"I'm *sorry*," Neely said again, scooting even closer,

which, since she was sitting right beside him on the bench seat, was kind of hard to do. "Who would have thought we'd run into your dad in the woods?"

"Yeah." Eli sounded dispirited.

"He was probably shagging my sister, you know."

"Yeah."

"Oh, God, Eli, here's the turn—you *missed* it!" She looked over her shoulder as he drove right past Fields Lane.

"You think I'm going right down the middle of the street?" Eli asked savagely. "What if they should be driving out, or something? I'm going back through the fields. Hang on."

The truck slowed, and seconds later pulled into a gravel lay-by, where Eli doused the lights. From there, they went bouncing over the fields in the dark.

"Can you *see* anything?" Neely hissed, hanging on to the dashboard with both hands.

"I can see Whistledown. Don't worry, I know what I'm doing."

Neely could see Whistledown too, a square, gracious shape on top of the hill just ahead. Lights glowed from the windows—both she and Alex preferred to leave the lights on when they were gone. The driveway seemed to be deserted. Beyond Whistledown, on down the hill, the Welches' house was dark.

"They must still be at Grandpa's," Eli said, sounding relieved as he echoed her thoughts.

"Told you."

The truck bumped to a halt not far from Whistledown's back door. Neely fumbled in her bag for her key.

"I'll wait here and keep a look out," Eli said. "Get in there and get the damned stuff and *hurry up.*"

Thus adjured, Neely scrambled out of the door.

Forty

✤

The predator was in Whistledown's basement, on his way down to Cassandra, when he realized he'd left his drill right in the middle of Alexandra's bed. Now that, he told himself, she would notice.

Of course, she would have no idea how it got there. It might be amusing to watch her try to figure it out.

But no, he cautioned himself. She might call the police. His fingerprints were on that drill. If the police came, if they were curious, if they ran a fingerprint check, they would come sniffing around him.

Life was like that. A series of *ifs*. A successful man always had to keep an eye out for the *ifs*.

So he headed back upstairs to retrieve his drill. He went up the back staircase, moving swiftly for his size because he was anxious to get down to Cassandra and then go on home. Really, with the late nights he'd been keeping lately, he was starting to feel a little run-down.

Maybe he should start taking Geritol. He smiled at the thought, and was still smiling when he heard footsteps hurrying toward him along the upstairs hall.

His eyes widened. He was near the top of the stairs—too late to go back. He looked around the narrow stairwell with its smooth walls: nowhere to hide. He could feel the adrenaline start to pump through his system at the idea that he was, perhaps, about to be discovered. In a way, because of the rush it gave the body, fear was almost as good as sex—wasn't he always telling Cassandra and the rest of them so?

He reached toward his back pocket, fumbling with the button, pulling out his taser. . . .

The little sister, Cornelia, appeared at the top of the stairs.

Forty-one

✢

For Alex, the ride home with Joe and Cary was a nightmare. Cary cursed explosively as he struggled in vain to free himself from his son's hold. Joe made only the occasional terse remark, interspersed with variations on telling his father to shut up. Alex, who was concentrating on driving, said nothing. The stench of liquor was so strong in the enclosed cab that she finally had to roll down a window or be sick. At last, as they neared their turnoff at Fields Lane, Cary did shut up. Surprised, Alex glanced around Joe to find Cary slumped against his son's shoulder.

"He's passed out," Joe said, sounding grim. They were driving past Whistledown now, and Alex spared a sideways glance for the dignified old house on top of the hill. With the interior lights that she always left burning when she was out at night shining through the windows, the house had an air of expectancy, as if it were waiting for her to get home. An instant later, her gaze snapped back toward the second-story porch. There was a man standing there, exactly where he had been before. With a brightly lit window as a backdrop, the image was clear. . . .

"For God's sake, Alex, watch the road!" Joe yelped.

Attention recalled to the road, Alex quickly corrected

her swerve toward the ditch. Then, wide-eyed, she glanced back at Whistledown again. The man was gone. She blinked, and looked again.

No one was there.

"Joe," Alex said urgently. "The man on the porch . . . I just saw him again."

"Oh, God, not tonight." Sounding dispirited, Joe looked toward Whistledown, but of course there was nothing to be seen. They had already passed it by this time, but when she glanced back at the house it was clear that the soft incandescent glow coming through the windows was unobstructed now.

"But Joe, I saw . . ."

"Honey, let me deal with one crisis at a time, will you please?" Joe sounded indescribably weary, and Alex, after a swift glance at his face, said nothing more. Whatever she had seen, she could worry about it later. There were more urgent matters to deal with at the moment. Maybe, she told herself, what she had seen was just her imagination, or a trick of the light.

But she didn't believe it.

The gravel lane that led to Cary's house began near Joe's driveway, then angled on around the barn and up toward the woods.

"Open the door, would you please?" Joe said to her when they were parked in front of the house, and he was hoisting his father over his shoulder. Alex nodded, and went ahead of him up the pair of wooden steps to the narrow porch that ran the length of the house. Unlocking the door, she swung it wide. Joe, with Cary limp as a bag of feed over his shoulder, walked past her into the house.

Alex followed him, closing the door and looking for a light switch as Joe, with the surety of someone who knew his way around, headed off through the darkened house, disappearing around a corner. She found the switch and flipped it. Immediately a lamp came on, and Alex discovered that she was standing in the living room. The house had a fairly open arrangement, and to her left, beyond a half wall that held a gray telephone sitting atop a phone book, was a small kitchen. The kitchen was strictly utilitarian, with inexpensive-looking wooden cabinets, white appliances, and a small round table in the center.

Ahead of her, a hallway branched left. As Joe had disappeared down it with Cary, Alex presumed that it led to the bedrooms.

The living room itself was small and neat, with plain white plaster walls, a comfortable-looking couch slipcovered in red corduroy, and a gold tweed armchair and a bentwood rocker, both placed at right angles to the couch. The white ceramic bean-jar lamp she had turned on with the flipping of the light switch sat on a pine end table at the end of the couch. Its twin, at the couch's other end, remained dark. An oblong coffee table sat in front of the couch, and a good-sized TV stood against the opposite wall. Framed pictures crowded the top of the TV, and Alex crossed to look at them. They were family shots, some of a much younger Joe and Cary with a woman and a girl who Alex presumed were Joe's deceased mother and sister, one of Joe in the black cap and gown of a graduate, and several of what were obviously school pictures of Cary's three grandchildren. The one that caught Alex's eye was a picture of Joe, younger and looking seriously handsome in a navy suit with a white shirt and a red tie, and a woman with Eli and Josh when they were toddlers. The boys sat on Joe's knees, and the woman stood behind him. The adults and a perhaps three-year-old Eli were smiling for the camera. Baby Josh looked like he was ready to howl. Alex's attention fixed on the woman: Joe's then wife. She was a pretty woman, in her early twenties, with thick straight golden blond hair that fell almost to her waist. Her hand rested proprietarily on Joe's shoulder. Alex studied her face. It was round and rosy, smiling and very young.

This was Eli's and Josh's and Jenny's mother. Joe's ex-wife. Laura, Joe had said her name was.

Alex was still looking at the picture when Joe walked into the room. Wide-shouldered and slim-hipped in his sweatshirt and jeans, he stood for a moment without saying anything, running a hand through his hair as he met her gaze. He was so handsome he made her heart beat faster, and so dearly familiar that just his presence made her feel warm inside. He looked tired, and slightly careworn. As his eyes touched on the picture, registering which one it was, Alex put it down and crossed the room toward him.

"Did you get your father taken care of?"

"Yeah. He's out cold. Won't surface before noon tomorrow, and then he'll have a hangover that won't quit." His gaze met hers, and his mouth twisted wryly. "God, this has been a hell of a day."

"I'm sorry about Neely," Alex offered quietly.

He made a sound that was a cross between a laugh and a snort, then picked up her hand and carried it to his lips, pressing his mouth to the palm. Her hand seemed to sizzle where his mouth touched.

"You are not your sister's keeper," he said with a slight, curling smile, holding on to her hand as he moved toward the couch and dropped down. He pulled her down beside him, and she snuggled close against his side while he wrapped an arm around her shoulders. Propping his booted feet up on the coffee table, crossing one ankle over the other, he tipped his head back against the cushions and slanted a look down at her. "I realize you can't control her. Just like I can't control Eli. When children reach a certain age, they have to make their own decisions. You hope they're going to be good ones, but you never can tell. I don't blame your sister for what Eli did, either. He knew better."

"What are you going to do to him?"

"Ground him until high-school graduation, probably, and work his butt off around the farm until he's so tired he won't feel like getting into trouble." His voice was grim. Then he took a deep breath, and looked up at the ceiling as the lines around his eyes deepened. "I would have bet my life Eli wouldn't do something like that. I guess I would have lost."

"Joe. He's a great kid."

Joe grimaced. "Makes you kind of wonder what else you don't know about them, doesn't it?" He looked at her again. "What are you going to do about your sister?"

Alex gave a helpless little shrug. "Talk to her. Send her back to boarding school. What can I do? She's not bad, not really. She's just—neglected, in the most profound sense of the word. We've always had every material thing we've ever wanted, but what Neely wanted was love. She didn't get much of that, to tell you the truth."

"You love her."

"Yes, but I'm her sister. It's not really the same thing. What she needed was a parent's love: my father's. She never really felt like she had it."

"I sometimes wonder if a father's love is enough anyway. Maybe what kids really need is their mother. I can't pick out the right clothes for Jenny, can't seem to get Josh out of what seems to be a perpetual bad mood, and now Eli's smoking pot." He gave a little laugh that was completely devoid of amusement. "I've tried my damndest to do a good job raising these kids, but I'm not sure that it's enough."

"At least you love them, and they know it."

"Yeah, I love them."

"Joe."

"Hmm?"

Her head was resting against the soft cotton of his navy sweatshirt. He smelled good, she thought, of fresh air and warm skin and smoke from the bonfire, with maybe a touch of Cary's booze (she probably smelled of it, too; the stench had permeated the cab) blended in. She tilted her head back a little so that she could see his expression more clearly.

"Tell me about your father. Has he been like this—the drinking I mean—since you were little, or . . ." She let her voice trail off.

His mouth quirked, and his gaze slid away from her to fix on the ceiling. He shifted position so that his shoulders lay flat along the back of the couch. Shifting with him, Alex ended up with her head resting on his shoulder instead of his arm, and her arms wrapped around his waist.

"Pop's been drinking for as long as I can remember, since before I was born, I guess. When I was a little kid, it wasn't so bad. He'd just drink until he passed out, not too often, maybe every couple of months, and one of us would cover him up wherever he happened to be and that was that. He was a trainer, a trainer of thoroughbreds, pretty big-time too—did you know that?" Alex shook her head. "He had a whole barn full of horses that he was training at Churchill Downs back then. One night he got drunk and passed out right there in the barn, and when he woke up Vince Atkinson's twelve-million-dollar stallion had his leg broke so bad that the bottom half of it was just hanging by a little piece of skin. Horse had to be put down, Atkinson collected the insurance on it—and the word went out that my father got a payoff, that he closed his eyes to the killing of that horse so Atkinson could collect the insurance. Atkinson went bankrupt a few months later anyway, and my father could never get another first-rate horse. His career just went downhill. The horses kept getting sorrier and sorrier, and the jockeys and racetracks too, until finally it was over—he was out of business. Couldn't even get a quarter horse to train. He had to sell insurance, for God's sake, and he wasn't very good at it. That's when he really started to drink. By the time my mom and sister were killed, he was pretty much a weekend drunk. Now he's drunk about half the time. That's why he lives here, instead of with me. I don't want him around the kids when he's like that. Usually he just gets drunk up here all by his lonesome and passes out. About every three or four months, he'll pull something like this performance tonight. I'm getting fed up with it, I can tell you. Did you see Eli's face back there? And Josh's? He's embarrassing my kids. And after tonight, you can believe that I'm going to let him know that he's setting a hell of a bad example for them, too."

"So what are you going to do about it?" Her voice was low, sympathetic. Her hand slid up his chest, smoothing the soft cotton sweatshirt and, through it, the hard-muscled chest beneath. Seemingly oblivious of her ministrations, Joe shrugged.

"I don't know. What can you do? Hold my breath until the next time, I guess." He slanted a look down at her, and his expression changed, warmed. He picked her hand up off his chest and carried it to his mouth. "You're beautiful."

Alex smiled a little at that and reached up to kiss him. He stopped her with his fingers placed gently over her lips.

"There's something I need to tell you before we go any further with this. Something that may make you change your mind."

Alex's eyes widened on his face. "What?"

"Tommy asked me to come by his office today," he said. "He had a lawyer there waiting for me, a friend of mine, Rob Mayhew, and he asked if he could tape-record our conversation. Then he showed me a woman's purse and shoes, and told me that they'd found some remains in a plastic garbage bag that they thought might be human." His eyes met hers. "The purse and shoes were Laura's. Tommy thinks the remains might be Laura's, too."

Alex sat bolt upright on the couch and stared at him as the implications of this became clear in her mind. "Oh, my God! The sheriff thinks your ex-wife was *murdered*? Josh and Jenny and Eli's *mother*?" Her thoughts flew to the pretty blond woman in the picture on the TV.

He nodded. "That pretty much sums it up."

"Here in Shelby County?" Her voice was incredulous.

"Apparently so. Of course, it's always possible that the remains that were found aren't human, or if they're human that they're not Laura's. That's what I'm hoping for, anyway. And I'm not going to tell the kids until we hear that they're hers for sure. Tommy said he'd keep it confidential until the lab lets him know one way or another."

"Oh, they're probably not," Alex said in relief. Then she frowned at Joe. "So what was there in that to make me change my mind about—us?"

He smiled at her, a slow and charming smile that ratcheted up her body temperature. "Us, huh? I like the sound of that." Then the smile faded. "If the remains should turn out to be Laura's, that means she was murdered. Right here in Paradise County. About eight years ago, apparently, in June, because of the dates on the contents of some items in her purse." He took a deep breath. "That was about the time I last saw her. She came to see the kids. We haven't seen or heard from her since, which has been fine by me.

But Tommy already thought I might have murdered her, and if the remains turn out to be hers a lot of people may think that."

Alex stared at him. "They couldn't."

Joe looked faintly rueful. "Apparently they can. I've known Tommy since kindergarten, and he tape-recorded our conversation just in case I might be going to confess."

"That's ridiculous!" Alex was indignant on his behalf.

Joe smiled at her. "You didn't ask me if I did it."

"I know the answer to that."

"Blind faith, huh?" His smile widened and warmed.

"I know the kind of man you are. Obnoxious and arrogant, yes, sometimes. Rude and impossible, yes again, sometimes. A wife killer? I don't think so."

Joe was grinning by the time she had finished. "Thanks for the ringing endorsement. Remind me never to ask you to be a character witness for me."

"Truth hurts." Alex parroted his long-ago words to her with a flickering smile. Joe picked up her hand from where it rested on his chest, carried it to his mouth, kissed her knuckles, then turned her hand over to press his lips to her palm. Alex felt the touch of his tongue against her skin and shivered. Her eyelids flickered and her lips parted in involuntary response.

"You don't really think I'm—what was it?—obnoxious, arrogant, rude, and impossible, do you?" His mouth slid down to rest against the pulse in her wrist. It quickened appreciably; Alex knew he could feel the increased pace of it against his mouth. Not that it mattered; she was equally sure he could read the intensity of her response in her eyes.

"On first acquaintance? Oh, yes."

"Now, that's strange. See, even when you were firing me, the precise words that kept running through my head were *What a babe.*"

"Liar." Alex said it abstractedly, her eyes busy absorbing the contrast between her pale, slender fingers and the strong brown hand that held them, her body preoccupied with assimilating a suddenly dry mouth, increasing respiratory rate, and a rapid weakening of all important muscle groups.

"I'm telling the truth, I swear." His eyes twinkled at her suddenly. "Surely you don't think I'd make up a story like that just to try to get inside your pants?"

Her gaze met his, and focused with an effort. "Wouldn't you?"

He shook his head. "I'm much more direct than that."

"Oh, really?"

"Mm-hm. For example, if I was trying to get inside your pants, I'd start by laying you back on the couch just like this"—sliding an arm under her knees, he tilted her backward until she was lying flat with her legs across his lap—"then I'd lean over"—he loomed above her—"and kiss you."

Alex was already reaching her arms up to wrap them around his neck when his mouth came down on hers.

Forty-two

❀

The kiss was gentle, slow, and languorous. His cheeks and chin were scratchy with stubble, and felt like sandpaper against her face. She loved the masculine feel of his beard against her soft skin. His tongue explored the inside of her mouth and his lips moved against hers in a leisurely way that gave the impression that he had all the time in the world. At the first touch of his mouth her body went to fever pitch, ready to take up where they had left off in the woods. Her tongue engaged his in a fierce war. Her lips demanded. She tugged at his shoulders until he was lying on the couch with her, half beside and half on top of her. She wanted him. God, how she wanted him.

But he clearly wasn't in any hurry, and, conversely, that made her response all the more urgent. She slid her hands under his shirt, running her palms up his bare back. The muscles there were firm and flexible. His skin was warm and smooth. His hand found her breast, flattened over it, and in answer she dug her nails into his shoulder blades. His back tensed, and his thumb teased her nipple through the layers of cashmere and silk. Alex whimpered into his mouth, arching her back to give him better access to her breasts. When he continued to do no more than gently rub his thumb across her nipples, she bit his earlobe in frustration, and moved so that her pelvis pressed up against his. But that contact with the hard bulge in his pants only made her want more. She kissed his neck, running her mouth over the warm prickly skin, rocking against him, trying to show him without words what she wanted him to do, how she wanted to be touched.

But still he was gentle with her, and slow—oh, so slow. He captured her face between two hands, and kissed her with deep, ravishing kisses. He caressed her breasts through her clothes, moving from one breast to the other, teasing the nipples with his fingers until they were quiveringly erect and she was aching with need for him.

But that was all he did.

Alex couldn't stand it. She couldn't wait another second. She wanted him naked and inside her, *now.* Reaching down between them, she ran her fingers delicately over the front of his jeans. Back and forth. Back and forth. The denim was stiff and smooth and faintly cool. The bulge that she wanted to set free was warm and hard. She closed her hand around it and squeezed. It pulsed beneath her hand. Sliding her hand upward again, she groped for the tab of his zipper.

He caught her hand, imprisoning it against the front of his jeans as he pulled his mouth from hers. Propped on one elbow, he looked down into her face. For a moment they stared at each other, sea-blue eyes locking with eyes of a darker, softer blue. With some satisfaction Alex saw that Mr. In Control was breathing hard too. A dark flush stained his cheekbones. His eyes reflected the yellow lamplight, making it look as if they were aflame.

"Wait a minute," he said. Although his voice was husky, a slow, wicked smile lit up his face. "The whole idea is, I'm supposed to be trying to get inside *your* pants."

Alex stared at him, narrow-eyed, as that registered. "You did that deliberately!"

"You think so?"

He looked so sexy smiling at her like that that Alex couldn't even feel affronted for long. What she felt was hungry—for him. Her eyes locked with his for a long, smoldering moment. He'd been deliberately trying to drive her wild with desire, she realized, and, she had to admit, he had succeeded. Now it was time to turn the tables.

He was still holding her hand flat against the front of his jeans. Alex wiggled her fingers, pressing on the pulsing hardness beneath them, watching him all the while. When his eyes darkened and his jaw tightened in response, she tugged her hand free and slid it inside the waistband of his pants.

His pupils dilated until his eyes looked almost black. Her fingers moved over the washboard-firm muscles of his abdomen to find and close over his hot, swollen shaft. He drew in a sharp breath, and clenched his teeth as she slowly, rhythmically moved her hand.

Then he reached down, grabbed her wrist, and pulled her hand out of his pants.

"My turn," he said, his voice thick.

Aquiver with desire, Alex lay back on the couch and watched as he unbuttoned her pants, pulled down her zipper, and delved inside. His palm was warm and big, and his fingertips were faintly rough as his hand slid over her taut stomach to find and caress the triangle of ash-brown curls between her thighs. She was wearing tiny silk bikini panties in a delicious leopard print, and the top part of them was just visible in the V of the open zipper. Watching his hand disappear inside them was the most erotic thing she had ever seen in her life. Then he was pushing his fingers on down between her legs, touching her where she wanted to be touched, pressing, caressing, sliding inside—and watching her all the while.

"Oh, God, Joe," she breathed, writhing convulsively under the ministrations of his knowing hand, her fingers digging into the soft couch cushions beneath her, her body on fire. "Make love to me. Now. Please."

"You got it, Princess." His voice was so hoarse that the words were almost a growl.

He sat up abruptly, his face flushed, his jaw clenched. Alex whimpered as his hand was withdrawn, but then he was scooping her onto his lap and standing up with her. Her arms looped around his neck, and clung. She looked up and met his eyes, which were bright and hard with desire for her, as he carried her out of the lighted living room into the shadowy hall, then turned from that into a darkened bedroom, where, reaching behind him, he closed and locked the door.

"Your father . . ." she whispered.

"Wouldn't hear an express train plow through the living room."

The curtains were open, allowing moonlight to pour into the room. There was a bed, Alex saw, a double bed with a dark nubby-textured bedspread. He yanked the bedspread back, and the top sheet, then put her down on the mattress with her head resting on one of the two pillows. The sheet was smooth and cool and faintly stiff, some kind of floral pattern. The pillow with its matching case was of too-firm foam rubber. The bed smelled clean, but the room had the air of one that had not been used in a long time.

Joe pulled his sweatshirt and T-shirt off in a single fluid movement. Alex caught just a glimpse of broad bare shoulders that gleamed bronze in the moonlight and a wide chest covered by a thick wedge of dark hair. His unzipped jeans sagged below his hipbones, revealing plain white jockey shorts beneath. He was gorgeous. . . .

Then he was bending over her, tugging at her pants, pulling them down.

"My boots." Alex struggled to sit up. "I have to take them off first."

He let go of her pants and moved down to her feet. Picking one up, he gave her high-heeled boot a peremptory tug. It didn't budge.

"Remind me to buy you some tennis shoes," he muttered, tugging harder.

"They unzip," she said, and did it herself, pulling off both boots then dropping them onto the floor, and shedding her blazer, which hit the floor, too. He tugged her sweater over her head, and then reached down and grabbed her pants, pulling them off. Alex was left wearing only her tiny bikini panties and matching push-up bra.

"If you got that at Victoria's Secret, Jenny's going to buy her underwear there over my dead body," he said, his eyes moving over her as, supported by her elbows, she lay waiting for him to join her on the bed. "That's the sexiest getup I ever saw in my life."

He sat down on the edge of the bed. Alex sat up and pressed her silk-covered breasts against his bare back, her hands sliding over his shoulders, measuring their breadth. They were so wide, and strong. . . .

"They have plain white cotton, too," she promised huskily as he struggled with his own boots. The first one hit the floor with a clunk. He was working on the second. She put her arms around him, running her hands over the hard contours of his chest. His chest hair was crisp, and curled around her fingers. His nipples were hard. . . .

"All right, that's it."

The second boot hit the floor, and then he turned suddenly, grabbing her upper arms and twisting at the waist so that he could kiss her. Gasping at his sudden fierceness, she wrapped her arms around his neck and kissed him back. Turning with her in his arms, he lowered her to the mattress and rolled on top of her, pushing her bra up out of his way, yanking her panties down her legs and throwing them aside, pulling himself free.

He pushed his jeans and shorts down his legs with a series of quick, impatient shoves. Then his knees slid between her legs, his hands grasped her hipbones and he plunged deep inside her. He was huge, burning hot, and just what, she thought, she had always wanted. She cried out, arching up to meet him, her heels pushing up off the mattress, gasping at the intense pleasure of it. He kissed her mouth, her throat, her breasts, suckling them like a babe. His mouth and tongue were as scaldingly hot as the rest of him. Alex loved him back with a wild passion, her nails scoring his back, her legs wrapping around his waist. He thrust inside her with an urgency that made her writhe and buck and strain—and beg for more. His hand slid down between their bodies to touch her where they joined, and stayed to tease and caress. Alex buried her face in the hollow of his neck to muffle sharp little cries of ecstasy, while her body quivered and burned and finally convulsed.

"Joe! Oh my God, *Joe!*" Her release, when it came, was shattering. She was trembling, shaking, dying with the sheer bliss of it.

But he didn't stop, didn't even give her time to catch her breath. He kept going until she was begging him not to stop, until she came again, until finally he took pity on her and found his own release, groaning his pleasure into her throat as he ground himself deep inside her shaking body.

In the aftermath, Alex lay on her back on the bed feeling vaguely like she had been run over by a semitrailer truck. She was too spent, too tired, too achy and shaky to move. Joe lay on top of her, and he weighed a ton. He was hot, sweaty, and his breath was stertorous in her ear. They were both naked. She could feel the rasp of his chest hairs against her breasts, and the solid strength of his thigh as it lay between hers. She moved a little, experimentally, and his mouth nuzzled her ear. His hand, which had been resting on her upper arm, slid down to fondle her breast. Then it slid lower, smoothing over her rib cage, sliding across her abdomen. . . .

"Joe," she protested, curling her fingers around his wrist to stop his hand and noting as she did so that his wrist was way too big for her fingers to come anywhere near to encircling.

"Had enough?" He lifted his head and looked at her, his eyes gleaming bright in the spill of moonlight.

"What I was going to say is . . ." She smiled up into his eyes, then wriggled on top of him so that she was lying full-length against him, breasts to chest, stomach to stomach, thigh to thigh, her toes curling against the hair-roughened hardness of his calves.

"My turn."

Then she wriggled up his body until she could kiss his mouth.

Forty-three

✦

"Neely." It was a whisper, just the teeniest breath of sound. The voice was familiar, achingly familiar . . . "Daddy?" she whispered, opening her eyes. It was so dark that she couldn't be sure whether it was day or night. So dark she could not see as far as the end of her nose. Dark as the inside of a grave. And cold and clammy as one, too. The air smelled of damp, of the earth after a rain. She was lying on something soft. A mattress? A bed? She could hear—what? A steady drip, as if from a leaky faucet. And a moan. . . .

"I'm here with you, Neely."

"Daddy?" She heard the voice, she knew she did, she was not just imagining it. She struggled to move. Her hands were tingling, asleep. She'd been lying on them. They were beneath her body. She shifted, stretching her aching arms. At least, she tried to stretch her arms. With a metallic rattle they moved—and then she could move them no farther.

There were metal bands around her wrists with something linking them together. Her arms were pinned behind her back.

Neely explored frantically. Moving out from the metal bands on her wrists, her fingers found smooth, cold metal links—a chain.

Her wrists were chained together behind her back.

She fought the chain, struggling madly, twisting, kicking—*her ankles were chained, too.*

My God, my God, what was this? She was chained hand and foot, lying on a mattress in a cold, damp place that was darker than the inside of a cave.

"Daddy," she whimpered, even though she remembered now that he was dead. Is that how she had heard his voice? Was she dead too? No, there wouldn't be chains, not even in hell.

There'd been a man at the top of the stairs—he'd grabbed her.

That was all she could remember.

She squirmed over onto her stomach, trying to twist free, to kick free, to get free any way she could, realizing as she did so that she was still dressed in her jeans and turtleneck. But she'd been wearing her jean jacket, too, and a pair of cowboy boots. She wiggled her toes: only her thin trouser socks covered her feet. Someone had taken off some of her clothes.

The thought made Neely's skin crawl.

"Neely?" Her dad's voice again.

"Where are you?" she sobbed, her head thrashing wildly from side to side as she fought to see through the darkness.

She could see nothing. Absolutely nothing. It was as dark as if she were blind. But she knew she wasn't.

She fought the chains. They clanked and rattled and held fast no matter what she did. She took a deep breath, opening her mouth to scream. . . .

"Be quiet," her dad's voice warned. And then she saw something: two dots, two small glowing dots, luminous green, just a few feet away. Like eyes in the night. . . .

Footsteps. She heard footsteps. Footsteps that grew louder as they approached where she lay.

This was not good. Neely didn't know how she knew it, but she did.

"Pretend to sleep." The voice was fading away. The dots of green light were gone. She was in the dark again, alone and terrified. She wanted to call him back, scream *Daddy* at the top of her lungs, but she was too scared, too conscious of the approach of something . . .

Evil. She didn't know how she knew that, either, but know it she did.

Instinct took over. Trying to get her breathing under control, Neely wriggled onto her back and assumed the approximate position in which she had awakened: supine, arms beneath her body, legs stretched out straight. . . .

There was light. It was coming toward her like the headlight of a train. A small headlight, without the accompanying rattle and roar—it was a flashlight, of course. Someone was walking toward her carrying a flashlight.

Just before she squeezed her eyes shut, Neely saw that she was lying on the bare mattress of a twin-size bed. It had been pushed lengthwise against the far wall of a small, cell-like room with rough stone walls and jail-like iron bars forming an entire fourth wall. The chamber she was in looked like the set from a horror movie. Vampires would feel right at home.

At the thought, Neely felt the hair rise on the back of her neck.

She heard a rattle as if of keys, and squeezed her eyes shut while the flashlight was still a couple of feet away from the iron bars. Then she forced herself to relax her face. . . .

"Hello, Cornelia," a male voice crooned. It was a

pleasant voice, not too deep, unmistakably Southern in origin.

It made her skin crawl.

"Are you awake yet?"

There was the sound of metal on metal, a faint click, and then the cell door swung inward and he was inside the cell with her, moving toward the bed.

Neely's heart raced. Instinctively she stiffened, then had to remind her terrified body to relax, go limp, feign sleep. . . .

"Still asleep?" He sounded disappointed as he played the flashlight over her body. "Well, that's all right. I've got plenty of time. All night, in fact."

He laughed, although it was more like a giggle, a weird little high-pitched giggle that made Neely want to scream. Only she knew she could not, knew she had to remain perfectly still, perfectly limp, as he set the flashlight down somewhere near the bed and touched her, rolling her onto her side. . . .

"Your hair is so pretty." He fingered one of the long, curly strands. "You dye it, don't you? Or are you blond all over? We'll see. . . ."

He was talking to himself as much as her, Neely realized. She realized, too, just what she was in for. Rape—*oh, God, oh, God*—after which he was probably going to kill her.

Stay limp. Keep your limbs heavy. Remember to breathe. She could almost hear the words as they scrolled through her mind.

"Let's make you more comfortable, shall we?" He rolled her onto her side so that her back was to him, and his fingers brushed her skin as he fumbled with the shackles on her wrists. Unlocking them, she realized, as first one hand and then the other was set free. To her surprise, he chafed her wrists, a kind gesture that was somehow almost scarier than violence would have been. "I'm sorry I had to leave you like this for so long, but there was something I had to do. You just missed the most amazing bonfire. It was in your honor, actually. Your predecessor just moved out."

His words made no sense to her.

Stay limp. Let your arms hang. They're dead weight, heavy. . . .

"We'll just chain this one little wrist to the wall, and then you can move about as much as you like. I don't want you to be uncomfortable. I'm nice to my girls, you'll see."

He rolled her onto her back again, then gently stroked her face. *Stay limp. Breathe. . . .* His hand was moist, sweaty. He leaned over her, his breath, which was warm and disgusting with a faint overtone of some kind of mint, all over her as he reached across her for her left arm, which was the arm nearest the wall.

"So you won't fight me, you know. I'd hate to have to hurt you." He picked up her wrist. Something metal was sliding around it. Fatter than a handcuff, more like some kind of shackle.

"You're not asleep, are you, Cornelia? Ah, ah! So naughty to try to fool me." He was touching her, stroking the shrinking skin of her neck, his hand gliding down over her turtleneck to close over her right breast, squeezing. "So pretty. . . ."

Neely couldn't stand it. She couldn't stand his hand on her, his breath on her, the knowledge of what was to come.

His hand slid beneath the hem of her turtleneck to creep over the bare skin of her stomach. . . .

Neely screamed. Without even knowing that she meant to do it. Right in his face. With the force of a factory whistle at quitting time. At the same time her eyes flew open and she bunched up her legs and kicked like a kangaroo, catching him full in the stomach with the soles of her feet and sending him careening backward.

"Help! Help!" she screeched, leaping off the bed and flying after him toward the door. She had to escape, had to escape, had to escape. . . .

Only she couldn't fly. Her ankles were shackled together, linked by a heavy iron chain that was, perhaps, three feet in length. She lurched in her stocking feet across the cold stone floor, tripped over something, nearly fell, caught herself—and found herself looking down at Eli, huddled and chained and apparently lifeless in the middle of the floor. But she could do no more than glance at him with horror because she had to get to the door. Had to escape before he recovered, before he caught her. . . .

She wasn't going to make it, she realized just inches from her goal, and stumbled to a halt. Her captor had regained his balance and was glaring at her, snorting like a bull before the charge, murder in his stance. There was no way she could get out that door and past him. . . .

"You did a bad thing, Cornelia, and I'm going to have to punish you for that," he said, and came at her.

He had stumbled back through the cell door when she had pushed him, and it had rebounded back toward her. Its black, floor-to-ceiling bars stood between them now, only partly ajar. Neely screamed again as he rushed her, and grabbed the cold iron bar closest to her, clanging the door shut in his face. It didn't lock. She had no way to lock it.

The door hit him in the forehead and he howled and staggered back a step.

"Eli! Eli, help me!" she shrieked, swinging a lightning glance around, but Eli didn't move and she was on her own. . . .

The metal bracelet was still around her wrist with the chain dangling from it, although he had not had a chance to snap the bracelet closed. Quick as the thought, Neely wrapped the chain around the bars as many times as she could, fastening them together, then pulled her wrist free of the bracelet. Even as he came at her again, shoving a beefy shoulder against the door, she clicked the bracelet shut around the coils of chain, locking the chain—and the door—in place.

"Open that door." The light from the flashlight threw his shadow against the stone wall behind him, making him look huge and menacing. "If you don't—look, Cornelia, look! Look what happens if you don't mind me!"

He walked a little away from the door, and turned on a camp lantern that was set in the middle of a table. Neely saw that the area beyond the cell looked much like a basement, with a card table and a big armchair and a TV. . . .

There was something hanging from the wall. Something black hanging from manacles set into the wall. Scorch marks on the stone as high as the ceiling . . . a tuft of singed blond hair still attached to a horribly burned head . . . a *corpse* . . . a burned-beyond-recognition *corpse*.

Neely screamed, then screamed again as she realized what she was looking at: that thing on the wall had once been alive, a human being, a woman from the look of that hair. . . .

"Her name was Cassandra, and she didn't please me. So I burned her alive. That's what will happen to you, Cornelia, if you don't please me. This is your last chance to try. Open that door."

Neely shuddered, and backed away.

He growled, and threw his full weight against the door with a tremendous crash and rattle of metal. The door gave, but no more than an inch or so. With the chain holding it in place, she saw to her relief, he wasn't going to be able to break through.

Straightening, he stood there for a moment just looking

at her. Then he smiled, a horrible smile that made her skin crawl.

"Uh-oh. I've got the key." He continued to smile at her as he reached into his pocket and extracted a small silver key. For a moment he dangled it where he was sure she could see it. Then he stepped forward and reached inside the bars. Looking through them—it was obvious that he could not quite see where the bracelet was—he began to feel for the bracelet, and the keyhole that would unlock it.

"Help! Help me!" Neely screamed. She glanced wildly at Eli. He was still unmoving, and she thought, feared, he might be dead.

"No one can hear you," her captor said.

She had to stop him from unlocking the chain. . . .

Frantically she looked around for something, anything she could use as a weapon to hold him off. She would fight for her life. . . .

She spotted her cowboy boots lying on their sides by the bed.

As a weapon, a boot wasn't much, but it was all she had.

He was having to feel for the keyhole with the end of the key. He found it. . . .

Neely made a headlong lunge for her boot, grabbed it, and turned around to see the key slide smoothly into the lock.

"No!" she screamed, leaping back over to the door and raising the boot high over her head at the same time. Panting with exertion and terror, holding the boot by its shank, she slammed the heel down on his hand with all her strength. It connected with the sound of a pumpkin smashing against pavement.

"Ow! Bitch! Bitch!" he screamed, withdrawing his hand

and leaping back—and the small silver key dropped with a tiny *ping* to the floor.

On Neely's side of the door.

She dived for it, landing on her stomach, snatching it up just seconds before his hand came through the bars, after it too. She scuttled backward, crablike, stopping only as she came up against Eli's inert body.

"Give me that!" Her captor was getting to his feet, a big man, enormous, glaring at her through the bars.

Her foot was in something wet, something that was soaking through her sock.

Glancing down, Neely realized to her horror that she was crouched in a pool of Eli's blood.

Forty-four

✦

He was in love. Those were the words that kept running through Joe's head as he lay on his back with his arms folded beneath his head, watching the dawn light creep into his bedroom. Outside, a rooster crowed from some nearby farm. Birds were just waking up, and their morning chatter made a familiar backdrop for the start-stop growl of the newspaper delivery man's truck, its tires crunching as it turned around right on schedule in Joe's driveway.

Alex was sleeping next to him, curled against his side. They'd left his father's house about two A.M. and driven back here. With Jen spending the night at a friend's house, and Josh, Eli, and Neely at the high school lock-in, there'd been no reason for her to go home.

So she'd spent what had remained of the night in his bed. As a consequence, he'd gotten maybe an hour of sleep.

And he'd fallen in love.

The very thing he'd feared most had happened: He had fallen head over heels in love with Princess Alex.

And he didn't mind a bit.

Turning on his side, he propped himself up on one elbow and looked down at her face. Her eyes were closed, her lips slightly parted. Her hair was tangled in a pale cloud across the pillow. The quilt was pulled up around her shoulders, hiding the rest of her from his view, but it didn't really matter. He'd have plenty of time to look his fill later.

He wasn't letting this woman go.

She might not know it yet, but she was his.

She stirred in her sleep, murmuring. Even when she took a sleeping pill she was a restless sleeper. He knew: he'd been listening to her slumber every night. Up and down, moving around her bedroom at all hours of the night. He was going to consider it his personal quest to replace her sleeping pills with good, honest nightly exercise. Maybe then he'd be able to get a decent night's rest.

Smiling at the thought of that exercise, Joe leaned over and dropped a soft kiss on her lips.

"Joe?" she murmured sleepily, one eye blinking open to peer at him.

"I'm going to go check the horses," he said, smiling at her. "It's only about six A.M. Go back to sleep."

She murmured something, and closed her eyes. Even before he swung his legs out of bed, her even breathing told him she was once again asleep.

Smiling, Joe got dressed and went out to check on the horses. When they were seen to he walked across the field to his father's house. It was scarcely past seven—pretty early to be waking a man who was sure to be nursing a massive hangover—but that was just too damned bad. Last night had been the proverbial straw that had broken his camel's back: it was time to deal with his father's drinking problem.

He was going to have to deal with Eli, too. *Eli.* The son he had always thought he knew as well as he knew himself. Apparently not.

Being mistaken in the character of the son he loved more than his own life hurt more than he would ever have imagined it could.

Today he lowered the boom.

Using his key, he let himself into his father's house and headed to the kitchen to make coffee. The coffee was for him. His dad would prefer something stronger: the hair of the dog. Mouth twisting, Joe pulled a bottle of Wild Turkey out of a cabinet stocked with a liquor store's worth of booze and poured a generous shot of it into a glass. He knew the exact amount needed to begin the transformation of his dad from a trembling, nauseated, woozy-headed wreck into a reasonably coherent human being: he'd been performing this anti-hangover ritual since he was a kid.

Taking the glass with him, he headed toward his father's bedroom.

"Hey, Pop!" The smell of sour mash was so strong in the room that Joe checked for a moment on the threshold. Then he recovered, and, setting the glass down on the nightstand, moved over to the single double-hung window and flung the curtains wide. Sunlight poured into the room. Joe opened the window to let some of the smell out so, hopefully, he wouldn't suffocate, and turned back toward the bed.

"Hey, Pop! Wake up!" Sitting down on the edge of the bed, Joe shook his father's shoulder, not roughly but not real gently either. Joe had stripped him down to his boxers the night before. Now he sprawled on his stomach on the bed, his still thick white hair looking like someone had taken an eggbeater to it, his mouth open, his snores loud enough to rattle the windowpanes.

"Pop!"

"Wha...? Joe? What?" Cary's eyes opened a slit.

Perceiving Joe, they blinked rapidly, then closed again as he groaned. "My head. . . . Who opened the damned curtains?"

"I did. Wake up, Pop, we need to talk."

"Hell's bells, son, did somebody die?" Cary groaned again, and flopped over onto his back. Like Joe himself, his father had a great deal of body hair. But the hair on Cary's chest had turned as white as the hair on his head. There were other signs of aging about his father, too, Joe noted. Somehow, without Joe noticing, he had developed an old man's turkey-wattle neck, and the skin on his face had grown loose enough so that it fell away from his bones. Despite his annoyance at the old man, these visible signs of his father's mortality moved Joe.

Despite everything, he loved the old fart.

"Sit up and drink this." His voice was a shade less brusque than it had been.

"Did you bring me my medicine?"

"Yes." *Pop's medicine* was the euphemism they'd used for years to describe the after-bender alcohol infusion that Cary invariably required. The term with its painful childhood associations made Joe frown.

"Oh, God." With much groaning, Cary managed to inch himself far enough up against the shiny pine headboard that he could take the glass Joe held out to him. But his hand shook so badly that Joe had to keep his own hand on the glass, too, and help guide it to his mouth.

Cary swallowed the contents in a series of quick gulps and then gagged, coughing. He leaned back against the headboard for a minute as Joe put the empty glass down on the nightstand.

"Into the shower," Joe said ruthlessly, grabbing his father by the arm and half-dragging, half-helping him from the bed. This, too, was part of the sober-up ritual.

"Jeez, no, I feel so bad—ah, Joe, can't you just let me alone?"

With Cary swaying on his feet, Joe hoisted one of his father's arms around his neck and force-marched him toward the bathroom. Once there, he helped him into the bathtub, where Cary, still in his undershorts, sprawled with one arm hanging over the rim while he alternately berated his son and begged for mercy. Unmoved, Joe removed the handheld shower from its holder, turned on the cold water full blast, and held it over his father's head.

Cary reacted like a fish suddenly flung onto dry land. He bucked and flopped and spit and spluttered, struggling to get up, yelling curses the whole while. Finally, when Joe judged he'd had enough, he reached into the tub, turned the water off, and hung the shower head back in its place.

With the cessation of the water, Cary lay there, shivering and spluttering, wiping the water from his face with both hands. Then he glared at his son.

"You're a ruthless son-of-a-bitch, Joe."

Joe tossed him a towel. Cary used it to wipe his face.

"Better?" Joe asked, unmoved.

"What the hell time is it?" Cary growled.

"Noon," Joe lied unrepentantly. "Can you get up by yourself?"

"Hell, yes, I can get up by myself." Cary grabbed hold of the edge of the tub on one side and the grab bar set into the tile on the other and heaved himself up. Joe caught his arm to steady him, careful not to get too close unless he had to so he wouldn't get all wet himself.

"I got it, I got it," Cary said irritably as he stepped out of the tub. "Go on into the kitchen. I'll meet you in there."

"You go back to bed and I'll haul your ass under the shower again," Joe warned.

Cary waved him away, and Joe went. In the kitchen, he

poured himself a cup of coffee, then poured another one for his father and got out two aspirin, which he set beside the coffee on the small round table.

A few minutes later, Cary came shuffling into the kitchen, wrapped in a shabby, ankle-length canary yellow bathrobe that Joe remembered from his childhood. An involuntary smile touched his mouth at the sight. *Big Bird—The Morning After* was what he and Carol had always dubbed scenes like this.

"Hell, boy, somebody better have died: it's only seven-thirty," Cary grumbled, having taken one look at the clock on the wall. "What the hell is the matter with you?"

"Sit down, Pop," Joe said, and with another glare at him Cary did as he was told, taking the chair opposite Joe. He picked up the aspirin and popped them into his mouth, then took a gulp of the coffee, gagging and coughing again.

"This needs something," he said, looking pointedly up at the cabinet where he kept the booze. When Joe failed to take the hint, Cary sighed, and took another swallow of coffee before looking his son in the eye.

"So what's on your mind?" Just like always, when he felt guilty, there was a hint of bravado in his voice.

"How much do you remember about last night?" Joe asked levelly.

Cary thought. "You brought me home and put me to bed."

That was such a safe guess that Joe didn't alter by so much as one iota his belief that his father didn't remember anything at all. Memory blackouts were part and parcel of the stage of alcoholism that Cary had reached.

"Yeah, I brought you home, Pop. Otherwise Tommy would have put you in jail. You punched him in the face because he took your car keys. You were so belligerent I had to hang on to you in the truck on the way home. Know who drove the truck, with you fighting and cursing and smelling like a damned brewery the whole way? Alex, that's who."

"Alex, huh? Now, there's a looker. You could do worse for yourself, son." Instead of inciting his father to shame, as Joe had hoped, this mention of Alex made Cary's eyes brighten. "You tried your luck there yet? Yeah, of course you have. I didn't raise no fool."

"Pop . . ." Joe's eyes narrowed warningly.

"Don't waste your time denying it, Joey. Think I haven't seen the way you look at her?"

"Pop, how I look or don't look at Alex is not the point. The point is, you're humiliating the family! Eli and Josh were there, and saw the whole thing. And their friends. And the whole town, practically, for that matter."

Cary winced, and this time he did look a little abashed. "Jenny there?"

Joe met his gaze. He was tempted to lie, knowing that Jenny was the apple of her grandfather's eye, but he didn't want to humiliate his old man that much.

"No," he said. "Just by pure luck is all, though."

Cary looked relieved. "Okay, son. You've made your point. I'm sorry for it, and I won't do it again. You have my word on it."

Joe laughed. It was a harsh and bitter sound. "Pop, I had your word on it back in September, too. And in August before that. And on back as far as I can remember. I hate to tell you this, old man, but your word's not worth a crap to me anymore."

Cary stared at him, his eyes widening a little. "That's a hell of a thing to say to your father, Joe."

Joe met his gaze, his eyes suddenly hard. "I'm a father now, too, Pop, and when it comes right down to it I've got to protect my kids. I'm not going to let you put Eli and Josh and Jenny through what you put Carol and me through. And you're setting them a bad example, too. I don't drink a drop, have you noticed? But here you are, getting falling-down drunk every two months, and they look up to you. Know what I caught Eli doing last night? Smoking pot. It's hard to say to kids, no, you can't get high, when the grandpa they love does it all the time. So here's the deal: Either you check into a residential treatment program and get some help or you're out of this house and out of our lives until you do."

His father stared at him. "You can't do that!"

"I own this house, Pop, and they're my kids. I can."

There was a moment of silence as the two exchanged measuring looks.

Cary shook his head sorrowfully. "That a son of mine could ever threaten me like that. . . ."

"Can it, Pop, I've passed way beyond guilt over this. I'm prepared to do what I have to do. So which is it? A treatment program or are you out of here?"

Cary frowned, and glanced around the kitchen before finally looking at Joe again. "I guess I could go into a program maybe sometime in the spring. . . ."

Joe shook his head. "Next Monday, Pop. I've been thinking about this since September. All I have to do is give your doctor a call, and it's all arranged."

"Joe, you're my son, and I love you more than any other living person, and you know that. But you've got a cold streak in you a mile wide, and you always have had. What your mother would say if she could hear you trying to bully me like this. . . ."

Joe's eyes narrowed. "Don't even go there, Pop. I mean what I say." He got to his feet.

"Okay. Okay, you stubborn . . . Okay. I'll go into some

fancy-shmancy treatment program if that's what you want. But I need to wait until after the first of the year, at least."

"There's no waiting, Pop, I told you." Joe started to turn away, ready to walk out of the room. "Monday or you're out."

"Son, there's something I got to tell you." Cary's voice was suddenly so desperate that Joe, arrested, turned back to regard his father through suspicious eyes. "There's a reason why I need to wait until after the first of the year.

"I entered Victory Dance in the Magna Futurity at Gulfstream Park." The words came out all in a rush.

"*What?*" Joe stared at his father. The Magna Futurity was run on the Florida track on the second Saturday in December. It was one of the most prestigious races in the game, with a half-million-dollar purse and a fifty-thousand-dollar entry fee. No way could his father have . . . "Pop, you couldn't have. You don't even have your trainer's license anymore. And we sure don't have fifty thousand dollars to spend on something like that."

His father chewed his lower lip and glanced away. "I used yours."

"*What?*"

"I said I used yours. I used your license, and I took an advance out on your equity line to pay the entry fee. I did it through the mail, and I signed your name to all the papers, too."

Joe was so flabbergasted that all he could do was stare at his father. Surely the old man was lying. . . . But he wasn't. Joe knew his father well enough that he could tell just by looking at him.

"That's god-damned forgery!" Joe let loose with a string of curses that put to shame Cary's diatribe of the night before. When at last he ran out of steam and stopped, Cary was looking a little more cheerful.

"You shouldn't oughta curse like that, boy," he said reprovingly. That nearly set Joe off again. Instead he glared at his father.

"If you were one of my kids, instead of the other way around . . ."

Cary cut him off. "I've been in the horse business my whole life, Joe. I'm telling you, this is the one. He can win. I know what I'm talking about. Let me train this horse, Joey. Please. Let me train him, and then I'll go into treatment, I swear."

"Jesus, Pop," Joe groaned. Visions of losing fifty thousand dollars danced in his head. Right when he needed to scrape together all the money he could, too.

"He can win," Cary repeated.

Joe saw the entreaty in his father's eyes and cursed himself for a fool even as he gave in. "Damn it, Pop. All right, train him, then."

Forty-five

✦

Eli wasn't dead, but he was hurt bad. Shot, Neely thought. The hole in his chest was no bigger than a pencil eraser, she saw when the monster was finally gone and she picked up the flashlight he'd left behind and pulled up Eli's shirt to check for the source of all that blood. But the blood oozing from the wound bubbled and the wound itself seemed to kind of suck in when he breathed. She thought that must mean that his lung was punctured. Vaguely she remembered hearing something about sucking wounds in a first-aid course she had taken at school.

His skin was cold to the touch, as if he were already dead. Neely shivered at the thought. He was lying on his side, curled into a fetal position. His wrists were chained behind his back. Another chain bound his ankles.

She had the key. The small silver key she had used on the chain around the door should work on this lock, too. It did, she discovered to her relief, and she removed the chains from his wrists and ankles, then rolled him onto his back, all the while glancing fearfully over her shoulder in case the monster should return.

"Eli! Eli!" She shook his shoulder, called him. He didn't respond, didn't moan or blink. Shock. Could he be going into shock? She had learned about shock, too, at school, but she didn't remember much about it other than that it could kill. She hadn't been paying attention, as usual.

Now she frantically searched her brain, trying to remember every scrap of first-aid information she could.

The first thing to do, of course, was stop the bleeding. But there was nothing to use, no sheets to tear up, nothing like that. Socks—her own were thin, flimsy trouser socks, but Eli was wearing thick white athletic socks, she saw when she pulled off his boots to check. She stripped them off his feet, then wadded them into a pad and pressed the pad over the hole in his chest with the heel of her hand. In a few minutes blood was soaking through the pad.

He was wearing a black sweatshirt with *Rockets* on the front, over a white T-shirt and sweats. The sweatshirt and T-shirt were pretty much soaked with blood, so she pulled off her own turtleneck—a little reluctantly, because when the monster came back she didn't want to be caught wearing just her bra; the thought creeped her out. Shivering now, whether from cold or fear, she wadded that up, too, and pressed it to the wound.

This time the blood didn't soak through. Eventually she felt confident enough to remove her hand. She tied the makeshift bandage in place with the arms of the turtleneck, then pulled his T-shirt and sweatshirt back down as the only warmth she had to offer him. It was cold in here, freezing really, and she was shivering.

Or maybe she was shivering from fear.

The floor was cold, so cold that her feet were numb even though she had what slight protection her socks afforded. Eli should not be lying on the floor, she realized. He needed to be kept warm—fat chance of that in here. She glanced at the bed. If she could get him on the bed . . .

But she was afraid to move him more than she had to,

and anyway she didn't think she could lift him. Eli was thin, but he was tall and, deadweight, he would be beyond her strength.

She pulled the mattress off the bed instead, positioning it awkwardly beside him—the room was tiny, maybe eight by ten feet, so there wasn't much room to maneuver—then rolling him onto it. By the time she had done that, she was sweating. Eli had moaned once, and his eyelids had fluttered, but that was it, even when she had tried to rouse him by calling his name and rubbing his hands and cheeks.

Finally, because she could think of nothing else to do, she settled down on the mattress beside him, pressed up against his back and put an arm around him, hoping the warmth of her body might help him. Then, reluctantly, to conserve the batteries, she'd switched the flashlight off.

Oh, God, please don't let him die, Neely prayed as she lay there shivering in the dark. But other than praying, there was nothing more she could think of to do.

Except wait for the monster to come back.

"Daddy," she whimpered aloud. But this time there was no reply.

Forty-six

✦

Ah, well, the predator thought. Things did not always go according to plan. But a little spontaneity was not necessarily a bad thing. It helped to keep life interesting.

So Cornelia was a fighter, was she? He mused as he drove along U.S. 60 in the bright light of a brand-new day, heading for his place of business. Pushed him out of the cell, locked the door with her chain—enterprising. Very enterprising. He had to give her that.

It actually made his opinion of her rise.

Taking her had been so easy—big surprised eyes staring at him from the top of the stairs, a grab of her wrist, a zap of the taser—that he had not expected her to put up a fight.

Expectations were a stumbling block on the road to success, he told himself. Expectations had fouled him up before. Charles Haywood—now, there was another case where his expectations and the reality of events had not meshed. And see what had happened? Haywood had ended up dead, thus bringing his daughters to Whistledown, thus leading to Cornelia in the cell.

And Eli, too. He was sorry about Eli, actually. If the boy had not come inside looking for Cornelia just as he'd been lugging her into the kitchen, he would never have thought of taking him. He'd been fast, too, Eli had, turning and running out the back door and jumping into his truck. Good thing he had had his Glock on him as well as his taser. He'd had to shoot the boy through the windshield. What a mess. Glass everywhere, the boy bleeding and no doubt in pain.

He'd meant to put the boy out of his misery last night, right after he'd finished with Cassandra. She'd cried when he'd chained her to the wall, knowing what was coming. He had some wonderful pictures of that—and of the flames licking up her body to blaze around her face just before she died. She had screamed, as they all did.

If only he could exhibit his photographs, he was sure he'd win some major prize.

Death's Heads, he could call them. Or something like that.

He'd meant to do Eli next. After finishing with Cassandra, he had been so hungry for new flesh, for fresh flesh, that he had decided to try Cornelia out first, to make her his. Then he had expected to clean up the mess that was Cassandra, and hang Eli up on the wall in her place.

Expectations again. Never have them, he warned himself.

He had nothing against the boy, no desire to harm him, and Joe was actually a pretty good guy.

It would take him a while to get over the loss of his son, but he would eventually get over it. A person could get over anything, he was firmly convinced.

Take himself as a case in point. His father took off before he was born. His mother, Jean—he could still remember her long blond hair; as a little kid he had liked to feel the soft, silken strands with his pudgy little hands—pretty Jean, who had been so sad, all the time, that she had eventually killed herself, and tried to kill him, by setting the house on fire as he slept.

He had awakened in time to run screaming from the inferno, his pajamas ablaze. Arriving firefighters had had to chase him. By the time they'd caught him, rolling him on the ground to put out the flames, he'd had third-degree burns over ninety percent of his body.

The only part that had been spared was his head and face.

Now, *that* was a trauma. He was sure anyone would agree. But he had recovered, and gone on to live a productive life.

Well, maybe he still had a few *issues*, as Sally Jessy would say.

But he was working them out.

The thought made him giggle.

All in all, he thought, smiling, it was shaping up to be a pretty good day.

Cornelia had confounded his expectations last night.

Tonight, he would confound hers.

She had wound a chain around the door, locked it in place, and contrived to get hold of the key.

Smart little girl. Resourceful little girl.

But not smart and resourceful enough.

He had a spare key.

Forty-seven

✦

They were missing. Neely and Eli. It was almost midnight before Joe accepted that. Alex had arrived at that conclusion several hours earlier. But then, Neely had run away before.

"Eli wouldn't just run away," Joe was still insisting after he'd talked to his friend Tommy and filed a missing-persons report with the police and called every single person Eli knew and driven over miles of road to see if his son might possibly have had an accident. "It's just not something he would do."

Alex looked at him. They were in his living room. She, dressed in a white sweater and tan corduroy pants, her hair pulled back in a sleek ponytail at her nape, was curled up on the shabby tweed couch and he, in jeans and a plaid flannel shirt, was standing in front of her. Josh and Jenny, both wide-eyed at the commotion and upset at the absence of their brother, had been sent protesting to bed at eleven. Cary, who was almost as upset as Joe, had gone home just a few minutes before.

Alex was spending the night at Joe's house by mutual agreement. Ostensibly, he was going to sleep on the couch and she was going to sleep in his bed. It had been his suggestion: he didn't want her to spend the night at

Whistledown alone, and she didn't want to, either. Number one, she didn't want to leave him under the circumstances. And number two, there was something about that house. . . .

Bad things happened at that house. Alex remembered the breathing, the sense she always had that she wasn't alone, the figure on the porch. Her father had died there; Neely had gone missing.

She shivered.

"I know, I know," he said dispiritedly, crossing the room to push the closed front drapes aside and look out the window into the silent black night. "I didn't think he'd smoke pot, either. God, if he's not lying in a ditch somewhere, or otherwise incapacitated, I am going to kill him for putting me through this."

Alex stood up and walked over to him, sliding her arms around his waist and resting her cheek against his back in wordless comfort.

"*Why* would he run away? That's what I don't understand. Yes, he was in bad trouble with me and he knew it. But he's not afraid of me. I swear he's not afraid of me. I've never lifted a hand to the kid in my life. He wouldn't be afraid to come home."

"Joe." Alex felt so sorry for him. He was going through hell, and it was obvious. She, on the other hand, was long inured to Neely's antics. It wasn't a stretch for her to picture Neely running away. Neely ran away from school or somewhere on the average of twice a year. "That friend of Neely's—Cinda Hawkins, remember—and her boyfriend gave them a ride from the pep rally to the school. Eli's truck is nowhere to be found. Neely was in trouble too. I was threatening to send her back to boarding school, remember; I'm sure Neely talked him into running away."

She could practically hear Joe grind his teeth. "Your sister is a menace."

She pressed her lips into his back. "I'm sorry. We've caused you so much trouble. I bet you wish you never saw a Haywood in your life."

"No," Joe said, turning around to cup her face with both hands and look down into her eyes, "I don't exactly wish that."

Then he bent his head and kissed her.

Forty-eight

✤

N eely." It was her father's voice again, rousing her
from an uneasy sleep. Since she'd been dreaming
about him, hearing his voice wasn't a surprise. In
fact, it made her feel warm, it made her feel loved.

"Daddy?" She opened her eyes. It was dark, and she
wasn't alone. There was someone beside her—a body,
faintly warm, that she couldn't see. Where was she?

Oh God. Memory came rushing in.

"Neely. He'll be coming back."

"Daddy? Where are you?" She sat up, looking around in
the dark. She *wasn't* just imagining his voice. She was
hearing it, she knew she was. The green dots were there
again, as luminous as before, seeming to look at her.
Reaching for the flashlight, fumbling, Neely found it,
aimed, and turned it on.

Hannibal was staring at her through the bars, tail
twitching.

"Hannibal. Oh, Hannibal!" The sight of the cat brought
her plight home. Her lips quivered and tears sprang to her
eyes. "Hannibal, how did you get here?"

But the cat looked over its shoulder, then turned tail
and vanished into the darkness. Seconds later Neely
understood why.

She could hear the approaching footsteps too.

Oh, God, he was coming back.

Panicking, she got to her feet, clutching the flashlight, crouching on the mattress. Eli was still alive, still breathing, but unconscious. He didn't know anything about their ordeal—for an instant Neely almost envied him—and would be no help.

The monster was coming back, and she was on her own.

He couldn't get in. She'd fixed the door so that he couldn't get in.

Unless he had a second key.

Where the thought came from she didn't know, but it widened her eyes and made her heart race with terror.

Of course he would have a second key. People always kept spare keys, didn't they? He would have a key, and he would be bringing it with him—and he would be able to get in.

"Oh, God!" Neely sprang to her feet, sobbing with fear, her stomach cramping and her knees turning to jelly and her chest heaving as she fought to breathe.

She needed a weapon: a gun, a knife.

No, she needed to barricade the door.

She could see the beam of his flashlight approaching. Oh, God, she was running out of time.

The bed. It was the only thing she could use. The frame was metal, sturdy. It was a twin. It would be six feet long. The box spring. How wide was it?

It didn't matter. It was all there was.

Desperation gave her strength. She put the flashlight down and shoved the bed frame against the steel bars. God, Eli and the mattress were in the way; she couldn't quite get it positioned right.

The camp lantern was switched on. Neely didn't even

look around. Her back was against the cold stone wall; she was sitting on the floor, her feet wedged against the mattress with Eli's dead weight on it, pushing it out of the way.

"Cornelia, what are you doing?" The perfectly normal-sounding voice made her break out in a cold sweat. The mattress moved, and she glanced at the monster, glanced his way because she couldn't help herself, because he terrified her. . . .

"Bad girl, Cornelia! Bad girl!" He was rushing over to the cell, his hand fumbling for his pocket. A key. She'd known he would have an extra key. Even with the bed shoved against the door, there was still plenty of room for him to get it open. A good three feet of space still remained between the foot of the bed and the rear wall.

His hand came through the bars with another key, just as she'd known it would. This time, she saw, the key was attached to his wrist by a braided strap—and in his other hand, aimed toward her face, was a can of pepper spray.

This time he had made sure she was not going to be able to knock away the key.

Panting, crying, Neely jumped to her feet and raced around behind the bed, wrestling the big, bulky box spring into place. It was not quite wide enough to fit; when she got it into position there was still space left between the spring and the wall.

But not enough. He pulled the chain off with a horrible rattling sound just as she got the spring into place, and shoved his shoulder against the bars. Neely jumped back out of the way as the spring smacked into the wall.

The door was open. He was coming through.

"Help!" Neely screamed, backing up into the far corner. "Please, somebody, help me!"

His arm was through the gap, and his shoulder—but that was all. It was not wide enough.

He could not get through.

Thank you, God, Neely thought, and, her bones having turned suddenly to jelly, fell to her knees.

He began spraying pepper spray at her through the gap.

Forty-nine

✦

The next few days passed with excruciating slowness. No word was heard from the runaways. An army of police and private investigators, courtesy of the Haywood estate, were searching for them, but so far not so much as a single sighting of a battered blue pickup truck carrying a tall black-haired boy and a pretty blond-haired girl had been reported.

Joe grew haggard. Jenny and Josh were pale and unnaturally quiet, growing more subdued with every hour that passed without word of their brother. They tended to trail Joe around, and he spent as much time with them as he could. Alex, too, was becoming concerned. Neely might run away—all right, she often *did* run away—but she always turned up again in a day or so. She couldn't imagine her sister just vanishing for this length of time without a word.

The worst thing about it was, there was nothing any of them could do. Joe had searched the area until there wasn't a single blacktop or gravel or dirt road left that he hadn't driven down; the police had searched the area, even dredging suspect ponds on the chance that the pickup might have somehow driven off the road; neighbors and friends had conducted a walking search of woods and

fields until the consensus was that the kids were not anywhere within a thirty-mile radius.

That left the whole rest of the country to be searched.

Andrea called, warning Alex that a reporter was interested in Neely's disappearance, and, sure enough, stories
about the case appeared in the national media. But they
were small stories, focused on the troubled life of a billionaire's teenage daughter, slanted so that Neely appeared as a
drug-abusing party girl with multiple body piercings
who'd made a habit out of being a runaway. The stories
caused barely a ripple, and, even with accompanying pictures, produced no leads at all.

In the midst of all this, some semblance of normal life
had to be maintained. After the second day, Josh and
Jenny had to go back to school. Joe had never really
stopped work, and Cary was training Victory Dance with
meticulous care. Having been told about Cary's entering
the horse in some important upcoming race, Alex was not
surprised. But Cary had lost his enthusiasm even for
Victory Dance, as Alex saw when he sat down to eat supper with them each night.

Alex was practically living in Joe's house now. They
were maintaining the fiction of sleeping in separate beds at
night for the sake of the children, but Joe had not slept
more than a couple of hours at a stretch since Eli's disappearance, and the truth was that they passed the nighttime
hours in his bed or on the couch in the living room
together, alternately talking and making love.

Tommy stopped by one night after supper to talk to
Joe. Upon seeing his car pull up, the whole family had
rushed onto the porch, hoping for news of Eli and Neely.
But after telling all of them that the reason for his visit had
nothing to do with that, Tommy took Joe outside and
spoke to him alone.

When Tommy was gone, Joe walked back into the kitchen, where Josh, Jenny, Alex, and Cary were cleaning up after the evening meal. Four pairs of eyes looked up at him expectantly as he entered.

"Josh, Jen, come on into the living room," he said, his voice very gentle. Alex's eyes widened in alarm as they met his. It was clear that whatever Tommy had told him, it was some kind of bad news. "Alex, you and Pop might as well come too."

When they were all seated in the living room, Joe on the couch with Jenny and Josh on either side of him and Alex and Cary in the adjacent chairs, Joe told them: Laura's body had been identified, and it appeared that she had been murdered in June of 1991, shortly after she had visited them for the last time.

"So that's why she never came to see us in all these years," Josh said thoughtfully. "I wondered. It's kind of strange, never seeing your mom at all, you know. Most kids who get divorced live with their moms, and if they don't see one of their parents it's, like, their dad."

"'Fraid you got stuck with me, pal," Joe said, obviously striving for a light note as he ran his hand over Josh's shorn head.

"That's okay," Josh said, looking at him quickly. Since Eli's disappearance, Josh had seemed almost to be walking on eggshells around Joe. "I don't mind being stuck with you. I mean, if you don't mind being stuck with me."

Joe's eyes sharpened on Josh's face. "What do you mean, if I don't mind being stuck with you? 'Course I don't mind being stuck with you. I love you. You're my son."

"Eli's gone and I'm not," Josh blurted in a rush, his eyes tearing up. "I keep thinking you wish it was me who was gone and him who was here."

"Oh, God." Joe sounded stricken. "Josh, no." He

wrapped an arm around Josh's shoulders and leaned toward him, looking earnestly into his face. "Josh, you're every bit as important to me as Eli, don't ever think you're not. You're the only Joshua I have. Whichever one of you is gone, it doesn't make any difference: I would hurt just as bad. I need you both here. I need you all three here."

Josh leaned over, gave Joe a quick, clumsy hug, then jumped up and, with a self-conscious glance around, left the room.

Joe started to get up, apparently meaning to follow him, but Jenny tugged at his arm.

"Daddy," she said, looking up at him with an almost stark expression in her eyes. "I've been thinking: If Mom came here and got murdered, then that means there's somebody around here who kills people. Maybe whoever it is got Eli and Neely, too."

✦ ✦ ✦ ✦

Later that night, after he had spent private time with both Josh and Jenny and they had gone to bed, Joe asked Alex if she wanted to go for a walk. Cary was still there, plopped on the couch with them watching TV. He'd been staying at Joe's house late the last several nights, usually until eleven or so. Like the rest of them, Alex guessed, Cary didn't feel like being alone.

"I'll stay here until you get back," he said, waving a hand at Joe. "Take your time. I'm not going anywhere."

It was a beautiful night, cold and clear, with scuttling clouds making a game of peekaboo out of looking up at a sky full of stars. The three-quarter moon was small and high overhead. The wind was up, blowing Alex's hair back from her face. Pale strands of it trailed across the sleeve of Joe's coat.

"I've got to go check on the horses up at Whistledown," he said, looking down at her. Her hand was tucked in his, and she was walking close against his side. "Feel like walking that far, or you just want to go down the road a little and let me come out again later?"

"Whistledown's fine," Alex said. "I need to stop by the house, anyway, and pick up some more clothes."

They walked down the road anyway, and up the driveway because the going was easier.

The house was dark because Alex hadn't been staying there. As soon as they got inside Joe walked through it, turning on lights as he went, glancing in all the rooms. Neely's room was almost poignant, Alex thought: the clothes she had worn on their last shopping trip still hung over the back of the chair in the corner, and her electric curlers sat on the dresser. Other belongings filled corners and niches, and her denim backpack lay on her bed.

Neely, where are you? she asked silently. Are you ever coming back?

It was the first time she had entertained the possibility that maybe, just maybe, her sister might *not* be coming back.

Maybe something terrible had befallen her. Alex's stomach knotted at the thought.

Something terrible had happened to Joe's ex-wife here, whether the locals called this place Paradise County or not.

"You okay?" Joe was beside her now, looking down at her. Not wanting to upset him with her imaginings—he was distraught enough over Eli without her adding to it— she nodded and smiled, and together they walked downstairs.

"God, I'm tired," Joe said as he headed into the den and collapsed into the big blue leather chair beside the couch.

He scrubbed his hands over his face and looked up to smile at Alex. "Sleeping with you is killing me. You're too restless."

He reached out and caught her hand, pulling her down onto his lap. She went willingly, curling her arms around his neck. "That's because I've gone cold turkey on my sleeping pills. I've found too many interesting things to do at night."

He laughed. "You were restless when you were taking those things. You drove me crazy when I was listening to you over the walkie-talkie. Up and down and walking around all night."

"I never did! Once I took a sleeping pill and fell asleep, I was out like a light."

"If you say so." His smile faded. "God, that was hard tonight. I didn't know Josh felt like that."

"How were they when you went upstairs to talk to them?"

"Josh was okay." He grimaced. "Jenny cried."

"Because her mother was dead?"

Joe nodded. "Can you believe that? Jenny was only a baby the last time she saw Laura. She couldn't possibly have any memories of her, fond or otherwise. But she cried."

"Laura was her mother," Alex said gently. "Whether she has any memories of her or not."

Joe took a deep breath, and slanted an unsmiling look down at her.

"She was the mother from hell," he said. "She was a drug addict, a booze hound, a party girl all the way. Once she got into drugs, I never felt safe leaving her with the kids. She would just up and leave them whenever she felt like it. She'd go off for days at a time with any man who'd buy her drugs. That's what I think happened to her: I think she got into some kind of drug deal gone wrong. All those years when the kids and I didn't see her I prayed to God to keep her away. You know what she did, the last time she came to see me? She said she'd take the kids away from me if I didn't give her the money she wanted. Understand, she didn't want them. She didn't even know them by that point. But she knew that I would pay through the nose to keep them. And I did."

He slanted a look down at Alex, and smiled humorlessly. "And then tonight Jenny cried for her. I sat with my little girl until she fell asleep, and I lied to her and told her how much her mother had loved her and wanted her and how proud she was of her. Hell, Alex, Laura didn't give the flick of her eyelashes about Jenny, or any of them. All she cared about in the end was coming up with enough money to get high."

Alex gave a wordless murmur of sympathy, and kissed the prickly underside of his jaw.

"I've never told anybody else what happened the last night Laura came to see me," he said, "just you."

Offering the only solace she could, Alex tightened her arms around his neck and pulled his head down and kissed him. She unbuttoned his flannel shirt and ran her mouth over his chest, then slid down to the floor so that she was kneeling at his feet. Nibbling at his flat belly, listening to the quickening rasp of his breathing, she unzipped his jeans, pulled him out and made love to him with her mouth. After the first swift intake of his breath he sat very still, with his eyes half shut and his hands clenched over the arms of the chair, watching her through slitted eyes the color of the sea.

Finally, growling with passion, he came down onto the floor with her, flipping her onto her back and stripping them both naked with swift efficiency. He kissed her all over, her mouth, her breasts, between her legs, until she was writhing and moaning and gasping with need. Then he took her with a fierce hunger that she matched with her own. When it was over, with their bodies still joined, he propped himself up on his elbows above her and looked down at her with a slight smile that made her heart turn over in her breast.

"I've got a news flash for you, Princess," he said. "I'm crazy in love with you."

Alex looked up at him, at the dark handsome face and sea blue eyes, at the wide bare shoulders that loomed over her, at the man who, in such a short time, had assumed center stage in her world: at Joe.

"I'm crazy in love with you, too," she said with a little laugh. Lifting her tired arms to link her hands behind his neck, she smiled at him, tremulously, and he bent his head to softly, gently kiss her mouth.

Later, he went out to the barn to check on the horses and she went upstairs to pack some clothes.

"I'll be back in fifteen minutes to get you," he promised. "But just to be on the safe side, set the alarm and lock the door."

Fifty

✦

The monster had started leaving the TV set on for, he said, her viewing pleasure. At first, because the screen was small and rather far away, Neely hadn't realized exactly what it was she was watching.

A picture of an empty room—big deal. But at least it provided some small degree of illumination, so that she was not left in utter darkness.

It was only when she saw a figure walk into that room that she realized, to her horror, exactly what she was watching. Alex's bedroom. Alex.

At first she had screamed at her sister, instinctively assuming she could hear, but of course Alex could not. Now she just watched dully as Alex infrequently appeared.

Neely had long since figured out that Alex could not be staying in the house. She was only in her bedroom for a few minutes at a time, and never seemed to sleep there. She probably didn't want to stay alone in the house.

Were they looking for her and Eli? Neely wondered achingly. She knew they were, knew that a frantic search must be under way. The real question was, would she and Eli be found?

She was afraid she knew the answer to that too.

Nobody was going to come to save them, at least, not in time.

She was going to have to save herself.

She had a plan. It wasn't a good plan, but it was the only one she could come up with. The bed frame had metal slats going across it to support the box spring and mattress. The slats were screwed into place. While she was sitting there in the semi-dark, she worked and worked until she managed to unscrew a slat. Once it was free, she had flicked on the flashlight and examined it closely. It was about three feet long, possibly a little more, with rounded corners, very sturdy.

She sat in the dark again, scraping one rounded end back and forth over the stone floor, endlessly it seemed, until she had worn it to a point on one side. Then she switched to the other side, scraping and scraping, for hours on end.

She was making a spear.

Once, long ago, in a comic strip somewhere, she had read about mole people. They were called that because they lived underground and never, ever surfaced or saw the sunlight. That's what she felt like. She could have been in this hole for years, or even centuries. The odds were that she was never going to see the sunlight again. She doubted that she would emerge from this vampire's tomb alive.

But she was going to try. She was growing very weak, she knew. It had been so long since she had eaten anything other than a bug that she was no longer even hungry. Bugs—cockroaches, crickets, disgusting insects with dozens of legs—were not very plentiful in her prison, but each day she managed to capture one or two. They crunched when she bit into them, but actually, if she didn't think about what she was eating they weren't so bad.

If it had not been for the drip in the corner of the ceiling, she would have died. Water came in there, beading on the stone, just enough to keep her from succumbing to thirst. Her tongue and lips felt swollen, though, and parched all the time. Already her skin stood up in tiny peaks if she pinched it, and this, she knew, was the hallmark of dehydration.

Eli had regained consciousness from time to time, moaning and tossing but not really lucid. He was in far worse shape than she was. She had torn a clean piece of cloth from the hem of his T-shirt, chewing at the cloth until it had given, and she used that to soak up moisture for him. Nine or ten times a day she would soak it and then squeeze the water out in his mouth, maybe getting a teaspoon's worth at a time. Several times she had tried squashing a bug and putting it in his mouth so that he could eat, but she couldn't get him to swallow.

If help did not come soon, or her plan did not work, he would die. They would both die.

The only question was how.

The monster visited regularly, bringing food and water each time. He would set it outside the door and walk away, hoping to make her think he was gone, hoping to lure her out. The smell drove her insane, making her stomach knot and growl. But if she succumbed to the trays he left for her, he would catch her, she knew. He was waiting for her out there in the dark beyond the door.

How stupid did he think she was, anyway? He had brought another chain, and a big padlock, which he used to secure the door when he left. When he arrived, he set out the food and took the chain off and walked away. An imbecile could figure that one out. But she'd always been stubborn, and she wasn't just going to let him win. She might die, but she wasn't going to die without a fight.

Her plan was to rearrange the barricade so that, with a little effort, he could get in. She would lie down beside Eli as if unconscious too, and wait. When he was inside, she would stab him with her spear.

But first she had to get the spear made.

Hannibal appeared while she was scraping. She had already figured out that the cat's eyes were the two glowing green things she had seen in the dark, and she knew, too, that her father's voice was all in her head. But at least he talked to her frequently, giving her good advice.

Hannibal's appearances invariably prefaced an appearance by the monster—he must somehow get into this place through whatever entrance the monster used—so when Neely saw him she immediately hid the spear under the bed.

Today, instead of approaching the bars—he was too fat to fit through—he jumped on the table, and sat, tail twitching, beside the TV set.

If he hadn't drawn her attention to it, Neely never would have seen Alex walk into her bedroom.

Neely watched, transfixed, as her sister walked across the room and opened the closet, rifling through her clothes. The image was small, but it was clear.

Watching, Neely felt her throat close up and her stomach clench.

Alex! She almost called her sister's name, but she remembered that the monster was coming and did not.

Deliberately she turned away from the screen. There was no point in torturing herself.

Neely. It was her father's voice again, talking inside her head. *Neely, use the cat.*

Use the cat. All of a sudden it became clear to Neely exactly what the voice meant.

She pulled off her one remaining sock and tied a quick

knot in it so that it formed a loop. For good measure she popped the diamond stud out of her nose and secured it to the sock. Then she crouched down. She didn't have much time, she knew.

"Hannibal! Here, kitty! Come here, Hannibal!"

To her relief, he came. Neely reached through the bars, grabbed him—and slipped her sock around his neck.

"Go!" she whispered to him. "Go!"

For a moment he just stood there looking at her, his green eyes glowing in the gloom. Then, with a twitch of his tail, he stalked away.

And the flashlight that always announced the arrival of the monster appeared.

Fifty-one

✦

Alex was just finishing gathering up what she would need for the next few days when she heard Hannibal. He was in her closet, and he was meowing his head off.

Had she locked him in there when she closed the door? She didn't even remember seeing him, but apparently she had.

She wanted to smile and cry at the same time, remembering Neely's comment about the dematerializing cat.

She opened the closet door and let the cat out. He stalked past her, waving his tail and jumped up on the bed, right in the center of her neat little pile of clothes.

And he sat.

"Shoo!" Alex said, waving her hands at him. But still he sat, fixing his eyes on her, as if he intended to stay right where he was until the end of time.

Joe would be back in a minute, and she really needed those clothes.

Girding her courage, she picked the enormous animal up.

And saw the sock tied around his neck.

Fifty-two

✢

The predator was smiling as he set the tray down on the floor.

"Aren't you hungry, Cornelia?" he asked genially. "You know, you'll starve to death if you don't eat."

Cornelia didn't reply. She sat huddled in a corner, refusing to look at him. Bad little girl. When he got his hands on her, he was going to make her pay. . . .

His gaze strayed to the TV screen. Ah, Alexandra was home! She'd been away lately, so it was a real treat to see her on Alexandra TV. At the moment, she was leaning over her bed, picking up that damned cat.

She was removing something from around the cat's neck. It looked like a noose. . . .

It was a strip of cloth with a knot in it.

She untied the knot and shook it out. All of a sudden her eyes went wide.

His eyes went wide too. His gaze slashed around to Neely, who was still huddled in the corner staring at the floor.

"You bitch!" he snarled, and raced for the stairs.

Fifty-three

✦

Alex stared at the sock in her hand. It was a pink trouser sock, grimy, stained with what looked like blood—with a diamond nose stud stuck through the toe.

Neely! Her heart raced. Her pulse pounded. Neely must have tied this sock around the cat's neck. . . .

Joe! She had to tell Joe! She hurried toward the bedroom door. Neely had to be somewhere nearby; Eli had to be somewhere nearby. . . .

From the state of the sock, Neely and Eli were in trouble. The sock was obviously an attempt to signal for help.

She pivoted, heading back toward the phone. In the weeks that she had been here, she had discovered that Paradise County did indeed boast 911 service. If ever anybody needed it, she needed it now.

Picking up the phone, fingers shaking, she punched the first two digits. . . .

And heard someone rushing at her from behind. She screamed, whirling, but it was too late. A hand twisted in her hair, nearly yanking it from her head as she was jerked backward. A heavy, muffling hand clamped across her face, locking her into a suffocating embrace, cutting off her scream.

She dropped the sock.

"Shut up! Stand still!" Her hair was released. A heavy metal object, round and cold, was shoved hard against her left temple. A gun barrel! Having never felt such a thing before, Alex nevertheless recognized it instinctively. Eyes widening, Alex stopped struggling and stood still. Her heart pounded; her blood ran cold.

"That's better." His grip didn't ease by so much as a millimeter. He was talking in her ear. The voice was vaguely familiar. She could not see him, but from the feel of him against her he was stocky and not as tall as Joe. "If you scream, I'll kill you right here and now. Understand?"

Alex shuddered in horror. Her stomach knotted with fear. She broke into a cold sweat. He was going to kill her, no matter what she did. She knew it as well as she knew her own name.

But she didn't want it to happen any sooner than it had to.

"Understand?" His voice was fierce. His fingers dug into the soft flesh around her mouth. The gun barrel ground against her temple, hurting her. Alex felt her knees weaken from sheer terror.

She nodded.

He bent and scooped up the sock, stuffing it into his pants pocket. He was wearing black pants, with a well-pressed crease. His shoes were black loafers with a slight coating of dust. His shirt was white and long-sleeved. He smelled of something she couldn't quite place.

She couldn't see his face.

Of course. She realized it then. This man must have Neely and Eli, too.

"Good girl. Now walk."

Alex was forced, stumbling, toward the closet.

"Open it," said the voice in her ear.

Alex obediently fumbled for the knob. Opening the door, she was pushed inside with such ferocity that she almost fell to her knees. The suffocating hand kept her upright. The gun barrel dug punishingly into her flesh.

The closet was big for the era in which it was built, long and narrow with the clothes all hung on one side, an old-time version of a walk-in. He swung her sideways, commanding her to close the door. Alex complied. In the dark now, with her clothes brushing against her on the left and his arm wrapped around her on the right, she was shoved to the back of the closet. All around her the familiar soft scent of the sachet she used hung in the air, adding to her sense of unreality.

This could not be happening. It was a nightmare.

"Remember, if you scream I'll kill you," the voice in her ear promised. Then he released her mouth, his hand reaching out toward the closet wall. Alex took a great gulping gasp of air, but did not scream. She had no doubt that he meant what he said. And anyway, unless Joe had returned to the house—and she didn't think there had been time—no one was around to hear.

To her amazement, as he pushed against it the back of the closet opened like a door. Alex was shoved into a passage so narrow that her shoulders brushed the walls on both sides. They were made of brick, rough and cold. Her captor released her mouth only to twine his hand in her hair, jerking her head back. The gun barrel moved to press against the nape of her neck. Her skin crawled with horror; she was so frightened she could barely breathe. He shoved her a foot or so farther along. Behind her, the door to the passage closed with a soft click. A flashlight was switched on. Its beam illuminated a long, narrow alley like the inside of a chimney that apparently ran the length of the upstairs.

"Walk," he hissed in her ear. Alex realized that he was

having to turn sideways to fit. He was a big man, heavy. The gun barrel jabbed hard against the base of her skull.

Alex walked. Her knees were trembling with fright.

At the end of the alley was a narrow set of stairs, no wider than the passage itself, heading down. Forced to descend, Alex realized that it was located in the wall behind the kitchen staircase. She realized, too, that the whole time they had been living in this house, her captor had had access to her bedroom, and probably the other bedrooms too.

As Alex remembered the breathing that had terrorized her on her first night in the house, her eyes widened.

She had her explanation now.

They reached the bottom of the stairs and turned on a tiny landing, then continued down. Heart sinking, Alex realized that they were descending into the basement.

It was hardly more than a coal cellar, and it reflected the age of the house. The air was chilly and smelled of damp. The floor was uneven, and she stumbled more than once. Except for the path illuminated by the flashlight, it was dark as a grave.

He seemed to relax a little now that they were in the basement.

"Ah, Alexandra! What fun we're going to have!" he said almost genially in her ear. His voice was familiar, but she could not place it. In the dark, even when she tried to glance around, she could not quite see. . . .

"Where is my sister?" To her dismay, her voice, which she had meant to be firm, shook.

They were almost across the basement now. It looked to Alex like she was being pushed straight toward the furnace. It was an old coal-burning furnace, black and ancient, no longer in use. Modern heating and air-conditioning units had been installed upstairs.

"Cornelia? Oh, she's a bad girl. I was very angry with her just a few minutes ago, but now I'm not. What she did is destiny, I've decided. I've been wanting you. Now you're mine."

His obvious meaning made Alex's skin crawl. "You have her, don't you? And Eli, too? Where are they? Have you hurt them?"

"You'll see them very soon."

At his calm statement, Alex felt something tight relax inside her heart. For a moment she felt almost overwhelming relief—until she realized that her finding Eli and Neely was not going to do anyone any good; she was just going to disappear, too.

Alex's stomach churned with terror at the thought.

Joe would miss her any minute. He would be coming in from the barn. . . .

"You know, you sleep very soundly. I've been in your room almost every night since you came, and you never knew I was there." He sounded almost cheerful. "Or maybe you did. Did you see me in your dreams, Alexandra?"

The thought of Joe gave her courage. He would search for her—he knew she had been in the house. If he had to, to find her, he would take Whistledown apart brick by brick. "I saw you on the upstairs porch. Twice."

"On the porch?" He sounded as if he were frowning. "Oh, no, you're mistaken. I'm a careful man. I wouldn't go out on the porch. Too dangerous. Someone might see me. You know, you and your sister have caused me a lot of problems. Your father, too. Very troublesome bunch, you Haywoods."

"My father. . . ." Of course. Here was the answer she'd been searching for. Her father hadn't killed himself; she had known it all along.

"You killed him, didn't you?"

He laughed, and pushed her around the furnace without replying. A small iron door was set into the stone wall. He reached around her, opening it, and it creaked loudly.

The moving flashlight beam showed her dirt floors, dirt walls, a pile of long-forgotten coal at the far end as she was shoved inside. Alex realized that they were in the old coal bin. He pushed her across it to the other side, through another small, creaky door, and once again they entered a chamber with stone walls and a stone ceiling and stone floors.

A hideous fetid smell hit Alex in the face. The room was illuminated by a faint bluish glow which emanated from a small TV. Alex saw that the room was outfitted almost like a den, with a big armchair and a table and a wall devoted almost entirely to photographs.

He let go of her then, shoving her violently forward, and Alex fell to her knees. She was wearing jeans and sneakers tonight—Joe had come home with the sneakers several days previously—but the impact with the floor still bruised her knees. However, it was nothing to the terror that raced like an icy finger down her spine. They had reached their destination. What would he do to her now?

"Cornelia!" he said, looking past her. "Here's your sister!"

Fifty-four

✦

From some distant place in the house, the damned cat was caterwauling like somebody was boiling it in oil. He'd heard it as soon as he walked in the back door. What was up with it?

The tinny wail of the security system reminded him to stop. He punched in the numbers of the code, and walked into the kitchen. God, he felt old. Older than his own father. And he was tired. Bone tired.

Eli. The thought of his son was a constant ache. *God, Eli, where are you?*

"Alex?" he called, walking into the hall and glancing around. No answer. She must be upstairs.

The cat was up there too, squalling like it was being barbecued.

He frowned as he climbed the steps.

"Alex?"

If it hadn't been for Alex, he didn't think he could have made it through this past week. For the first time in his life, he had needed someone to lean on. And she'd been there.

"Alex!" He was walking along the upstairs hall now, his voice a little louder. Her bedroom door was closed. From the sound of it, the cat was in there.

"Alex?" He opened the door, glanced around. The cat surged around his feet, rubbing against him, meowing its lungs out.

Except for the cat, the room was empty. Joe stepped inside, looked around, checked the bathroom. Alex was not there.

The cat continued to cry.

Calling for Alex, he turned and walked back down the stairs.

Fifty-five

✦

A lex had landed in a corner, a dark, shadowy corner, bounded by the damp chill of the stone on one side and a wall of iron bars on the other. Instinctively she got her feet beneath her and turned so that she faced her captor, backing up as far into the corner as she could get.

Her head came up, and she got her first look at him. He was moving toward the table, and as she watched he turned on the lantern in the center. His bald head glistened in the sudden bright light. His face was round and florid, with an almost pleasant expression. Her mouth opened and her eyes widened in shock. She knew she had recognized the voice: Homer Gibson, proprietor of the Dixie Inn.

A hand reached through the bars to touch her back.

"Alex?" The voice was a hoarse rasp.

"Neely?" Alex's head whipped around. There, crouched on the other side of the bars, was her sister. She was dirty and disheveled, clad only in a pale blue bra and jeans. Alex shuddered to think of what she had suffered, but at least she was alive. "Thank God! Neely, are you all right? Where's Eli?"

"He's here. He's hurt. Oh, Alex, I'm so sorry for getting you into this. I didn't . . ."

Looking beyond Neely, Alex saw the huddled shape of Eli curled in a fetal position on the mattress that seemed to take up most of the floor.

"Well, ladies, I'm glad I was able to provide you with this touching family reunion. Cornelia, dear, you now have a problem. You see, if you don't open that door and let me in, I'm going to chain your sister to the wall and make a bonfire out of her."

Alex's head snapped back to the front. She regarded him warily. Her heart started to pound. What did he mean? A bonfire. . . . Suddenly she saw the black scorch marks on the wall to her right. They rose to the ceiling. . . .

Homer crossed to the door of what she now saw was her sister's cell and put his hand through the bars, fumbling with the chain that secured it. With a loud rattle, he pulled the chain free.

Behind her, Neely sounded as if she were hyperventilating.

"Oh, God, oh, God. . . ."

"Neely, what . . ."

"Alex, oh, no, Alex. . . ."

"It's your choice, Cornelia. You can open the door, or . . ."

His voice trailed off. He was staring fixedly at the TV. Alex followed his gaze. Her lips parted in shock.

The figure on the small screen was unmistakably Joe. He was in her bedroom, walking around.

"And here we have another problem. Are there no end of them tonight? Do I go up there and bring him down here too? I don't want him, and there really isn't room. . . . Ah, he's leaving. Maybe he'll just go away." Tapping one finger thoughtfully against his teeth, Homer seemed to be talking more to himself than to Neely or her, Alex thought. The hand holding the gun hung limply down at his side.

For a split second she thought about running for it, but a glance toward the door dissuaded her. He could have the gun snapped up and firing in an instant. She could not possibly get past him and out the door.

As Alex watched the TV, Joe walked out of her bedroom. The screen now showed just the empty room. There were her clothes on the bed. . . .

"There's a camera over my bed." The realization brought an unpleasant, creepy feeling with it.

"Yes indeed. And in your bathroom, too. I call it Alexandra TV. All Alexandra, all the time."

At the idea that this pervert had been watching her in her most personal moments, Alex felt sick.

"I was watching you at the inn, too, you know. When you spent the night? I have a very nice videotape of you and your sister. You put on quite a show."

"You have cameras in your hotel?" Alex burst out in horror.

He smiled at her. "Oh, yes. All my rooms are wired: video and audio. The things that go on in a hotel—adultery, fornication—all kinds of chicanery. For example, I have your father on tape bribing our esteemed Lieutenant Governor Whelan." His face darkened. "I was hoping to make quite a bit of money from that tape, actually, but your father wouldn't play ball. I suppose I'll have to take the matter up with Mr. Whelan, but he really doesn't have any money so it all just seems a waste."

"Is that why you killed him? Because he wouldn't play ball?" Alex was conscious of something hard and cold being passed through the bars between her body and the wall, where Homer could not see. Neely was passing her something—Alex ran her fingers over it experimentally: cold flat metal with a sharp point on the end.

"Well, you know, I had him on *tape*." Homer sounded

aggrieved. "He and Whelan had breakfast in my restaurant then went into a room that had been rented in someone else's name. Your father wanted a permit for a certain number of hospital beds, and Whelan was glad to oblige—for a price. Money changed hands. I've got it all on tape." He frowned at Alex. "Your father was a very rich man. I didn't think there would be any problem. He asked me to meet him in the barn at Whistledown on a certain night at a certain time, told me he'd bring the money if I brought the tape, so I did. I even brought a bottle of whiskey along to celebrate. But he said he wasn't going to pay me a dime and pulled a gun on me! I believe he meant to kill me. But I had my taser with me—you know my taser, don't you, Cornelia? It's broken now—and I was able to zap him while I was handing over the tape. Spilled every bit of the whiskey while I was doing it, but no matter. When he was unconscious, I could see there was really only one thing to be done. If I didn't, he'd just keep coming after me. So I put the gun in his hand, pressed it to his head, and pulled the trigger. Instant suicide. I *am* sorry for your loss, by the way." The TV caught his eye again. His tone changed to one of vexation as he added, "There he is back!"

Fifty-six

✦

Alex was nowhere in the house.

At the realization Joe felt cold stark terror grab him by the throat. He knew as well as he knew morning was coming that she hadn't walked back down to his house in the dark by herself.

Joe picked up the phone in the kitchen and dialed Tommy. Calling 911 was not nearly so efficient as knowing the sheriff's home phone number, Joe had found.

"Haul your butt over to Whistledown now!" Joe's grip on the phone was so tight his knuckles showed white. "I can't find Alex! She was in the house, and she's disappeared!"

Tommy had obviously been asleep when he'd picked up the phone, but his voice was alert as he answered, "On my way."

He'd known Joe long enough not to ask questions: if Joe said it was an emergency, it was.

Then Joe went back up to Alex's bedroom. The clothes she had planned to take with her were on the bed. The damned cat had been on the bed. A depression and a few orange hairs on top of the pile of clothes made that obvious. Whatever had happened to Alex had most likely happened in her bedroom.

He walked inside and stood looking around. His heart was pounding, and the harsh taste of fear was bitter in his mouth. He couldn't lose her, not now. . . .

He didn't think he could bear to lose another person he loved. Hannibal emerged from under the bed. He looked at Joe, yowled, and walked toward the closet with his tail held high.

The cat. . . .

Arrested, Joe followed him, and opened the door. The cat walked right into the closet and stopped in front of the back wall, waving his tail gently from side to side, and turning to meow at Joe for all the world as if he were asking to be let out.

Joe let out his breath as a truly horrific thought struck him, and put his shoulder to the wall.

It gave way.

Fifty-seven

❧

"Well." Homer sounded faintly regretful as they watched Joe enter the closet in Hannibal's wake. "I guess it's destiny. Yours—and mine."

He walked over to Alex. Even as she tried to jump up, tried to stab him with the spear, he grabbed it from her hand.

"Bad girl!" he said, and hit her over the head with the gun.

Alex saw stars. By the time she recovered, he had chained one of her wrists to the wall.

"You're lucky I didn't shoot you," he said. "But then again, maybe you're not. Anyway, bullets ricochet down here."

In the cell, Neely was sobbing.

"Alex! Alex! Oh, no, please! Alex. . . ."

Alex felt her heart begin to pound. Her mouth went dry. Her eyes were wide with fear as she watched him pocket the gun and walk to the opposite end of the room from the cell.

He'd threatened to chain her to the wall and make a bonfire out of her.

She broke out in a cold sweat, and began to fight the chain that held her. It rattled and clanked, but it was a heavy chain fastened to a solid iron ring set into stone, and it didn't give.

When he returned, he was carrying a red metal gas can. Panic almost overwhelmed her.

He was going to burn her alive. Neely was keening now, a high-pitched sound of sheer terror.

Alex began to shake. "Please, Homer. Please. Don't do this. Please. . . ."

"This is not how I meant this to turn out, Alexandra," Homer said regretfully. "I meant to keep *you*. But since Joe is obviously coming this way, and I see no way of avoiding having my little home away from home discovered, the only thing to do is remove all the evidence by burning the entire place. When they find you and Cornelia and Eli in the ashes down here, they'll know what happened. But they won't know who did it." He started splashing kerosene around. The stench rose up to choke Alex as the liquid hit near her feet. "After all, he who turns and runs away lives to play another day."

He poured kerosene near the cell, splashed some through the bars, and backed away, pouring a stream of kerosene behind him as he went.

"Good-bye, Alexandra," he said, opening the door. Then he reached into his pants pocket, withdrew a book of matches, and struck one. Alex watched in horror as the flame flared brightly in his hand.

Then he dropped it, and the world turned orange with a *whoosh*.

Fifty-eight

✦

A lex! Alex!"
"Neely! Oh, God, Neely!"
Alex screamed as bright orange flames danced across the floor, raced around the room, climbed the walls. Smoke rose in its wake, curling toward the ceiling, reaching oily fingers toward her, clogging her mouth and nose. Neely was screaming too, Alex heard her, saw her sister burst through the door of the cell and run toward her, dodging a line of flames that was growing taller and more furious by the second.

"Alex!" Neely was fumbling with her wrist, with the manacle around her wrist, fumbling to insert a key which she produced from somewhere, God knew where, while Alex gagged at the smoke and tried to shield her face from the intense heat with her hand.

"Leave me! Leave me!" She was going to die, she knew it, she and Neely and Eli in this monstrous place, consumed by flames, screaming. "Neely, run! Leave me!"

"Please God, please God, please God . . ." Neely was sobbing the words as the flames climbed higher up the walls, heating the air, sucking the oxygen from it. . . .

The crackling roar was the most terrifying thing Alex had ever heard. The walls were beginning to char. She estimated that they had about a minute before the room was fully engulfed, before licking tongues of flame were climbing up their skin. . . .

The manacle came free.

The door at the back of the room burst open. The influx of oxygen caused the flames to soar. Joe appeared, leaping over one small line of flames, one arm up to shield his face. . . .

"Alex!" His bellow was louder even than the roar of the fire.

"Eli! Eli is in the cell!" Neely shrieked as she ran toward him. Alex turned toward the cell; she couldn't leave Joe's son. . . .

"Get out of here!" he screamed at her, running past.

The smoke was getting worse; her eyes were watering. She couldn't breathe, couldn't see. . . .

Her skin was crisping in the heat.

She couldn't leave Joe.

Panic welled like vomit in her throat. Joe was in the cell, bending over the mattress, hauling Eli up. . . .

And the flames had reached her feet. Sheer black terror overwhelmed her.

Alex ran, screaming, leaping like a deer, beating at the fingers of flame that grabbed at the legs of her jeans. The superheated air made it almost impossible to breathe.

The door; the door. Heart pounding, feet racing, she made it to the door. She burst through it, out into the dark earthen safety of the coal bin, beating at her legs, gasping for air, and turned just in time to see Joe, with Eli slung over his shoulder, come leaping out of the flames.

Fifty-nine

❦

B y twilight of the following day, they were all out of
the hospital except Eli, who was going to be there
for a couple of weeks, the doctors told Joe. He'd
already undergone surgery for the bullet wound in his
chest, and would, with time, recover fully.

"I haven't had a chance to thank you yet," Joe said to
Neely as he accompanied her and Alex back to
Whistledown to get their things. The house was badly
damaged; no one would be living there again unless extensive repairs were made. It had also been declared a crime
scene by the police, and was cordoned off with tape.
They'd had to get permission to enter to collect their
things. "You saved Eli's life."

"I have my good points," Neely replied with a cocky
grin. Like Alex's, her hair was singed to the point of frizzi-
ness and she had a few superficial burns. The burns to
Joe's legs were a little more serious, but they were ban-
daged and didn't seem to be slowing him down.

"I admit it. You do," Joe agreed. This conversation took
place in the upstairs hall, and Alex, who was in her bedroom packing, listened in with a smile. In her opinion,
which she had already expressed, Neely was a heroine.
Her sister had saved her life, too.

Joe walked into Alex's room, and she paused in her packing long enough to smile at him. He had constituted himself her and Neely's bodyguard for this visit, although the danger was past. Tommy had arrested Homer about twenty minutes after he'd gotten the whole story from Neely, Alex, and Joe. Homer had simply gone back to the Dixie Inn, confident that he had eliminated all witnesses. The state police, to whom Tommy had turned Homer over, had said that if he hadn't been stopped Homer would certainly have killed again: he had already killed twenty-two women and four men. He'd kept an extensive photo collection of his victims in his house; its duplicate had been displayed on the walls of the room in Whistledown's basement, and had been destroyed.

As soon as he was taken into custody, Homer had confessed. Laura Welch had been one of his victims, as they had already guessed. After her last visit to Joe, she'd spent the night at the Dixie Inn. Homer had taken her as she'd slept.

"Tell me something: Why are there secret passages in my house?" Alex asked, shifting so that she could look up at Joe. "It's not some kind of weird local custom, like basketball worship, is it?"

Joe grinned at her.

"Apparently Whistledown was part of the Underground Railroad," he answered. "It dates from before the Civil War, you know. They used to hide runaway slaves down in that room beyond the coal bin. The passages were there to slip them in or out of the house in case the slave catchers came. There was another passage leading out of the basement too, toward the creek. It's half caved-in since the rains, but apparently that's where Homer was stashing the bodies, stowing them very neatly in plastic garbage bags.

That big rain we had the night you got here apparently washed some of the bags out."

"How did Homer know about it?" This was Neely, calling from her room.

"He grew up at Whistledown. His family owned it about twenty-five years ago. The passages weren't a secret, really. Everybody had kind of forgotten about them, is all."

"Believe me, I didn't know anything about them," Alex said firmly. "I wouldn't have spent the first night in this house if I had known."

"Actually, you didn't," Joe said under his breath, and Alex, remembering her panicked run down the hill, grimaced at him.

He came around the side of the bed toward her and crossed his arms over his chest, looking at her consideringly. Alex lifted an inquiring eyebrow at him and continued packing.

"Now that you don't have a place to live anymore, I guess you'll be starting to think about heading back to Philadelphia," he said.

Alex stopped packing and met his gaze. "That depends," she said.

"On what?" His eyes were suddenly very intent on her face.

"On you."

"Oh, yeah?" He started to smile.

"Yeah."

"Alex." He reached over, caught her hand, and pulled her toward him. But when she would have wrapped her arms around his neck he held her a little away from him so that he could see her face.

"Marry me." His voice was husky.

Looking up at him, at the sea blue eyes and the beautiful mouth and the tan, strong face, she felt her heart turn over.

"Yes," she said, smiling at him. Then she wrapped her arms around his neck and rose up on tiptoe to kiss his mouth.

"Did I hear what I just thought I heard?" Neely shrieked from the doorway. "Did you just say you'd marry him?"

"You got a problem with that?" Joe asked, lifting his head. Alex turned around in Joe's arms to smile at her sister.

"Well, no," she said, and grinned impishly at Joe. "I don't know how I'm going to adjust to having Eli for a nephew, though."

Joe groaned.

"We'll work it out," Alex said firmly.

A little while later, possessions packed, they were ready to go back down the hill to Joe's house. Joe was already carrying suitcases downstairs.

"Have you seen Hannibal?" Neely asked Alex. Alex had already been looking for him, and shook her head. "We can't leave him."

"No," Alex agreed. The cat had been one of the biggest heroes of all. And remembering that, she suddenly had an idea where to look.

"Come on," she said to Neely, who frowned at her but followed.

When Alex stepped out onto the upstairs porch, a rush of cold air hit her in the face. It was the time of day when twilight turns to night, and the porch was deep in purple shadows. The sisters walked along it, calling for Hannibal. All of a sudden, he came walking toward them from the far end of the porch, purring loudly, his tail proudly erect and waving.

Beyond him, shimmery and indistinct but unmistakable for all that, was the image of a man.

Alex stared. There was no mistake: her father was

standing there, smiling at her and Neely, his hands in his pockets, his silver hair gleaming, his blue eyes warm with love. He was dressed as she had often seen him, in a tweed sport coat and open-collared shirt tucked into khaki slacks.

As she watched, eyes wide and lips parted in wonder, he began to fade. He lifted a hand in farewell, and then he was gone as completely as if he had never been there at all.

Only deep purple shadows remained in his place.

"Daddy!" Alex and Neely cried at the same time, as Hannibal twined around their ankles. Then they exchanged glances.

They had both seen him. There was no mistake.

"Alex!" Joe was bellowing, clearly faintly alarmed at not being able to find her.

"Let's go," Alex said. Neely scooped up the still-purring cat, cradling it in her arms. Then the sisters turned away, walking from the cool purple shadows of the porch into the bright warmth inside.

Epilogue

✣

On a bright Saturday in December, Joe leaned on the rail near the finish line at Gulfstream Park. On one side was his dad, jumping up and down and yelling fit to kill. On his other side was his new wife, Alex, who was jumping and screaming, too. All four kids were bouncing like kangaroos around them, and the noise level for the group was several decibels more than his ears could normally stand.

But this wasn't normally. This was watching Victory Dance sweep the Magna Futurity by six lengths. He couldn't believe it.

Two thoughts went through his mind as he watched that skinny fleabag of a horse run his way to half a million dollars and a piece of glory, and caught a glimpse of his shrieking wife at the same time.

The first was, When you're hot, you're hot.

The second was, Dreams do come true.

POCKET BOOKS HARDCOVER
PROUDLY PRESENTS

TO TRUST A STRANGER

✦✦✦✦

KAREN ROBARDS

Available December 2001
from
Pocket Books Hardcover

Turn the page for a preview of
To Trust a Stranger. . . .

I don't want to hurt your feelings or anything, MacQuarry, but you sure are one ugly-ass woman."

Mac shot his partner a withering look. Hinkle, walking beside him, was snickering openly. It was a sweltering Friday night in July, and the two of them had just met up in the parking lot of the Pink Pussycat, one of Charleston's most notorious gay bars.

"Hey, I feel pretty, all right? Back off."

"I wouldn't date you, that's for sure."

"You are dating me, so shut the hell up." Mac's spike heel caught on a crack in the pavement and he stumbled, nearly twisting his ankle. Grabbing Hinkle's arm, he recovered his balance with no harm done beyond a warning twinge. "Shit. How women walk in these things beats the hell out of me. My feet hurt already. I'll be a cripple before the night's over."

Chortling, Hinkle pulled his arm free. "You better be keeping them hands to yourself, homes. Rawanda's the jealous type. She'll kick your ass, she catches you molesting me."

"You're just lucky the guy's prejudiced. Otherwise your black ass'd be in this getup."

"I'd be lookin' good, too, unlike some people I could name. Hey, man, you can't go scratchin' yourself if you're gonna hang with me. It's not ladylike."

"I'm not scratching myself, I'm pulling up my pantyhose." Mac gave the waistband, which seemed more determined to head south than General William Tecumseh Sherman on his Civil War–era march to the sea, another savage tug. "Shut up, here we go."

They joined the throng on the sidewalk in front of the bar.

Located in the middle of a run-down block taken over long since by girlie bars and porn shops, the Pink Pussycat was a three-story cinderblock building painted flaming flamingo with a giant, reclining neon cat swilling a martini affixed to the front wall. The small curtained windows were outfitted with black iron bars like a prison. A bouncer checking IDs stood just outside the door. It was near midnight, and there was a line. At least half the patrons, Mac was relieved to see, looked as freaky as he felt. He was six-one barefoot, maybe six-four or six-five in the damned spindly-heeled shoes, which meant that at the moment he towered over the crowd. Oh, well, at least being able to see over everybody's head would make it easier to spot their target.

According to his sources, Clinton Edwards had a thing for buxom blond drag queens. And since Edwards' wife was paying through the nose so she could nail him good in their divorce, Mac was willing to turn himself into a buxom blond drag queen, wired for pictures and sound, to get the dirt. He hated domestic cases, hated them with a passion, and this one was even slimier than most, but MacQuarry and Hinkle, private investigators, were not successful enough to be particular about the jobs they took.

In other words, if it paid, he sashayed.

"That'll be ten bucks." The bald, multi-earringed bouncer looked them over without interest. In the spirit of getting into his role, Mac almost batted his heavily mascaraed eyelashes at him. But nah, the guy was shorter than he was but stocky, one of those weight lifter types, and who knew, he might get into it. Fending off a two-hundred-pound-plus lovestruck fruit was not on tonight's agenda.

Well, it was, maybe, but in any case not this particular lovestruck fruit. Edwards weighed somewhere north of two-fifty, according to his bio, but he was sixty years old and all lard.

Yumyum, Mac thought with an inward sigh. Just his type.

The things he did to earn a living.

Hinkle paid, and they walked inside. It was dark and smoky and smelled of beer and b.o. Plastic palm trees adorned the corners, and the DJ was playing "Margaritaville." Couples, some male-male, some female-female, some who-knew-what, swayed on the tiny dance floor in the middle of the room. Up on the stage, a blond with boobs the size of basketballs stripped in time to the music. She was peeling off her leopard-print panties before Mac realized to his horror that she wasn't a woman. Averting his gaze, he forced his mind back to business and scanned the room for their quarry.

Somebody grabbed his ass.

"Yow!" Mac was so surprised he jumped a foot straight up in the air. Landing on his spike heels, he wobbled, tottered and nearly went down. Catching himself on a table, he got his ankles straightened out and turned around. It was all he could do to stop himself from reaching for his Glock, which was conveniently holstered in his eighteen-hour bra.

"Hey, now, don't you be grabbin' my bitch." Hinkle's grin as he warned the bespectacled accountant type who was looking Mac up and down with clearly lascivious intent made Mac long to pop him one.

"Sorry, man, I didn't realize she was with somebody." The accountant held up both hands in a gesture of peace, leaned back in his chair, and picked up his beer. Over the mug's rim, his eyes met Mac's with an unmistakable message. Seeing that Hinkle's attention was briefly elsewhere, his lips pursed in a silent kiss.

Mac's eyes widened. Then he gritted his teeth and managed a saccharine smile.

"See you around," the accountant said.

"Yeah, see ya." It was his best falsetto. Careful to keep his assets out of reach, Mac turned and minced toward the bar. Christ, now both ankles were giving him trouble. He had to remind himself again just how much Mrs. Edwards was paying them. If he hadn't, he would have turned tail there and then and gotten the hell out of Dodge.

"From now on, you watch my back," he growled over his shoulder at Hinkle. But Hinkle wasn't looking at him. He was staring across the room, an arrested expression on his face.

"Shit, there he is."

"Where?" Alert now too, Mac followed his gaze. Sure enough, Edwards was seated with a gorgeous-looking blond—Mac had to remind himself that the babe was a *guy*—at a little round table in the corner. As he watched, the blond stood up, smiled flirtatiously at Edwards, then headed across the room. She disappeared inside a door adorned with a neon sign that read LADIES.

Jesus.

"Looks like you're on, boss," Hinkle said under his breath.

Mac looked at that door, looked back at Hinkle, and resigned himself to the inevitable. Sometimes a man had to do what a man had to do.

"You know," he said in his creaky falsetto, "I think I have to go tinkle."

With Hinkle laughing like a juiced-up hyena behind him, Mac teetered off to make a girlfriend of the blond. If she could be persuaded to invite him and Hinkle to join her and Edwards at their table, his life was suddenly made a whole lot easier. If not, he was going to have to go to Plan B. He didn't even want to think about Plan B. It involved getting friendlier with Edwards than he ever wanted to be with someone who didn't have two X chromosomes.

Either way, he thought as he pushed through the door into the soft pink lighting of the little girls' room, it was going to be a long night.

He should have listened to his grandma and become a lawyer.

Julie Carlson turned another corner, took a quick look around, and, for the third time in five minutes, pressed the button that secured all four car doors just to make sure they really were locked. All right, so driving a shiny silver Jaguar deep into Charleston's bustling red-light district in the middle of a Friday night was probably not the smartest thing she had ever done. But then, when she'd left the house, she hadn't known where she was headed, so she really couldn't be convicted of total stupidity. She'd just followed Sid blindly, desperate to know where her husband went when he snuck out of their house after he thought she was asleep, and she'd ended up here. Not exactly a positive reflection on their marriage, was it?

All up and down the street, neon signs blinked GIRLS! LIVE!

ONSTAGE! and ADULT MOVIES and XXX. Acknowledging their import, Julie felt the knot that seemed to have lodged permanently in the pit of her stomach twist itself several degrees tighter.

Sid was forty years old and healthy as a horse as far as she knew. She was twenty-nine, with a slim curvaceous figure she worked hard to keep, great legs if she did say so herself, long black hair that waved naturally in the sauna-like heat, and a face that had taken her far from her wrong-side-of-the-track roots. She was clean and sweet-smelling and bought her lingerie at Victoria's Secret. In other words, there was absolutely nothing about her that might turn a husband off.

She and Sid hadn't had sex in more than eight months. And it certainly wasn't from lack of interest or effort on her part. But trying to entice her own husband into bed without success was ego busting, to say the least.

Especially for someone who had once been called the prettiest girl in South Carolina.

Sid's excuse, when she confronted him about their dead (not dying—*dead*) sex life, was that he was under a lot of stress at work, so he'd appreciate it if she would just let him the hell alone. He was a contractor who owned his own very successful business, developing subdivisions and building luxury homes across the state. She had no doubt that he *was* under a significant amount of stress.

But enough stress to keep him from having sex? Uh-uh. No way.

It had taken a while for the other shoe to drop, but finally it had when she'd found diamond-shaped blue Viagra pills mixed in with some vitamins in his medicine cabinet. At first hope had flared, and she waited with anticipation, sure he'd decided to see a doctor to fix their little problem. But nothing had happened. There'd been eight pills when she'd discovered the cache on Monday. By this evening—Friday—when she'd checked again, only four were left.

Sid was having sex all right . . . just not with her.

At least he'd apparently been telling the truth about stress impairing his sexual functioning.

Ever since she'd made the discovery, she'd been sick to her stomach. It was hard to admit that her Cinderella, rags-to-riches, fairy tale marriage had about as much life left in it as yesterday's roadkill. To make matters worse, her whole family was now dependent on Sid: her mother and stepfather lived in a house he owned; her sister's husband worked as a vice president at his company, a job which paid Kenny perhaps three times what he was worth, enough for Becky to stay home with their two girls.

Divorce was such an ugly word. But Julie had a sinking feeling that she was looking it right in the face.

Until she had discovered the vanishing Viagra, she hadn't allowed herself to seriously consider ending her marriage. Maybe, she kept telling herself, things would get better. Maybe work stress really was the reason why Sid wasn't interested in her sexually anymore. Maybe there was also a perfectly reasonable explanation as to why he was so cold and brusque to her most of the time, and why he slept in the spare bedroom, and why he snuck out at night after she had gone upstairs to bed.

Yeah, and maybe there was an Easter Bunny, too.

She'd asked him about all those things before her Viagra discovery, which had left her almost too sick to talk to him at all. His response had been that the stress of keeping her in the style to which she was definitely not accustomed had both robbed him of his manhood and given him insomnia. He slept in the spare bedroom because he didn't want his insomnia to keep her awake, and when he couldn't sleep he sometimes went out driving around his subdivisions. Looking at houses he'd built relaxed him.

Uh-*huh*.

But still, coward that she was, she had wanted to believe. A stable home and a stable marriage were precious to her. As a child, she and her mother and sister had been so poor, they'd sometimes lived in homeless shelters. Hunger wasn't some abstract concept involving starving children in Africa— from experience, she knew exactly how it felt. Her looks had gotten her and her family out of that hell and had won her

Sid, the ultimate handsome millionaire prize she'd been dreaming of all her life. She'd fallen wildly in love with him when she was barely twenty, and he, in turn, had seemed to adore her. But somehow, over the course of eight years of marriage, it had all gone wrong.

The love had disappeared from their marriage like air escaping from a tiny hole in a balloon: the loss was so gradual no one noticed until the thing went flat.

So here she was, at quarter till one, caught in a snarl of traffic on this X-rated street just around the corner from the Citadel, spying on her husband—who had certainly not built a home anywhere in the vicinity that she knew of.

She should just turn around and go home, Julie told herself. Sid would kill her if he caught her following him, and she'd lost him, anyway. She'd seen his big black Mercedes turn onto this street and that was it.

When she had turned the same corner just a few minutes later, nothing. At least, no Sid.

Plenty of people who made her think that driving the Jaguar had been a bad idea, though. Like the promenading hookers eyeing her wheels from the sidewalk with dollar signs in their eyes. And the sleazy john-types who cast furtive glances her way before disappearing into the XXX doorways. And the shirtless, tattooed bald guy who crossed the street right in front of her, thumping a fist on the hood and waggling his metal-studded tongue suggestively at her as he passed.

That was it. Abort mission. She was going home. She who turns and runs away lives to follow her husband another day.

Julie hung a right into the nearest parking lot, swung the Jag around, and frowned to find her exit blocked by a beat-up blue pickup that had pulled in behind her.

Her frown deepened when the doors opened and a pair of muscle-bound skinheads in sagging jeans and wife-beater undershirts got out. As they approached the Jag, Julie's eyes widened. A quick glance around told her that there was no place to go. Parked cars ringed the lot on all sides. There was only one exit—and the pickup loomed between her and it.

Instinctively she punched the lock button again. It clicked

vainly. The doors were already locked. The windows were up. The punks kept coming. What else could she do? Julie grabbed her shoulder bag, ripped open the zipper, thrust her hand inside and rooted frantically around. A hairbrush . . . makeup . . . a jumble of miscellaneous junk. Where oh where was that cell phone?

Just as her fingers closed around it, knuckles rapped on her window. Julie looked up to find an Eminem clone grinning through the glass at her.

"Hey, open up."

His tone was almost friendly, but the gun in his hand was not.

Julie's heart began to pound. Oh, God, she was about to be mugged, or car-jacked, or worse. What was she going to do? What *could* she do? He was armed with a gun. She was armed with a cell phone.

If it came down to a duel, she was willing to bet that he could shoot her before she could punch in 911.

Whichever way it worked out, there would be no keeping this a secret. Sid was bound to find out. And if her husband discovered that she'd followed him into Charleston, he would kill her.

Always assuming that she was still alive to be killed, of course. The thought of Sid knowing what she'd done was scary, but the delinquent at her window was a more immediate threat.

"I said open the goddamned door, bitch." Her assailant didn't sound friendly at all this time. He'd just been kind of holding the gun at waist level before. Now he was leveling it at her.

Julie imagined a bullet shattering the glass and tearing into her flesh.

Her pulse raced. Her mouth went dry. Her fight or flight impulse kicked in, and it didn't come down on the side of fighting. Slamming the transmission into reverse, she stomped the gas pedal and rammed the heel of her hand down on the horn at the same time. The Jag shot backward. The horn blared. The thugs cursed and gave chase.

And the Jag crashed into the side of a black Chevy Blazer that was just at that moment backing out of a parking space.

The impact threw her forward, and brought the Jag to a shuddering stop. At about the same time her window shattered, showering her with glass. Her head whipped around in time to see the punk who had knocked on her window thrust his arm into the car and pull up the lock. Before she could do anything but gasp, her door swung open, the punk leaned across her cool as a Popsicle to unfasten her seat belt, and she was yanked from her seat.

Her butt and elbows hit the pavement hard and she cried out. The punks jumped into the car. She barely had time to roll out of the way before her Jag and the pickup that had blocked it peeled rubber out of the parking lot.

The bad news was, her Jag had been stolen. The good news was, she was relatively unharmed.

The plaintive lament of a slide guitar and voices, both reaching her ears from a little distance, brought her out of her first shocked immobility. Her phone, she discovered, making a quick inventory, was still in her hand. She'd lost her car, but she still had her phone. Frantically she punched in 9, then paused, recovering enough wit to think the situation through. She was sprawled on her stomach in the parking lot of some girlie joint deep in the heart of Charleston, lying on pavement that was hot enough to toast bread even so long after sundown, wearing nothing but her hubby-come-hither sleeping attire of hot-pink satin tap pants and a skimpy matching top, along with a pair of Nikes. Her butt was bruised, her elbows stung—and her car was gone. How was she ever going to explain this to Sid?

Oh, God, what if it hit the papers?

Maybe calling 911 was not the best idea, she thought with her finger poised above the button. But what else was she going to do?

"Have a fight with your boyfriend?"

The voice was masculine. The vision that filled her eyes as she glanced up in response was anything but. Pointy-toed black patent stilettos big enough to swim in. Muscular calves in opaque black panty hose. A red-sequined skirt that stopped several inches above a pair of athletic-looking knees. A shiny black blouse with a deep décolletage that was filled in with a red and black polka-dot scarf. Breasts the size and shape of traffic cones. Long platinum blond hair. A lean hard chin and manly features whose gender was given the lie by garish makeup ladled on thick. All this on a broad-shouldered, narrow-hipped frame that stood easily six and a half feet tall. The overall effect was Dolly Parton morphed with the Terminator.

She must have been gaping, because the question was repeated with a hint of impatience. It recalled her to the full dimensions of her dilemma, and the oddity of her questioner was forgotten.

"They stole my car! Those two punks—they stole my car." Julie peeled herself off the pavement and scrambled to her feet. Stabs of pain from her butt and elbows were ignored as she stared helplessly in the direction in which her car had disappeared. The street and sidewalks were still clogged with traffic, vehicular and otherwise, but her car was no longer in sight. Neither was the pickup. There was an intersection just half a block away. They could have turned left or right.

Her legs went rubbery, and she swayed a little before she could lock her knees into place. A surprisingly masculine feeling hand closed around her upper arm, steadying her.

"Are you drunk?" The voice was surprisingly masculine, too, given the appearance of its owner, and faintly disapproving. Glancing up, Julie confronted the full glory of twin arches of sky-blue eyeshadow above sea-blue eyes and gleaming scarlet lips above a strong chin with the faintest hint of five o'clock shadow, and knew despair. There was no help to be had here.

"No!" Impatient, she jerked her arm free, raised the phone, and added a 1 to the 9. Then she paused. Sid . . .

"You know, you banged into my car pretty good. You have a license? Insurance?"

"What?" She was so busy performing a fast mental search through the pros and cons of a variety of actions that she had pretty much blocked out everything else.

"License? Insurance? You know, the kind of information most people exchange when they've had a wreck?"

Julie took a deep breath, and tried to focus on what was being said to her. One problem at a time. Arnold and Dolly's bastard offspring was obviously afraid that he . . . she . . . oh, whatever . . . was going to be stuck for the damage to his car. A glance beyond him told her that it was pretty substantial. The dent extended from the middle of the right rear door to past the wheel well.

"Yes. Yes, of course I have a license and insurance. Oh, my purse is in the car. *They stole my car.* I have to get it back." Her finger shot to the final 1 and then she paused again, glancing despairingly toward the intersection. No doubt about it: the Jag was long gone. There was no way to keep this secret from Sid. She might as well go on and bite the bullet and call the police and be done with it.

Still she hesitated, racking her brains to come up with an—any—alternative. She glanced up appealingly, only to find that he was giving her the once-over. Julie was almost sure of it. She had been on the receiving end of enough of those looks to recognize it for what it was.

A bubble of near-hysterical laughter rose in her throat. How much worse could this night get? Her probably cheating husband had snuck out of their home after she'd gone up to bed. She'd chased him onto a block that looked like vice cops should be swarming all over it. There she'd had a wreck, been assaulted, and her Jaguar had been stolen. Now she was standing in her skimpy satin husband-bait in the parking lot of some sort of sex bar with a drag queen checking her out.

About to call the cops.

Life didn't get much better than that.

He finished his perusal of her body, glanced up, and their gazes met and held. Hers was indignant, challenging. She was *not* in the mood to be sexually harassed by what looked like the humongous hooker from hell. His had something she thought she recognized as being very male in it. After the briefest of pregnant moments he broke off eye contact, and his gaze dropped down her body again. Blatantly this time.

Julie bristled and opened her mouth to slay him with a few choice words.

He beat her to it.

"Girlfriend, you really should be wearing heels with an outfit like that," he said in a slow, faintly disapproving drawl.

He'd been checking out her *shoes*? Julie felt insane laughter bubbling up her throat again. She swallowed it, along with the blast she'd been getting ready to flatten him with, took a deep, calming breath, and glanced around.

People had entered the parking lot since she'd jumped to her feet: an entwined couple and an extravagantly dressed woman, walking separately, heading for their cars. It said a lot for the standards of the area that they didn't even give her in her sexy pj's and Amazonia in all her jaw-dropping glory a second glance.

Not that it mattered. The only thing that mattered was getting her car back and getting home before Sid. The problem was, how was she supposed to do that?

"Damn Sid anyway," she muttered aloud. This entire disaster was every bit his fault.

"Miz Carlson?" Amazonia asked then, on a faintly disbelieving note. Julie's eyes widened and shot to his face. Her previous conviction to the contrary, the night had suddenly gotten much, much worse. Whoever or whatever this person was, he knew her name.

Julie's heart began to slam against her breastbone. She met his gaze wide-eyed. A denial trembled on her lips, but she realized almost at once that it would only make her look foolish, and the situation even more questionable. There was no hope of concealing anything now. Might as well just punch in the final 1 and get it over with.

"Y-yes."

There was the tiniest pause as the heavily made-up eyes narrowed and the bright red lips thinned.

"Well, now," he said as his gaze ran over her once more, with an entirely different expression. "If that just don't absolutely beat all."

Julie wasn't sure what he meant by that, but she was sure she didn't like the sound of it.

"Hey, Deb-*bie*," a slurred voice interrupted. Julie glanced around. The couple—an overweight, obviously drunken man in a rumpled suit and a beautiful blond in an elegant black cocktail dress who clung possessively to his arm—came up behind them and paused, the woman obviously supporting the man, who was a little unsteady on his feet. The scent of booze emanating from the man was unpleasantly strong. Wrinkling her nose in instinctive protest, Julie realized that the greeting, uttered by the man, had been addressed to Amazonia. Debbie? Julie shot him a glance. The name seemed far too ordinary for such an extraordinary individual.

"You still got the address? It's gonna be a hell of a good time." The man's gaze shifted from Debbie to Julie, and moved over her in a way that creeped her out. "Your pretty friend here's welcome, too."

"Oh, Clint, you know I wouldn't miss it for the world." Debbie smiled and spoke in a mincing falsetto that in no way resembled the growling masculine tone he'd used with her. "You and Lana go on ahead, sugar. I'll be along shortly."

"Remember, we've got lots of blow. All you need to bring is maybe your little friend, and we'll party all night. There's plenty of fun to be had by all." Clint gave Julie a leering smile. Julie recoiled. As Lana pulled Clint away, she glanced back over her shoulder at Julie.

"You stay away, bitch," she mouthed. Then, waggling her fingers at Debbie, she added aloud, "See you later, sweet cheeks."

Sweet cheeks? Debbie? It hit Julie with the force of a blow: Lana was a man. She gaped after the pair as they resumed their lurching journey toward the far end of the parking lot. The beautiful, shapely blond swaying so sexily in four-inch heels was a *man*.

"She thinks *I'm* a man!" Julie exclaimed as revelation struck.

She caught Debbie's eye just then, and discovered that he was grinning.

"Close your mouth, Miz Carlson, you'll catch flies," he chided in his masculine voice, and gently tapped her slack jaw with a forefinger. Her teeth clamped together with an audible click. "You should feel flattered. You made Lana jealous. You notice she's not jealous of *me*."

For a moment Julie felt something like Alice after she fell down the rabbit hole. This was definitely a parallel universe. Then she remembered the mess she was in, and everything else was wiped from her mind.

"My car," she groaned, and started to punch in the final 1 before hesitating once more.

"You gonna call the police or not? I got places to go and things to do here. And we're going to need that police report for the insurance."

When a six-and-a-half-foot transvestite crosses his arms over his eye-popping chest, gives you an impatient look, and starts tapping his pointed patent leather toe, the effect is galvanizing, Julie discovered. She clutched the phone tighter, but could not quite bring herself to punch in that last 1.

If she did, all hell would break lose the minute she got home.

"Look, I've got a problem, okay? I don't want my husband to find out I was out tonight," she confessed, her shoulders slumping in defeat as she lowered the phone. Debbie knew who she was and therefore almost certainly knew Sid in some way or another, although her mind boggled at picturing mucho macho Sid having an acquaintance with a drag queen. But Debbie was such a bizarre figure that it seemed all right to confide, a little, in him. He would have his share of secrets, too. Besides, she'd wrecked his car, he wanted to call the police, and she was just now fully beginning to comprehend what a really bad idea that was. She was willing to bet good money that every cop in South Carolina knew or knew of her husband, and once she called them she might just as well take out an ad in the paper describing the night's debacle and be done with it. If telling Debbie a little of the truth would win her enough sympathy to give her time to think, Julie was all for that.

"Oh, yeah?" Debbie sounded interested rather than sympathetic, but interested worked too. More people were coming into the parking lot now, and a candy-red Corvette drove past them on the way to the exit. It honked, and a manicured hand tipped in long, bright red nails waved gaily out the driver's window. Lana and Clint.

"If you know who I am, then you must know I'm good for the damages to your car," Julie said. "But I really don't want to call the police."

"Is that right?" Debbie was looking at her speculatively. "Suppose we get in my car where we can have a little bit of privacy and you tell me all about it. Maybe I can help you out here."

Debbie's very masculine feeling hand curled around her upper arm again before Julie could answer, urging her toward his damaged vehicle. Julie glanced up, registered once again the mind-boggling dichotomy of platinum curls bouncing against breasts roughly the size of the Himalayas on a linebacker's broad-shouldered frame, then allowed herself to be persuaded. Turning to a flamboyant, gender-bending stranger for help was probably only a little less stupid than chasing after Sid in the first place, but under the circumstances none of the other options she could think of were any more appealing.

Debbie opened the Blazer door for her, and Julie slid into the black leather seat. It was only as he shut the door behind her and walked around the hood to get in himself that it occurred to her that maybe getting into a car with a strange man in women's clothes might not be the smartest thing she had ever done.

Visit
◆ **Pocket Books** ◆
online at

---

www.SimonSays.com

Keep up on the latest new
releases from your favorite
authors, as well as author
appearances, news, chats,
special offers and more.

SIMON & SCHUSTER
A VIACOM COMPANY
www.SimonSays.com

Pocket Books

2381-01